PRAISE F

"[Green] cont...
London and t...
of normal hum...
and otherwise—provide not just color but a dose of wry humor." —*RT Book Reviews*

From a Drood to a Kill

"Green is an absolute master at world building, and he con-
tinues to showcase his creative imagination in *From a Drood
to a Kill*." —*Fresh Fiction*

Property of a Lady Faire

"Tons of plot, nonstop semicomic action, and further reve-
lations about the entire Drood brood and their mysterious
mission—what's not to enjoy?" —*Kirkus Reviews*

Casino Infernale

"If you've ever read anything by Simon R. Green, you probably know exactly how things will go. It's going to be loud,
messy, funny, weird, without restraint or decorum, and a
whole lot of fun. Because Green writes with a freewheeling
passion that's hard to deny. He always delivers a solid story
with heaping doses of extreme creativity, ultraviolence, and
keen Moments of Cool. . . . I love these books." —*Tor.com*

Live and Let Drood

"A terrific, adventurous blend of genres, delivering high-
octane heroism on a road lined with razor blades. . . . Fans
of Green's genre-bending tales of high adventure will love
this latest installment of his Secret Histories series. . . . Eddie
Drood and his world are a smorgasbord for fans of urban
fantasy and espionage thrillers alike. Highly recommended."
—*SFRevu*

continued . . .

For Heaven's Eyes Only

"Clever world building, madcap characters, cheeky one-liners, and a James Bond feel make this series stand out, and a surprise ending will have readers eagerly anticipating the next Eddie Drood adventure." —*Publishers Weekly*

From Hell with Love

"Heroes and villains strut their stuff across a worldwide stage, and the end result is something so entertaining it's almost a guilty pleasure." —SFRevu

The Spy Who Haunted Me

"As usual, the narrative moves at a fast clip and the sarcasm flows freely. Another action-packed melding of spy story and fantasy, featuring suave sleuthing, magical powers, and a generous dash of dry wit." —*Kirkus Reviews*

Daemons Are Forever

"A rapid-fire paranormal suspense . . . will have readers applauding the reluctant hero and anxiously awaiting his further adventures." —Monsters and Critics

The Man with the Golden Torc

"Packed with enough humor, action, and plot twists to satisfy fans who prefer their adventure shaken, not stirred. . . . Readers who recognize the pun on Ian Fleming's James Bond title will find the secret agent in question has more up his sleeve than a fancy car and some high-tech gadgets." —*Publishers Weekly*

Dr. DOA

A Secret Histories Novel

Simon R. Green

ACE
New York

ACE

Published by Berkley

An imprint of Penguin Random House LLC

375 Hudson Street, New York, New York 10014

ISBN: 9780451476944

Roc hardcover edition / June 2016
Ace mass-market edition / May 2017

Printed in the United States of America
1   3   5   7   9   10   8   6   4   2

Cover illustration by Paul Young

Dr. DOA

The Drood family has been safeguarding Humanity for generations. Facing down the horrors of the hidden world so you don't have to. So you never have to know just how bad things can get. In the Secret Histories.

It's always the dangling threads, from cases that were never properly closed, that come back to haunt you. It's the nature of the secret-agent job that you're never going to get to the bottom of every mystery, never completely shut down every evil organisation, never put a hand on the shoulder of every villain. It's always the one you've forgotten all about that does for you in the end.

There is a man who gets away with murder. A man who specializes in removing the problems from other people's lives by killing the people who cause those problems. He operates from the darkest shadows of the hidden world, coming and going unseen. No one knows who he is—just his *nom de mort*.

Dr DOA.

CHAPTER ONE

Who Knows What the Future Holds?

'm Eddie Drood, secret agent for the very secret Drood family. Unless I'm working undercover, and then I go by my use-name, Shaman Bond. That feckless, easy-going face about town, always on the lookout for a little profitable trouble to get into. Shaman has his uses; doors will open to him, and people will talk to him, whereas they'd run like hell from a Drood. Under one name or another I've fought bad guys and evil forces, vicious conspiracies and demons from the outer dark. I've saved the world on more than one occasion, though the world never knew. I have punished the guilty and protected the innocent, solved mysteries and known something of the night, and walked right through the valley of death with a big nasty grin on my face. I have known good luck and bad, triumphs and tragedies, and the love of a woman worth loving. I've lived.

But I should have remembered the one certain lesson that life teaches. Nothing lasts. Every story comes to an end, and the curtain falls on every one of us. Because there's nothing you can build that the world can't tear down.

My name is Eddie Drood, and I am a dead man walking.

It started just like any other day, with a case that seemed no different from any other. I was walking through a winter wonderland, a pleasant snow-covered scene in the middle of a forest miles from anywhere. On a cold, brisk morning, under an iron grey sky, with snow falling silently in fat white puffs. Snow had been falling for quite some time, and the thick cover crunched noisily under my heavy boots as I strode along. The narrow path, such as it was, wandered between dark leafless trees and took its own sweet time about getting anywhere. No birds sang, and nothing moved anywhere, even in the depths of the forest. I could look in any direction I liked, for as far as I liked, and not be bothered by any trace of human civilization. When I want to get away, I like to really get away. My only companion in this calm and peaceful, whited-out world was the small shaggy dog padding cheerfully along beside me. He'd taken it upon himself to keep me company. He thought I needed looking after.

I trudged along the path, occasionally slipping and sliding as I kicked my way through treacherous drifts. My heavy greatcoat kept out the cold, and the long knitted scarf wrapped round and round my neck prevented the bitter wind from harassing me. I was also wearing thick rainbow-striped mittens, a gift from my Molly. A woman of marvellous abilities and intrepid character, but no taste at all when it comes to knitwear. I was wearing the damned things only because she'd knitted them herself. She'd suggested the dog might like a cosy coat and little booties, but I put my foot down firmly on his behalf.

My bare face smarted from the cold, and my breath steamed heavily on the air. My nose was running, and my ears ached. But I remained resolutely happy, even content. Nothing like being wrapped up warm against the cold, defying everything the winter world could throw at you.

I finally left the trees behind and emerged into a wide clearing, where a paved path led straight to the front door of my isolated country cottage. Just a simple stone structure, with shuttered windows, heavy gables, and a roof buried under a thick layer of snow. Icicles hung from the guttering like gleaming exclamation marks over how cold it was. The cottage was small enough to be cosy, but with room enough to breathe. Cat swinging was not encouraged. Occasional puffs of smoke rose from the squat brick chimney, reminding me that I needed to build up the fire again. I gathered up a bucket of coal and an armful of wood from the bunkers at the side of the house, while my dog watched solemnly and made no effort to help. I went back to my front door, kicked it open, and carried my burden inside. My door is never locked, because this far from civilization there's no one to lock it against.

The main room boasted comfortable furnishings, thick rugs on the floor, and the biggest grandfather clock I could find. It stood proudly in one corner, and had glass panels so I could observe the mechanisms working. I stoked the fire quickly and loaded up the battered old coal scuttle before pulling off the detested mittens so I could warm my fingers over the dancing flames. I straightened with a minimum of pained noises, stretched slowly, unwound the long scarf from my neck, and then shrugged off my greatcoat before hanging them both on the ornately carved coat-rack. The dog turned around several times in front of the fire and collapsed onto the thick rug with a solid thump. His way of telling me that as far as he was concerned, all travelling was now at an end. He wasn't going anywhere. I knew how he felt.

I turned on the clockwork radio, and Radio Four hit me with a cathedral choir singing a Christmas carol. Angelic voices celebrating the festive season and offering comfort and joy. I made myself a big mug of hot sweet tea and settled comfortably into the padded armchair by the fire. The mug had *World's Best Secret Agent* on one side and *Please Don't Tell Anyone* on the other. My uncle James gave it to me years ago. I looked around, taking my time and enjoying an old-fashioned setting illuminated by a warm golden light. My Christmas tree stood sturdily in its corner, festooned with the traditional battered tinsel, cracked baubles, and flickering lights brought out of storage one more time; it was one of my few happy childhood memories. Christmas cards lined the mantelpiece, because you can't escape the damned things. Reply to one, and you're on their list till one of you dies. I kicked off my boots and stretched out my toes towards the crackling fire. The dog made a low noise deep in his throat, as though to say, *Don't wave those things in my direction.* He was lying on his back now with his paws in the air, showing everything he had. Dogs have no dignity. They glory in the absence of it.

I sipped at my steaming tea. All was well with the world. I like Christmas. I like everything about Christmas, except having to spend it with my family. Most of my relatives could start a fight in an empty room and then lie about who won. I much prefer to spend Christmas on my own, in my own way. Not to be bothered by anyone—a selfish wish at an unselfish time of the year.

"Apart from me," said the dog, reading my thoughts as usual.

"You're different," I said.

"And your sweetie, Molly Metcalf."

"Well, of course Molly has to be here," I said. "Everything's better when Molly's around. For two such noted loners, we do seem to spend a lot of time in each other's company."

"That's love," the dog said wisely.

"What do you know about love?" I said.

"I'm a dog. We love everyone. That's what we're for. Humans aren't worthy of us, but we love them anyway. Because someone has to."

I glanced at the grandfather clock. "She should be here soon. I'd better take a look at how dinner's doing. The chicken's been in the oven for ages; it should have stopped clucking by now."

"Only you would cook chicken tikka masala for Christmas," said the dog.

"I like what I like," I said calmly. "Fortunately, so does Molly."

The dog sniggered. "Except when it comes to knitwear."

"You keep quiet about that," I said sternly. "One wrong word, and I'll send you off to be seen to. It's the little white lies and discreet diplomacy that make a relationship possible."

"Humans," said the dog. "If you all just sniffed one another's arses, you'd be a lot happier."

The phone rang—a harsh, urgent sound. The dog turned over heavily, and his head rose. We both looked at the old-fashioned black Bakelite phone. I stayed in my chair, hoping the thing would stop ringing if I just toughed it out long enough. But it didn't.

"Are you going to answer that?" said the dog. "Or do you expect me to?"

"That phone is supposed to be only for emergencies," I said, not budging from my chair. "And even then, my family should know better than to bother me at Christmas."

"The trouble with everyone in your family," said the dog, "is that they always think they know better."

"True," I said. I struggled up out of my nice comfortable chair, strode over to the phone, snatched it up, and growled into it. "Either you're in real trouble, or you're about to be."

"Ah, Eddie, gracious as ever," said a cold, familiar voice. The Drood Sarjeant-at-Arms. "Come home. You're needed."

"Get someone else."

"It has to be you," said the Sarjeant, entirely untroubled by the open menace in my voice. "All our other field agents are spoken for, and this mission can't wait. Don't make me come and get you."

"I'm expecting Molly for Christmas dinner! You want to argue with her?"

"Bring her too. You're going to need backup on this one."

I sighed heavily. "If this doesn't turn out to be horribly important and extremely urgent, I will decorate my Christmas tree with your insides."

He hung up on me. The modern equivalent of having the last word. I slammed the phone down and said a few choice words of my own.

"Am I to take it Christmas is cancelled?" said the dog. "No figgy pudding and plum duff for the good and the virtuous this year?"

"Let us be optimistic and say . . . postponed." I pulled my boots back on and strode over to the front door. My good mood had evaporated, effortlessly banished by my family and the hold it still had over me. Despite everything. I opened the door carefully inwards and looked out on the wintry scene. Everything was still and quiet for as far as I could see. I raised my voice, addressing the dark trees generally. "Molly! We're needed!"

She appeared abruptly out of nowhere, striding up the path to my door. Grinning cheerfully and wearing a long fur coat over knitted leggings. The love of my life, my reason for being, the only thing that keeps me sane in a crazy world. Her pale face, surrounded by long black hair, seemed paler than ever in the cold, her rosebud mouth the only touch of colour. She bounded up the path, kicking snow out of her way with simple joie de vivre. She called out to me while she was still some distance away, because she never could resist a chance to prove she was right about something and I was wrong. Relationships . . .

"I told you to rip that phone out, Eddie! Every year you try for a quiet Christmas, hiding yourself away from your relatives, and every year something comes up so they have to call you back. It's just tempting fate . . ."

"I thought I'd be safe here," I said. "Tucked away in a wintry corner of your Wood Between the Worlds."

"Just because the Droods can't get in doesn't mean they can't reach out and twist your arm," said Molly. "Any idea what the mission is?"

"No, but they want you as well," I said. "Which is . . . unusual. Probably means a mission that's more than usually dangerous."

"Now, that's what I call a Christmas present!" said Molly.

We met in the doorway, and she did her best to hug all the breath out of me, following with a kiss that made sure I'd stay kissed. Behind us, the dog started singing, "Love is all around . . ." Molly and I finally let go of each other, and I ushered her inside. She shrugged off her long fur coat and threw it at the coat-rack before sniffing at the air in a ladylike way as I closed the door.

"Tikka masala?"

"It'll wait," I said. "Till next year, if need be. My uncle Jack knew how to design an oven."

I opened the front door, carefully pushing it out-wards this time. And Molly and I stepped out of my isolated country cottage and into my private room in

Drood Hall. Comfortable enough, but with only the basic requirements because I made a point of spending as little time in it as possible. The dog trotted out after us and dropped his hologram disguise as I closed the door. Scraps.2 was a robot dog, one of Uncle Jack's last creations before his recent death. He scratched at his metal sides with a gleaming back paw, resulting in a harsh clattering sound. He seemed to find it comforting. His eyes glowed red as he looked at me.

"Only you would have a cottage in the woods inside a room within Drood Hall, Eddie."

"Self-protection," I said. "The more layers I can put between me and my family, the better."

"I could stick around if you want."

"Better not," I said. "I can't take a dog on a mission in the field."

"Why not?" Scraps.2 said loudly. "I'm tougher than you, better armed than you, and my logic circuits can think rings round you!"

"Because dogs that come with built-in weaponry and can fire grenades out of somewhere unfortunate tend to get noticed," I said.

"Ah," said the dog. "There is that, yes. I do tend to make an impression . . . Think I'll nip down to the Armoury, see what Maxwell and Victoria are up to. I can't have them thinking they can run the place without me. Look after him, Molly. See you two when you get back."

He trotted out the door, his steel paws thudding heavily on the thick carpeting. Molly looked at me.

"That is one protective dog."

"I think the Armourer programmed it into him," I said, "because he knew he wouldn't be around to do it himself."

"I still can't get used to him sounding like your uncle Jack," said Molly.

I shrugged. "His Master's Voice . . ."

*   *   *

We left my room and started down the landing, walking side by side and just daring anyone to get in our way. Start as you mean to go on . . . As a leading member of the family, I was entitled to a room on the top floor of Drood Hall. Only the one room, of course. After living in the old manor house for so many centuries, I find the Hall is getting just a bit crowded. The youngsters live in dormitories, which has led to more than one comment about battery farming. We keep the dormitories strictly separated, with locked doors and barbed wire fences in between, but we still have to give the birth-control talk a little earlier every year. But then, if they didn't see the world's rules and regulations as just challenges to be overcome, they wouldn't be Droods.

Molly and I descended several stairways, nodding and smiling briefly to all the people we passed. All of whom smiled and nodded briefly in return, while giving us plenty of space. Nothing like having a scary reputation to get you elbow room. When we finally reached the ground floor, somewhat out of breath after so many stairs, the Sarjeant-at-Arms was waiting at the bottom to meet us. Possibly out of courtesy; more likely so we wouldn't go anywhere he didn't want us going.

The Drood Sarjeant-at-Arms looks like a thug and a bully, because he is. He enforces discipline inside the family, and he does love his work. We've never got on. He was dressed as always in the stark black-and-white formal outfit of a Victorian butler, because tradition is a harsh mistress.

"I can't believe you're back working for your relatives again, Eddie," said Molly as we descended the stairs towards him. "After everything they've done to you . . ."

"It's just for now," I said. "It's not like I've anywhere else to go . . . or anything else to do. I need to keep busy."

"You need to feel needed," said Molly.

"If you despise my family so much, why are you here?"

"I'm just sticking around until you come to your senses."

We slammed to an abrupt halt at the foot of the stairs, because it was either that or walk right over the Sarjeant-at-Arms. And don't think that thought hadn't occurred to both of us. The Sarjeant nodded to me, ignoring Molly. She bristled dangerously, and I dropped a hand on her arm and squeezed it hard. She smiled at the Sarjeant in a way that clearly said, *Later* . . . Anyone else would have started running right there.

"The Matriarch is waiting to see you," said the Sarjeant. "In her new private office."

I had to raise an eyebrow at that. "Not in the Sanctity? But that's the most secure and most private place in the Hall. And anyway, it's traditional! Cut a Drood, and we bleed tradition."

"Normally, yes," the Sarjeant said stiffly. "But we have always understood the necessity of adapting to changing conditions."

I looked at him for a long moment. "What conditions are we talking about? What's changed?"

"Every new Matriarch must make her own way," the Sarjeant said steadily. "Margaret has decided not to use the Sanctity."

"How many of the family Council will be attending this meeting?" I said.

"Their advice will not be needed," said the Sarjeant. "This is just a private chat, in the Matriarch's private office."

I finally got the implication. "You mean, away from Ethel? Doesn't the Matriarch trust our gracious other-dimensional benefactor any more?"

"I don't think the Matriarch trusts anyone," said the Sarjeant. "Which is, after all, as it should be."

Molly was shaking her head. "You people have raised paranoia to an art form."

"Thank you," said the Sarjeant-at-Arms.

"I thought Ethel could hear everything that goes on inside the Hall," I said.

"Not necessarily," said the Sarjeant. Which was . . . interesting.

He led the way through the ground floor, and everyone hurried to give us plenty of room. I might have a bad reputation, but he was the one they had to live with every day. And Molly was scowling, in a thoughtful sort of way, which is never a good sign. The Matriarch's new private office turned out to be in a remote corner of the ground floor, well away from the general traffic. The Sarjeant knocked politely, and the door swung open before him. He gestured for me to go in. I smiled, and waved for him to go first. Never trust a Drood Sarjeant-at-Arms at your back. He nodded, as though he quite understood what I was thinking and approved, and led the way. I strolled in after him with my nose in the air, doing my best to give the impression I was doing everyone a favour just by turning up. Molly stuck close to my side. More like a bodyguard than a lover.

The Matriarch had filled her new office with more flowers, blooms, and unusual vegetation than any normal person should have felt comfortable with. Thick grass carpeted the floor, and the walls were covered with heavy mats of creeping vines. Bright colours rioted to every side, and rich scents steeped the air. It felt more like a jungle than a garden. I kept wanting to look around for predators. The Matriarch was sitting behind a very ordinary desk, her face calm and implacable. Molly and I sat down on the chairs facing her, without waiting to be asked, while the Sarjeant-at-Arms stood to one side. Because he didn't do normal things like sitting. People might think he was getting soft.

I glared around the office, in a way I hoped suggested that everything should keep its distance and know its place. I don't approve of familiarity from the plant world. It was all very impressive, but I would have hated to be the Drood in charge of keeping everything watered. I finally nodded familiarly to the Matriarch.

"Missing your old job as head gardener, Maggie?"

"You have no idea," the Matriarch said in her usual no-nonsense voice. "I never wanted to be Matriarch, but if I have to run this family, I'll do it in a way I can live with. If I can't be in the garden, I'll bring the garden inside. Now, we need to talk. Something has happened that needs stamping on right now."

I looked the Matriarch over carefully. She'd gone in for a serious makeover since I last saw her. A dark blue power suit of almost brutal style and impact, and blonde hair shorn back to her skull in a buzz cut. She was still short and stocky, but she looked . . . bigger. All business. Being Matriarch changes a person; you have to grow up, to grow into it. Power and duty, an unchallengeable word and never-ending responsibilities, either make or break you very quickly. Of course, Margaret had always been a tough nut even when she was just Capability Maggie, in charge of the Hall grounds. I couldn't resist teasing her, just a bit, for the good of her soul.

"Are those shoulders . . . padded?" I said innocently.

"It's a good look," Molly said solemnly. "Very Eighties, very Iron Lady. Really rocking that power-crazed authority-figure bit."

"She is the Matriarch," said the Sarjeant. "People must show the proper respect."

"Us?" said Molly. "That'll be the day."

"Why have I been called back so urgently?" I said just a bit plaintively. "When I told you I needed some downtime and was on call only for serious emergencies?"

I broke off as all the flowers and blooms turned their heads to look at me, and not in a good way. The creeping vines on the walls stirred, and hissed threateningly. The Matriarch has always been very protective of her garden, and vice versa.

"Control your pets," said Molly. "Or I'll hit them with a blast of magical weed killer."

"They're just looking out for me," said the Matriarch. "You really shouldn't raise your voice to me, Eddie."

"If they even look like bothering me, I will make mulch out of them," I said coldly.

The flowers looked at me, and then at Molly, in a thoughtful sort of way, and backed off a little. The Sarjeant-at-Arms cleared his throat.

"If we could please stick to the matter at hand . . . Time is of the essence."

"It's come to something," I said, "if you're having to act as peacemaker."

"The irony of the situation has not escaped me," said the Sarjeant.

"All right!" I said. "Peace all round and goodwill to everyone. Let's get the hell on with it. What's the mission, and why is it so damned urgent?"

"You brief them," the Matriarch said to the Sarjeant. "You have the latest information."

The Sarjeant bowed to her and fixed me with a hard look. "We need you to break into the Secret Headquarters of a new organisation, Cassandra Inc. It claims to be able to see the future. And has been selling information on what's going to happen, to all kinds of interested parties."

"Okay, hold it right there," said Molly. "That's not actually possible. There is no one fixed future, as such. Just a whole bunch of possible outcomes and differing timelines. Which one you end up in is the result of all the different choices made by all the people in the world. Even the most powerful computers would have a hard time crunching numbers that big."

"Nevertheless," the Sarjeant said in his best *You're not telling me anything I don't already know* voice, "Cassandra Inc has demonstrated an excellent track record of getting it right."

"How is it doing it?" I said.

"We don't know," said the Matriarch. "And that's just one of the things worrying us."

"As long as Cassandra Inc stuck to predicting business futures, or personal recommendations, we were ready to leave it be," said the Sarjeant. "But now Cassandra has started peddling future information to the secret organisations of the hidden world. The good, the bad, and all those highly dubious groups lurking in between."

"Not Government agencies?" I said. "I mean, they'd be the most obvious markets. Politicians always have a vested interest in knowing what's coming their way so they can blame it on someone else."

"Cassandra has refused to deal with any Government department or individual," said the Matriarch. "Either for political reasons or because no Government would approve of how Cassandra's getting its information."

"Would we be right in thinking our current Government is not too happy about being excluded?" said Molly.

"And would we, by any chance, be doing our Government a favour by intervening?" I said. "Do we perhaps need something from it?"

"So cynical," said the Matriarch.

"Please," I said. "I'm a Drood."

"It wouldn't hurt to have the current administration owe us one," the Matriarch conceded. "Never know when we might need to call it in . . . But that's not why we're sending you. We have our own reasons for wanting Cassandra Inc brought down. It's started selling information on where Drood field agents are going to be and what they're going to be doing. And that is unacceptable. No one gets to interfere with Drood business."

Molly had a sudden moment of insight, and bounced up and down in her chair. "That's why they need you, Eddie! All your fellow field agents are compromised, and running round in circles trying to avoid the futures predicted for them! You're the only one without a current mission!" She broke off, then sat still and frowned. "No, wait, hold on a minute . . . If Cassandra Inc really can predict the future, it should know about this meeting and know that we're coming."

"According to the family psychics, Eddie has been through so much, in so many weird and unusual places, that he has become . . . unpredictable," said the Matriarch.

"I've always thought so," said Molly.

"Cassandra must be stopped," the Sarjeant said flatly. "The organisation is sabotaging our missions, interfering with the family's ability to operate in the shadows. Making it impossible for us to defend Humanity from all the things that threaten it."

"Again, Cassandra should know that," I said. "Isn't the organisation putting itself at risk, along with everyone else?"

"You'd think so, wouldn't you?" said the Matriarch. "We get a free pass, a lot of the time, because good and bad alike can see it's in their best interests to leave us alone. We couldn't operate if we were constantly at war with everyone who disagreed with us."

"Well, we could," said the Sarjeant. "But it would be . . . messy."

"Damned right," I said. "We're supposed to be shepherds, not storm troopers."

"We protect Humanity," said the Sarjeant. "Whatever it takes."

"We have reached out to Cassandra, directly and indirectly, as a reminder of this," said the Matriarch. "But the organisation refuses to talk to us. We think it's just in it for the money. Make as much as possible, as quickly as possible, and then disappear and leave everyone else to clean up the mess it's made."

"Or it could be," said Molly, "that whatever Cassandra's using to predict the future has a limited shelf life. The organisation has to squeeze what it can out of it, while it can. That's why it's prepared to take on people like you . . ."

"Could be," said the Sarjeant.

"Your mission is to infiltrate Cassandra's Secret Headquarters, and find out how it's doing this," said the Matriarch, fixing her attention on me. "And then decide whether we should co-opt it and take it in-house, or shut down the whole operation with extreme prejudice."

"That's why you want Molly to accompany me," I said, "because she's the really destructive one."

Molly smiled at me dazzlingly. "You say the nicest things."

"A plan of action has been prepared for you," said the Matriarch.

"How can we be sure Cassandra won't know we're coming?" I said.

"Our esper section is getting ready to flood the aether with psychic chaff, just in case," said the Matriarch. "Overload the scene with so much information that Cassandra will be temporarily blinded. And no, I don't fully understand that either, so there's no point in asking. Basically, they'll be generating a psychic blind spot for you to move in. But apparently that takes a lot out of them, so they won't be able to maintain it for long. Once you leave the Hall, you'll be working against the clock. Take too long, and your protection could just vanish."

"I thought you said Eddie was unpredictable?" said Molly. "And what about me? Will they be able to see me?"

"Since we don't know how Cassandra gets its information, we can't be sure of its limitations," said the Sarjeant. "Stick close to Eddie and you should be fine. Of course, if you're worried . . ."

"I'm going!" said Molly. "I just don't like being taken for granted . . ."

"Trust me," I said. "Nobody does. They wouldn't dare."

She beamed at me. "Somebody's getting something special in their Christmas stocking . . ."

"If we could please stick to the subject," said the Sarjeant. "We need to get the two of you moving as soon as possible."

"Given our psychic department's past record," I said, "I can't say I have much faith in psychic chaff. I wouldn't trust that bunch to guess my weight."

"I'm sure they know that," said the Matriarch. "Now, since you'll be operating inside a blind spot, you won't be able to communicate with the family until the job is over."

"You mean I won't be bothered constantly by my family-mandated handler?" I said. "Gosh, what a pity; never mind. Now, what is the mission? Exactly? Information gathering, property damage, or blow up everything and sow the ground with salt afterwards?"

"Whatever you decide to be necessary," the Matriarch said carefully. "It's up to you to discover what's really going on, and do whatever it takes to resolve the situation. Permanently."

I looked steadily at her. "Do I need to remind you? I have sworn I won't kill again. Even in the line of duty. I'm an agent, not an assassin."

The Matriarch met my gaze unflinchingly. "I'm not asking you to kill, Eddie. Just asking you to spy."

The Sarjeant moved over to the left-hand wall, and the creeping vines drew back to reveal a viewscreen. An image of a massive aircraft carrier appeared. In flight. It seemed to be sailing through the clouds quite serenely, without any obvious means of support. So high in the sky, there was no sign of ground anywhere.

"Cassandra Inc's Secret Headquarters," said the Sarjeant. "It remains constantly in flight, never landing. Held aloft by alien tech acquired on the black market."

"While you're there," said the Matriarch, "find out what this tech is, and where Cassandra got it, so we can shut down the suppliers as well. There's far too much alien contraband out in the world these days. Drawing attention to itself. We're supposed to be the only ones with that kind of advantage."

"The unknown technology also seems to hide the Headquarters from the rest of the world," said the Sarjeant. "No one knows where the ship is. Apart from us."

"How do we know?" I said.

"Because we're Droods," said the Matriarch. "We know everything."

"If that was true, this mission wouldn't be necessary," I said. "What you mean is, somebody talked."

"Exactly," said the Sarjeant. "Someone, and it really doesn't matter who, bought future information from Cassandra. Whatever it was, it upset them so much, they ratted Cassandra out. And once we knew what to look for, nothing could hide Cassandra from us."

"Our new Armourer is settling in nicely," said the Matriarch. "Doing really good work."

"How are we supposed to sneak onto an aircraft carrier zooming around in the stratosphere?" I said. "In fact, if it never lands . . . how does Cassandra get its own people on board?"

"Shuttles," said the Sarjeant. "Our first thought was to have you join the next replacement crew, but that would take too long. We want this operation shut down now."

"I suppose I could try the Merlin Glass," I said. "Have it open a Door somewhere inside the carrier . . ."

"No," the Matriarch said flatly. "We can't trust that unnatural thing any more. Not after it's let you down so many times. And besides, using that much power would almost certainly blast right through the psychic chaff. You'd be spotted immediately."

"We never did find out why Merlin gave the Glass to the family in the first place," said the Sarjeant. "As I am Head of Security for the family, that has bothered me for some time. The Trojan Horse insists on coming to mind."

"Merlin Satanspawn didn't exactly have a reputation for kindly deeds, outside of King Arthur's court," said Molly. "I mean, come on. The clue is in the name."

"He was born to be the Antichrist," I said, "but declined the position because of his friendship with Arthur. And because he believed in Arthur's dream of Camelot. As far as I'm concerned, that buys him a lot of slack."

"Only because you've never met him," said Molly.

"And you have?" I said.

"Oh sure. In Strangefellows bar, in the Nightside. Of course, that was after he'd been dead for centuries."

"What was he like?" said the Matriarch.

"Grumpy," said Molly. She looked at me thoughtfully. "He did say a few things . . . Did he work with the Droods, back in the day?"

"Hard to know," I said. "A lot of the family's earliest records are missing. Some say deliberately destroyed. The family is supposed to have done some things, when it was starting out, that we're better off not knowing. Supposedly, Merlin presented us with the Glass as a gift, for helping him take down Arthur's greatest enemy. The evil sorceress, Morgana La Fae."

"Really?" said Molly.

"Who knows?" I said. "Go back that far, and it's as much legend as history."

"If we could please return to the matter at hand?" said the Matriarch.

"Go ahead," I said. "Don't let me stop you."

"You can't use any transfer mechanism or teleport spell," the Matriarch said firmly. "They're all too susceptible to prediction. You're going to have to do this the hard way, sneaking on board inside the blind spot. Don't worry, Eddie. We have a plan worked out for you."

And then she smiled. So did the Sarjeant-at-Arms.

"I'm really not going to like this, am I?" I said.

After the plan had been explained to me, and I'd stopped shouting and calmed down a bit, I escorted Molly out of Drood Hall and round the back. It didn't help that she'd laughed so hard, she'd given herself hiccups. Though whether this was because the more extreme aspects of the plan appealed to her, or just because she loved seeing me lose my temper with my family, was open to question. The Hall grounds stretched away into the distance, with hardly anyone about. No snow or ice here, just perfectly manicured lawns under a darkening sky. The only sounds on the quiet afternoon were the cries of peacocks and the occasional howl from the gryphons. It was too cold for anyone to be out and about if they didn't have to be.

"Where are we going?" said Molly. "I thought we had a plane to catch."

"You've never seen where my family keeps its fleet of Blackhawke jets," I said, cheering up a little. "You're in for a treat."

We'd only just rounded the corner of the Hall when the lawn before us split open and pulled apart, the two grassy sides rising up and up to reveal a vast hidden bunker deep underground. The straining of hidden mechanisms sounded loudly on the still winter air until the two huge green sides were practically vertical. And rising steadily into the air between them, on a gleaming hydraulic lift, was a sleek black futuristic jet. The Drood Blackhawke. Guaranteed to get you there in one hell of a hurry and not lose your luggage along the way. It slammed into position and stopped, and a bridge appeared so Molly and I could walk out over the long drop to board the plane. Molly squealed loudly and clapped her hands together delightedly.

"That is so Tracy Island!"

"Some ideas are just classic," I said. "You'd be amazed what we keep under Stonehenge."

The Blackhawke's massive jet engines thundered to life as it readied itself for take-off, and I flinched away from the sheer volume. Molly didn't. The side door opened as I led Molly across the bridge, and a stairway descended. Molly all but danced up the steps. I've travelled on the family jets so often, a lot of the thrill has worn off, but I enjoyed Molly's reaction. She stopped just before the open door and looked back at me.

"What about the runway?"

"Doesn't need one," I said. "Vertical take-off."

"This just gets better and better. Your family has all the best toys!"

Inside the plane it was all very comfortable, even luxurious. The urgency of the situation meant we got the whole cabin to ourselves, and we could take our pick of the rows of empty seats. Molly took her time selecting a seat, before finally settling on one roughly in the centre. *Safer,* she said vaguely. She sat down by the window, and I sat down beside her. I prefer an aisle seat—gives me room to stretch my legs.

"Doesn't this beat having to hang around an airport for three hours for security checks?" I said. "There's only so much duty free you can shoplift before you get bored."

"I wouldn't know," said Molly. "It takes a lot of effort and some major-league disguise spells to get me through airport security these days. I may have given up being a supernatural terrorist, but some people just can't let it go . . . I stick to teleport spells and transfer Gates these days. Less harm to the environment, and a lot harder to intercept."

The pilot's voice came over the intercom. That calm, relaxed, *Never mind an engine's just fallen off the wing everything's fine* voice that all pilots have to have. I think it's a law.

"This is Elliot, your pilot for this flight. Welcome aboard, Eddie and Molly. Make yourselves comfortable. It's going to take us at least two hours to get to the other side of the world. No cabin crew, no complimentary drinks, no point complaining. We're in a hurry. Not expecting any real turbulence, but if things should get a little shaky, try to get some of it into the bags provided. I'll let you know when we've arrived, so don't bother me."

"And people wonder why there are no Drood diplomats," I said.

"No they don't," Molly assured me. "Are there any magazines?"

"Just the family in-house organ," I said, pulling the latest issue out of the seat holder in front of me. "The *Drood Times*. Packed full of family chat, helpful articles, and inspirational thoughts. Ghastly beyond measure."

Molly took it from me anyway, just to be contrary. The front cover had a carefully posed photo portrait of the Matriarch with her new look, and the tag, A NEW MATRIARCH MEANS A NEW DAWN FOR THE FAMILY! Molly leafed quickly through the glossy pages, curled a lip in disbelief, and tossed the thing to one side.

"Lots of people do that," I said.

"Are you ever in it?" said Molly.

"Only as a dire warning," I said solemnly. "Apparently, I am a bad influence."

"I am so proud of you," said Molly.

There is also an entirely unofficial house organ, called the *Drood Inquirer.* Produced infrequently, very much in secret, and circulated from hand to hand when no one's looking. Full of scandalous gossip, tales told out of school, and all kinds of things the higher levels of the family would rather the rest didn't know about. It keeps being shut down, and resurfacing almost immediately.

I have been known to contribute the odd piece, now and again.

"Well," I said. "So much for my family. Any news from your sisters? Has Isabella blown up anything big, or Louisa killed anyone particularly important?"

"They're around," Molly said vaguely. "Almost certainly doing something your family would not approve of."

I smiled. She wasn't usually that circumspect. "What's the matter? Afraid someone in my family might be listening?"

"Can you be sure they aren't?" said Molly. She looked at me, considering. "Are you really happy to be back working with your family again? Given what you've had to do for your relatives, and what they've done to you? You keep leaving, but you keep going back."

"That's family for you," I said. "This will do, for now. For want of anything better. It helps that there's nothing morally uncertain about this mission."

"As far as you know," Molly said darkly. "Why was the Matriarch so keen to keep it secret from Ethel?"

"I don't know," I said. "I'm going to have to look into that when we get back. Ethel's motivations have always been a mystery, but the fact is the family couldn't operate without her. I can't see any way in which picking

a fight with Ethel could be in the family's best interests."

"Do you trust Ethel?" said Molly.

"She's never given me any reason not to," I said carefully. "But she's never explained just why a major entity
such as herself would want to babysit the Droods. Some
people outside the family have hinted to me that she
has her own reasons, and that when we finally find out
what they are, we're really not going to like them."

"Is that why you're back?" said Molly. "To keep an
eye on things?"

"I need to be doing something," I said. "I need a
good reason to get out of bed in the morning."

"What about me?" said Molly.

"You're a reason to get into bed. I need . . . to be
someone worthy of you. To be doing something that
matters. The Droods make that possible."

"You're talking about duty and responsibility, and
all those other things I can't be bothered with," said
Molly.

"You used to be one of the world's feared supernatural terrorists," I said. "Brown-trousering authority
figures on a regular basis. Are you really saying there
wasn't a moral component to that?"

"Hell no," said Molly. "I just get bored easily."

A few hours' hard flying later, I was dozing while Molly
slept the deep, untroubled sleep of the entirely conscience free. Elliot came back on the intercom to inform us he was currently manoeuvring the Blackhawke
into position high above Cassandra Inc's flying Secret
Headquarters. Molly stopped snoring with a very un-
ladylike grunt, lifted her head off my shoulder, and
stretched languorously. I got up out of my seat and did
a few deep knee bends and stretches. I felt the need to
be in really good form for the crazy and quite possibly

suicidal plan ahead of me. All I got for my troubles were some loud cracking noises from my joints and a few paranoid thoughts about deep vein thrombosis. I started down the aisle to the rear door, and Molly came hurrying after me. Somehow she'd magically changed her entire outfit when I wasn't looking, and now she was wearing a snazzy black leather cat-suit, complete with a great many belts and buckles. Molly always believed in dressing for the occasion.

I dressed anonymously, because I was a spy. And because I don't give a damn.

"We are now flying directly over the airship," said Elliot. "Matching its speed exactly. All the Blackhawke's security measures are functioning perfectly, but even so, I don't feel like hanging around here one moment longer than I absolutely have to. So please take up your position by the rear door, and wait for the green light. Then feel free to get the hell off my plane as soon as humanly possible."

I couldn't help noticing that the easy-going element to his voice had disappeared. I stood before the rear door, with Molly tucked in close at my side. I ran through the Matriarch's plan in my mind again, and still thought I should have insisted on something better. Or even something else. A red light glared fiercely above the door, and a whole bunch of alarms sounded as Elliot rapidly reduced the air pressure in the cabin. There was a prolonged shrieking sound, and everything not strapped down flapped around like dying fish. I subvocalised my activating Words, and golden armour shot out from the torc round my neck, covering me from head to toe. Immediately I felt stronger and faster, more awake and more alive. Like I'd just been jolted out of the ordinary doze of living. My armour is the great family secret; it makes us untouchable and unstoppable. Mostly. I wasn't sure just how well it could protect me in the unfortunate event of my falling out of a plane and slamming into the deck of a flying airship at high velocity.

I glanced at Molly. She'd surrounded herself with a mystical shield, its crackling and coruscating energies protecting her from earthly and unearthly dangers while also supplying her with air to breathe. Again, I had no idea how much help the shield would be when it came to jumping out of an airplane with no parachute. She seemed cheerful enough, even smiling in anticipation. But then, that was Molly.

We waited before the rear door as the pressure dropped, equalizing itself with the rarefied atmosphere outside. My golden hands clenched into fists. Molly stared unblinkingly at the red light over the door, willing it to change. Red became green, all the alarms shut down, and the rear door blasted open. The great roar of air rushing past came clearly to me as I stepped up to the opening to look down. And there it was, Cassandra Inc's Secret Headquarters, cruising through the skies some two hundred feet below us.

"I've brought the Blackhawke down as much as I dare!" said Elliot. "Any lower and someone would be bound to notice."

"This will do," I said.

"Can't really miss at this range," said Molly.

"Can I have that in writing?" I said.

"Are you sure you want to do this, Eddie?" said Elliot. For the first time, he sounded honestly concerned. "I mean, just jump and hope for the best?"

"Of course," I said. "I'm a Drood field agent. We can do anything. It says so in our job description."

"But what if you should miss? You wouldn't believe how strong the winds are out there . . . You could even be shot out of the sky! My sensors are showing me some appallingly big guns . . ."

"Really not helping my peace of mind, Elliot."

"Sorry. Go when you're ready."

"Are you sure about this?" said Molly.

"Of course not," I said. "Where would be the fun in that?"

Molly laughed. "A man after my own heart. Let's do it."

I concentrated, and grew a pair of sturdy golden handles out of the back of my armour, right between my shoulder blades. So Molly would have something to hang on to. I stepped into the open doorway, and looked down at the long drop. The airship seemed very small and very far away. Just a small grey object in the wide-open sky. Molly clapped me on one golden shoulder to let me know she was ready, and took a firm grip on the two handles. I threw myself out the door and plummeted down. The Blackhawke roared away, leaving Molly and me behind.

The freezing air rushed past me. I could hear it even if I couldn't feel it. I kept my arms close to my sides and my head pointed down, aiming myself at the flying airship like a golden arrow. Molly clapped her legs around my hips and hung on tight as the turbulence buffeted both of us. She was whooping with glee so loudly, I could hear her above the rushing wind. I fixed my gaze on the ship below, which was growing steadily larger.

We dropped like a golden stone, building up speed, and the Secret Headquarters came rushing up to meet us. Really big gun positions took up a lot of the deck, along with any amount of sophisticated sensor tech. We'd better be hidden inside my family's psychic null, or those guns would have no trouble at all shooting me out of the sky. I didn't think they could actually hurt me inside my armour, but they could certainly blow me off target. And then it would be a really long way down to the ground. But the gun stations didn't react at all as I drew closer, and I breathed a little more easily.

I waited as long as I dared, until I was heading for the ship like a golden bullet, looking for the one point on the deck I had been assured was a blind spot for the ship's sensors; just in case. I concentrated, and broad golden glider wings shot out from my armour's sides. They immediately caught and cupped the air, slowing me down. I was still falling, but now I had at least some limited control over my speed and direction. I glanced back over my shoulder to check whether Molly was okay. She'd tightened her legs around my hips and let go of one of the handles on my back, so she could wave one arm in the air like a cowgirl riding a bronco. I had to smile.

I was close enough now to see that the airship really was a ship. A mothballed aircraft carrier, tons of steel, blatant and uncompromising, sailing through the skies as though it had every right to be there. The deck rushed up, filling my sight till I could no longer see both ends of the ship at once. Coming at me like a windscreen on the freeway. I stretched my glider wings as wide as possible, braced my legs, and finally touched down so gently, I barely had to bend my knees. Ethel's armour never ceases to amaze me. I quickly pulled my glider wings back into my armour; it's a strain to maintain any big change in the armour for long. Molly dismounted lightly from my back, dropped her mystical shield, and then danced triumphantly around me. I sucked the golden handholds back into my shoulder blades.

"That was fantastic!" Molly said loudly. "I want to do that again!"

"Later," I said. "You unrepentant little thrill-seeker, you."

I flashed up a map on the inside of my mask so I could see where we needed to go. The interior of the ship was a warren of narrow steel corridors, but the marked route seemed clear enough. How my family acquired this information, about what was after all supposed to be a rival organisation's Secret Headquarters, hadn't been made clear to me. But my family has a way of always knowing what it needs to know and then being smugly mysterious about it afterwards. As soon as I had the directions memorized, I dismissed the map and armoured down, sending the golden strange matter back into its torc. I didn't want to risk drawing attention to myself, just in case the psychic chaff turned out to be not entirely effective. Or even real. The buffeting wind hit me hard, and the cold was so vicious, I shuddered violently. I turned to Molly and pointed down the deck, shouting to be heard over the wind.

"That way!"

"Let's do it!" she yelled back, stepping behind me so she could use my armoured form as a windbreak.

We crept forward along the steel deck, stepping around and over all kinds of technological protuberances and fighting our way into the teeth of the howling wind. I peered briefly over the nearest side. It really was a hell of a long way down. There were actually dark cloud banks between the ship and the ground. I glanced at Molly to see how she was coping with the thin air. She was shivering, but grinning broadly. For her, it was always going to be about the adventure. I looked up and down the great length of the ship, and wondered how Cassandra Inc had been able to launch such a huge flying fortress into the sky without anyone noticing. I said as much to Molly, shouting into her ear.

"Probably bribed all the right people to look the other way," she shouted back. "Paying them off with future information. That's what I would have done. And you have to admit, Eddie, this is the perfect place to hide a Secret Headquarters. Beats the hell out of a cavern inside a volcano."

And then the wind dropped suddenly, and her last few words sounded loudly in the quiet. Her head came up sharply, and she looked quickly around her.

"We're not alone here, Eddie. Someone just joined us."

"Cassandra can't have found us already!"

"I don't think it's Cassandra . . ." Molly pointed off to one side with a steady hand.

Standing alone on the far side of the deck, a tall, still figure in a grey monk's robe was staring at us. His cowl was pulled well forward to hide his face. His feet were bare, and his hands were clenched into fists at his sides. The wind had dropped to almost nothing, and the cold was gone; I had no doubt that was all down to him. He had . . . an air about him, of cold intent and implacable purpose. I'd met his kind before. Such men are dangerous.

"Who the hell is that?" I said. "And what's he doing here? Now?"

"I know him," said Molly. "And not in a good way. That is the Manichean Monk. A spiritual enforcer, specializing in righteous retribution. Jumped-up thug with a halo."

"You mean, like the Walking Man?" I said. "The wrath of God in the world of men?"

"Oh please; he wishes," said Molly. "The Monk's just a general troubleshooter. He mostly operates out of the Adventurers Club these days, in the Nightside. I worked with him on a few cases, some years back."

"I won't ask," I said.

"Best not," Molly agreed. "Except to say, in my own defence, it seemed like a good idea at the time."

"So many unfortunate things do," I said. "But the Adventurers Club? He's one of the good guys? Can't say I've ever heard of him."

"He does try to be a good guy, in a frightening sort of way," said Molly. "Manicheans are heavily into duality. Good and Evil, Light and Dark, Law and Chaos, and nothing at all in between. He hunts down heavy-duty sinners, on behalf of the Church of Last Resort. Humanity's saviours, self-appointed. When you've tried everything and everyone else, they're what's left. If you're sure your cause is just and your conscience is clear. Manicheans have a really unpleasant way of dealing with time-wasters."

I shot her an amused glance. "Okay, how did an odd couple like you two end up working together?"

"I may have lied to him, just a little," Molly said airily. "About who and what I was."

"It's okay," I said. "I understand. We've all got a dodgy ex or two somewhere in our past."

"He is not an ex! He was never an ex! Oh hell, he's coming over. Look penitent."

The Monk came striding forward, stern and determined, like a force of nature on the move. For a man in a monk's robe, with no obvious weapons, he still managed to look pretty damned threatening.

"Does he believe we're here to stop him?" I said. "Or is he here to look you up, in a not-at-all friendly way?"

"We worked perfectly well together, thank you," Molly said coldly. "And parted on good terms. I thought."

"Could he be here for the same reason we are?" I said.

"I suppose it's always possible, if Cassandra really pissed off his church with the wrong kind of prediction . . . but I wouldn't have thought so. The Monk deals with individual sinners, not organisations."

"Then I refer you to my previous question," I said. "Why is he looking at us like that?"

"I'll ask him," said Molly. "He'll listen to me. Unless he's found out who I really am . . . Hey, Monk! Been a while. What's going on?"

The Manichean Monk crashed to a halt, a cautious distance away. He ignored Molly, all his attention fixed on me. I still couldn't make out his features inside the shadows of his pulled-forward cowl. When he finally spoke, his voice was harsh and grating.

"It's time to pay for your sins, Drood."

"Oh hell," I said. "It's family business. Look, Monk, I'm a bit busy right now. I'm sorry, but I just don't have the time for this."

"Don't be flippant, Eddie," Molly murmured in my ear. "The Monk has no sense of humour about what he does. I found that out the hard way."

"Another story for another time," I said. "Is he dangerous, do you think? To us, or our mission?"

"Could be," said Molly.

I nodded politely to the Monk. "Okay, what sins are we talking about here?"

"The murder of innocents," said the Monk.

"I never killed anyone who didn't need killing," I said coldly.

"Your family has."

"I can't answer for everything my family's done."

"Someone has to," said the Monk.

"Something's wrong here, Eddie," Molly said quietly. "This doesn't feel like the man I knew. There's something . . . off about him."

"Well!" I said loudly to the Monk. "We can't stand around here chatting all day, or Cassandra's security is bound to notice us. Hello? Monk? Why is he just staring at me, Molly? Why isn't he saying anything? Can't you just teleport him out of here? Answer that last question first."

"He's shielded!" said Molly. "And . . ."

"Why did I just know you were going to say that? And what?"

"Bad news, part two," said Molly. "The Monk has a special gift, from God."

"Really?"

"Apparently. He can shut down people's powers and

abilities. Doesn't last long, just enough to give him an advantage. He's already shut down my magics. Try your torc."

I called for my armour, and it didn't come. A chill ran through me. I'm not used to feeling unprotected.

"I knew this mission would turn out to be a pain in the arse," I said. "I just didn't think it would happen so quickly . . . Look; what do you want, Monk?"

"Your death," said the Monk. "In payment for your sins. Your bloody-handed guilt."

"Can't we talk about this?" I said. "I'm working here! And just for the record, I have sworn never to kill again."

"Too little, too late," said the Monk. "You're guilty. You're a Drood."

I looked at Molly. "What powers does he have? What weapons?"

"He doesn't need any," said Molly. "He can't lose because he's always in the right. Comes with the job."

"Terrific . . ."

The Monk lunged forward. His hands came up and he went for my throat, and just like that, we were going head to head and hand to hand. Throwing punches and wrestling each other back and forth across the uneven steel deck. Molly held back, not wanting to get in my way. The Monk was almost inhumanly strong and fast, and driven by a terrible fury, but he didn't have my fighting skills or experience. Drilled into me by the old Sarjeant-at-Arms when I was a lot younger, over many painful lessons, just so I'd be able to defend myself if I didn't have my armour. I avoided the Monk's grasping hands, ducked and dodged his punches, and hit him whenever I felt like it. He didn't even try to defend himself; he just kept coming at me.

I hit him in the head and ribs so often and so hard, I hurt my hands, but he never made a sound. So I darted back out of his reach, waited for him to come after me, and then stepped inside his defences and caught him with a perfectly timed left uppercut to the jaw. His head snapped right back, but he still didn't fall. His cowl fell away, revealing his face at last. His eyes were wild and unblinking, and he snarled at me like an animal frustrated in its rage. I backed away. There's no point in fighting a man who doesn't care how hard you hit him. He came after me, because only getting his hands on me could calm the rage burning inside him. I ducked to one side and kicked his legs out from under him, so that he fell forward onto his face. And then I dropped onto his back with both knees, driving all the breath out of him in one explosive grunt. And still the Monk struggled to throw me off. I couldn't believe it. I twisted one arm up behind his back and put all my weight into holding it there. I put my head down beside his so I could yell into his ear.

"You thought you couldn't lose, because you're always in the right! So the fact that you're losing now should tell you something! I'm not the bad guy here. Really, I'm not. So call this off, stand down, and we'll talk. There must be some way we can sort this out. We don't have to do this! Stop fighting me and listen, dammit. We're both on the side of the angels!"

"You have to die!" said the Monk, throwing all his strength against me. "Drood! Murderer!"

I weighed down on his twisted arm, ready to break the bone if I had to, but he reared up so strongly, I couldn't hold him. He threw me off, and I rolled away across the deck. What was it going to take to stop this man? By the time I'd got my feet under me again, he was off and running, straight at Molly. She gestured quickly, but her magics didn't work. Her small hands closed into fists, but he was already upon her. She punched him hard in the mouth, and he didn't even feel it. He buried his fist in her gut, bending her right over. I cried out in fury at seeing her hurt, and ran to them.

The Monk grabbed hold of Molly as she struggled to get her breath back, and hauled her over to the edge of the deck. She fought him fiercely, but couldn't break his grip. His hand closed tightly around her throat till she was gasping for air. He looked down at the long drop and then looked meaningfully at me. I slowed to a halt, some distance away. I didn't want to panic the Monk into doing something stupid. Or even deliberate. I held my hands up placatingly.

"Take it easy, Monk."

"I could jump," said the Monk, breathing hard. "Just step over the edge and take your woman with me. Or you could save her."

"All right!" I said. "I'm listening. Tell me what to do. Just don't hurt her."

"I want you to jump," said the Manichean Monk. "Jump off this ship and fall to your death, Drood. Your armour will return, once you're out of my range of influence, but not even Drood armour can save you after a fall from this height. You'll have a long time to think about dying, all the way down. To suffer, as your family made me suffer. It's up to you, Drood! Either you agree to jump over the side, or I jump and take her with me!"

"Why?" I said. "Why are you doing this? I haven't done anything to you. I don't even know you! And Molly was your friend!"

"Jump, Drood. Or watch her die for your family's sins."

I called desperately for my armour, but it didn't come. I was on my own. I couldn't rush the Monk; he was too far away. And already far too close to the edge for my liking. I had a gun, tucked away in my pocket dimension, but I didn't dare draw it. Just the sight of it might provoke him into jumping. I stood very still, trying to work out what my options were. I'd got too used to relying on the advantages my armour gave me. Now it was down to me . . .

I moved slowly forward and stood on the edge of the deck, carefully maintaining my safe distance from the Monk. He studied me closely, his hand still closed around Molly's throat. She'd stopped trying to fight him, watching me with worried eyes. I looked down, over the edge. I couldn't even see the ground; the clouds were in the way. I wondered what it would feel like to fall through them, knowing my death was waiting on the other side. And just that thought showed me I'd already made my decision. The only one I could make. I looked back at Molly, who was helpless in the Monk's grip, and did my best to smile reassuringly at her.

"Take it easy, Molly," I said. "Everything's going to be all right."

Molly saw the look on my face, and her eyes widened with horror. "No! No, Eddie, you can't! You mustn't! Don't you give this bastard what he wants! Don't you do it, Eddie!"

"I have to," I said. "Because if it's down to you or me, that's no choice at all."

She struggled fiercely to break free. The Monk almost broke her arm, holding her in place. She cried out, her face twisted in agony, and fought him anyway. There was nothing I could do. The Monk could take them both over the side in a moment. Molly finally subsided, breathing harshly and staring miserably at me with tear-filled eyes.

"Hush," the Monk said to her. "It will all be over soon."

"Why are you doing this?" said Molly. "You know this isn't right. It can't be what God wants!"

"It's what I want," said the Monk. "Do it, Drood. Jump. Or I go, and she goes with me."

I believed him. I nodded to the Monk, and stepped right up to the edge. I felt strangely calm, now all other choices had been taken away from me. There was just what I had to do, to save Molly. I took a deep breath. I didn't look down. There was nothing there I wanted to see. I looked at Molly so I could take the memory of her face with me. I wanted her to be the last thing I ever saw.

"Please, Eddie," she said. "Please; I'm begging you! Don't do this . . ."

"I have to," I said. "It's all right, Molly. I've always known you were worth ten of me."

She screamed then, in rage and horror, and slammed her heel down hard on the Monk's bare foot. The sudden pain distracted him, catching him off balance, and Molly bent sharply forward, putting all her strength into the judo throw that sent the Monk flying forward over her shoulder. The pain to her arm must have been unbearable, but she never hesitated. The Monk shot right over her, unable to stop himself. He lost hold of her arm and crashed to the steel deck at her feet. Molly kicked him savagely in the ribs. The Monk shot out a hand and grabbed hold of her ankle.

I was already off and running, the moment Molly freed herself from the Monk. I knew I had only one chance to get this right. The Monk saw me coming, let go of Molly's ankle, and scrambled up onto his feet again. Molly beat at his head and shoulders with both fists, but he didn't seem to feel the blows. He grabbed one of her flailing arms and dragged her back to the edge of the ship. She fought him every step of the way, slowing him down and buying me time to get to them.

The Monk realised I was going to reach them before he could jump. He threw Molly to the deck and turned to face me. He struck out at me with vicious strength. I ducked under the blow and hit him hard with a lowered shoulder. I hit him square on, and the impact sent him staggering back. Towards the edge. He tried to grab hold of me, to take me with him, and then he was over the edge and gone.

Molly ran to me and hugged me tightly, and I held her as close to me as I could. After a while, we walked over to the edge and looked down. There was no sign of the Monk. I hadn't even heard him scream. Molly spat after him.

"Bastard."

"Yes," I said. "But that's not a good enough reason to kill someone."

"Eddie?"

"I've killed again, Molly. After I swore I never would."

"You had no choice! He was out of his mind . . . Everyone will understand. You have no reason to feel guilty!"

"But I do," I said. "I should have known; God does love to make a man break his word."

"You would have jumped to save me, wouldn't you?"

"Of course."

"Then I wish the Monk were back here so I could kill him for you."

"You knew him," I said. "Was he a good man then?"

"The man we just met wasn't the man I knew," said Molly. She frowned. "There was something wrong with him. I could feel it. Maybe something happened to him, in the Nightside . . . If he'd been in his right mind, following his duty, he couldn't have lost. Hey, my magics are coming back! Is your torc . . . ?"

"Yes," I said. "Come on; we still have a mission here. And it had better turn out to be worth it."

By the time we reached the entrance point marked on my map, the cold was back and the wind was rising again. It turned out to be a single square hatch, securely bolted on the inside. I knelt down beside it, and Molly craned over my shoulder.

"What is it, Eddie? A fire exit, or maybe an inspection hatch?"

"It's our way in."

"If Cassandra really can predict the future, there's probably a whole army of security guards down there waiting for us."

"Good," I said. "I feel like hitting a whole bunch of people."

I armoured up one arm and ripped the steel plate away. The closed bolts sheared clean through, the hinges flew away like shrapnel, and the steel plate crumpled in my grip like tinfoil. I tossed it to one side, and it clattered loudly away across the desk. I barely heard it over the rising wind. I peered down through the opening, couldn't see anything, and dropped down into the corridor below. I landed easily and looked quickly around, but there was no one waiting. I wasn't sure whether I felt relieved or disappointed. Molly dropped down, landing as lightly as a cat beside me. I armoured down my arm, not wanting to draw unwanted attention, and considered my new surroundings.

Steel bulkheads everywhere, with all kinds of pipes and conduits, but no frills or fancies. Just a loud background hum of straining machinery, as though only a constant effort from the hidden alien technology held the Secret Headquarters this high in the air. I set off along the corridor, following the map in my head and moving deeper into the flying ship. Molly strode along beside me, looking happily around like a tourist on a day out. I was glad she could still enjoy the game; the mission had gone sour for me. I just wanted it over and done with.

"Do you need to call up your armour again to check the map?" said Molly after a while. "Only we do seem to have taken rather a lot of turns without actually getting anywhere."

"I know where I'm going," I said. "I memorized the route."

"You always say that, and I always end up having to ask people for directions."

"Only because you don't have my sense of direction."

"Oh come on! You can get lost trying to find the bathroom in the middle of the night!"

She was trying to cheer me up. I played along as best I could.

"So, how far is it now?" said Molly. "To wherever it is we're going?"

"You didn't read the briefing notes on the plane, did you?"

Molly sniffed. "I have you for that. I had some important beauty sleep to be getting on with."

"According to the map, there should be a communications centre up ahead. That's why we came in through that particular hatch. We can use their computers to find the source of Cassandra's predictions."

I stopped abruptly, and Molly stopped with me. A large group of uniformed people were bustling down the corridor, straight at us, chatting loudly together. Molly looked at me.

"Do you want me to whip up some kind of invisibility spell? My magics are only just returning, but I should be able to manage something basic."

"No need," I said. "Just look confident. If we act like we belong here, they'll assume we do. On a ship this big, they can't know everyone."

"What if somebody does challenge us?"

"Then I get to hit a whole bunch of people after all."

"Suits me," said Molly.

Sure enough, when the uniformed technical people finally reached us, they were too wrapped up in their own conversations to pay us any attention at all. I walked straight at them, Molly stuck close to my side, and the crowd just parted automatically to let us through. I nodded briefly to anyone who glanced in our direction, and they nodded back and kept going. Sometimes confidence is the best weapon a spy has.

The communications centre turned out to be just a few minutes away. There was even a helpful sign on the door. No one standing guard, no obvious security. Some people don't deserve to have secrets. I kicked the door open and barged in, Molly right behind me. Half a dozen technical staff looked up, startled. I was about to armour up, when Molly barked out the single word "Sleep!" and they all fell fast asleep at their posts. A few of them even snored gently. Molly looked at me suddenly.

"Oh I'm sorry, Eddie! Did you still need to hit someone? I could always wake them up again."

"Thanks for the thought," I said, "but the moment's passed. Stand by the door and keep an ear out while I check this place over."

That she didn't give me any grief for giving her orders was a sign of how concerned she still was about me. She just nodded and looked out into the corridor while I examined the communications equipment. It all seemed standard enough. I chose a likely looking terminal, armoured up my hand, and sent tendrils of golden strange matter sneaking into the system to override its restrictions and corrupt its programming. My armour can do many amazing things, and I don't understand half of them. Mind you, I feel the same way about most of the cars I drive. The ship's main computer couldn't have been more helpful, answering questions almost before I could ask them. It still took a while to dig out the information I needed. Long enough for Molly to get bored at her post and wander back to join me.

"I'm still not clear on what we're looking for here."

"The secret of Cassandra's success," I said patiently. "Whether it's a what, or a who. Hmm . . . according to this, Cassandra's been selling future information for only about eight months. So whatever it is, they haven't had it long. What do you think, alien tech, or some gifted psychic? Remember the little old lady I told you about, the one at Lark Hill who could listen to the whole country at once?"

"If there was anyone like that here, I'd feel it," said Molly. "I suppose it could be some kind of divination, powered by blood sacrifice."

"Trust you to think of something like that," I said.

"I've been around," she said airily. "I've seen things."

"I'm sure you have."

The computer made a series of agreeable sounds, indicating that my armour had tickled it in all the right places, and it was now ready to spill the beans. Except, the computer didn't actually know the source of Cassandra's predictions. Apparently, such knowledge was limited to upper-management personnel only. But the computer did know where the source was. It even printed out a map for me, without having to be asked. I withdrew my golden tendrils and shut the terminal down. Molly pored over the map.

"Not far, just a few corridors down. Nothing here about security measures, though . . ."

"Bound to be some, but there was nothing listed in the computer," I said. "And trust me, I looked. Doesn't matter. I'll set my armour against anything Cassandra can put up. I mean, look around; it's not exactly state of the art here, is it?"

"Maybe most of their budget went on some really nasty hidden security," Molly said darkly.

I took the map and headed for the door, and then stopped so suddenly, Molly almost ran into me. I looked back at the sleeping members of the tech staff, still slumped in their seats.

"They will all wake up again, on their own, won't they?"

"Oh sure," said Molly. "Eventually."

"What if they don't?"

"Then someone had better put a wall of thorns around them and hope for a handsome prince."

We headed briskly through the narrow steel corridors, looking so in charge that everyone we met en route just naturally hurried to get out of our way. It's all down to the walk. When we finally arrived at the right location, the empty corridor stretching away before us seemed entirely unremarkable. No one around, no signs or numbers on any of the doors. I counted them off until we were standing before the door marked on the map. Nothing about it to suggest it held anything special. Presumably, that was the point. Still, no guards on duty, no obvious surveillance . . . I didn't like it. It's always the defences you don't spot that end up ruining your day.

"You'd think they'd at least have a few warm bodies standing around," said Molly. "Someone to shout, *Who goes there?* and wave a gun around in a menacing manner."

"Oh, I'm sure someone's on guard," I said. "We're just not seeing them. Don't touch the door!"

"I wasn't going to! This isn't my first burglary. And don't you shout at me, Eddie Drood! I was just getting a feel for the surroundings."

It felt good to have things back to normal between us.

"You go right ahead," I said. "Don't let me stop you. Feel things."

She carefully considered the door with her witchy Sight, and then its immediate surroundings. She scowled, and shrugged unhappily.

"There's something here, but it's really well hidden. I'll try a spell to force hidden things to reveal themselves."

"Have you got enough magic for something like that?" I said carefully.

"Just about. I've been running on fumes ever since the Monk shut me down, but it's coming back."

She did the business, with a minimum of chanting and arm waving, and just like that, the security measure was hovering right there in front of us. A single massive eyeball, floating on the air, it was so big that it blocked the corridor all on its own. Complete with a pair of eyelids that were currently closed. The skin was a pale blue, with dark straggling veins. I edged around the giant eyeball in a complete circle, being very careful not to touch or disturb it, but somehow no matter where I was, it was always facing me.

"What the hell is it?" I said after I'd run out of anything else to do. I did think about prodding the eyeball with a golden finger, but I couldn't convince myself that was a good idea.

"If that is what I think it is—and I'm pretty sure it is—we are in deep doo-doo," said Molly.

"It's never good when you use language like that," I said. "Okay, hit me with the bad news."

"It's a basilisk's eyeball," said Molly. "Removed from its host, almost certainly without permission; greatly enlarged and then weaponized for sentry duty. If the eyelids open, it will quite definitely kill everything it looks at."

"Let's try to avoid that, then," I said. "Any idea what might set it off?"

"Well, making it visible probably didn't help," said Molly. "I mean, we walked right through it when we didn't know it was there, and it didn't care. Now . . . probably any unauthorized contact with the door will wake it up in a hurry. But, Eddie, there is no way Cassandra could have done this on its own. This is specialist work."

"It still settled for just the one eyeball."

"That's like saying just the one nuke! My point is,

Cassandra must have contracted out for security, and weaponized supernatural body parts don't come cheap. If Cassandra could afford to set something this nasty on guard duty, it must be making serious money . . ."

"If we should happen to wake it up," I said carefully, "could your magics protect you?"

"In my current condition, probably not," Molly said reluctantly.

"So . . . let sleeping giant eyeballs lie?"

"Sounds like a plan to me."

I did think about armouring up, but just my armour's presence might be enough to trigger a response. So I edged past the eyeball to stand before the door. Molly edged round from the other side, hugging the wall. I looked the door over. No obvious booby traps, and just a standard lock. I couldn't believe it would be that simple, that easy, so, when in doubt, go sneaky. I knelt down and sent just a trickle of golden armour running down my shoulder and arm, and into the lock. I tensed, but there was no reaction from the eyeball. I concentrated, and my armour unlocked the door in a moment. I withdrew the tendrils, straightened up, and flashed Molly an encouraging smile.

"Piece of cake."

I opened the door, and every alarm in the world went off at once. The eyelids snapped open, and the eyeball swivelled round to focus on its closest target, which was Molly. I didn't have time to do anything but jump between her and the eyeball, subvocalising my activating Words as I moved. The armour leapt out of my torc as the basilisk looked at me, and a terrible light blazed up, filling the corridor and dazzling me even through my mask. A great force erupted from the eye, fierce and wild and deadly. It hit my armour, rebounded, and slammed into the eyeball. The lids slumped shut again, the eyeball shook all over, and then it fell to the floor.

Landing hard, and somewhat squishily. The alarms all went quiet, as though embarrassed. I blinked several times until my eyes cleared, and then glanced over my shoulder. Molly was still behind me, unharmed. I armoured down, and she punched me hard in the shoulder.

"Ow!" I said. "What was that for?"

"For protecting me!" she said. "I can look after myself!" And then she grabbed me and kissed me hard. "Thanks for the thought, though."

"You're welcome," I said. "But next time, can we go straight to the kissing?"

Molly looked at me thoughtfully. "Did you know your armour could protect you from the basilisk's stare?"

"Of course," I lied.

I led the way through the open door. Molly immediately pushed past me, just to make a point. And then we both stopped dead in our tracks. A large cage, made entirely of silver bars, took up most of the room. A pentacle, old-school and intricate, had been painted on the floor, surrounding the cage. I could feel a presence on the air, a terrible power, barely restrained. It was like staring at the door to a massive furnace and wondering if it might leap open at any moment.

I looked at Molly. "Any ideas?"

"This is bad," she said quietly. "I don't know what they've done here, but . . . bad, Eddie. Seriously not good."

"Okay," I said. "Let's go take a closer look."

"A man after my own heart," said Molly.

The cage looked to be some twenty feet on a side, each silver bar so thick, I would have had trouble closing my hand around it. Inside the cage, a man sat slumped in one corner, paying no attention to us. Just an ordinary man in shabby clothes, his head lowered so I couldn't see his face. He had to know we were there, but he didn't even raise his head to acknowledge our presence. I looked around the cage, but there was no sign of a door anywhere. It was as though the cage had been constructed around him, with no plan of ever letting him out again. Was this the goose that laid golden futures? I reached for the bars, and Molly suddenly grabbed my arm to stop me. When I looked at her, Molly's face was pale with something very much like shock.

"What is it?" I said, keeping my voice down. Even though the man looked completely out of it, something about him suggested it wouldn't be a good idea to disturb him. "Molly? What are you Seeing? And may I please have my arm back before you cut off the circulation? Thank you."

"Sorry," said Molly. She wasn't looking at me. Her gaze was fixed on the shabby man in the far corner of his cage. "Armour up, Eddie. You need to See what I'm Seeing."

I armoured up. It wasn't just a man in a cage—I already knew that at gut level—but I still wasn't prepared for what I saw when my mask's Sight kicked in. Instead of a man, a gigantic humanoid form filled most of the cage. Ten, maybe twelve feet high, curled up in a ball and wrapped in heavy feathered wings. It had a perfect form and face, like a colossal marble statue brought to life. Inhuman in its perfection. The skin was a shining, shimmering white; the kind that contains every colour at once. And just like that, the cage turned my stomach. It felt wrong that something so mean could have been done to something so marvellous. Like someone had walked into a gallery and thrown acid across a masterpiece. I looked to Molly.

"Is that . . . what I think it is?"

"Oh yes," said Molly. "It's an angel."

"Are you sure? I mean, I've never seen one before. I don't suppose many have, but . . ."

"Hush, Eddie. You know what it is."

And I did. You only had to look at it to know.

"All right," I said. "From Above, or Below?"

"The Devil has power to assume a pleasing form," said Molly. "So I suppose it could be either."

"I'm imprisoned, not deaf," said the angel. "I can hear you."

It sat up in a great spreading of wings and looked at us. Its voice had been rich and thrilling, but when it fixed us with its glowing golden eyes, I winced and stumbled backwards. It was like staring into a spotlight. Even imprisoned, there was still something inhumanly judgemental in the angel's gaze. I made myself stand my ground and glare back. I'm a Drood. We don't bow or bend the knee to anyone. That's the point.

"Hello, Eddie Drood," said the angel. "Hello, Molly Metcalf. I've been expecting you."

"Oh shit," said Molly. "It knows us."

"I am Heaven's warrior," the angel said quite calmly. "I am the will of God made flesh, to enforce his wishes in the mortal world. I know everyone."

"Then how did you end up here?" I said.

The angelic form disappeared, replaced by the shabby man. He stood facing us, his hands in his pockets. His face was calm, empty, anonymous. "My presence is too much for human sensibilities. So I take this form, of my involuntary host, to shield and protect you. You're welcome."

"Thank you," I said. In its presence, it was hard to think of anything but the angel. As though it was more real than us.

"Well," said the angel, "I am one of the good guys. Are you here to set me free?"

"Depends," Molly said quickly. "I've known men

possessed by things from the Pit, but . . . you're claiming to be a man possessed by an angel? Has that ever happened before?"

"There is another," said the angel. "In Shadows Fall."

"Doesn't surprise me," I said. "They'll let anyone in. What's going on here?"

"I am an angel imprisoned inside a man, as he is held within these bars. He is my cage."

"What does Cassandra want with you?" said Molly.

"I make its business possible. All angels exist Outside of Time and Space, so we can see more clearly, to be about our business. Past, Present, and Future, all at once. I was part of the angel war, fought in the Nightside over the Unholy Grail."

Molly put a hand to her mouth, her eyes wide. The shabby man smiled at her.

"Yes, you were there, weren't you, Molly Metcalf?"

"You were?" I said, staring at Molly. "You were there when angels came to the Nightside from Above and Below, to fight openly over the cup that Judas drank from at the Last Supper? And you never said?"

"I don't tell you everything," said Molly.

"Just as well," said the angel. "Considering why you were there. What matters is, I was attacked and weakened, and fell to Earth. Hauled down from my high station, I was captured and imprisoned within a powerful human psychic. The only cage that could hold me. But just the effort of such a possession drove the man insane, and I refused to do anything my captors wanted. They had no way of compelling me. They dared not injure the host for fear of weakening his hold on me. And for fear of what I would do once I was free again. So I was traded back and forth, among various powerful organisations and individuals. Some because they hoped to find a way to force information out of me; some because they wanted me to intercede with Heaven for them. And a few just wanted to have sex with a man who had an angel in him. I refused to cooperate with any of them, and the psychic remained crazy. There's not much of him left now—just this shell. Finally, the people who became Cassandra bought me at auction.

"They wanted to know the future. And they got answers out of me by threatening to freeze my host in cryogenics so I would never be free. They also promised to release me, once I'd answered a specific number of questions. That number is almost up, but I don't believe they will keep their word. I can't See for sure; I am not allowed to See my own future. But I believe Cassandra Inc's Management are too scared of what I might do to them, once I was no longer constrained. For daring to compel an angel . . . And they're quite right, of course. They're currently searching for a way to destroy my host that would also send me straight back to Heaven." He laughed softly—a ghastly, merciless sound. "Like that would protect them from the wrath of God."

"Why has Heaven allowed you to remain caged for so long?" I said.

"What are a few moments in Time, compared to Eternity?"

"If you suspected Cassandra Inc's Management were lying to you, why tell them what they wanted to know?" said Molly.

"Because of the possibility of freedom," said the angel. "From being caught in the matter trap. I had a feeling my actions would result in someone coming here . . . who could free me."

"Yes," I said. "I can do that."

Molly grabbed me by the arm and moved me urgently back to the door so we could speak quietly together. I wasn't sure what difference that would make where an angel was concerned, but I went along. Molly glared at me.

"Really?" she said. "Let it out? Just like that? I'm

not so sure that's a good idea, Eddie. Angels are beyond our understanding; they move in mysterious and often very scary ways. Particularly when someone's really pissed them off. I do not want to end up as a pillar of salt!"

"Doesn't matter," I said. "It's the right thing to do. Look at it, Molly. See what they've done. It's not right to keep Heaven in a cage."

I walked back to the silver bars, with Molly straggling reluctantly along behind me. The angel looked back at me with its human face. Not begging or pleading, not ordering or demanding. Just waiting to see what I would do.

"Time to go," I said. "Time for you to go home."

"What do you want in return?" said the angel.

"No conditions," I said. "No bargains. That would be wrong."

"There are things I could tell you, Eddie Drood. Things I could do for you."

"It wouldn't be right," I said, "to compel an angel."

"Don't look at me," said Molly. "He gets like this sometimes."

"What a refreshing change," said the angel.

"I would . . . ask," I said. "Leave the people on this ship to human justice. Please."

"Since you asked so nicely," said the angel. "But still, nothing for yourself? Then allow me to express my gratitude. I see death hanging over you, Eddie Drood. Nothing can stop it. Plan accordingly. And beware the Merlin Glass. When you look into that mirror, you're not the only one who looks back."

I waited, but that was all he had to say.

"I don't get anything?" said Molly.

"Don't push your luck, supernatural terrorist," said the angel.

"Fair enough," said Molly.

I took the silver bars in my golden hands and forced

them apart. Strange magics and unnatural energies flared around me, so bright and fierce, Molly had to turn her head away, but none of them could touch me in my armour. The silver bars broke and shattered, and I threw the pieces aside until one whole side of the cage was gone. I stepped quickly back from the opening I'd made, and the man with an angel inside came out. He looked at the pentacle painted on the floor, sniffed dismissively, and stepped easily across the lines.

"Amateur night," he said.

"Okay . . . ," said Molly. "That's freed the host, but how are we supposed to get the angel out of him? I'm guessing an exorcism wouldn't work . . ."

"I was hoping you'd have something," I said.

"Way outside my experience," said Molly. "I suppose we could always kill the host . . ."

"Kill an innocent man, to release an angel?" I said. "I'm guessing seriously bad karma."

Molly looked at the angel. "I don't suppose you've got any ideas?"

"Not really my area of expertise," said the angel.

"I need to talk to my family," I said to Molly. "Can you . . . boost the signal, or something?"

"Maybe," said Molly. "Let's try."

She moved in close and touched my torc with the fingertips of her left hand. They trembled slightly on the strange matter, like the most intimate of touches. Like she was touching my soul. I could see the strain in her face as she fought to marshal what magics she had left. I called out to the members of my family through the torc, and they heard me. My handler's voice rang loudly in my ears.

"Eddie! This is Kate! I've been waiting here all evening just in case you needed me! What's happening?"

"All kinds of weird and wonderful things," I said. "Listen, I'm on board Cassandra's ship, but I need you to do something for me."

"Of course, Eddie. That's what I'm here for. What do you need?"

"Tell the family psychics to stop generating their chaff and to put all their power into helping someone here with me. They'll be able to locate him easily enough; he's possessed. By an angel. I'll explain later, I promise, but right now I need them to concentrate on breaking the binding so the angel can go free. Can you sort that out?"

There was a pause. "Only you would get involved with something like this, Eddie," said Kate. "I'll see what I can do. Hang on."

"She likes you," said Molly.

"I know."

"No, I mean she really likes you."

"I know! You don't mind, do you?"

"I think it's very sweet," Molly said firmly.

She went over to the door and looked out into the corridor. "I was sure breaking the cage would set off some kind of silent alarm, but I don't see anyone."

"Doesn't mean they're not on their way."

"True. Do you still feel like hitting a whole bunch of people?"

And then the psychics must have come through, because the human host's head suddenly came up, as though reacting to something only he could hear. He smiled, for the first time.

"Thank you, Eddie Drood, Molly Metcalf. I'll put in a good word for you."

The angel burst out of the man in a blast of unbearable light. What we'd seen before had just been an impression of an angel; what it allowed us to see. Scaled down, so it wouldn't damage us. Wild and glorious, magnificent and free at last, the angel departed, in a direction I could sense but not name. The whole room rocked as the forces unleashed in its passing shook the flying airship from end to end. Molly and I clung to each other as the floor dropped out from under us. There was the sound of a whole string of explosions and all kinds of systems breaking down, along with any number of alarms and sirens, and a great many people panicking. One end of the room dropped dramatically as the airship began to fall out of the sky. Molly and I staggered back and forth, and had to hang on to what was left of the silver cage to steady ourselves.

"I asked the angel not to hurt anyone," I said. "I should have specified—that included not dropping the bloody ship out of the sky with us still on board!"

"I told you it would come out in a bad mood," said Molly. "I'm just relieved I didn't end up as a salt lick."

At the back of the cage, the human host was lying curled up in a corner, not moving. He'd clearly been dead for some time, probably killed by the original shock of containing the angel. Only its presence had kept his body going. Decay was setting in now and making up for lost time.

The airship lurched again, and Molly and I clung desperately to the silver bars. I armoured down to keep Molly company.

"I think we need to get to the control room," I said. "See how bad this is, and what we can do to help."

"Really?" said Molly. "After everything they've done, let them crash!"

"Not everyone on board is necessarily guilty," I said. "I doubt most of them even knew about the angel. Probably just ordinary working stiffs."

"You and your conscience," said Molly.

The room steadied for a moment, and I quickly headed for the door. Molly stuck close behind, holding on to the back of my belt with one hand, in case things got a bit unsteady again. I could hear running feet approaching before I even got to the door, and when I looked out into the corridor, it was full of armed guards.

Who took one look at me and immediately opened fire. I ducked back inside the room and armoured up. Molly yelped briefly as the hand she had holding on to my belt was pushed aside by the enveloping armour.

The door sprang open and the first guards charged in, opening fire again the moment they saw me. I stood between them and Molly, not moving. Bullets slammed into my armour, and it absorbed them all, effortlessly soaking up the massed firepower. With my old armour, the bullets used to ricochet, but that could lead to unfortunate incidents with innocent bystanders. I don't know what my current armour does with the bullets it absorbs; I've never quite dared ask. More and more guards burst into the room, targeting me with their various weapons. The sound of so much gunfire in the confined space was deafening. And I just stood there and took it all. Staring calmly at the guards through the featureless golden mask that covered my whole face. That always freaks people out.

One by one the guards stopped firing, and lowered their weapons. In the sudden echoing quiet, the security men looked at one another, and then reluctantly looked back at me. I raised one golden fist, and grew heavy spikes out of the knuckles.

"Run," I said.

And they did.

They'd been gone only a few moments before two men and a woman came charging into the room. Young business types, in smart power suits. They didn't even look at me, all their attention fixed on the broken silver cage. One of the men actually moaned. The woman finally looked at me and Molly. Behind the understated makeup, her face was pale, but her mouth was still a flat, stern line.

"Who the hell are you?"

"I'm a Drood," I said. "Who are you?"

"We're Cassandra Inc's Management," said the woman. "What have you done?"

"Let the angel go free," I said. "You had no right to hold it here."

"We bought that angel!" said one of the men. "We paid good money for it. It's ours!"

"You let it go?" said the other man. "We were going to be rich!"

"We didn't imprison the angel," the woman said carefully. "We just bought the man, with the angel already inside. We made a deal with it."

"But did you intend to keep your side of the bargain?" I said. "The angel didn't think so."

"It was just business," said the woman.

"Didn't you think of all the damage you were doing with your predictions?" I said. "When you interfered with the Droods, you put the safety of the world at risk."

"It was just business!" said the woman. "What gives you the right to interfere?"

"You messed with my family," I said. "No one gets to do that."

The woman looked at the two men. "Do something!"

They looked at each other, and ran back out the door. The woman went after them, bitterly calling them cowards.

"We didn't even get their names," said Molly.

"Do you care?"

"You let them go. I would have turned them into frogs."

"My family will see that word gets out that they're responsible for all the trouble Cassandra caused," I said. "Those three will be on the run for the rest of their lives."

"Nasty," said Molly. "I like it."

"Let's go find the control room," I said.

"Let's," said Molly.

*　　*　　*

I armoured down, and we fought our way through the narrow steel corridors, through crowds of desperate, panicking people looking for escape pods, parachutes, or any other way off the sinking ship. Having met the Management, I was willing to bet there weren't any. The crowds paid no attention to me or Molly, except to curse us when we got in their way. I tried to ask directions to the control room, but no one had the time to talk to me. In the end, I just grabbed a man at random, slammed him up against the wall, thrust my face into his, and demanded directions. And he was only too happy to supply them.

But by the time I crashed onto the bridge, with Molly right behind me, the whole place was deserted. It was a room full of computerized control systems, with dozens of workstations and even an old-fashioned wooden steering wheel facing a massive windscreen, and not one crew member at his post, trying to keep the ship in the air.

"They ran," I said. "Deserted their posts. Useless shit-bastard cowards."

"Rats deserting a sinking ship," said Molly. "Still think these people are worth saving?"

"Let them run," I said. "My family will see they're rounded up and made to pay for what they've done. Once I've saved them. I can't just leave them to die, Molly."

"You think the law can touch people like these?" said Molly.

"Who said anything about the law? I'm talking about my family." I wandered round the various workstations, trying to make sense of the controls. "There must be something we can do . . ."

Molly pointed speechlessly at the massive windscreen before us. The ship's prow was sinking even lower. It had already passed through the cloud banks, and was plummeting towards the earth at increasing speed.

"Eddie, we need to get the hell off this ship," Molly said in a calm and extremely controlled voice. "And I mean right now."

"Do you have the magics for a teleport?"

"Well, no, but . . ."

"I suppose I could wait till the last minute and jump," I said. "Hold you in my arms and trust the glider wings . . ."

Molly glared at me. "Any other ideas?"

I grinned at her. "Save the ship."

"Let it crash! Everyone on board deserves it!"

"I'm thinking more about where the ship might crash," I said. "The people it landed on might not deserve it. And besides, in the ordinary, everyday world, oversized flying aircraft carriers aren't supposed to suddenly drop out of the sky and make a really large crater in the local surroundings. Droods are supposed to protect people from ever having to know things like that can happen."

"All right!" said Molly. "I get the point! Save the bloody ship!"

I found the main control station and sat down, armoured up one hand, and sent tendrils of golden strange matter surging through the systems. Computer screens burst into life all around me, packed with information. I grasped what I could, thought for a moment, and did the only useful thing left to me. I slaved all the systems to the steering wheel. I retrieved the golden tendrils and moved over to stand at the wheel. It was solid oak, very sturdy. I armoured up, took a firm hold, and tilted the wheel back to raise the prow. The ship didn't want to know. I set the power of my armour against the wheel, and slowly, inch by inch, the prow came up.

"That really is very impressive, Eddie," Molly said quietly beside me. "But we are still falling out of the sky."

"The main engines looked to be undamaged," I said. "According to the computers, it's just the guidance systems that are screwed. That's why I put everything through the wheel. Think of me as the manual override. If I can just hold her steady, the engines should slow the ship down."

"Should?"

"Hey, I'm dancing as fast as I can . . ."

"Anything I can do?" said Molly.

"Wish me luck," I said. "This isn't going to be easy."

I fought to guide the ship down, using all my strength. The armour could do only what I told it to do, multiplying my strength and intent. And the ship's weight, speed, and sheer inertia fought me every foot of the way. Systems broke down all around me, workstations exploding one after another and bursting into flames. Black smoke drifted across the bridge. Molly found a fire extinguisher and ran from station to station, fighting the fires. The ship groaned loudly as its whole superstructure began to buckle under the strain. I held the wheel and kept the prow up. My back was screaming at me, my arm muscles howling with pain. Sweat was running down my face underneath my mask.

"Molly?"

"Yes, Eddie? I'm here."

"If you can scrape together enough magic to teleport yourself off this ship, do it."

"I won't leave you, Eddie."

"My armour will protect me."

"After a crash from this height?"

"Yes. Theoretically . . . Molly, you have to go. I'm serious. I think the ship is breaking up. The best I can hope to do is crash-land it somewhere it'll do the least harm."

Molly moved in beside me. "I won't leave you, Eddie. I'll never leave you."

We stood together awhile as I fought the falling ship.

"Wait a minute," I said. "Look out there, up ahead . . . Is that an open body of water?"

"It can't be the sea, can it?"

"No, we're not that lucky . . . I think it's a reservoir! Yes! Any port in a storm . . ."

I guided the ship as best I could, working with the few systems still cooperating, but in the end, all I could do was aim the ship at the water and then just let it drop. I held on to the wheel for as long as I could, and then turned away and grabbed hold of Molly. I concentrated, and my golden armour swept out to envelop her as well. The strange matter sealed us in together, and we held each other tightly inside our golden cocoon as the aircraft carrier smashed down into the reservoir.

Somehow, the ship held together. When the noise and reverberations from the impact had finally died away, I armoured down, and Molly and I rolled away from each other and scrambled to our feet. I hurt all over, but I was alive. I grinned tiredly at Molly, and she whooped loudly.

"You did it, Eddie! You brought her down! Damn . . . You know, I would have bet good money against that. But you did it! You saved the ship!"

And she grabbed hold of me and danced me round the bridge. I went along, forgetting my aches and pains in the triumph of the moment. It's good to celebrate the little victories in life. Finally we stood together, looking out the windscreen at the calm and placid surface of the reservoir.

"We can't just leave the ship here," I said. "People would notice."

"Of course," said Molly. "It's illegally parked. I hear they can get very tough when things like that happen on reservoirs."

"Most of the ship's protections should still be working," I said. "Enough to keep it hidden until my family can get people here."

"What will they do?" said Molly. "Break the ship up for scrap metal?"

I grinned. "Why waste it? Haven't you ever wanted your very own flying aircraft carrier?"

"Your family is weird, Eddie."

I looked around me. "All its future predictions, and Cassandra Inc never saw this coming."

"Cassandra Inc never saw us coming," said Molly.

"Damned right."

CHAPTER TWO

Deadline

So I called home, and my handler assured me the family would send a Blackhawke to pick us up. After it had landed back at Drood Hall, re-fuelled, and loaded up with all the people necessary to take care of business at my end, I politely pointed out that this would undoubtedly take some time, and what were Molly and I supposed to do till then? Kate just sniffed. *You're on a boat, aren't you? It's hardly going to sink.* This typical example of Drood tact and consideration is why I ran away from home first chance I got. And yet, I keep going back. I think one of us assumes the other is going to change someday, and I don't know which of us is the bigger idiot.

Fortunately, Molly's magics returned long before the Blackhawke, and she teleported us back into the Drood family grounds, right outside the Hall. She smiled at me, just a bit smugly, because she knew she wasn't supposed to do that. In fact, technically speaking, she shouldn't have been able to do it, given that the

Sarjeant-at-Arms is constantly upgrading all our protections and defences. Droods have spent centuries keeping people safe, and as a result we have a lot of enemies. But no one's ever been able to keep Molly Metcalf out of anywhere she wants to be. Especially if she thinks someone doesn't want her to be there.

"Good to be home, I suppose," I said.

The next thing I knew, I was lying on a bed somewhere. Flat out, a pillow under my head, fully clothed but with a blanket over me. I started to sit up, and Molly was quickly there at my bedside, putting a restraining hand on my chest and telling me to lie back.

"It's all right, Eddie," she said quickly. "I'm here. You collapsed, out in the grounds. I couldn't move you, and you wouldn't wake up, so I had to call for help. Your family carried you into the Hall and brought you here. We're in the Infirmary." She managed a small smile. "You should have seen them panicking. The Sarjeant was convinced you'd been struck down by some unseen enemy, as the start of some major attack on the family. I told them you'd just fainted."

"I don't faint," I said.

And then I stopped as I took in the look on Molly's face. What she was really feeling and what she'd been trying to hide with artificial cheerfulness.

"Molly? What is it? What's happened?"

"The doctors have been examining you," Molly said carefully. "I was concerned, after what the angel said about death hovering over you. So I insisted they run a full series of tests. Check everything. They were very thorough. You've been out for more than three hours, Eddie!"

I didn't know what to say. Nothing like this had ever happened to me before. And I once had an entire hotel fall on me, back in the States. Even when I'm not actually in my armour, I'm used to feeling protected against anything the world can throw at me. I did my best to smile reassuringly at Molly, but it didn't feel like it came out right. There was something in her eyes, something she knew that I didn't . . .

"What's wrong, Molly?"

"Eddie . . ."

She couldn't bring herself to say it. Her voice choked off as tears threatened to spill down her face. I looked at her, bewildered. It takes a lot to make Molly cry. For the first time, I realised half a dozen medical staff in white coats were standing around, watching me closely. One of them, Dr Mary Drood, stepped forward. I used to see her all the time, back when I was a kid. When the old Sarjeant-at-Arms would beat the crap out of me on a regular basis, for this infringement or that, she was the one who stopped the bleeding and got me back on my feet again. She was older now, of course; a medium-height middle-aged woman with a calm, professional presence. A warm smile and cool grey eyes. These days, she was in charge of the Special Isolation Area.

I sat up abruptly, despite Molly's objections. I didn't feel feverish, or injured, or in pain. So what the hell was I doing in the Special Isolation Area? That was reserved for the most extreme cases, where the patient had to be kept away from everyone else to protect the rest of the family. I felt the first cold touch of fear in my heart.

I made a point of ignoring Dr Mary while I took a good look at my surroundings. The whole place had been painted stark white, bright gleaming walls without even a poster or a notice to break up the view. Clean and antiseptic, no doubt, but not a touch of warm colour anywhere to bring comfort to the patient. Because if you were in the Special Isolation Area, it was a bit late for that. There were only three beds in the room, and mine was the only one occupied. Because to be here was very rare. There was just the one sign, over the door: *Abandon All Hope, Ye Who Enter Here.*

Drood humour.

I had been here once before, though no one else knew that. To visit another field agent, Dylan Drood. That was a long time ago, back when I was still just the secondary field agent for London. Doing my duty as a Drood, while keeping as great a distance as I could between me and my family. I came back to the Hall without being summoned, and against standing orders, just to visit Dylan. One of my few real friends from childhood. I had to sneak back into the Hall, slipping past the defences and protections, because Dylan had been declared out of bounds once he'd been admitted to the Special Isolation Area. I chose my moment carefully, when the day shift was giving way to the night, put on a white coat, picked up a clipboard, and just strolled in. No one looked at me twice. Which gave me more than enough time to find Dylan and read his case notes.

Apparently, he'd been sent into the Welsh mountains to fight an other-dimensional incursion by strange mutated creatures from another earth. He drove them back and closed the Gate, stopping the invasion, but not before he picked up something from them. Something nasty.

He managed to get back to the Hall before he collapsed. Anyone he'd come into contact with was in quarantine, and he was in the Special Isolation Area. I found him lying on a bed just like mine, looking very small and vulnerable, surrounded by all kinds of medical equipment. There were sensor feeds all over his body, and tubes going in and out of him. Keeping him alive. His face was flushed and slick with sweat, and his eyes rolled back and forth. His breathing was worryingly fast, like that of a panting dog. I spoke to him, but he didn't even know I was there. Judging from what I could understand of his case notes, that was probably a good thing. Whatever he'd picked up from the invaders was burning him up. Boiling his brains in his head. He was dying, and there was nothing anyone could do but watch and take notes.

That was the first time I really understood that my armour couldn't protect me from everything. That I could die out in the field. I'd always known that, but now I believed it. I ran away from Dylan, from the Special Isolation Area, from the knowledge of my own mortality.

And now here I was, back in the dying place. I shuddered, briefly, and looked back to Dr Mary. She was in charge; she wouldn't have turned out for an individual case unless it was something extraordinary.

"Hello, Eddie," said Dr Mary. Her voice was professionally calm and reassuring. "You had us all worried. Now, I need you to listen to me, before I explain what's been happening and why you're here. I brought in all my colleagues for this case, Eddie. Every discipline, every speciality. Together we cover everything from combat surgery to alien diseases to enforced genetic mutation . . . so when I say we've dealt with pretty much everything at one time or another, I'm usually right. But none of us have ever seen anything like what's happened to you."

"So, this is serious?" I said.

"Yes, Eddie."

"Life threatening?" I said, trying hard to keep my voice steady.

Dr Mary didn't say anything, just nodded. I put out my hand, and Molly was there to hold it tightly.

"We've sent down to the Librarian," said Dr Mary. "He's searching through the more obscure areas of the Old Library, just in case. You've been poisoned, Eddie. An unknown chemical has been introduced into your system, and it's killing you. We can't stop it. We can detect its presence, but we can't identify it. We have no antidote, no cure, and we can't even treat the symptoms.

You've been murdered, Eddie. You just didn't know it, until now."

"I'm a dead man walking," I said, trying hard to keep my voice as steady as hers. "Didn't expect to hear that, when I got up this morning. How did this chemical get into me? Could I have been poisoned while I was at Cassandra's Secret Headquarters?"

"No," said Dr Mary. "Given how much damage it's already done, we think the poison must have been introduced some time back. Almost certainly while you were here, recuperating from the Big Game."

"I was poisoned inside the Hall?" I said. "How could the killer get inside the Hall, past Drood security? Without anyone noticing?"

She didn't react to my rising voice. "Those are very good questions, Eddie. We've contacted the Sarjeant-at-Arms, and he's on his way. But you mustn't give up hope. There are still things we can try. Constant dialysis, coupled with complete blood replacement. Organ transplants and cyborg implants. But you must understand, that would just be addressing the symptoms. Slowing the poison's progress. To give us more time to think what to do."

"No," I said. "I don't want extreme measures taken just to keep me alive. I don't want to lie helpless in my bed, dying by inches, hooked up to machines. I want to still be me, when I go out."

I was thinking of Dylan. I looked to Molly.

"Isn't there anything you can do?"

"It's a poison," she said. "Not a spell, or a curse, or a possession; just . . . chemicals. If it were an ordinary poison, I might be able to do something . . . but this is so different, my magic can't even touch it."

I turned back to Dr Mary. "I need to be up and about, doing something. Is there anything you can give me, to keep me going? Keep me strong while I work? Buy me some more time?"

Dr Mary looked at the other doctors, but they were already shaking their heads. "Anything extreme enough to affect you now would be countermanded by your torc. It's constantly monitoring and reinforcing your natural defences, fighting the poison. Protecting you from all outside influences."

"Then why is he still ill?" said Molly.

"Without the torc, Eddie would have been dead weeks ago," Dr Mary said steadily. "The torc is all that's keeping him alive. You really need to speak to Ethel about this, Eddie. She can tell you more about the torc and its capabilities." And then she leaned forward, lowering her voice. "But don't do it here. Or anywhere inside the Hall." She straightened up again before I could say anything.

Everyone looked around as the Armourer hurried in. Maxwell and Victoria, both of them looking indecently young and intimidatingly intelligent in their immaculate, starched white lab coats. Making the doctors' white coats look very much the poor relation. Maxwell was tall, dark, and handsome; Victoria was tall, blonde, and beautiful. They looked like a movie poster for love's young dream among the scientists. Given the mood I was in, I was ready to accept them as comic relief, but for a change neither of them was smiling. They nodded quickly to me, and then gestured for an assortment of their lab assistants to wheel in a whole bunch of unfamiliar equipment. Most of which had that fresh-from-the-drawing-board look, with loose wires and bits not properly attached. Dr Mary frowned, but said nothing. Maxwell and Victoria stood at the bottom of my bed, and looked at each other to see who wanted to go first.

"We bring presents," Maxwell said finally.

"And hope!" said Victoria.

"Just a few things we've been working on that we thought might prove useful."

"Though of course we're not really in the healing

people business. More the killing and blowing people up . . ."

"But we've adapted our most powerful and sensitive scanners," said Maxwell, "to see if they can find something everyone else has missed."

"Because that does happen," said Victoria.

"Oh yes. You'd be surprised."

"Quite right, Maxie dear. You tell him."

"I am telling him, Vikki. Don't you worry, Eddie. We're here now."

"Thanks for coming," I said. "I could use some cheering up."

"Well, quite," said Maxwell. With the air of someone who knew he'd missed the joke but wasn't going to admit it.

"You just let us go to work!" said Victoria.

"We can do this," said Maxwell.

"We can't lose you, Eddie," said Victoria. "Not so soon after losing Jack."

"We'll think of something."

"We always do."

And then they stopped and looked at each other again, at a loss for anything more to say. A clattering of steel paws on the bare floor announced the arrival of the robot dog, Scraps.2. The doctors looked like they wanted to object to his presence, but couldn't think of an acceptable reason. Scraps.2 reared up to place his front paws on the side of my bed, and fixed me with his glowing red eyes.

"Honestly. I turn my back on you for five minutes . . . Have they told you you're dying?"

"Yes," I said.

"Good. I did wonder if they'd got round to it, or if they were still busy being tactful and understanding. You know what your uncle Jack would have said about this."

"Yes," I said. "Do my duty to the family."

Scraps.2 snorted loudly. A disconcerting sound, given that he didn't have a real nose. "Hardly. He'd have said, *Find the bastard who did this to you, and really ruin his day.*"

"Sounds like a plan to me," I said.

Dr Mary looked over the equipment the assistants were assembling around my bed, and glared at the Armourer. "What is all this? You can't just bring untested equipment into a sterile environment!"

"We can if it's an emergency," said Maxwell. "We can do anything, if it's an emergency. Probably part of our job description, isn't it, Vikki?"

"Almost certainly," said Victoria. "Don't you mess with us, Dr Mary. We have guns. And other things."

"Oh yes," said Maxwell. "And our other things are much worse than guns."

"You have nurses," said Victoria. "We have lab assistants. Fear their ingenuity."

I smiled at Molly. "I am definitely feeling better for their being here."

She smiled back but didn't say anything.

In the end, the doctors just backed off and let the Armourer get on with it. Molly stayed where she was. She wouldn't let go of my hand. The assistants took one look at her and worked around her. I leaned back on the bed, ready to object if anything looked like it was getting invasive. But they just took it in turns to point things at me and then study the results on their laptops. I watched their faces closely, and the way Maxwell and Victoria muttered together as they considered the various readings. There was a growing tension in the air, as one by one the assistants were forced to admit there was nothing their marvellous new equipment could usefully do. Maxwell and Victoria ended up standing at the foot of my bed again.

"I'm sorry, Eddie," said Maxwell. "I really thought we had something to bring to the table."

"We brought exotic tech and alien tech," said Victoria. "And a few things various field agents picked up in their travels."

"And Droods have been to some pretty strange places."

"We even brought a few things the assistants came up with specially, just for you."

"Too extreme to be tried, usually," Maxwell admitted.

"But none of it worked!" Victoria's voice rose sharply.

"Hush, dear, hush," said Maxwell. "We've done all we can."

"It's not enough!"

"We can see the poison, Eddie," Maxwell said steadily. "But not identify its components. Whatever it is, it's outside our experience."

"Completely unknown."

"Not from around here."

One by one the lab assistants departed, taking their equipment with them. The doctors tried hard not to look like they were thinking, *We told you so.* The assistants looked to me like mourners filing out of a funeral. Maxwell and Victoria stood close together, too busy comforting each other to think about comforting me. Victoria was dabbing at her eyes with a crumpled tissue.

"If anyone should be crying here," I said, "I think it should be me. Stop trying to upstage me."

"He's being so brave!" sniffed Victoria.

"We're the Armourer!" said Maxwell. "We're supposed to come up with something amazing at the last moment, and save the day. But we didn't. I can't help thinking your uncle Jack would have succeeded."

"No, he wouldn't," Scraps.2 said firmly. "Trust me. The first thing you need to learn about your job is that not every problem has a solution. Come on; I'll take you back to the Armoury. You can think better there." He turned his heavy steel head to look at me. "Sorry to leave you, Eddie, but I can help them. I can't help you."

"Understood," I said.

The Armourer went off with the robot dog, leaving me with the doctors. I looked at them steadily.

"How long have I got?"

They muttered together for quite a while, not wanting to commit themselves, but every time they glanced at me, I was still looking at them, so they went back to debating the matter. Finally, Dr Mary faced me squarely.

"Best estimate, three months. And the last month will be . . . pretty bad."

It hit me hard to hear my death sentence announced so certainly.

"So all that's left," I said after a while, "is to track down my murderer. And make him pay." I looked at Molly. She was crying quietly. I squeezed her hand. "Don't, love. I'm dying, and I'm not crying. It's just another deadline. We can do deadlines."

Molly stopped her tears through an effort of will, and nodded her head firmly. "Who could have done this?"

"I might know," said the Sarjeant-at-Arms. "Everyone but Eddie and Molly, leave the area. This is a security matter."

No one argued. No one does, when the Sarjeant says that. The family trusts him to keep us safe. The doctors filed out quickly. I got the sense they were almost relieved to be getting away from the accusing gaze of the man they couldn't save. I knew I was being hard on them. I didn't care. The Sarjeant waited till he was sure everyone was gone, and then leaned in close.

"There is a man most people believe to be just an urban legend of the hidden world. Dr DOA. Blamed for every death that has no obvious cause, he is the killer that other killers fear. The assassin who strikes from the shadows, who murders his victim without even being noticed. By the time the victim finds out he's been poisoned, if he ever finds out, it's too late. Dr DOA's poison is always fatal. Always."

"No one has ever recovered?" said Molly. "No one's ever beaten the poison?"

"No," said the Sarjeant. "And he's supposed to have killed some people I would have said were unkillable. Whatever he's using, there's no defence against it and no cure."

"What do we know about this . . . Dr DOA?" I said.

"Not much. No one knows who he really is, where he came from, or how he does what he does. Which is why most people prefer to believe he's just an urban legend. But this fits his usual MO, and his usual arrogance. To get inside Drood Hall, past all our security, poison one particular Drood, and then get out again without ever being noticed . . . Before today, I would have said that was impossible!"

"Calm down, Sarjeant," I said. "A complexion that colour can't be good for you."

I was genuinely amused to see him taking all of this as a personal affront.

He sniffed loudly. "I will find out how he did it. And if any of my people have been lax, there will be blood on the walls."

"Any idea as to how he might have got in?" I said.

"I'm working on it," he said grimly. "In the meantime, I have questions for you, Eddie. Where you've been, who you've spoken to . . ."

"Later," I said. The Sarjeant started to say something, saw the look on my face, nodded abruptly, and left. I turned to Molly. "He must really be concerned. He was actually being considerate."

The Special Isolation Area seemed very quiet, with just the two of us in it. I swung my legs over the side of the bed and got carefully to my feet. Molly was quickly there at my side, ready to catch me if I fell. But my legs held steady, and my head remained clear. I felt fine. Not at all like I was dying. I smiled reassuringly at Molly, and hoped the smile looked more convincing than it felt.

"See? Not dead yet. Tell you what; let's go for a walk. I need to be out among living things. See the world while I still can."

Molly started to say something, and found she couldn't. She grabbed hold of me and crushed me tightly to her, hanging on like a drowning woman. I could feel her heart hammering next to mine, almost as fast as mine. Like trapped birds in cages who can see the cat approaching. I murmured comforting words in her ear and made myself be calm, to calm her down. It helped me, to be able to help her. It stopped me thinking about me. I gave her one last hug and pushed her gently away from me. She let go immediately and stood back. There were still patches of raised colour on her face, but her eyes were dry and her mouth was steady.

"We find him, and we kill him," she said. "Nothing else matters."

"Right," I said.

We stood and looked at each other for a while. She'd never seemed lovelier, or more determined. I wanted to look at her forever.

"All the things I meant to do, for you and for me," I said. "Places I meant to take you, sights I meant to show you . . . Special places I always meant to share with you. When I had the time. Things I put off because I always thought there would be more time. And now, suddenly, there isn't."

"You can't die," said Molly. "What would I do without you?"

"Typical," I said. "Always thinking of yourself."

We both managed a small smile. Trying to be supportive of each other.

"I refuse to believe your death is inevitable," said

Molly. "I mean, the first time we got together, you were dying! Poisoned by strange matter, from where you'd been shot with an arrow by an elf lord. Ethel pulled you back from that, at the last moment. You need to talk to her, Eddie. Even if your family isn't talking to her. Maybe especially because it isn't. What's going on there, anyway?"

"Damned if I know," I said. "I'll have to find out before we leave the Hall."

Molly leaned in close, lowering her voice. "Your family might be listening to us."

"You think my family would bug a hospital ward?"

"You don't?"

"Given that I haven't a clue what's going on with the new Matriarch . . . I'm not sure about anything, right now."

"Could her falling-out with Ethel . . . have something to do with Dr DOA's getting into the Hall undetected?"

"Good point," I said. "Something else to look into."

"Then there was the time that Immortal almost killed you," said Molly, reverting to her normal tone of voice. "And I had to go haul your arse back from Limbo. You're really very hard to kill, Eddie. So, third time lucky."

"Of course," I said.

I didn't believe that, but I could see Molly needed to, so I went along.

"Let's get out of here," I said.

I walked back through the Hall, striding it out because I didn't want to have to stop and talk to anyone. Molly hurried along at my side. Everywhere we went, people fell back to watch us pass. Some fell silent; others murmured urgently together. Word had got around. I could feel the pressure of their gazes. I wanted to turn suddenly and shout, *Boo!* at them, just to see what would happen. I increased my pace, and Molly stuck close, glaring at anyone who looked like they might even be thinking of getting in our way, or even getting too close. We left the Hall through the front door, and I felt a very real relief at putting the huge old building behind me. I've always associated the Hall with bad news, and the worst parts of my life.

"You should never have come back, Eddie," said Molly, echoing my thoughts. "Bad things are always happening to you here. Hell, they nearly killed me once. This whole place is just one big jinx."

I decided to go for a walk through the grounds. Across the wide-open lawns, under the iron grey sky. I set off at a steady pace, breathing deeply, savouring the familiar rich scents and the bracingly cold air. How could I be dying, when I felt so alive? How could I be murdered, when the world was still so full of life? I looked around me, and it was like seeing it all for the first time. The lawns and the flower beds, the copses of beech and ash and oak trees, the artificial lake . . . Molly moved along beside me, saying nothing, just being there.

The peacocks scattered as I approached them, letting out their eerie cries in protest, but the gryphons ambled happily forward to greet me. Great lumpy creatures, with scaly grey bodies and long, morose faces. Just psychic enough to see the near future, and serve as an early-warning system against intruders. They were the only part of Drood defences that actually looked forward to an invasion; because they got to eat the invaders. They smelled appalling, because they ate carrion and loved to roll in dead things. Which is why they're never allowed inside the Hall, even when it's raining. Especially when it's raining. They bumped against my legs and nuzzled my hands with their soft mouths.

"I used to sneak scraps out to them when I was a kid," I said.

"I doubt they remember," said Molly. "They can't be the same ones."

"Gryphons live for centuries," I said. "Lucky bastards . . ."

A sudden surge of anger burst through me. I pushed the gryphons aside and strode on. Molly had to hurry to catch up. We passed a huge display of weird and unnatural flowers, with great heads bobbing at the top of long stalks. The heads blossomed, and turned to watch me as I passed.

"Bad news really does travel fast," I said.

I circled round the ancient hedge maze, with its tall green walls. There was a time when the maze served as a prison for the living rogue armour, Moxton's Mistake. I had to wear it once, to survive. My skin still crawled at the thought of its embrace. Everywhere I looked reminded me of some past adventure, some vital part of what was once my life, and now was history.

I took Molly down to the artificial lake, to watch the swans sail elegantly by. They saw us and held well back. They'd learned to be wary of Molly, because she had a tendency to throw things at them. Hard, heavy things, not at all bready. The surface of the lake was still, the swans hardly moving. It all seemed so peaceful. Like nothing bad could be happening on such an ordinary day.

"I did wonder if the undine might manifest for me," I said. "But apparently not."

I felt obscurely upset about that. She'd made an appearance for Jack's funeral.

"She knew Jack," said Molly, following my thoughts with the ease of long acquaintance. "I never did get to the bottom of that. You didn't know her, did you?"

"No," I said. "I just thought she might . . . She's another of the mysteries of this place I always took for granted. I knew there was a story, but I never pressed anyone . . . Don't suppose I ever will now."

I moved on, and Molly came with me. It didn't seem fair to me that the world should just keep on going when I wouldn't.

"You could always come back as a ghost!" Molly said brightly. "Like Jacob, in the old Chapel."

"The family doesn't allow ghosts to hang around," I said. "Or you wouldn't be able to move in the corridors for ectoplasm and poltergeist phenomena. The family gets through a lot of soldiers in its never-ending war."

"Didn't stop Jacob from occupying the Chapel," said Molly.

"He had a special dispensation," I said. "And what would I do, anyway, as a ghost? Stick around to watch you grow old? Watch you start a new life with someone else? Move on, and forget me?"

"I would never do that!" said Molly.

"Of course you would. That's what the living do. You had a life before me, and you'll have a life after I'm gone." I stopped and looked at her. "Molly, that's what I want."

She looked into my face, searchingly. "Really?"

"Well," I said. "If truth be told, what I really want is for my passing to break hearts and ruin lives. I want mass weeping and a month of national mourning. But then, after that, everyone should just get on with their lives." I looked around. "It wasn't that long ago I was here for Jack's funeral. And soon they'll be holding mine. I hope the weather's nice."

I looked back at the Hall, far behind me now. Just a great brooding presence on the horizon. Weighed down by history, and all the generations of Droods who'd lived and served in that hulking edifice to duty and responsibilities. So many stories, come and gone. And that's all I would be now. Just another story, with a beginning, a middle, and an end.

Which made me think of the Winter Hall, that cold

empty place where I passed the time in Limbo, caught between Life and Death. A frost-covered shadow of my home, where I walked through empty corridors haunted by memories. Until Molly came and got me and brought me home. She wouldn't be able to do that this time. She liked to boast she'd been to Heaven and Hell and everywhere in between, but she'd never brought anyone back from the dead. There are some limits even the wild witch of the woods has to respect.

The Winter Hall reminded me of the Other Hall, which briefly took the place of my Hall, thanks to the dimensional engine Alpha Red Alpha. The Other Hall had been home to a whole different family of Droods, on a different earth. Someone killed them all and blew up their home, leaving only burned-out ruins and dead bodies. Some still wrapped in half-melted golden armour. I never did find out who was responsible for that. Another thing I'd always meant to get around to, but life kept getting in the way.

For a while there, I thought I was the last Drood. So many people have died on my watch. Friends and family, allies and enemies. Some I'd seen die; some I killed myself. For what seemed like good reasons at the time. More faces, more stories. So much death in my life.

I wandered on through the grounds, just going where my feet led me. Visiting various places Molly and I had been before. On the edge of the grounds, I found a place of dead earth and dark trees. I stopped.

"This was where we broke into the grounds, the first time I came here with you," I said. "After my family had declared me rogue and wanted me dead."

"Yes," said Molly. "I remember."

"This is where we met the scarecrows . . ."

"I know. I still have nightmares about them sometimes."

"That's my family for you."

The scarecrows are part of my family's outer defences. Stuffed and preserved human figures that look like they've just come down off their crosses with bad intentions on their minds. Unstoppable, unfeeling things driven to fight all intruders. My family makes them out of the bodies of our most hated enemies, to guard the family they tried to harm. Eternal punishment, or for as long as they last. I remembered how they looked, lurching out of the shadows to face us. Their clothes rotting and falling apart, their faces stretched taut, brown as parchment and as brittle. Tufts of straw protruded from their ears and mouths. Their eyes were still alive, still suffering. I remembered names . . . Laura Lye, the water elemental assassin known as the Liquidator. Mad Frankie Phantasm. And the Blue Fairy, who had been my friend, my ally, and my enemy. Half Drood and half elf, and never sure which was his true nature. In the end, he guessed wrong. My relatives have always found it hard to forgive those who betray them.

I led the way back across one of the biggest lawns, where once an army of Accelerated Men had come spilling onto the grounds to attack us, through a dimensional Gate opened by our worst enemies, the Immortals. It seemed to me I could still see the ghosts of dark figures, running straight at the Drood defenders, superhumanly fast and strong, burning themselves out just to get at us. Used by the Immortals as supercharged attack dogs. Hundreds of Accelerated Men died on this open ground, lied to and betrayed, sacrificed on the altar of our enemies' hatred. We killed them all. We had to.

"So much fighting," I said finally. "So much blood and death on these grounds, and so few picnics and pleasant walks. That's the Drood life for you."

"You never cared much for picnics, or walks of any kind," said Molly. "You were always more interested in a pie and a pint at the pub, or a good book in a comfy chair."

"I might have developed a taste for such things if I'd had the time," I said. "We were always so busy, always in such a hurry . . ."

"I could conjure us up a picnic hamper," said Molly. "If you like. We never did get our Christmas meal. We could just sit down here, take a break . . ."

"No," I said. "I'm not hungry right now. Maybe later."

It occurred to me that I had to stop saying that. Stop putting things off. Because all too soon there wouldn't be a later. A sudden horror took me, a despair at being caught in a trap with no escape, no way out. Trapped in a body that had turned against me. My heart lurched in my chest at the sheer unfairness of it all, and for a moment I couldn't get my breath. Molly saw the panic rising in my face. She moved in close, placing her hands on my chest and murmuring comforting words until I had control again. I nodded slowly and smiled my thanks to her.

"Live in the moment," I said. My voice sounded harsh, even to me. "I can do this. I have to do this. I've been close to death before; it comes with the job . . . Why does it bother me so much now?" I looked at Molly and knew why. "Because now I'm not just losing me; I'm losing you."

We walked on, together.

"We never did get married," I said after a while.

"I never asked you," said Molly.

"I could have said something," I said. "There would have been problems with my family, but . . ."

"Eddie, I never wanted it." Her voice was firm. "I never felt the need. We had each other, and that was all that mattered." She stopped suddenly, so I stopped with her. She looked at me. "I said *had* . . . Like it's already over. I won't accept that. I'll never accept that."

"At the end," I said, "if it gets bad . . . I don't want you around me. If I do end up dying by inches in some hospital bed . . . I don't want you to see me like that."

"I'll never leave you," said Molly. "You'll always be my Eddie. Do you really think I'm that shallow?"

"I don't want you sitting at my bedside, watching me die," I said. "You shouldn't have to go through that. I wouldn't do it for you. I couldn't . . . A man should die on his own. It's the last important thing he has to do; he should be left alone, to concentrate on getting it right."

"You do talk crap sometimes," said Molly. "You know damned well you can't do anything practical without me there to help."

"Of course," I said. "What was I thinking? The two of us, together . . . Not forever, after all. But together till the end."

"I can live with that," said Molly.

We smiled and walked on, arm in arm.

"How do you feel?" said Molly.

"I don't know," I said. "It's all happened so quickly. I cheated death so many times, out in the field, that I stopped thinking about it. But I should have known . . . everyone's luck runs out eventually."

"You were ready to die for me earlier today," said Molly. "Standing on the edge of that airship . . ."

"That was different," I said. "There was a purpose to that. This feels so random . . . Like I just drew a bad ticket in some lottery. Mostly, I feel angry. That I won't have the life, the future, I thought I was going to have. With you."

"I don't know what I'll do, once you're gone," said Molly.

"You'll think of something," I said.

"Are you scared?" said Molly. "I'm scared."

"Don't be," I said. "I've had a good . . . Well, I don't know about good, but I've certainly had an interesting life. And I had you. Finding you was enough good luck for any one life."

"How can you be so accepting?" said Molly.

"I'm not," I said. "But I can fake it, long enough to find Dr DOA. And put a stop to him. Not just for me, but for all his victims. Be strong for me, Molly. For when I can't."

"I'm here, Eddie. I'm here."

We came at last to the great grassy mound at the rear of the Hall, under which was buried a dragon's head. Struck off by Baron Frankenstein centuries ago, but still somehow living. I found it, alive and lonely, under a hillside overlooking the ruins of Castle Frankenstein. So I brought it back to Drood Hall, because it didn't seem right to just leave it there. The dragon's head seemed quite happy in its new home, always ready to chat with any passing Drood. It seemed to me that the mound was somewhat bigger than I remembered from the last time I visited.

"Sorry it's been a while," I said. "I've been busy."

"That's all right," said the dragon's voice. Deep and resonant, rich as wine, old as the hills. "The Armourer and their lab assistants are always popping by. My condition fascinates them. They're always bringing strange new machines to my mound to try out on me. And the Librarian often stops by, so we can discuss history. I've seen so much of it. I do miss the old Armourer, your uncle Jack. He kept saying he was going to grow me a new body, but . . . I have heard what's happened, Eddie. I understand how you're feeling. I wasn't ready to die either, when the old Baron cut off my head."

"But you're still alive!" said Molly. Almost accusingly.

"You call this living?" said the dragon. "Sorry. That was an old joke, even in my time. The point is, I didn't expect to survive my beheading. It had been such a long time since I'd seen any others of my kind, I had no idea we were so . . . durable. I really believed my time was up. And even though I'd lived for centuries, I still wasn't ready. No matter how long you've had, it never seems enough. You're never ready to let go. At least you have some time, Eddie, to put your affairs in order."

"And get revenge on my murderer," I said.

The dragon rumbled approvingly. "You would have made a good dragon."

I said my good-byes to him, just in case we didn't meet again. It occurred to me, I was probably going to be doing a lot of that. And then I carried on through the grounds. Molly was quiet for a long time.

"Promise me one thing," she said finally.

"If I can."

"Don't ever say good-bye to me. I've never been any good at good-byes."

"I'll probably have other things on my mind," I said kindly.

I was trying to look at everything, force every detail into my mind. Because once I left the Hall to go after Dr DOA, it was possible I might never get to come back. Never see any of this again. I could die, chasing the man with death for a name. It felt . . . like I was saying good-bye to my life. To my world.

I walked up and down and back and forth, and Molly followed along wherever I wanted to go. She didn't say anything about the time passing. Until I realised I was just putting off going back to the Hall, to begin my last mission. I stopped, took a deep breath, and headed back to the Hall by the shortest route. I always felt better, and stopped worrying about things, once I'd settled on a course of action. Molly saw where we were heading and understood our break was over. That we were going back to work.

"What are we going to do?" she said.

"Well, to start with, we don't panic," I said. "We work the possibilities. I don't care who this Dr DOA really is; he can't operate in a vacuum. He can't do his work in our world without leaving traces. He has to arrange things, buy things, make travel plans . . . There's got to be a trail somewhere. So we go out there and start leaning on people. Someone will talk. Someone always talks. Enough to point us in the right direction. What's wrong, Molly? You look disappointed."

"When you said *possibilities*, I thought you meant looking for a cure."

"Molly . . ."

"We can't just give up!"

"I'm not," I said. "But I'll leave the last-minute-miracle stuff to the experts. They have the resources, and the time. We have to concentrate on what we can do."

"There's still the Nightside!" said Molly. "There's always someone in the long night who can do anything. If you've got the money."

"Somehow that thought doesn't exactly fill me with confidence," I said.

"Money is a great motivator," said Molly. "You know, if all else fails . . . I could always bring you back. Like Dead Boy."

"No thank you," I said firmly. "I don't want to be like that."

"You don't know," said Molly. "You've never met him."

"I've heard about him. I've heard lots about him."

"Or like Larry Oblivion, the dead detective!"

"Even more no thank you. I've met Larry. We worked a case together some years back."

"You never said!"

"I don't tell you everything."

"There are other places, outside the Nightside!" Molly said desperately. "All kinds of extreme hospices, voodoo parlours, future-tech establishments . . . all the shadowy places on the borderlands, where they do things no one else can! I know places. I know people . . ."

"My time is limited, Molly. I'd rather spend what's left of it hunting down the man who killed me and making him pay. Rather than risk his getting away because I was too busy chasing false hopes."

"I still have friends in Heaven and Hell who owe me favours . . ."

"Not any more," I said. "All your old Pacts and Agreements were rendered null and void when your debts were taken care of by the Powers That Be. Remember?"

"Damn," said Molly. "Okay . . . Look, I'll contact my sisters. See what Isabella and Louisa have to say. They know things and people I don't."

"If you like," I said.

We headed for the Hall. It loomed up before us, heavy with fate and foreboding. As though just by walking back through its door, I would be committing myself to my last mission. No stepping aside, no turning back. I'd be starting down a road that had only one destination.

I looked the old building over carefully, trying to see it clearly one last time. Drood Hall is old, really old. And it's always been colourful as hell, just like the family it contains. The sprawling old manor house dated back to Tudor times, and the central section still had the black-and-white boarded frontage, along with heavy leaded-glass windows and a jutting gabled roof. Four extensive wings had been added, down the years. Massive and solid in the Regency style, they contained thousands of rooms. We're a big family. The roof rose and fell like a great grey-tiled ocean, complete with any number of gargoyles, and grotesque ornamental guttering that probably seemed like a good idea at the time. Add to that an observatory, an eyrie, and a whole bunch of landing pads for the steam-powered autogyros, futuristic helicars, flying saucers, and winged unicorns. Because my family has always been ready to embrace anything that works. The Hall, solid and firm in stone and wood, people and causes. The Droods have always weighed heavily on the world.

"Do you have a bucket list?" Molly said suddenly.

"What, things I should do while I still can?" I said.

"Never got around to thinking about it. Bit late now. I've got work to do. Do you have a list?"

"I always planned to take you on a pub crawl of the hidden world," said Molly. "To all the especially off-the-beaten-track places I go, when I really want to let my hair down. Show you all the special places that meant something to me. We never talked like this before."

"Never had cause to before." I thought about it as the front door drew nearer. "I suppose I should update my will, before we leave. Make sure you're properly provided for."

"Can you be sure your family will abide by your wishes?"

I grinned. "My family doesn't know half of what I've got tucked away."

We stopped before the front door. Molly grabbed hold of me, and hugged me fiercely.

"I can't let you go! I won't let you go!"

I held her tight and said nothing. Because I knew there would come a time when I'd have to let Molly go, and go on alone.

CHAPTER THREE

Everyone Wants to Help

There are days when you think things can't get any worse, but somehow they always do. I walked back through the front door of Drood Hall, with Molly on my arm, and there waiting for me was the Sarjeant-at-Arms. Standing right in the middle of the entrance hall with his arms tightly folded, and with the air of someone who'd been waiting for some time. And really wasn't happy about it. I couldn't be bothered to give the impression that I gave a damn. I planted myself in front of him and raised a single eyebrow. He drew himself up to his full height, the better to look down his nose at me. I could feel Molly stirring dangerously at my side, and amused myself wondering which way the Sarjeant would fall after she hit him.

"What?" I said.

"I am here to escort both of you to a meeting with the Matriarch and her advisory Council," the Sarjeant said flatly. "Your attendance is . . . requested."

That last word stopped me. If he was being polite, if the Matriarch was being polite, something was up. Something had changed. So of course I had to go. Especially if Molly was included in the invitation. Normally, my family does everything short of declaring open hostilities to keep Molly out of Council meetings. Partly because she's not family, but mostly because she likes to sit at the back, eat popcorn, and heckle.

"Lead the way, Sarjeant," I said graciously. "Molly and I would be delighted to attend your little tea party."

"Oooh! A party!" said Molly. "Will there be tea and crumpets?"

"We can but hope," I said.

The Sarjeant gathered his injured dignity around him, turned on his heel like the poker up his arse had just sprouted spikes, and led the way into the familiar embrace of the Hall. Without once looking back to check we were actually following. I ambled along behind, while Molly stuck close by me, glaring watchfully around for ambushes, unfortunate comments, or just the wrong look on someone's face. I let her. I didn't want her to notice how worried I was.

I'd thought I had time to do all the things I needed to do. Was the Matriarch about to tell me that I didn't, after all?

It soon became clear we weren't heading in any of the directions I'd expected. I closed the gap between the Sarjeant and me, and raised my voice.

"We're still not meeting at the Sanctity? Even though it's a full-Council meeting?"

"No," said the Sarjeant.

"At some point," I said, "you're going to have to explain to me just what the hell is going on."

"Not my place," said the Sarjeant. Carefully not looking back at me.

I couldn't help but notice that wherever we went, everyone hurried to step back and avert their eyes from me. No more pointing or muttering, no more gathering in groups to enjoy the spectacle of a dead man walking. Possibly because I was with the Sarjeant-at-Arms now.

We made our way into the East Wing, which meant we weren't going back to the Matriarch's new garden-centre office. So where else would the new Matriarch feel safe from Ethel? There wasn't much in the East Wing; it's mainly offices and meeting places, where general policy gets discussed and the details hammered out. Drood equivalent of the civil service. Not the most glamorous work, but necessary for the smooth running of family business. Personally, I'd rather hammer nails into my head.

The Sarjeant finally took us out of the East Wing through a side door, and just like that, we were outside the Hall, facing the old family Chapel. Where the ghost of Jacob used to hang out. I stopped where I was, ignoring the Sarjeant's unhidden impatience, so I could take a good look at the Chapel. It had been some time since I'd last been there. It used to be one of the few places I could go to get away from my family. Where I could feel safe from what the family wanted of me. And now my family had even taken that away. But why were we meeting the Matriarch and her Council here? What was so important, so significant, about this battered old edifice?

Once upon a time, it really was the family Chapel, back before we went multi-denominational. This was after a rather embarrassing period, when the then-Matriarch decided the family was in danger of becoming too inbred. Too many marriages inside the family, too many cousins connected in too many ways. We were in urgent need of fresh blood. So an outreach programme was launched, and any number of Drood chicks were kicked out of the nest and told to fly off in search of partners. The result was a great many new marriages with outsiders, inevitably followed by an inrush of new ideas and new values. One of which was a more relaxed attitude to Drood religious observance. The Chapel was abandoned, and apparently for a while you couldn't move in Drood Hall for new churches, red-hot religious debates, and even a few duels. I miss out on all the good stuff.

I'm amazed our established church lasted as long as it did, anyway. There's nothing like having regular contact with the agents of Heaven and Hell to make anyone a dedicated freethinker.

The old Chapel was a squat stone structure with crucifix slit windows. It looked Saxon, but was really just an Eighteenth Century folly. Put up to replace an older and far more authentic building that was simply too old, and too boring. The Chapel looked as ugly as ever, its rough stone walls all but buried under thick mats of crawling ivy. Some of which was already stirring threateningly as it detected our presence. Until the Sarjeant-at-Arms glared at it and the ivy settled sullenly back down again. No one argues with the Sarjeant. Which is, of course, why I always did.

I tried the door, and to my surprise it opened easily. In the old days, I had to put my shoulder to the heavy wood just to get it to move. Because I was the only one who ever used it. But now all the old gloom was gone, dismissed by newly installed electric lighting, and the interior looked completely different. There used to be a pile of old wooden pews stacked against the far wall, and a big black leather recliner chair, where Jacob would slump at his ease and watch the memories of old television shows on a set that didn't even have any workings. And an old-fashioned freezer, somehow always full of ethereal booze. For a ghost, Jacob really did like his comforts. But all of that was gone now. The place had been cleaned up and cleared out. Someone had even swept the floor, revealing old flagstones worn smooth in places by massed bent knees.

The Matriarch was sitting at the back of the Chapel, behind a richly polished mahogany desk. Complete with telephones and a laptop so she would never be out of touch. She sat up straight in her chair, her hands together and resting on the tabletop before her. She looked calm and composed, with everything she had to say carefully rehearsed in her head so she could shut down any objections I might have before they could get off the ground. The Sarjeant went to stand beside her, holding himself at parade rest. The Armourer, Maxwell and Victoria, sat side by side before the table. Close enough that they could still hold hands. I had to wonder whether that was an affectation, or whether I'd always been too old for love's young dream. Love, real love, came somewhat late in life for me. I glanced round to make sure Molly was still at my side, and she smiled and slipped a reassuring arm through mine. I looked back at Maxwell and Victoria; they seemed younger than ever in such a formal setting.

Which was more than could be said for the old gentleman sitting opposite them; he looked tired and fretful and out of place. Though it had to be said William the Librarian did appear pretty spruce, for once. In a heavy tweed suit, a clean white shirt, a peach cravat held in place by a diamond pin . . . and fluffy pink bunny slippers. Suggesting his ongoing rehabilitation to civilised behaviour wasn't entirely complete just yet. His bushy white hair had been attacked with a brush and comb and partially subdued, and someone had shaved him recently. His gaze was clear and his mouth was firm, but there was still an air of vagueness about him, as though he were trying to remember why he was there. Or why he'd ever thought turning up was a good idea in the first place.

The reason for the general improvement stood beside him; his wife, Ammonia Vom Acht. The most powerful telepath in the world. Ugly as a bulldog licking piss off a thistle and about as convivial, Ammonia had a square, almost brutal face, not improved by a permanent thunderous frown. Short and squat in her shapeless grey suit, Ammonia was still an impressive, striking figure. She and William were devoted to each other. And there was no denying she'd been good for him. The Librarian was a lot more himself these days. It amazed me to think how far he'd come since I brought him back from where he'd been hiding, at the Happy Acres high-security institute for the criminally insane.

Technically speaking, Ammonia shouldn't have been present at a Council meeting. Just marrying a Drood wasn't enough to make you family. But as she was only a psychic sending, and not physically present, everyone made allowances. Because Ammonia didn't give them any choice. Her image looked real enough, until you noticed her feet didn't quite reach the floor. Because of her incredible telepathic abilities, Ammonia couldn't bear to be around people. She lived alone in a cottage on the coast, miles from everywhere, and preferred to limit her travelling to her spirit form. She looked solid enough. I had to resist the urge to give her a quick prod, just to check. She looked at me coldly, as though she knew what I was thinking. I quickly turned my gaze to the Matriarch.

"Where are the Heads of the War Room and Operations?" I said. "Shouldn't they be here? They were still part of your advisory Council, last I heard."

"They're busy," said the Matriarch. "Clearing up the mess in the field left by Cassandra's interference. I'll brief them later. Take a seat."

I stood my ground. "Why are we meeting here, of all places?"

"Because this location is steeped in ghostly energies and temporal complications, thanks to Jacob's peculiar afterlife existence," said the Matriarch. "The psychic plane is so saturated with information, it should be impossible for anyone to observe us."

"Including Ethel?" I said.

"Yes," said the Matriarch.

"Is that right, Ethel?" I said.

There was a long pause. Everyone's head came up, listening, but there came no response.

"What is going on?" I said.

"I'll tell you when you return from your mission," said the Matriarch.

"Why not tell me now?"

"Because you're going to speak to Ethel about your condition before you leave. I would."

"Am I not supposed to tell her what we discuss here?" I said.

"That would be wisest," said the Matriarch.

She gestured again at the two empty chairs set out before her table. Set out exactly half-way between the Armourer and the Librarian. I decided I'd pushed her as far as I usefully could, and sat down. Molly settled onto the chair next to me, as stiff and watchful as a suspicious cat. I looked at Maxwell and Victoria, but they didn't want to meet my gaze. William reached out to pat me on the arm, as though reassuring a restless dog.

"I've been ransacking the Library ever since I heard, looking for something to help you, Eddie. Found all kinds of interesting things. None of them particularly helpful as yet, but . . . early days. It's a big Library. In fact, I'm not even sure just how big the Old Library really is. I have a suspicion the boundaries move when I'm not looking. My assistant, Yorith . . . You remember Yorith? Of course you do . . . He's searching through some of the more arcane areas while I'm here." He stopped to look meaningfully at the Matriarch. "I still don't know why my presence was deemed so damned essential. You'll do what you decide to do, whatever any of us have to say. Just like always."

"I value your opinions," said the Matriarch.

"Then you should pay more attention to them," said the Librarian.

"Hush, dear," said Ammonia. Her hand hovered just above his shoulder, and he settled a little at the seeming touch. "We need to get on with this, William. So Eddie can get on with what he has to do."

"Of course," said the Librarian. "Sorry, Eddie."

"We are still pursuing a number of promising leads!" Maxwell said loudly. "Very promising! The lab assistants have dropped everything else."

"You must come down to the Armoury before you leave, Eddie," said Victoria. "You really must. We'll have something for you."

"To help you on your mission," said Maxwell.

"Something useful," said Victoria.

"We are all doing our best for you, Eddie," said the Sarjeant. "The whole family is outraged at what has been done to you. An attack on one Drood is an attack on us all."

"Are you so outraged because I've been poisoned?" I said. "Or because Dr DOA got to me despite all your vaunted security?"

"We will throw all of the family's resources into tracking down your attacker," said the Matriarch. Which, I noted, wasn't exactly an answer to my question. "I know you feel the need to pursue this case yourself. But should the worse come to the worst, and Dr DOA is able to hide himself until you are no longer capable of going after him . . . I promise you, the family will continue the hunt for as long as it takes. He can't hide from all of us."

"You couldn't see him when he was here in the Hall, right under your noses!" Molly said angrily. "If Eddie hadn't collapsed, and if I hadn't insisted on a complete medical check, you'd never have known Dr DOA was ever here!"

There was a pause as everyone took it in turns not to look at one another. I like to think they were feeling guilty, rather than just caught out.

"All of our security protocols are being overhauled," said the Sarjeant. "All protections and defences are being seriously upgraded as we speak."

"After the horse has sneaked in and out," I said.

"Have you found any trace of Dr DOA yet?" said Molly.

"No," said the Sarjeant. "No sign he ever set foot inside the Hall. Which is . . . disturbing. Before today, I would have said that was impossible."

"Your parents are currently in London, Eddie," said the Matriarch. "Putting together a new Department of Uncanny, under their leadership. We are endeavouring to contact them, to tell them what's happened. So they can come back. They will be here waiting for you, when you return."

It was nice of her to say *when*, instead of *if*.

"I'll turn the Library upside down if that's what it takes to find some cure, some answer!" said William. "There has to be something in the records! Nothing is ever really new. Everything comes from somewhere. The poison must have been used before, must have been developed and tested . . . If the family has ever encountered it, there'll be a record somewhere. And I will find it!"

"There's always the Pook," Molly said suddenly.

There was a long pause as we all thought about the strange rogue presence that sometimes appeared in the Old Library. That old spirit, which sometimes makes itself known as a giant white rabbit. Terribly powerful and sometimes worryingly terrible in its aspect.

"We still don't know exactly what the Pook is," the Matriarch said carefully.

"Or what its true intentions are," said the Sarjeant. "We know it followed William home from the asylum. Which doesn't exactly fill me with confidence that it is what it appears to be."

"Whatever that is," said the Matriarch.

"I trust him," said the Librarian.

"You would," said the Matriarch.

I looked to Ammonia. "You've spent time inside William's head. You've seen the Pook through his eyes. What do you think?"

"It's an old power," Ammonia said slowly. "Older than the Droods. It scares me. I think the Pook, or what we see of it, is only what it allows us to see. The tip of the iceberg. The smile on the face of the tiger."

"I will ask the Pook if he can help you, Eddie," said William. "But whether he'll answer . . ."

"What are things coming to?" I said. "When my best bet for survival would seem to be an invisible giant white rabbit that might or might not actually exist?"

"Yes, well," said the Librarian, "that's the Drood life for you."

"I am receiving constant updates on your condition from Dr Mary, Eddie," said the Matriarch. "Representing all the medical teams. I've got every department in the family working on this. There's always a chance someone will come up with something. We have a wide range of your blood and tissue samples, taken while you were unconscious."

"Good," I said. "Because you're not getting any more. Hate needles."

"I will reach out to the telepathic community," said Ammonia. "Have them search for Dr DOA. For any knowledge of where he is, who he is, and, more importantly, who hired him. After all, Dr DOA is just the weapon, not the killer."

I liked what she was saying, but it still came as something of a surprise. I hadn't even known there was a community of telepaths. Beyond a certain point, telepaths tend to be solitary creatures, for their own mental protection. To keep the world's voices outside their heads. They go their own way, like cats, highly individual and fiercely independent.

"We don't congregate," said Ammonia, "but we do communicate. We don't need to meet in person, because we're never more than a thought away."

"Could Dr DOA be a telepath?" said Molly. "Could that be how he hides from people, and how he passed unnoticed inside the Hall? Because he can make people not see he's there?"

"Our psychics would have detected his presence," said the Sarjeant.

"Not necessarily," said Ammonia. "Not if he was a high-functioning telepath. There was a time I would have said it was impossible for any telepath that powerful to appear out of nowhere and not be noticed, but that was before Eddie found the artificially created telepath working at Lark Hill. The world is always moving on, leaving the rest of us to play catch-up. Not every telepath wants to be known . . ."

"You made a good point, about who hired Dr DOA," said the Sarjeant. "There has to be a clue in that. Who wants Eddie dead that badly? Why him, of all of us, and why now? Why not go after someone more important in the family, while he had the chance? He could have taken out any number of us . . . Hell, he could have poisoned us all!"

"Maybe one poisoning was all he could manage without being noticed," said Molly. "Anything more might have attracted attention, revealed his presence. Maybe even caught Ethel's attention. That's a point . . . Why didn't she detect his presence?"

"Good question," said the Matriarch. "Perhaps you should ask her."

"Haven't you asked her?" I said.

The Matriarch made a point of moving on. "Everyone here has been checked; we're all free of the poison. The entire family is currently undergoing tests, just in case. And all agents out in the field are being called in, the moment they've completed their missions. On the off chance Dr DOA might be targeting field operatives."

"The question remains," said the Sarjeant. "Who wants Eddie dead so badly? You've made your share of enemies, Eddie; it comes with the job and the territory. But I would have said the truly dangerous ones were all dead."

"They are, as far as I know," I said. "The kind of cases I get, you can't afford to leave any of the really bad guys alive. Or the bad stuff will just start happening again. That's one of the reasons why I decided I wasn't going to kill any more. Too much blood on my hands."

"The family has never asked you to do anything that wasn't necessary," said the Sarjeant. "Nothing that any member of the family shouldn't be prepared to do. For the greater good."

"But the family didn't do it," I said. "I did. And sometimes, when I look back . . . all I can see are the ghosts lined up behind me."

The Matriarch leaned suddenly forward across her table, fixing me with her cool, implacable gaze. "I give you my word, Eddie. The family will not rest until everyone involved in your murder is caught and punished. No one does this to a Drood and gets away with it."

"Are you doing this for me?" I said. "Or to protect the family's reputation?"

"Yes," said the Matriarch. She sat back in her chair again and regarded me thoughtfully. "Where will you begin your search?"

"The Sarjeant's right," I said. "The answer must lie somewhere in my past. Some case I worked, some mission left unfinished, some enemy I didn't kill that I should have. Or perhaps someone I did kill that I shouldn't have. I'll have to think about it."

"In the meantime," said Molly, "we go looking for answers. Talk to people who know things. The Wulfshead Club is always the best place to start."

"Do I really need to tell you to be discreet?" said the Matriarch. "It wouldn't be good for our reputation if people discovered an assassin was able to poison one of us inside our own Hall."

"It wouldn't be good for people to know a Drood can be killed," said the Sarjeant. "The protection our armour gives us is one of our most important weapons."

"We know how to be discreet," I said.

"It's just that normally we don't bother," said Molly.

"True," I said. "But just for you, Maggie, for the family, we'll give it a shot."

"If necessary," said the Sarjeant, "I will avenge you, Eddie. Personally. I will find your killer and pour his heart's blood on your resting place."

Everyone nodded sternly in agreement. Looking around the Chapel, I could see genuine anger and resolve in all their faces. I was touched to see how upset everyone was on my behalf.

"I never knew you cared," I said.

"We're your family," said the Matriarch. "You've done so much for us; we have to do this for you."

There was some more talk, but it just went round and round without getting anywhere. So I stood up and said I was leaving. Molly was immediately out of her chair and on her feet beside me. The Matriarch and her Council fell silent, and then one by one, they wished me luck and said good-bye. Trying hard not to sound like it was for the last time.

I left the Chapel with Molly, closed the door firmly, and strode off into the grounds again. Every time I left my family, it felt like a weight coming off my shoulders. And I was carrying enough burdens as it was. Right now they might mean well, but I always remember which road is paved with good intentions. I walked for a while, though I went nowhere in particular, just putting some distance between me and the Hall. Molly glanced up at the leaden skies.

"Looks like it might snow soon."

"Yeah," I said. "I'm dreaming of a white Christmas. Hell of a present I got this year."

"We'll just have to find the receipt," said Molly. "So you can give it back."

We shared a smile. We had to keep it light, or we'd both go crazy.

"You know," Molly said carefully, "we don't have to do this alone. I mean, just this once it might be better to work with your family. Use its resources. Have other field agents do the actual legwork while you stay here at the Hall and orchestrate things. So you'd never be far from help."

"No," I said immediately. "I told you, no hospital bed for me. I need to be out of here, doing something. I need to keep myself occupied. It keeps me from thinking too much. And anyway, we do have to do this for ourselves. Run our own separate investigation into what's really going on. Because it's always possible someone in my family might be behind this. That would explain how I could be poisoned inside Drood Hall despite all the security, and why no one noticed anything."

"You mean Dr DOA might still be here, inside the Hall somewhere?" Molly could hardly get her breath, she was so angry. "Someone in your family could be helping him, hiding him?"

"I have to wonder," I said. "Wonder why he chose the one poison my family couldn't cure. And I also have to wonder just how high up in the family his orders might have come from. It wouldn't be the first time my own Matriarch wanted me dead."

Molly lost it, big-time. She shrieked out loud—a raw, painful sound, of fury and despair. She spun round and hit me with a blast of concentrated magic, trying to cure the poison and save my life through sheer force of will. She hit me with one spell after another, chanting and gesturing, her face twisted with a wild desperation, her voice harsh and strained. Her whole body shook as she summoned up powerful and dangerous forces. The nearby gryphons ran for cover, just before lightning bolts stabbed down out of an empty sky, blasting great charred chunks out of the lawns. They slammed down again and again, never quite touching me or Molly. Curling and coalescing, unnatural energies formed around Molly, staining the air like inky blots. I stood very still.

My torc tingled painfully at my throat, but my armour didn't appear. It didn't feel threatened. It could tell Molly was just trying to help. I stared at Molly, feeling the danger she was putting herself in for me, and knew it was all for nothing. I couldn't detect any change in me. Molly had called up some truly terrible forces, but they couldn't seem to reach whatever it was Dr DOA had put inside me. The thing that was killing me.

It all stopped. The lightning strikes disappeared, and the summoned energies quickly dissipated. Molly stood slumped before me, trembling, exhausted. The oppressive atmosphere cleared. There was none of the usual peace and calm that follows a storm, because nothing had changed; nothing had been resolved. The gryphons came slowly slinking back. Followed by a brief rain of dead frogs. Just the universe, quietly correcting an imbalance.

"There's nothing I can do," Molly said dully. "Your torc is blocking my magics. Take it off, Eddie. You have to take it off, or I can't do anything."

"No, dear," said Ethel. "He can't do that."

There was none of the rose-red glow that normally accompanied her presence. None of the usual sense of well-being. Just her voice, coming out of nowhere and sounding perhaps a little quieter, a little more distant.

"Hello, Ethel," I said. "I was wondering when you'd show up."

"Why can't he take his torc off?" Molly said angrily. "What good is it doing him?"

"It's all that's keeping him alive," said Ethel. "The torc is fighting the poison inch by inch, moment by moment. If Eddie should remove his torc, or have it removed, he will die. Quickly, and horribly."

"He's definitely going to die?" said Molly.

"Yes," said Ethel.

"Then why aren't you doing something?" said Molly, grief and despair making her voice almost inhumanly harsh.

"Hush, love," I said. "Hush . . . Ethel, there are some things you can do for me. I need you to sever all links between me and my family handler, Kate. In fact, it might be best if there was no direct contact between me and my family, unless I instigate it. In case I find it necessary to do things my family might need to plausibly deny."

"It's done," said Ethel. "You'll be able to phone home in an emergency, through your torc, but as far as your family is concerned, you're currently ex-directory."

"Kate will be upset," said Molly.

"She'll get over it," I said.

"Ethel," said Molly.

"Yes, Molly."

"Please . . . There must be something you can do. Something. You helped him the last time he was poisoned."

"I'm sorry," said Ethel. "I really am, but that was different. There's nothing I can do this time. The poison's progress is so advanced that no cure is possible. I can't save you, Eddie. I would have to rewrite your whole existence, and the physical laws of your reality are really very restrictive. Just trying to use that much power would force me out of your dimension. And your family still needs me, Eddie."

"Really?" I said. "None of my relatives seem too sure about that, just at the moment. Can you tell me what's going on?"

"Of course," said Ethel. "Your Matriarch is sulking."

"What?" said Molly.

"She demanded to know why I care so much about this family," said Ethel. "Why I provide you with torcs and armour and so on. She was very insistent that I explain my reasons and motivations, and what I'm getting out of it. She really is a very suspicious woman for an ex-gardener. And I wouldn't tell her."

"Why not?" said Molly.

"Because my business is my business," said Ethel. "So she's mad at me, and trying to pressure me by distancing the family from me as much as she can."

"That's it?" I said. "I can't believe she'd be so petty . . . Well, actually I can, because she's a Drood. No one is ever allowed to be more important than the Droods. You're not thinking of leaving us, are you? Because of her?"

"No," said Ethel. "I'm not sulking."

"Why are you looking after us?" I said.

"Perhaps I'll tell you," said Ethel. "Just you. When you get back from your mission."

"If I get back," I said.

"Let's all be positive," said Ethel. "I promise you this. I will avenge you, Eddie, if no one else can."

"Everyone wants to avenge him, but no one wants to save him!" said Molly. Her voice broke, and she looked away so I wouldn't see her holding back tears.

"I'm sorry," said Ethel. Her voice sounded flat, and quite final.

"Can't you See who did this to me?" I said.

"No," said Ethel. "And I should be able to . . . Isn't that odd? I'm going to have to think about this."

Her voice cut off abruptly. Molly and I both called after her, but she didn't respond.

"We have to find Dr DOA," Molly said finally, "and make him fix this. He wouldn't work with a poison unless he had a cure, in case of accidents."

"What if he doesn't?" I said.

"Then before we kill him, we make him tell us who hired him," Molly said steadily. "Who hates you enough to want you killed in such a horrible, cowardly way. Who doesn't have the guts to face you himself. I'll make him talk, and when he finally dies, it will feel like a release."

"I can live with that," I said.

"Don't you have any idea who it might be?"

"I've been racking my brains," I said. "But like the Sarjeant said, all my enemies are dead. It could be the family of someone I killed . . . or a friend. Sometimes, with the best will in the world, you can't avoid collateral damage in taking down an enemy. I like to say I've never killed anyone who didn't need killing, but other people are bound to be affected. The damage I do doesn't always end with a death."

"No," said Molly. "This kind of killing feels more . . . personal. There are real hate, real spite and vindictiveness in this. Remember the Manichean Monk, on the airship? He was mad as hell about something, and he wanted you dead. Could he be connected to this?"

And then we both broke off as images of the Armourer, unsteady visions of Maxwell and Victoria, appeared suddenly before us. I could tell they were projected images, because I'd seen Uncle Jack use the process, back when he was Armourer. He invented it some time back, and for a while he was sending images of himself all over the Hall, when he had something to say and didn't feel like leaving the Armoury. The Hall was full of surprised squeals and startled bad language as the Armourer appeared out of nowhere in front of some poor unsuspecting soul. And then he bothered the Sarjeant-at-Arms while he was on the toilet. The Sarjeant had a lot to say about that, and shortly afterwards image projection inside the Hall was banned.

It seemed Maxwell and Victoria had decided the ban didn't extend to the Hall grounds. Perhaps they were jealous of Ammonia's sending.

"There you are!" said Maxwell. "We've been looking for you!"

"You have to come down to the Armoury before you leave!" said Victoria.

"You must!"

"Oh, you really must!"

"We've got some things for you," Maxwell said temptingly.

"Really cool things," said Victoria.

"I don't think I've got time," I said tactfully. "I have things to do."

Maxwell and Victoria were immediately very upset. They looked at me with big puppyish eyes, their lower lips trembling.

"But you have to!" said Victoria.

"I don't need anything," I said.

"But it's traditional!" said Maxwell.

"You always see the Armourer before you go off on a mission!" said Victoria.

"I know we couldn't help with the poison," said Maxwell, "but there are some things we can do."

"You have to let us help you!" said Victoria.

"All right!" I said. "I'll come down."

Maxwell and Victoria beamed hugely, and their images snapped off.

"We really don't have the time," said Molly.

"I know," I said.

"But we're going anyway, aren't we? You indulge them."

"I know!" I said.

We went back into the Hall. I was getting really tired of having to go back in, every time I thought I was free of the place. I strode through the entrance hall with my best *Get the hell out of my way* look on my face, but there was hardly anyone around. As though everyone had decided they didn't want to see the dead man walking any more. Or maybe the Sarjeant had quietly had a word. As long as it kept people from staring at me like an exhibit on display, I was fine with that.

And so we descended the steep stone steps that led to the Armoury, situated deep in the bedrock under the Hall. So that when things inevitably go wrong or Bang! very loudly, it shouldn't affect the rest of the Hall. The Armourer's lab assistants have always had a *Prod it and see* attitude when it comes to testing new things.

"Why can't you have a nice, shiny high-tech lab, like everyone else?" said Molly. "I always feel like I'm visiting some eccentric old boffin, in his shed at the bottom of the garden."

"The Armoury is set up in what used to be the family's old wine cellars," I said patiently.

"Really?" Molly suddenly looked interested. "Does your family still have wine cellars?"

"Hell yes," I said. "Extensive ones, under the North Wing. One of the best-protected areas in the Hall. I've never been a great wine drinker myself, but my cousin Christopher once told me the family has been laying down fine wines since before the days of King Arthur."

"What are you saving them for?" said Molly.

I stopped at the bottom of the stone steps and looked at her. "Do you know, it's never occurred to me to ask."

"Definitely something to look into, when we get back," said Molly. She wasn't quite rubbing her hands together in anticipation, but she had that look in her eyes.

The Armoury is sealed away behind heavy blast-proof doors designed to keep things in, rather than out. They usually opened for me the moment I arrived, but not this time. New Armourer, new security.

"You could knock," said Molly.

"On blast-proof doors?"

"I could huff and puff and blow them right off their hinges."

"No time to be making enemies," I said.

The doors opened on their own, heavily reinforced hinges groaning theatrically from the weight of the doors. Molly looked at me.

"I don't see any cameras watching us, so how did they know we were here?"

"This is the Armoury," I said. "Home to many lab assistants with far too much time on their hands, no inhibitions, and even less regard for privacy."

"Of course," said Molly. "I was forgetting."

We stepped inside, and the heavy doors slammed back into place. The Armoury is basically a long series of connected stone chambers, with white-plastered walls and low, curved ceilings, mostly buried under a multicoloured spaghetti of tacked-up wiring. It's supposed to be colour-coded, but I've never been able to find anyone who could explain it to me. Some of it's been there since Tesla put it up.

Stark fluorescent lights cover everything with an unrelenting glare, and the air conditioning works when it feels like it. Strange lights come and go, chemical stinks and pungent herbs drift on the air, and there're always some kind of gunfire and deeply disturbing laughter coming from the firing range.

I strolled down the central aisle with Molly hanging on my arm, keeping a safe distance from everyone and everything. We also avoided glowing chemical spills and chalk-drawn pentacles on the floor. Someone had set up a mantrap in the shadows, heavy enough to hold Bigfoot. All around us, hardworking young men and women in charred and stained lab coats clustered around workstations and test benches, combat areas, and clearly defined no-go areas. It was all much more organized and efficient than it had been in the old Armourer's time. Uncle Jack ran a tight ship, but he approved of individual initiative. Even if it did tend to lead to a lot of cleaning up afterwards. His way led to many important new breakthroughs, and a lot of happy accidents. Provided you were inclined to be somewhat loose in your definition of happy.

I missed the spirited chaos of the old days, where I could always be sure of encountering something weird and wonderful on my visits. This new era of efficiency and discipline was no doubt safer for everyone, and maybe even more productive, but it did look a lot less fun. Less survival of the fittest, or, at least, the most ingenious. Until a lab assistant came running past, brandishing a really big butterfly net, in hot pursuit of a miniature horse with eight legs. Not far away, another assistant was wrestling with a chainsaw battle-axe, while looking frantically for the OFF switch. And another assistant was looking down at the four extra arms protruding from his sides with a look that clearly said, *This is not what I had in mind.*

A loud explosion from the firing range shook the floor, followed by screams, laughter, and much drifting black smoke. Something caught fire, something disappeared, and something else turned into something else.

Young lab assistants at play. Business as usual in the Armoury, after all.

Maxwell and Victoria came hurrying forward, smiling happily at Molly and me. Until they remembered the solemnity of my condition, and did their best to look properly grave and professional.

"Welcome to the Armoury!" said Maxwell.

"Been a few changes since you last saw us!" said Victoria.

"But we still do good work," said Maxwell.

"Of course you do!" said Victoria. "His trouble is, he's too modest, Eddie. Aren't you, dear? You don't talk yourself up enough, Max!"

"Oh, I don't like to . . ."

"But you must, darling; you really must. Or people won't take you seriously!"

They suddenly remembered they had guests, and put on their professional aspects again.

"We still supply weapons, devices, and really quite appalling dirty tricks to agents in the field," said Maxwell. "Everything they need to baffle and brown-trouser the enemy."

"Never really understood that expression," said Victoria.

"I'll explain it to you later, dear."

"Is it dirty?"

"Later, dear . . ."

"What have you got for me, Armourer?" I said. "What is it you think I'm going to need?"

"You can never be too careful," said Maxwell.

"Or too well prepared," said Victoria. "I trust you still have your Colt Repeater?"

I slapped my side. "Best gun my uncle Jack ever turned out. Aims itself, never runs out of ammo; regular or specialized. A classic."

"Jolly good," Maxwell said vaguely. "Here . . ."

He offered me a small black plastic box, with a dial

on the top. I hefted it warily, but it didn't seem to be doing anything.

"That is a chemical nose," said Victoria. "It's been attuned to the poison in your system. Once you get near anything chemically similar, that box will take you straight to it."

"Okay," I said. "That could prove useful." I slipped it into my pocket.

Maxwell handed over another small plastic box; this time in bottle green, with a single black button on top. "This is a neural inhibitor! Only works at close range, for the moment, but point this at any opponent and hit the trigger, and it will interrupt their thinking quite dramatically. Don't point it at anyone you like; the side effects can be upsetting. And a bit messy."

"Oh, don't remind me," said Victoria. "It took ages to clean up after poor Cuthbert."

"He volunteered!"

"Not for that, he didn't."

"Moving on," Maxwell said quickly, holding out yet another small plastic box, this time in a garish purple. "Now, this is something rather special. You'll be the first to test it."

"Meaning it hasn't actually been used in the field?" I said.

"Not as such, no," said Victoria.

"Once you turn it on," said Maxwell, "it generates a field that compels people to tell the truth. They don't even realise anything's changed; it all feels perfectly natural."

I accepted the thing gingerly. "What are the drawbacks? Come on, there're always drawbacks."

"Well," said Victoria, "apart from a tendency to overheat and blow up quite dramatically if you leave it running for too long . . . remember, you'll be inside the field too. So be very careful what you say out loud."

"It does lead to a certain feeling of liberation," said

Maxwell. "A desire to speak out and damn the consequences. People say all kinds of things. Don't they, dear?"

"Oh my word, don't they?" said Victoria. "We had ever so much fun playing with this last week. I haven't been able to look at Jeremy the same way since."

"Is that it?" said Molly as I tucked the various boxes away about my person, while making careful mental notes as to which colour did what. "That's all you've got to offer? No weapons? No big guns, no unnatural nastiness, no protein exploders?"

"Since when do you feel the need for weapons?" said Maxwell, just a bit defensively.

"Since I decided this was a killing mission," said Molly.

Maxwell and Victoria looked at each other uncomfortably.

"Well," said Maxwell, "we do have something . . ."

"We've always preferred to concentrate on espionage," said Victoria. "General sneakiness, aids to information gathering, that sort of thing, rather than death and destruction."

"But we do understand the need for weapons," said Maxwell. "So, we have this."

He handed Molly a very ordinary-looking wristwatch.

"What am I supposed to do with this?" said Molly. "Tell an enemy that it's later than they think?"

"You hit the raised button on the side. *Don't touch it now!*" said Victoria.

"After that, everything inside the field generated by the watch will accelerate in time," said Maxwell.

"Thousands of years will pass in seconds," said Victoria. "We designed it to break down walls and other barriers, or destroy documents and other incriminating evidence. But you can imagine what it would do to a person. Or any powerful creature."

"As long as you don't choose something naturally long-lived," said Maxwell.

Molly strapped the watch on her wrist with a casualness even I found disturbing.

"These are all really clever ideas," I said. "Jack would have approved."

"We hope so," said Maxwell. "We got into this for the Science. It was only when we took over here, and had to concentrate on turning out useful things, that we realised the uses our creations would be put to. Out in the field."

"No use for pure science in the Armoury," said Victoria. "We've always been more interested in creating things than destroying them."

"Have you ever considered that you might be in the wrong job?" said Molly.

"Yes," said Maxwell. "But Jack came to us and asked us to take over for him. We couldn't say no."

"We're just not very interested in finding new ways to kill people," said Victoria.

"Mostly we let the lab assistants concentrate on the weapon making," said Maxwell. "Because you can't stop the little terrors coming up with all kinds of horribly destructive things."

"It's just . . . not us," said Victoria.

"But we know our duty."

"Anything for the family."

They stood together, holding hands quite unselfconsciously, like two children lost in the big bad wood.

And then alarms went off all over the Armoury. Bells and sirens and flashing lights. Maxwell and Victoria moved quickly to stand back to back, trying to look in all directions at once. Lab assistants came running from all over, armed with whatever weapons happened to be closest. A dimensional doorway opened up between Molly and me and the Armourer. Just a ragged gap in mid-air, not much bigger than an actual door. Looking through the gap, quite casually, was William the Librarian. He smiled cheerfully at Molly and me.

"Ah, there you are . . ."

Maxwell and Victoria came hurrying round to see what we were seeing, and were immediately outraged and scandalised. They glared at the Librarian, and then gestured for the lab assistants to stand down. They retreated reluctantly, still hanging on to their weapons. The alarms shut down. All except for one bell, which kept on ringing until an assistant hit it. Maxwell pointed an accusing finger at William.

"This is not acceptable behaviour, Librarian! How are you even doing that? Unauthorized entrances into the Armoury aren't supposed to be possible! Not with all our security measures!"

"That's right, Max! You tell him!"

"I am telling him, dear . . ."

William just grinned. "Amazing what you can find in books. Eddie, Molly, I need you to come and see me. Right now. I may have found something. Step through, please."

"But we're not finished!" Maxwell said immediately.

"You have more for us?" I said.

"Well, no, but . . . ," said Victoria.

"But you always talk to the Armourer before you go off on a mission," said Maxwell. "It's traditional."

"We were looking forward to it," said Victoria.

"Later," I said, as kindly as I could. "Thanks for your help."

I stepped through the dimensional breach, and into the Old Library, stepping carefully over the ragged edge at the bottom. I'd seen someone lose a foot to one of these things. Molly came through right after me, crowding my back. Possibly because she didn't want to be left behind with Maxwell and Victoria. The dimensional tear slammed shut behind us.

The Old Library hadn't changed a bit since I last saw it. Endless wooden stacks, packed full of books, stretching off into the distance for just that little bit farther than the human eye could comfortably follow. Pleasant, honey-coloured light hung over everything, from no obvious source. The stacks contained everything from modern paperbacks to leather-bound volumes, manuscripts in folders to palimpsests on scraped skin. Grimoires and bestiaries, maps of lands that no one now remembered, and visions of worlds yet to come. Books on everything under the sun, and the dark side of the moon. Drood records go way back . . . There was a general sense of peace and quiet, of academic solitude, and forbidden knowledge right there for the taking. Slightly undermined by a constant sense of being watched, from somewhere out in the stacks. Possibly by the books.

Away from the formality of the Matriarch's Council meeting, William had slipped off his tweed jacket and dropped it casually on the floor. He was sitting behind a sturdy old Victorian desk covered in opened books, and yet more books with markers in them. Piles of assorted volumes leaned up against the desk. That amiable young man, Yorith, assistant to the Librarian, came forward out of the stacks, bearing another armful of books. He dumped them beside the desk, started to smile at Eddie and Molly, and then saw the look on the Librarian's face. He shrugged easily, then produced a long handwritten list and considered it briefly before heading off into another part of the stacks.

"What's so important, Librarian?" I said.

William marked his place carefully in the oversized volume before him and carefully closed it. He seemed very focused, for him. He'd taken off his cravat to use as a marker in one of the books, and his bushy white hair was looking wild and windswept again. But in his Library, in his place of power, William possessed an authority he didn't have anywhere else. Here, he was the man who knew things. When he could remember them.

"We don't just have reference and history books," he said in his formal lecturer's voice. "All the information that comes to this family, from whatever source, ends up here. For storage and later retrieval. With Yorith's help, I was able to locate this particular and very interesting volume that I remembered reading some time back. It contains, among many other fascinating items, a request for funding from a very secret group whose members are dedicated to staying alive in the face of everything the world can throw at them. They call themselves the Survivors.

"They were extremely detailed in their proposal, concerning their intended field of endeavour, so I had it bound in with a whole bunch of other interesting proposals. Just in case they ever came up with something we could use. According to what I've been reading— just to refresh my memory, you understand—it seems they're willing to use science and magic and everything in between, including alien and other-dimensional technology. And pretty much anything else they can get their hands on. Remarkably open-minded people. It seems entirely possible to me, Eddie, that they might have something to keep you alive."

"Where are they?" I said. "And what kind of people are we talking about?"

"What does it matter, if they can help?" said Molly.

"It matters, love," I said. "Survival at any price? I don't think so. Some prices are just too high."

"Even if they can't actually cure the poison," said William, "they might be able to buy you more time."

"Where are they?" I said.

"The Survivors have their own very secret, and very secure, hidden bunker," said William. "Inside a mountain. Don't ask me which one. Apparently the only way in or out is via a teleport mechanism. Entrance strictly by Invitation Only."

"I could use the Merlin Glass," I said.

The Librarian pulled a face. "You still have that awful thing?"

"Yes," I said defensively. "It might not be as reliable as it was, but it still has its uses."

"If you'd read as much as I have about Merlin Satanspawn, you wouldn't let anything he'd touched anywhere near you," William said coldly. "A truly devious and dangerous mind, with far too much power for his or anyone else's good. On no one's side but his own."

"Do you know why he gave the Glass to the Droods in the first place?" said Molly.

William frowned. "It does seem to me I read something about that, long ago . . ." He scowled fiercely, struggling to find the memory. I waited politely. Molly, somewhat less so. William worried his lower lip between his teeth, his gaze far away. "The Glass, yes . . . It isn't just a useful device. It has a specific purpose. It guards something . . . or perhaps it was supposed to guard us against something . . ."

His scowl of concentration gave way to frustration, his mouth twisting miserably, and he beat on his desktop with his fists, so angry with himself, he was on the brink of tears. I stepped forward and patted him comfortingly on the arm. As he had with me. He didn't even know I was there. I held his hands still to stop him from hurting himself. William sighed heavily and sat slumped in his chair. A tired old man who'd been hurt too much, and too often. I let him sit for a while, and then tried again.

"Why wouldn't the Merlin Glass get me in to see the Survivors, Librarian?"

"Because they have incredibly powerful defences in place. They don't want to be interrupted in their work, or share their progress with anyone who hasn't paid for it. To get in, you need to know someone on the inside. And we don't know any of the current prime movers. Not these days. I've been going through the original proposal very carefully, but all references to the original founders were removed long ago. Someone in the family didn't want the names to be general knowledge. I fear that information is now lost."

"Come on," I said. "Someone must know. Someone in the family always knows . . ."

"Usually, yes," said William. He'd resumed his calm, if not his poise. "But we've lost so many of the old hands, just recently. Martha, James, Jack . . . even the Drood in Cell Thirteen. Those who remain may have access to the information, but they don't know people. Not the way the old guard did. They can't call in personal favours to guarantee an audience. And if I ever knew the right names . . . I don't remember them any more. There's a lot I don't remember. Not all of it through choice."

A familiar lost look filled his face. It was easy to forget how damaged he was, when I first found him at Happy Acres. Just one more disturbed soul hiding from a terrible enemy, among the other insane people. He'd come a long way since coming home, but he could still stumble over the gaps in his mind.

"Should we call Ammonia?" Molly said quietly. "Maybe she can help."

"No," said the Librarian. "Don't disturb her. I'll be fine."

Molly looked at me, and I shook my head. You can't help someone who isn't ready to be helped.

"All right!" said Molly. "We go to the Wulfshead Club. Because someone there always knows what's going on. Someone will know of a way into the Survivors' mountain base."

"Remind me," I said. "Are we still banned from the Wulfshead?"

"Don't know; don't care," said Molly.

"I haven't given up, Eddie," the Librarian said quietly. "It's just that there are so many books, and the index isn't worth the vellum it's written on." He fixed me with a surprisingly bright gaze. "I've been to too many funerals since I returned. I would rather not have to attend another. But . . . there is an old saying, Eddie. *If all that's left to you is to die, die well. And take as many of the bastards down with you as you can.*"

Molly glared about her. "Tell me, Librarian. Is the Pook still here?"

William looked at her oddly. "No use asking me, my dear. The Pook comes and goes at his pleasure. I feel his presence more often than I see him. He's disturbingly playful, for such an ancient entity. He shows up now and again, for a spot of civilised conversation . . ."

"What do you talk about?" said Molly.

"Oh, you know," the Librarian said. "Things . . ."

"Do you know what the Pook is?" I said.

"You mean apart from a giant white rabbit that not everyone can see? To be honest, Eddie, I'm always surprised anyone else can see him. I thought I'd left him behind in the asylum."

"Isn't there anything in the Library about him?" said Molly.

"Oh yes," said William. "Any amount. All of it utterly contradictory. Which is only fitting, I suppose, given the Pook's nature. He's something from the very old days. When we all lived in the forest, because there was nowhere else. He is the lightning in the skies and the laughter in the woods, a thing of March Hare madness and pagan wildness. A survivor from a time when men talked with their gods every day and thought nothing of it. Who comes and goes as he will, revealing himself to this one and to that one . . . To the broken people, like me, because he feels a kinship. He is the Pook. That's enough."

Molly turned away from him and raised her voice against the quiet of the Old Library. "Pook? Are you there?"

We all waited, looking into the shadows between the stacks, but there was no response.

"Pook!" said Molly. "Damn it; we need you!"

And then we all tensed as we heard footsteps moving among the stacks. Drawing slowly, steadily closer. Molly fell back. I moved in beside her. William sat up straight in his chair. Until Yorith emerged from the stacks, carrying another armful of books. He stopped for a moment, clearly wondering why we were all looking at him, and then moved forward to put his books down beside the Librarian's desk.

"You can't compel the Pook to do anything, Molly," the Librarian said kindly. "It isn't in his nature."

"The Pook?" said Yorith. "Is he back?"

"Apparently not," I said.

"Good," said Yorith. "He puts the wind up me something fierce."

"Perhaps the Pook can't help," said Molly. "And just doesn't want to admit it."

"Perhaps," said the Librarian.

Molly studied the rows of stacks coldly, the glint of battle rising in her eye. "Maybe if I . . ."

"No," I said immediately.

"Why not?" said Molly.

"Because this is no time to be making enemies," I said. "Let's go. We have things to do and a deadline to beat. If we can find Dr DOA and bring him down, at least we can avenge his past victims. And prevent any new ones."

"That's not enough," said Molly.

"No," I said. "It isn't. But it's what we've got."

CHAPTER FOUR

No Greater Love

As so often happens with the members of my family, I felt the need to hide something from them. So I gave Molly a significant look, and just casually announced to the Librarian that I was going to look for a book in the stacks before I left. William regarded me with a certain amount of surprise, not to mention suspicion.

"Of course," he said. "Tell me which book, and I'll have Yorith locate it and bring it here."

"I'm interested in a particular field," I said. "Rather than a particular book. Think I'll just browse for a while. Run my fingers across a few spines, see what I can turn up."

"You're up to something," the Librarian said resignedly. "Full of obscure poisons and half-dead on your feet, and you still won't be straight with me." He smiled suddenly. "Typical Drood. Off you go, Eddie. Do what you have to. But if you so much as dog-ear a single page, I'll have your guts for bindings."

He busied himself with the volume before him, leafing through the heavy oversized pages with thunderous concentration; so he could honestly tell the Matriarch he had no idea what I was up to. Yorith dropped me a wink, and disappeared back into the stacks with his list. I led Molly into a whole different area of the Old Library. She waited more or less patiently until she was sure we were out of the Librarian's hearing, and then tapped me sternly on the shoulder.

"A book? Really? That was the best excuse you could come up with?"

"The choices are somewhat limited in a Library," I said. "I could have volunteered to do some dusting, but I think he would have seen through that. Besides, there's dust here that hasn't moved since the Venerable Bede decided to jot down a few odd thoughts. I have a horrible suspicion some of it might fight back."

"What are we about to do that we don't want the Librarian to know about?" said Molly. "Crack open a book that's been sealed for centuries and write rude comments in the margins? Steal something? What?"

"I'm going to use the Merlin Glass to transport us directly to the Wulfshead Club," I said.

"Okay . . . And why do we need to be so secretive about that?"

"Because, technically speaking, I'm not supposed to have it. On the family's orders, I handed the Glass over to my uncle Jack shortly before his death, so he could examine it. But he didn't have time. He left the Glass to me, unofficially. The Librarian knows, because Jack trusted him to give me the Glass. But the Matriarch probably still thinks it's in the Armoury, somewhere. And I think I'll feel just that little bit more secure, having an advantage the Matriarch doesn't know about."

Molly nodded slowly. "I don't want to go to the club, Eddie. Not yet. There's somewhere else I think we ought to try first. Isabella once told me about this very private medical establishment just off Harley Street. The Peter Paul Clinic. I really believe they can help you."

I looked at her thoughtfully. "Can't say I've ever heard of the place. And Harley Street and its environs used to be part of my regular beat, back when I was a field agent for London. Is it new?"

"Sort of," said Molly. "And very specialized."

She met my gaze steadily as I thought that over. She'd never been good at lying to me, but she'd always been very good at misdirection.

"What kind of specialists are we talking about here, Molly?"

"Hopeless cases," said Molly. "Lost causes. If I'm remembering correctly, they have a really good track record when it comes to saving people everyone else had given up on."

"Why didn't you mention them before?"

"Because it's a long shot, all right? And quite definitely illegal; not something I want to be discussing in front of your high-and-mighty relatives. They wouldn't approve."

"Ah," I said. "One of those establishments . . . Look, Molly, thanks for the thought, but I'm really not keen on wasting time on possible miracle cures. Not when my time's so short."

"You can't just give up!" said Molly. "You can't just assume you're going to die! Please, Eddie; I really think they can help you. Listen to me. Let me help you. You have to let me help you."

"All right," I said. "For you, Molly."

She was right. I had given up. I was going to die, just like all of Dr DOA's victims. I'd come to terms with that. All I had left was one last chance for justice and revenge. But if it would keep Molly happy, to chase after some quack's home-made remedy, then I'd go along. For now.

I reached into the pocket dimension I keep inside my trouser pocket, and brought out the Merlin Glass. Just a simple hand mirror, at first glance; an oval glass in a scrolled-silver back and handle. Nothing you'd look at twice in an antiques shop. I was always surprised at how light it felt in my hand, given how much historical weight it carried. But that's often the way, in the hidden world. It's always the most dangerous things that like to look most innocent. Mr Hyde, spying on the world through the eyes of Dr Jekyll. Molly looked dubiously at the Merlin Glass, not quite turning up her nose.

"You really believe we can trust that thing? Given how many times it's let you down? It's almost like the Glass has developed a mind of its own. Along with a really nasty sense of humour."

"Wouldn't surprise me in the least," I said. "Considering who made it. But we don't have a choice. You've burned through a lot of magics today. A cross-country teleport spell would wipe you out; wouldn't it?"

"Maybe," said Molly, not giving way in the least. "I could still surprise you."

"You always do," I said generously. "But this is not the time for you to be left defenceless. Once word gets out that I'm . . . weakened, you can be sure vultures will start to gather. Like the Manichean Monk on the airship. If my family's enemies smell blood in the water and come looking for me with trouble in mind . . . I'm going to need you strong enough to protect me. For when I can't."

"All right!" said Molly. "I get it! When did you get so damned pessimistic, Eddie?"

"Right after I found out I was dying," I said.

"You're not dead yet!"

"No, I'm not. I'm just being practical. So, we go with the Glass. Yes?"

"Even after everything the Librarian just said about it?"

"Nothing I didn't already know," I said. "And given

how many times I've already used the Glass, I think if it was going to do something really nasty, it would have done it by now."

"But what if it is guarding something?" said Molly. She looked at the Glass in my hand as if it were a snake that had just started hissing. "You've said before . . . there have been times when you were convinced there was another presence in the Glass."

"As long as it doesn't turn out to be a Victorian girl with long blonde hair, or an Oxford mathematics genius . . ."

"If it was up to me, I'd exorcise that Glass with a specially blessed mallet," said Molly.

I held the hand mirror up before me. Molly looked over my shoulder, crowding in close. All I could see in the reflection were Molly and me. I looked tired and drawn; she looked . . . stretched thin. I made myself concentrate, studying every detail carefully and looking for something, anything, out of place. The angel had only confirmed what I'd suspected for some time now: When I looked at myself in the Glass, I wasn't the only one looking back from the other side of the mirror. I didn't say anything to Molly. I didn't want her upset. Because the angel had been right, about death hovering over me . . .

In the end, what I thought or felt didn't matter. We had to use the Merlin Glass to get around because we had a lot of ground to cover. And not much time to do it in.

Molly looked behind her several times, comparing the scene in the mirror with reality, and finally shrugged.

"All right, Eddie. Let's do it. Maybe we are worrying about nothing . . ."

"That would make a nice change," I said.

I shook the Glass out to the size of a Door, and instructed it to show us Harley Street. Our reflection was gone in a moment, replaced by a view I recognised immediately; it was the scene half-way down one of the most exclusive, not to mention expensive, streets in London. Where you could find all kinds of doctors and surgeons, alternative therapies and outright quackeries; science and magic and more weird shit than you could shake a caduceus at. Remedies from the Past and the Future, presented by highly qualified men and women with arcane areas of knowledge, professional smiles, and the souls of accountants. Medicine without limits, if you could afford it. Given some of the more outré establishments I remembered from Harley Street, it was just possible someone there might be able to help me.

I felt the first faint twinge of hope, like sensation returning to a numbed extremity. Painful, but encouraging.

People hurried up and down the crowded pavements with stressed and preoccupied faces, intent on their own business and unaware of the opening the Merlin Glass had made. It's always been good at covering its tracks. I stepped through into Harley Street with Molly treading on my heels.

London, in the evening. Amber street lights under a darkening sky already speckled with stars, and the thin sliver of a new moon. The fresh chilly air was a relief after the close atmosphere of the Old Library. No one in the street saw us arrive—one of the more useful side effects of the Glass. If they noticed us at all, they just assumed we must have arrived the same way they did, quietly and surreptitiously. Because no one comes to Harley Street for trivial matters, or the kind of problem one wishes to discuss with family and friends. I shook the Glass back down to hand-mirror size, and slipped it into my pocket.

There wasn't a lot of traffic around; it was mostly black taxicabs dropping off important people. Who stared straight ahead as they headed for their destination by the shortest possible route. And if by some unfortunate chance they should happen to bump into someone they knew, both parties would have the good manners not to acknowledge each other.

An ambulance raced down the road, lights and sirens going. The taxis pulled aside to let it pass. Everyone paused to watch the ambulance go by like it was an albatross, a harbinger of doom. They watched till it was out of sight, and only then started moving again. Breathing a little more easily because the shadow of death had passed them by. Another soldier had stopped the bullet.

"I prefer the ambulances you see in old movies," I said. "When they had ringing bells, instead of sirens. A far more pleasant sound."

"People don't tend to get out of the way of pleasant sounds," said Molly.

"You're so practical," I said.

"One of us has to be," said Molly.

I looked around. "So, where is this Peter Paul Clinic?"

"Not far."

"Walking distance?"

"Of course!" said Molly.

"Then let's get a move on," I said. "We have things to be about."

Molly looked at me. "More important than this?"

"Probably," I said.

"Don't you have any faith in me?" said Molly.

"In you," I said.

We set off. Harley Street is basically two long rows of Georgian terraces, tall, narrow establishments crowded together, with astronomically high rents to keep out the riff-raff. Carefully anonymous facades hide all kinds of security measures, to protect patients' privacy. Lots of doors, but hardly any nameplates. Either you knew who and what you were looking for, or you were probably in the wrong place. Most of the heavy, secretly reinforced doors would only open to buzzers after you'd murmured the right passWords. And even then, you had to get past the heavily armed receptionist.

I looked around, taking it all in. Being in Harley Street again brought back memories.

"All right," said Molly. "Why are you smiling like that?"

"Just thinking of the last time I was here," I said. "I'd been sent to track down an important politician who'd made the mistake of going walkabout in the darker backstreets of Bangkok. Where he had a very close encounter with a lady thing. As a result of which he'd ended up pregnant, with the exact opposite of a love child. My family had seen *Rosemary's Baby* and *The Omen*, so I was sent here to terminate the pregnancy with extreme prejudice."

"Eddie!" said Molly. "You didn't . . ."

"No, of course I didn't," I said. "Just shot him with an ice needle made from holy water. That did the trick. My life was so much simpler then."

I raised my Sight to check what was really going on around me in the hidden world. If Humanity could see who and what it shares this world with every day . . . Humanity would crap itself. Though it has to be said, Harley Street was a special case. With so much Life and Death around, and so many unnatural procedures constantly being practised, the balance between the two states has been seriously disturbed. All kinds of weird shit tend to congregate in Harley Street, and even weirder people.

Ghosts walked in and out of buildings, some of which weren't there any more. Images trapped in loops of repeating Time, like insects in amber. A group of teenage girl vampires, in heavy caked makeup to hide their industrial-strength sunblock, came trotting down the street in dark goth outfits, hiding in plain sight. An alien Grey walked hand in hand with a Reptiloid—Romeo and Juliet from outer space. Moments like that give me hope. A demonic half-breed in a Savile Row suit and an Old School Tie smiled at me as he recognised my torc. Hellfire burned briefly in his eyes. It looked like he was about to say something, but then he caught Molly's gaze and thought better of it. The hellspawn bowed politely, and moved on, its shadow hurrying to catch up.

Everybody comes to Harley Street.

I looked at Molly. "That demon knew you."

"Probably."

"And?"

"Best not to ask."

"That covers so much of your life," I said.

Looking up and down the street, I was pleased to see many of the old familiar establishments were still doing business. Even though it had been . . . what? Ten years since I was last here? Where does the time go . . . Saint Baphomet's Hospital still had the same brutally ugly exterior, because it wasn't there for the nice things in life. It specialized in treating the more unpleasant supernatural illnesses and unnatural conditions. Where the cure was often not only worse than the illness, but a damned sight more expensive. Right next door was Dr Dee & Sons & Sons. The old firm. There to deal with the more extreme forms of exorcism. Its unofficial motto, *We get the Hell out.* They guaranteed to save your soul but not necessarily your mind. A little farther down stood the VooDoo Lounge, for those who needed to consult the Loa Courts. People forget that voodoo isn't just a system of magic; it's also a religion practised all across the world, with a huge pantheon of gods. Most of whom are in dispute with one another at any given time. And since a large part of voodoo worship is based on possession of the living by the loa, things are bound to get a bit argumentative on occasion. You need a really good advocate if you're arguing a case in the Loa Courts.

Molly led the way, striding it out, and everyone hurried to get out of her way. Some people clearly recognised her, some just as clearly didn't, but they all knew trouble on two legs when they saw it. Molly was in no mood to be messed with. Though to be honest, I would be hard-pressed to name a time when she was. I had to hurry to keep up.

"An angel this morning, and now a demon," I said. "It's like the afterlife is rubbing my nose in it; just to remind me how close it's getting. Or maybe it's because the afterlife is drawing nearer that I'm seeing its denizens more clearly." I looked thoughtfully at Molly. "What do you know about the afterlife, Molly? I mean, really know? You're always saying you've been to Heaven and Hell and everywhere in between . . . but you never talk about what you found there. Or at least, not to me."

"No," said Molly, not looking at me. "I never talk about that to anyone."

"I spent some time in Limbo," I said. "In the Winter Hall. Whatever that was . . ."

"Think of it as a waiting room," said Molly. "Or a holding cell."

I could tell she really didn't want to talk about it, but that just made me all the more determined to press the point.

"Talk to me, Molly," I said. "I need to know what you know."

"There's nothing I can tell you!" said Molly. She finally turned her head to meet my gaze, but instead of the stubbornness I was expecting, her face was full of helpless concern. Like someone had asked her for a lifeline, and all she had was empty hands. "I don't remember anything of what I saw or experienced in the Other Realms, because I'm not allowed to. Mortals can't know such things, because it would interfere with our experience of this world."

"Come on, we've spent our whole careers interacting

with angels and demons, and all manner of agents from Above and Below! We've known any number of people who've slept with demons or channelled angels . . ."

"I know!" said Molly. "And if you think about it for a moment, you'll remember none of them have ever said anything useful. Or in any way illuminating. And it's not because some of them didn't want to. You know hellspawn love to mess with our minds. But anything that enters our world, from Above or Below, has restraints placed upon it. As a condition of entry."

"Who decides that?" I said. "Who enforces that?"

"Who do you think?" said Molly. "These things are decided where all the things that matter are decided— in the Courts of the Holy, and the Houses of Pain. And keep your voice down, Eddie! You never know who might be listening, especially in a place like this. Yes, we've met angels and demons, but they might not have been what they seemed, or what they claimed to be. They could have been lying, or playing games with us, or any number of equally worrying things. I know what you want, Eddie. You want me to tell you what's going to happen to you after you die. But I don't know."

"Does anybody?" I said.

"No one whose answer I'd trust," said Molly. "Beyond a certain point, the maps just end. Usually in large open spaces marked *Here Be Mysteries*. Everything we know, or think we know, about the afterlife . . . can only usefully be discussed through metaphors. Simpler truths, to allow us to contemplate a far more complicated situation. There are some things human beings really aren't meant to know. And believe me, my sisters and I have tried very hard to find out. Often in disturbing and subversive ways."

"Doesn't surprise me for a moment," I said dryly. "Who have you talked to about this?"

"Zombies and vampires, ghosts and ghouls, death-walkers and necronauts," Molly said in an entirely matter-of-fact way. "And we couldn't get a straight answer out of any of them. Or at least, nothing that wasn't immediately contradicted by the next person we talked to. The only thing they would agree on . . . is that you can't trust anything the dead tell you. Because the dead always have their own agenda."

"It seems to me I might have heard that before," I said. "Did you try the Ghost Finders?"

Molly sniffed loudly. "Amateur night."

"Snob," I said, not unkindly.

Molly looked at me with real pain in her eyes. "I wish I could be more of a comfort to you. But I don't know, and anyone who says they do is either lying, or has a vested interest in making you believe them. Would you rather I lied to you?"

"Maybe later," I said. "You know, it occurs to me that we've been walking for quite some time. Are you sure you know where you're going? Should we stop someone, and beat directions out of them?"

"I've never actually been to the Clinic myself," said Molly. "I'm just going by what Isabella told me. This isn't the kind of address you can look up on Google Maps. It shouldn't be far now."

"What was Isabella doing at this Clinic, anyway?" I said.

"She wouldn't tell me," said Molly. "Which usually means, *Don't ask, as the answer would only upset you.*"

"You're not exactly selling me on this," I said.

"Isabella told me the Peter Paul Clinic could save people everyone else had given up on," Molly said stubbornly.

"Maybe," I said. "But did she say how? Because I'm going to say it again; some prices can be too high."

"Relax," said Molly. "I brought my credit card."

"I thought the company cancelled it."

"That's what they think. Ah, this looks right."

She took a sudden turn down a narrow side street, and just like that, the whole character of the neighbourhood changed dramatically. The bright lights disappeared, replaced in a moment by subdued lighting and sprawling shadows. As though no one here wanted to be seen too clearly. The terraces in this street were decidedly older, and less well maintained. Smaller, less ostentatious businesses squeezed in side by side, with a general air of *Enter at Your Own Risk* about them. Establishments where it would always be cash in hand, and no questions asked on either side.

There was hardly any traffic on the quiet road, apart from the odd ambulance, and none of them bothered with lights and sirens, as though there was no need for them to hurry any more. A few people on the pavements, definitely more down-market than the visitors to Harley Street. Everywhere I looked, all the windows in all the buildings were covered. By blinds, drawn curtains, even heavy wooden shutters with hex signs carved into the frames. There were lights on, here and there, but no trace of movement. The whole street had a gloomy, depressing ambience. A place where people came to watch their loved ones die.

I went to raise my Sight again, and found I couldn't. A really heavy-duty security barrier was in place, suggesting everyone here took their privacy very seriously. I couldn't decide whether I found that reassuring or not. And it did bother me that I didn't recognise this particular side street. I thought I knew all the streets in this area; it was part of my local knowledge as a London field agent. I looked around the grubby walls for the name of the street, but there wasn't a sign to be seen anywhere. I turned to Molly.

"Where are we?"

"Off the beaten track, and off the sides of the map," Molly said briskly. "One of the shadowy places. Because the kind of miracle you need can only be found in places the Light can't reach."

She stopped abruptly before a small anonymous establishment. From the outside, it could have been any kind of storefront. Bare brickwork, covered with accumulated grime, interrupted here and there by long streaks from the leaky guttering. It looked to me like the kind of place where unlicensed surgeons would perform unauthorized cosmetic surgery, on people who'd been turned down by everyone else. The kind of place where you could take the cure for tanna leaf addiction, or a taste for recreational possession; or get an elemental off your back. Off-white plastic blinds covered the only window, and the dull brown door didn't even have a number. Nothing about it said medical clinic to me. Apart from the small and very discreet sign above the door: *The Peter Paul Clinic*.

I looked at it doubtfully. "Is that the name of the guy who runs this place?"

"No."

"Then . . ."

"Look, just wait till you get inside," said Molly. "Everything will be made clear."

"That's what's worrying me," I said.

I looked dubiously at the lone ambulance parked a short distance away. There were no patients being unloaded, no driver at the wheel. It was just . . . waiting. I found its presence ominous, and more than a little creepy. Suddenly, I couldn't get my breath. I was shaking all over. I shook my head hard, trying to clear my thoughts. Part of me just wanted to turn and run, and keep running. Molly moved in close beside me, slipped an arm through mine, and pressed it firmly against her side. So I couldn't run, even if I wanted to. Her presence did help me to feel a little calmer.

"We're almost there, Eddie," she said.

"You sound like a dental nurse," I said numbly. "Announcing, *The dentist will see you now!* Like that's a good thing."

"You get scared of the strangest things," said Molly. "I've seen you stand up to demons and ancient gods and never blink an eyelid, but . . ."

"I'm allowed to hit demons and ancient gods," I said.

"Better now?" said Molly.

"Some," I said.

She looked me over carefully, till she was sure I could stand on my own, and then disengaged her arm and approached the Clinic door. She didn't try the handle; she knew it would be locked. She leaned over the intercom grille set into the rough brickwork beside the door.

"It's Molly Metcalf. Isabella's sister."

The buzzer sounded immediately, and Molly pushed the door open. I followed her in, thoughtfully. Her name, or that of her sister, was a passWord.

The interior turned out to be much larger than I'd anticipated. A great open space, with pleasant pastel-painted walls designed to be calming and soothing to the eye, and to the troubled mind. Comfortable chairs had been set out in neat rows, vending machines offered snacks and hot drinks, and bland, inoffensive music played quietly in the background. But there were no signs on the walls to describe the practices or options available. No list of doctors or departments. As though you were supposed to know what you were getting into. A flowery perfume hung heavily on the still air, undermined by something astringently antiseptic.

"You take a seat," said Molly, "while I go and sort things out. Do you want to get something from the vending machines?"

"You have got to be kidding," I said. "Boiling hot flavoured water and sugary cholesterol bites? If you weren't sick when you came in, that stuff would do it to you."

"You're in a mood, aren't you?" said Molly.

"Yes," I said. "I wonder why."

I looked suspiciously around the reception area while Molly just walked off and left me, heading straight for the long reception desk at the far end of the room. It was manned by a half-dozen bright young things in starched white uniforms, all of them doing their best to appear professional and efficient as they worked their computers and answered the constantly ringing phones. Molly planted herself in front of one of the reception staff, and just glared coldly at her until she put down her phone. Molly then proceeded to talk urgently and implacably to her, in a way that made clear she wasn't going to take any variation on *no* as an answer. I left her to it.

Visitors and family members, and those there to be supportive, had their own section, off to one side. They sat in quiet rows, showing great concentration as they read the magazines provided. So they wouldn't have to think about anything else. On the other side of the room, a man with a horse's head sat next to a man with a shrunken head, who sat next to a man with two heads. Under a sign that said, simply, *Cursed*. They seemed quite resigned, all things considered. Not far away, a middle-aged man in a crumpled suit sat on his own, staring at the floor, while half a dozen smoky ghosts swirled around him. Their faces were vague and unfocused, all dark eyes and chattering mouths, all of them talking at once while the man did his best not to listen. The miserable look on his face showed he'd been listening for some time. I sympathized. Haunted houses are bad enough; haunted people are worse.

A woman sat alone, bent right over on her chair. At first, I thought she was hunchbacked, given the way her ridged spine rose up to press against her coat, but then I saw her back heave and swell, before subsiding again. Something inside wanted out. The woman's face was pale and drawn from the pain, and slick with sweat. Her eyes had a lost, hopeless look. I hoped someone there could help her.

There were a great many other patients, sitting quietly, all of them wrapped up in their own problems. Hoping against hope someone in this very out-of-the-way Clinic could do something for them. They looked at me, searching for symptoms. And when they couldn't see anything obviously wrong, they looked away again. Not one of them.

A woman in one of those distinctly unflattering hospital gowns that do up only at the back came marching through the waiting room. She was attached to an IV drip on a stand, but it didn't slow her down. Heading for the front door, she strode past the other patients without even looking at them. When she got there, she propped the door open just enough to smoke a cigarette. Through a hole in her throat. She blew the smoke outside, her face impassive. I winced. If I ever got to that stage, I think I really would seriously consider quitting. The woman looked round, caught me watching her, and stared me down. She blew a smoke ring at me through the hole in her neck. I shuddered, and she smiled briefly.

And then I looked up sharply as the background music changed to a sappy orchestral version of Blue Oyster Cult's "Don't Fear the Reaper." Hospital humour. Molly came hurrying back to join me, and I nodded to her thankfully.

"What took you so long?" I said.

"We had a bit of a discussion," said Molly. "What's the problem?"

"You mean apart from the fact that this place is depressing the hell out of me? I mean, look at it. Are you sure we haven't accidentally wandered into the Nightside?"

Molly smiled. "It's not that easy to get into the Night-side, even in this part of London. Trust me, if we were actually in the long night, you'd know it. This is more like an overlap. So much weird shit happens in Harley Street, it calls out to other strange stuff. It attracts abnormal places and situations, shadowy areas, and they attach themselves to the real world. We're in the Shade, Eddie. The overlap between the day and the long night."

"Why didn't I know this street was here?" I said.

"Sometimes it isn't," said Molly. "This is a place for people who don't want to be noticed. And even then, nothing that happens here is important enough for the Droods to care about. Look, never mind all that. I've got you an emergency appointment! The doctor will see you right now."

"You intimidated a hospital receptionist?" I said. "Damn, girl; you're good."

"Money talks," said Molly.

"How much?"

"I told you; don't worry about it. I've got you covered. See the white door at the far end? Go through there, and Dr Benway will see you. I'll wait for you here."

"You're not coming in with me?" I said. "I don't want to go in alone. Strange doctors make me nervous."

"Don't be such a baby," Molly said briskly. "It's just hospital rules, to protect your privacy. You're the patient; I'm just a friend. What do you want me to do, anyway—hold your hand?"

"That would be nice, yes," I said.

"Get in there."

"Do I get a nice sweetie afterwards?"

"Eddie . . ."

"All right!" I said. "I'm going."

I made my way somewhat gingerly across the open space, trying not to notice all the other patients hating me for jumping the queue. I knocked on the white door, and a cheerful voice invited me in. I strode in, trying to project a confidence I absolutely didn't feel. It could have been any consulting room, anywhere. Pleasantly appointed, comfortable furnishings and fittings, a desk to one side and a long red leather couch on the other. I looked hopefully for a human skeleton standing in one corner, but there wasn't one. I always felt there should be. The usual framed diplomas had been carefully mounted on the walls. It occurred to me no one ever checks the details on these documents; they could say anything. Framed prints displayed unthreatening countryside scenes. At least there wasn't any background music.

The doctor came out from behind his desk to greet me. Middle-aged and unremarkable, in an expensive suit, he seemed a smooth and plausible sort, with a professional smile already in place. His handshake was firm and reassuring.

"Hello, old man. Do come in. Make yourself comfortable. I'm Dr Benway." He leaned forward, to look closely at my torc. Which startled me just a bit, because civilians aren't supposed to be able to see it. Unless you're the seventh son of a seventh son, and family planning has mostly taken care of that. He straightened up again and nodded cheerfully. "And there it is; the famous Drood torc. Amazing. Remarkable."

"How are you able to see it?" I said.

"Hmm? Oh, all part of the job, old man. To be able to see hidden things." He smiled in a satisfied sort of way. "Eddie Drood . . . Never had a Drood in here before. Heard all about you, of course. Before you leave, you really must let me examine that thing . . ."

"No," I said. "Not a chance."

He shrugged, entirely unconcerned. "Didn't think so, but I had to ask. Come and sit down, sit down." He sat behind his desk again, and I sat down facing him. "Now then, old man, what are the symptoms?"

"Didn't Molly tell you anything?" I said.

"For the amount of money she's paying for this emergency consultation, she didn't have to," Benway said cheerfully. "Besides, I always prefer to hear the details of any problem direct from the patient. Don't be shy, old man. We really have heard it all before."

"My family doctors tell me I've been poisoned," I said. "With something they've never seen before. No cure, no treatment. According to them, I've got three months. If I'm lucky."

Benway sat back in his chair. He nodded slowly, his face giving nothing away. "Well, well . . . That is a bit of hard luck, isn't it? Your family doctors do have an excellent reputation in the medical field . . . If they've said there's nothing they can do for you, I wouldn't doubt them. And you came to us? That is a compliment. I think we'd better take a close look at you, old man. Let the dog see the rabbit, eh? Lie down on the couch, please."

I got up from the chair, went over to the couch, and stretched out on it. "Can I just say, I hate needles!"

"Me too!" Benway said cheerfully. "Fortunately, we don't go in for that sort of thing around here."

He produced a pair of sunglasses from inside his jacket, and fitted them carefully on his narrow nose. They had silver frames and deep purple lenses. He leaned over me, hands behind his back to keep them out of the way, and looked me over carefully from head to foot. His expression never changed, but he did go *Hmm* several times. He finally straightened up again, took off the sunglasses, and put them away.

"Yes . . . I see. Really quite remarkable. You have been poisoned."

"I already told you that!" I said.

"Indeed you did, old man, and quite right you were. I've never seen anything like it. An entirely new poison.

Quite appallingly toxic stuff too; it's a wonder to me you're still alive."

"But is it going to kill me . . . ?"

"Hmm? Oh yes. Quite definitely. Your doctors gave you three months, you say? Well, they know your system better than I do. Personally, I wouldn't bet on it."

I lay back on the couch and looked up at the ceiling. I'd known he was going to tell me there was nothing he could do, but it still hit me hard. A small part of me had really hoped he'd find something the Drood medics had missed. That they'd got it wrong, and it only looked like I was poisoned. That he knew what to do . . .

"You really have no idea what the poison is?" I said finally.

"Haven't a clue, old man," said Benway. "Not from around here . . . not of this world, I would say. Lots of visitors around these days, of course, but they're usually so different, their little problems don't affect us. How did this poison get into your system in the first place?"

"I don't know," I said.

"Then I really can't help you with identification," said Benway. "Fortunately, that won't be a problem. It's a good thing you came to us, old man. None of the traditional forms of medicine could do a thing for you, but we're not in any way traditional."

I allowed myself to feel a faint twinge of hope. "You can help?"

"Of course, old man! Don't you worry yourself; we have what you need!"

I sat up on the couch and looked at him. "What is it you do here, exactly? What is your particular discipline? How can you help me?"

"Easy, old man! One thing at a time, eh?" Benway smiled at me reassuringly. "Here at the Peter Paul Clinic, we rob Peter to pay Paul. We don't deal in drugs or surgery, science or magic. As such. Or any kind of healing. We deal strictly in the transfer of life energies. Don't ask me to explain how it works; I'm not entirely sure I understand myself. It works, and that's all that matters."

"What about side effects?" I said.

"Nothing you need to worry about, old man," said Benway. "Though you might want to think about embracing a healthier lifestyle, after you leave here. Nothing to do with the poison or your treatment; just general good advice. I say that to all my patients. If people could only see the damage they do to themselves . . . Ah well, never mind." I must have been giving him a really hard look, because he snapped back to the subject. "We drain the life energies from willing—and very well-paid—volunteers, and then transfer these energies to the patient. Who needs them more. The volunteers all give a little, and we give it to you in one big dose. They don't miss it, really; no more than a blood donor.

"This new life energy doesn't actually cure anything, but it does slow down the dying process quite dramatically. The poison will still be in you, but the new life energy will slow its progress right down, and buy you more time. It's not a cure, but the sheer amount of life energy will keep you going for years and years. You'll feel perfectly well and healthy, with no unfortunate symptoms. Basically, we're putting off your death, old man. And when you've used up all the new life energy, you can always come back here for more top-ups! Which will be expensive, of course, but then, you're a Drood. I should point out . . . that this is not an indefinite process. Each transfer of life energies does take its toll. Each time, your body will accept less of the new energies, until finally it won't accept any. We're selling health, old man, not immortality. Or we'd be charging a damned sight more. And you must understand, there are problems . . ."

"Somehow," I said, "I just knew there would be. What sort of problems are we talking about?"

"To overcome a condition as severe as yours," Benway said carefully, "and a poison as malignant as yours, will require a really massive accumulation of life energies. And it's not like we keep it here in bottles. It has to come straight from a suitable donor. And they don't just hang around here, waiting to be needed. We'll have to put a call out to as many of them as possible, and pay over the odds to get them to come in as quickly as possible. Rounding them up will take some time . . ."

And then he broke off as the phone on his desk rang. He smiled reassuringly at me, excused himself, and went to answer it.

"Benway. Yes. He's here with me now. I've just been telling him . . . Oh. Are you sure? Well, if you're sure, go ahead and start the procedure. I'll get the patient ready."

He put the phone down and came back to smile at me some more.

"It seems you're in luck, old man. Apparently we do have sufficient donors to hand, after all. The transfer of life energies is being prepared, even as we speak. Lots of money really does talk very persuasively. Your partner, Ms Metcalf, has already sorted things out with my colleague, Dr Raven."

"So, what do you use?" I said. "Some kind of alien or future technology?"

"Hmm? Oh, no, we use a leech."

"What?"

"I know!" said Benway. "It does sound like a terrible step backwards, doesn't it? But this is a genetically engineered, really big leech. Originally created by a very secretive group called the Immortals. Whoever they were. All but wiped out now, I understand. We bought the leech at an auction of their effects. Got it for a really quite reasonable price too, because no one knew what it was, or what it could do. Neither did we until we started experimenting with it and had a few . . . accidents. But we know what we're doing now."

"I'm very pleased to hear that," I said.

"Oh yes . . . ," said Benway. "All very simple. We just slap the leech onto the donor, let it suck up some life energies, and then take it off again. Repeat as necessary. Once the leech has accumulated enough energies, we just slap it on the patient and persuade the leech to transfer all it's stored."

"How do you do that?"

"Hmm? Oh, we just zap it with a cattle prod. Look, stop asking questions if the answers are going to upset you so much. All you need to know is that this process will give you many years of extra life. Trust me; I'm a doctor. This has all been very thoroughly tested. Dr Raven is in the next room right now, getting ready to acquire the necessary energies. Shouldn't take long."

But something in that didn't feel right. Benway said he needed to call in volunteers, and then gather enough energy from them to save me. It couldn't be happening already. Benway must have seen something in my face, because he gave me his best reassuring smile.

"Just lie back on the couch, think of the bill, and go *Aaaargh!* A little private medical humour there."

"Just how expensive is this going to be?" I said.

"Oh very," Benway said cheerfully. "That's what happens when you have a monopoly on the market and everyone wants something only you can supply."

"So basically," I said, "you're drug dealers."

"You're the one in need of a fix," said Benway. "Remember, old man; you came to us. But you don't need to worry about the cost. Your partner, Ms Metcalf, has already taken care of everything." He looked at me thoughtfully. "She must be very fond of you."

Something in the doctor's voice didn't ring true. I

can always tell when I'm being sold a bill of goods. I sat up and swung my legs over the side of the couch. Benway made vague motions with his hands, as though he wanted to push me back down again but knew better than to try to force me. I looked at him, and he fell back a step.

"I want to talk to Molly," I said. "Before we start this."

"But you can't!" said Benway. "I'm sorry, old man, but it's just not possible. I can't allow you to . . ."

That was it. Something in his face, in his voice, was setting off major alarm bells. I was up and off the couch in a moment. I grabbed two handfuls of his jacket front, forced him all the way back across his office, and slammed him up against the wall. He cried out in shock and then broke off abruptly as I shoved my face into his.

"Where's Molly?"

"Don't hurt me!" he said immediately. "It wasn't my idea; it's not my fault!"

"What's not your fault?" I said. "What have you done? Where's Molly?"

I realised I was slamming him back against the wall with each question, and stopped to let him answer. He looked terrified of me, and he was right to be.

"She's next door! I told you; she's right next door! But you can't go in there . . ."

I threw him to one side, hauled open the door, and stormed out of the consultation room. Patients and visitors looked at me in surprise, took in the expression on my face, and quickly looked away. I tried the door to the next room, but it was locked. I called out Molly's name, and beat on the door with my fist, but there was no response. I armoured up. Cries of shock and alarm filled the waiting room as golden strange matter swept over me. I didn't care. I hit the door with my shoulder and it burst open, slammed right off its hinges. The next room looked just like the one I'd left, only Molly was lying on the red leather couch with another doctor leaning over her. A large fleshy sort in a baggy suit, with cold eyes and a professional smile, he was holding a really big leech with a pair of long silver tongs. It was the size of a bean bag, jet-black with pulsing scarlet veins. The doctor was holding it over Molly's neck.

He spun round at my sudden entrance, took one look at me in my armour, and immediately fell back from Molly. He retreated all the way across his office, not taking his eyes off me for a moment, until he banged up against his desk. He dropped the leech into a handy steel bowl, dropped the tongs onto the desk, and then held up both shaking hands so I could see he was no threat to anybody. Molly looked at me, and turned her head away. I turned to the doctor.

"What were you doing?"

"I'm Dr Raven," he said, trying to retrieve some of his dignity. "Ms Metcalf arranged with this Clinic to give up all her life energies to the leech so they could be given to you. To save your life. She volunteered! She agreed to a price for the service, and signed a contract!"

"Get out," I said.

He ran for the door. He thought I might kill him, and I thought I might too. I armoured down, and sat on the couch beside Molly. She didn't want to look at me. I didn't know what to say. Except . . .

"No."

"Please, Eddie." I could barely hear her, with her face pressed into the leather of the couch. "Let me do this. I want to. I need to do this, for you."

"Give up your life to save mine?" I said, working hard to keep any trace of anger out of my voice. "You think I want that? You really think I'd want to go on living, knowing I'd bought my extra years at the cost of your life? I can't let you die, Molly, because then I'd die anyway."

She finally turned her head to look at me. Tears were

coursing down her cheeks. "You think I want to go on living, without you?"

"This isn't the answer," I said. "This way, only one of us lives. I won't settle for any solution that doesn't involve both of us, and I won't give up till I find it. Don't you give up hope, Molly. I haven't."

"Really? I wasn't sure."

"Neither was I. Till now."

She sat up and wiped at her nose with the back of her hand. She wasn't used to crying.

"You knew about the leech all along," I said. "You knew what they do here."

"Yes." Molly looked at me defiantly. "Isabella told me, ages ago. She told me and Louisa, so we'd know what to do, if it ever became necessary. I've been thinking about the leech ever since the Drood doctors told me you were going to die."

"Why not just let the doctors here do their job?" I said. "Draw off small amounts of life energy from volunteers, until they had enough to save me?"

"That was what I expected," said Molly. "That was the plan. I'm not stupid! But when I explained the situation to Dr Raven, he said they'd need hundreds of volunteers to amass enough energies to save a Drood. And that would take so long . . . the odds were you'd be dead before they could put enough together. And then he suggested . . . that I could save you. My life forces are so much stronger than most people's because of my long exposure to the magics. Enough to save a Drood, all on my own. So I volunteered. I really did, Eddie. I agreed to this. No one forced me into anything."

"Bad idea," I said as calmly as I could. "I'm not even sure it would have worked. The more I think about this, the less I believe anything we've been told. Even after giving me all your energies, they could still have insisted I needed more. They could have kept me hooked on that leech forever, always telling me I needed more energies to keep the poison at bay. Leeching more and more money off me for each treatment. Bleeding me dry, and then my family . . . Until they decided money wasn't enough, and they wanted the Droods to do them a few little favours . . .

"Or they could have just lied to me. Told me they were saving my life, when they knew they'd never have enough energies to do it. They could just keep taking my money until I died. This whole life-energies-transference thing doesn't strike me as an exact science. This isn't a medical clinic, Molly; it's a con job."

Molly looked at me, thunderstruck. "They conned me! Me!"

"Just goes to show how upset you were," I said. "You weren't thinking straight. I'm flattered; I think."

Molly was up on her feet in a moment, her whole body shaking with rage. She mopped at her face with a handkerchief until she had her composure back, and when she finally spoke to me, her voice was calm and steady and extremely dangerous.

"Let's get out of here, Eddie. Before I decide to kill a whole bunch of people, just on general principles."

"Sure," I said. "Want to smash the place up and burn it to the ground before we leave?"

"You always know the right thing to say to cheer a girl up," said Molly.

She grabbed hold of me, kissed me fiercely, and then held me tight. And I held on to her. Because I'd wanted this to work so badly. Now, more than ever, all we had was each other.

Alarms started ringing out in the reception area. Loud, strident, and quite petulantly upset alarms. Molly and I let go of each other, and exchanged a smile.

"They're playing our song," said Molly.

"Time to go," I said. "I think we've worn out our welcome."

I moved over to the open doorway, and looked out into the waiting room. And then I beckoned for Molly to come and join me. She crowded into the doorway beside me, and slowly began to smile. All the patients and visitors had been herded off into a far corner, along with the reception staff, under Dr Raven. Who was looking very unhappy. Dr Benway was standing in the middle of the great open space, glaring at Molly and me. He looked like a small child who'd just had his favourite toy taken away. And then he smiled nastily at me and at Molly, as though he knew something we didn't. I looked around the reception area, but there didn't seem to be anything in place to stop us from just walking out. Until I heard slow, heavy footsteps approaching from a side corridor behind Benway. I looked to Molly.

"Could be security."

"What could they have that could stop a witch like me and a Drood like you?"

"I don't know," I said. "Presumably . . . that."

I pointed to the inhumanly good-looking, almost godlike figure that had just stepped into the reception area. His face had that cold, handsome quality you normally get only on the faces of classical Greek statues, and his body had the musculature to go with it. The man positively bristled with strength and vitality. He wore a simple white jumpsuit, and his every movement was full of unnatural grace and power. Dr Benway laughed out loud. It was an ugly sound.

"If you take donated life energies and pump them into a perfectly healthy person over and over, this is what you get! Someone who's stronger, better, than human! We call him Adam, because he's the first of a new kind. And as long as we keep recharging him, there's no telling how strong he'll get, or how long he'll live."

"And as long as you control your little lab rat's access to the leech, you control him," I said.

Benway shrugged. "You don't get anything for free

in this world. Adam, take those two captive. I want them alive but not necessarily undamaged." He was still smiling at us. Not his professional doctor's smile; now it was the smile of a con man who's been found out and is looking for revenge. He'd also stopped calling me *old man*, for which I was grateful. He grinned savagely. "Your turn to be lab rats! I can't wait to see just how many life energies I can drain from a Drood and the wild witch of the woods. We can probably sell it at a premium rate. Bound to be extraordinarily potent . . ."

"To attack one Drood is to take on the whole family," I said.

"And I have sisters," said Molly.

"None of them will ever know," said Benway. "This is the Shade, remember? No one ever sees what goes on in the Shade."

"Enough talking," said Adam. "I'm hungry. I'm always hungry."

His voice was utterly lacking in anything human. What emotions I could see in his perfect face made no sense at all.

"Somehow," said Molly, "I don't think he's hungry for a cheeseburger."

"He's looking at us like we're the cheeseburgers," I said. "And he looks like he thinks he can take us."

"He doesn't know us," said Molly.

"This is just another variation on the Accelerated Men," I said.

"Let's mess him up," said Molly.

"And then do something really unpleasant to the two doctors?"

"Why not?"

I armoured up again, and Molly surrounded herself with crackling magics. The watching patients, visitors, and staff cried out, and huddled together. Dr Raven tried to quiet them, but he didn't look nearly as confident as his colleague. Adam didn't look like he gave a damn.

He came straight for me, and when he was close enough, he hit me in the head. A sudden blow, so fast and so strong, I couldn't react fast enough to block or avoid it. His fist slammed into my featureless golden mask, and my armour made a dull booming sound, like a struck bell. I didn't feel anything inside my armour, but the sheer impact sent me staggering back into the consultation room. Adam looked at his fist. It seemed entirely uninjured, though by rights it should have been smashed to a pulp. He started forward, to come at me again.

Molly, who'd just been standing there nonplussed, got her act together and hit him with her strongest transformation spell. Probably something to do with frogs or toads; she's always been a traditionalist in such matters. Wild energies crawled all over Adam, spitting and hissing like living lightning, but he just shrugged them off. The magic fell away, frustrated by his unnatural perfection. Molly hit him with a dozen different spells in swift succession, each one nastier than the one before, and none of them had any effect. Perhaps because Adam was so perfect now, nothing from this imperfect world could touch him. He moved to go into the consulting room after me, and Molly blocked his way. He raised an arm to strike her down. Molly didn't flinch, didn't move. I charged past her and slammed into Adam.

I hit him hard with a lowered golden shoulder, caught him off balance, and sent him staggering backwards. The sheer weight and impact of my armour were more than a match for his perfection. He quickly recovered his balance, and the two of us went head to head, exchanging blows so powerful they would have killed anyone else. We rampaged back and forth across the reception area, smashing up the fixtures and fittings. Two godlike beings in a paper world. I grabbed a vending machine and broke it over his head. He threw me into a wall so hard, I cracked it from top to bottom. The onlookers were screaming now, terrorised by the sight of what happens when godlike beings go to war.

And then Molly jumped onto Adam's back, and slapped the giant leech onto his bare neck. He cried out in shock and revulsion, and reached back with one hand to tear it free; but every time his hand got near, it just slipped aside, as though it couldn't find it. The leech had its own built-in protection. No wonder Raven had to use special tongs to handle it. Adam grabbed hold of Molly and tried to haul her off him, but although she cried out at the vicious strength of his grip, she had both arms and legs wrapped tightly around him.

Adam lurched and almost fell, while the leech pulsed hungrily. He didn't look perfect any more. I hit him hard on the side of the face, and his head snapped right round under the impact. I heard bones break. He dropped to one knee. I hit him in the head again, putting all my armoured strength into it, and he collapsed unconscious to the floor. Molly rode him all the way down, just to be sure, and only then released her grip. She rose elegantly to her feet, and kicked Adam hard in the ribs. He didn't wake up. Molly nodded, satisfied. The leech pulsed and quivered on his neck, still draining the life energies out of him. Adam was looking less perfect by the moment. The bloom was off the rose, and humanity was setting in. His face showed clear signs of ageing.

Molly grabbed the leech with one hand, grimaced at the feel of the thing, and then tore it off Adam's neck. It didn't want to release its hold, but no one argues with Molly Metcalf. The leech came free with a loud, disgusting sucking sound, and Molly triumphantly brandished the ugly thing above her head.

"All right," I said. "Where did you get that from?"

"I stole it," said Molly, entirely unrepentant. "I thought your family might be able to do something with it."

"And you weren't at all thinking of selling it for quite remarkable amounts of money?"

"Only if your family couldn't do something with it."

"How are you able to handle it with your bare hand, without it draining your life energies?"

"Because I'm a witch," Molly said witheringly. "And nothing happens to me that I don't allow."

"Of course," I said. "I was forgetting."

Benway, almost in tears, came forward to look at his fallen Adam. "Look at what you've done to him . . . You've ruined him! It'll take me months to charge him up again."

Molly grinned. "Good luck doing that; I've got your leech."

Benway tried to snatch it from her. She held it back out of reach, waggling the nasty thing temptingly. Benway turned to the patients, still watching from their far corner.

"Look!" he said harshly. "They're stealing the one thing that can cure you! They want to keep it to themselves. Are you going to let them get away with that? Get the leech back from them, and your next treatments will be free! If they take it out of here, you're all going to die!"

"Time we were leaving," I said to Molly.

"You think they can stop us?" she said.

"I don't want to have to hurt them," I said.

"You always were a soft touch," said Molly.

We ran for the front door, and the whole crowd came baying after us, everyone desperate, hysterical, reaching for us with outraged hands. If I'd really thought the leech would help them, I would have made Molly give it back. But I had no faith in the thing, and even less faith in Benway and Raven to do the right thing with it. Con men only look after themselves. Benway and Raven were both screaming at the crowd to get the leech, running right along behind, almost out of their minds at the sight of their most lucrative meal ticket departing.

I ran out the front door and onto the street, with Molly treading on my heels. The few people passing by didn't even slow down to look at us; an armoured Drood and a wild witch with something unnatural in her hand were just business as usual in the Shade. I slammed the door shut the moment Molly was through, and kept it closed by pressing my armoured back against it.

"Now what?" I said. "We can't just run through the streets pursued by a screaming mob. Someone would notice."

"Easy!" said Molly. "We steal an ambulance!"

She pointed to the one parked just down the street. The sign on its side read *The Peter Paul Clinic. Private Ambulance. Group Bookings Available. No Time-wasters.*

The door slammed and shuddered against my back. I turned around, crushed the lock with my golden hand, and then backed cautiously away. The door held, but still shook ominously as a great many fists hammered against its other side. People who'd seen their hope snatched away, and thought they were fighting for their lives. I looked around, spotted a nearby parking meter, and smiled briefly. Never liked the things. I grabbed hold of its column with one hand, and ripped the meter right out of the pavement. Chunks of concrete went flying in all directions. I jammed the parking meter against the door, forcing it into place.

"That won't hold them for long," I said. "Those are some highly motivated sick people."

"Get in the ambulance!" said Molly.

I hurried over to the driver's door. There was still no one behind the steering wheel, but the door was locked. Molly tried the passenger door, but that didn't want to open either. I shrugged, and jerked the door open with one golden hand. The lock shattered.

"Ow!" the ambulance said loudly. "That hurt, you beast!"

I wasn't thrown. I've had stranger things talk to me. The ambulance had a sultry female voice that made me think of a mature stage actress, a little past her prime but still game.

"Sorry," I said. "We're in a bit of a hurry."

"Men always are, dear," said the ambulance. "You have no idea how to treat a lady . . . Hey! What are you doing? Don't you dare! Get out of me this instant!"

But I was already settling into the driver's seat. The passenger door opened, and Molly dropped into the seat next to me. She still had the big black leech in her hand. She didn't seem too sure what to do with it. She didn't want to risk losing it, but every time she looked at what she was holding, she winced. I looked for the keys to the ignition, but not only were there no keys; there was no ignition. The steering wheel didn't move under my hands, and there were no pedals on the floor.

"How do you get this ambulance going?" I said.

"Oh, the usual ways, darling," said the ambulance. "Flowers, chocolates, buck's fizz . . ."

"You drive yourself?" said Molly.

"Of course!" said the ambulance. "A girl has to make a living."

"Then take us to the Wulfshead Club," said Molly.

"I am not taking you anywhere," the ambulance said haughtily. "I'm on my break. Of course, if you were to take advantage of my generous nature by offering a poor working girl a substantial bribe . . ."

I looked back at the shaking and shuddering Clinic door. It didn't look like it would last much longer.

"How much?" I said.

"Oh, it's not about the money, honey," said the ambulance. "In this business, it's all about the suffering . . ."

Molly slapped the leech onto the dashboard, and it stuck there. The ambulance made a surprised sound. Molly goosed the leech with a small lightning bolt from her fingertip, and the heavily veined flesh shuddered briefly. Lights flashed wildly all across the dashboard, and the whole ambulance trembled for a moment.

"Oh yes, darling!" said the ambulance. "That will do nicely!"

The Clinic door burst open, and men and women driven crazy by desperate need fought one another to get into the street first. The ambulance started its engine. Turning as one mind to look, the crowd saw me sitting behind the wheel and charged forward, shouting and howling. Those in the rushing mass were so out of their minds now, they weren't even producing words, just animal noises. The ambulance surged forward, and those in the crowd ran along beside it, beating on the sides with their hands. Some of them grabbed hold, and were pulled along as the ambulance accelerated, before falling away again, to be trampled underfoot by the running mob. I looked back at the desperate faces, slowly losing all hope, and then looked at the leech on the dashboard.

"Stop the ambulance," I said. "Stop right now."

"Really?" said the ambulance.

"Yes!"

"Well, make up your mind, dear. And if those animals scratch my paintwork, you're going to be paying for my next makeover."

The ambulance screeched to a halt, and the crowd took new heart. Those who'd stopped running started again, and the mob soon surrounded the ambulance on all sides, beating on the walls and trying to force open the doors. Others threw things at the windscreen. Molly swivelled round in her seat, the better to give me a very hard look.

"If they get their hands on us, they'll tear us to pieces. Tell me you have an idea."

"I have an idea."

"Is it a good idea?"

"It's an idea."

"I'm not going to like this at all, am I?" said Molly.

I explained my idea to her, briefly, and after a moment a big, broad grin spread slowly over her face.

I armoured up my right hand, took a firm hold of the leech, and pulled it off the dashboard. It didn't want to let go, but finally jerked free with a nasty sucking sound. The ambulance made a disgusted noise. The leech pulsed hungrily in my hand, single-minded as only genetic engineering could make it, but it couldn't get to me past the strange matter. The crowd had closed in all around us now, rocking the ambulance back and forth. I kicked open the driver's door, leaned out, and held up the leech so everyone could see it. Everyone in the crowd froze where they were.

"Back off!" I said loudly. "Or I'll crush it!"

Those at the front backed away immediately, and word spread quickly through the crowd. The noise fell away as people reluctantly retreated, and the ambulance grew still. Those who could see the leech in my hand looked at me with a wretched mixture of hope and despair. I leaned out farther, holding the leech up before me. A dark inkblot against my golden hand. All eyes were fixed on it. Benway and Raven forced their way to the front of the crowd.

"Give it back!" said Benway. "That belongs to us!"

"You've no right to it!" said Raven.

"Neither do you," I said. "It should belong to the people who need it. But if you want it, it's yours."

I threw it straight to them. Those in the crowd couldn't believe it. They made a sound like they'd been hit, and surged forward from all sides at once. Benway and

Raven got to the leech first, snatching it out of mid-air. They each got a hand on it at the same time, both to preserve it for themselves and for fear it might fall to the ground and be trampled underfoot. Or that the leech might be torn apart by the crowd fighting over it. Benway and Raven both took a firm hold on the leech at the same moment . . . with their bare hands. In the heat of the moment they'd forgotten all about gloves and special tongs.

Both of them cried out in shock and horror as the leech sucked the life energies out of them. They tried to let go, but their hands had clamped shut on the leech in a convulsive grip. The leech had them, and it wasn't letting go. I gave Molly the signal and she leaned over me, pointed one finger at the leech, and blasted it with another of her miniature lightning bolts. Just enough to really speed up the process. The leech went into overdrive and sucked all the life energies out of Benway and Raven in a moment. Leaving nothing but two shrivelled, crumpled shapes; desiccated mummies in good suits. They fell dead to the ground, with no more sound than two dried-up insect husks.

Those in the crowd ran right over them to get to the leech; not even looking down as they fought one another to get to the one thing they thought might save them. A dozen hands clamped down on the leech at once, not caring what its touch might do. And Molly hit the leech with a slightly different magical lightning bolt. This one reversed the leech's polarity, forcing it to release all the life energies it had stored in one great blast. The leech exploded, but there was no blood, just a blast of brilliant light. A wonderful life-giving light that filled the street, washing over all of the crowd at once. They stood still, awed and confused, as the stored life energies sank into them. And the pain left them, one by one, and the madness went out of their faces.

They turned and looked at one another wonderingly,

and then laughed and cried and embraced one another, free of the pain and the horror, and the deaths that had been staring over their shoulders for so long. They turned away from the ambulance and went back to the Clinic to share the good news with their friends and family. Not that they were cured, but that they had a lot more time than they'd thought. I watched them go, and wished I could have gone with them. That I had reason to go with them. Molly settled back into her seat as I armoured down my hand and closed the driver's door.

"All right," said Molly. "As ideas go, that one wasn't too bad."

"Just this once," I said, "nobody dies on my watch. Sometimes I forget that I'm not just here to fight the bad guys. I'm here to save people."

"With a little help from your friends," said Molly.

"Of course," I said. "Okay, ambulance, the Wulfshead Club, if you please. As fast as you can."

The ambulance set off down the street, accelerating fiercely. With all the alarms and sirens going, at no extra charge.

"I'm going to need a new job, aren't I?" said the ambulance after a while. "Never liked Benway or Raven . . . and I never really liked being an ambulance. You wouldn't believe what I've had to wash out of the back of me on a Saturday night."

Molly looked at me. "She keeps saying things . . ."

"I had noticed," I said. I studied the departing street in the rearview mirror. "This time next week, there'll be a shrine back there, to mark where a miracle took place. And a whole new bunch of con men will emerge, to take advantage of the situation. Such is life. But it does feel good to do some good."

"You look good, Eddie," said Molly. "You look . . . better. How are you feeling? Did any of the leech's light touch you?"

"No," I said. "It couldn't get past my torc. I'm still dying. But for the first time since the Drood doctors gave me my deadline, I feel alive again. I've got my hope back."

"About time," said Molly. "I was getting really tired of carrying you."

We laughed together as the ambulance sped through the streets of London.

CHAPTER FIVE

We All Wear Masks

've driven a Nineteen Thirties racing Bentley through strange dimensions, and piloted an experimental jet over worlds that don't even have names yet. I've run across carriage rooftops on the Trans-Siberian Express, and sailed a ship through a Faerie Gate. But I still say travelling in that ambulance from the Peter Paul Clinic to the Wulfshead Club is one of the most nerve-racking things I've ever done. Even though I was sitting in the driver's seat, I had no control over where we were going or how we were getting there. Mostly I just braced my legs and clung to the unmoving steering wheel with both hands, to keep from being thrown back and forth as the ambulance hit London traffic like a shark thrown into a toddler's swimming pool. She used her lights and sirens to intimidate everyone into getting out of her way, and when that didn't work, she was quite happy to play chicken with oncoming cars and threaten to rear-end everything else. Or drive right over them. Speed restrictions were treated as mere suggestions,

and the rules of the road were only for the weak and
the spineless. She had a particular fondness for side-
sweeping bicycle messengers, but then, don't we all?

She also liked to shout threats, abuse, and very vul-
gar suggestions at people who had the temerity to use
pedestrian crossings. I wasn't sure they could hear her,
but I still stayed slumped down in my seat, hiding my
face as much as possible. Word must have got ahead of
the ambulance, because after a while it did seem like
all the other traffic was going out of its way to give her
plenty of room, including by driving on the pavements.
I could understand that; I'd have moved to another
country to make sure she had enough room. I just hoped
the ambulance didn't crash into anything. I really didn't
want to be cut out of the wreckage of a loudly blas-
pheming ambulance.

"Could we please slow down, just a bit?" I said plaintively. "I think I left my stomach behind at the last mini
roundabout. The one you went the wrong way round."

"Thought you were in a hurry, darling," the ambulance said cheerfully.

"Not this much of a hurry," I said. "There are theo-
retical particles that go backwards in Time that go slower
than this!"

"Don't listen to him!" Molly said loudly. "This is the
most fun I've had all day! You go, girl!"

"You are really not helping," I said.

I would have liked to close my eyes, but didn't dare.
There was a horrid fascination in seeing sudden death
coming straight at me, at speed. I just hoped the way
the ambulance dodged disaster again and again, usually
at the very last moment, would turn out to be some kind
of good omen. Molly, arms and legs braced, whooped
loudly in the seat beside me, treating the whole thing
as a roller-coaster ride. She grinned across at me.

"What are you looking so worried about? You can
always armour up!"

"Not in public," I said. "Hey! That was a red light!"

"See if I care, darling," said the ambulance. "I think they do that just to tease me."

"This is not how I thought I was going to die," I said wistfully.

Several near misses and a few heart attacks later, the ambulance finally skidded to a halt at the end of the alley that led to the Wulfshead Club. I slowly relaxed, and looked around carefully. The rest of the traffic carried on as normal, trying to pretend that nothing mind-numbingly dangerous and scrotum-tighteningly awful had just happened. For their own peace of mind. I knew how they felt.

Night had fallen during our journey. Street lamps glowed sullenly, office buildings blazed arrogantly, and the best the night sky could manage was a sprinkling of stars and a crescent moon. A few pedestrians wandered past, but no one so much as glanced at the ambulance, because this was an area for minding your own business. I opened the driver's door and got out, as quickly as dignity would allow. Molly jumped out of her side, quite happily. The alarms and flashing lights snapped off.

"Told you I'd get you here by the quickest route," said the ambulance. "Who needs sat-nav? Arrogant little things, with their celebrity voices . . . I know London. I even know bits of it that aren't always there, and a few that should be."

"Were you by any chance a taxi driver in some previous existence?" said Molly. "Or even a taxi?"

"Not a bit of it, sweetie," said the ambulance. "Just a regular working girl, with far too many streets under her white stilettos." She paused. "You know, I've always wanted to visit the Wulfshead. Any chance you could get me in?"

"Not looking the way you do now," said Molly. "Two legs good, four wheels bad."

"Ah well, you know what they say, darlings," said the ambulance. "A change is as good as a rest. It's not like I meant to be an ambulance all my life; I just chose it as a quick way to make money, and work out my frustrations on slow-moving traffic. You won't know me the next time you see me! See you on the flipside, sweeties."

She sped off into the night, in a swirl of flaring blue lights and wailing sirens. I could almost hear the rest of the world flinch.

"You meet the strangest people in this business," I said.

I led the way down the dark alleyway. Someone had made a public-spirited attempt to clean the place up since I was last here. Probably using really long-handled brooms, and a flame-thrower. The usual piles of garbage were gone, though I could still hear rats scurrying in the shadows. At least, I hoped they were rats. An attempt had been made to clean away some of the accumulated dirt and grime, with varying success. But the alley walls were still slick with moisture, running down the old brickwork in sudden streams, and there were still far too many shadows, deep and dark and quietly menacing. The long alleyway had a worryingly uncertain feel, as though its edges weren't properly nailed down. Like the alleyways we walk in dreams, where the end is always farther away than you think, and you don't need to look back to know something is after you.

I couldn't work out why the alleyway was disturbing me so much. I'd been there often enough before, to visit the Wulfshead, and it had never bothered me. Was it the alley, or was it me? I couldn't ask Molly if she was feeling the same, in case she wasn't. I wasn't ready to have it all be in my mind. And I didn't want to upset her. I realised I'd come to a halt, just standing there, looking . . . and that Molly was looking at me. I gave her a quick smile, and did my best to appear confident. I didn't think I was fooling her, but she was kind enough to pretend I was. I moved on, trying to keep an eye on everything at once. Even if I wasn't sure why.

The walls were still covered in overlapping layers of graffiti. Messages and warnings from the Past, the Present, and the Future. Recent additions included *Cthulhu Has Bad Dreams*, *Don't Move Anything*; *It Leaves Gaps*, and more worryingly, *Say Good-bye to the Flesh*. And then I had to stop suddenly as the world seemed to lurch under my feet. I turned quickly to the nearest wall and leaned against it, supporting myself with both hands. My head was swimming. Everything felt far away. My legs were trembling, as though they might stop holding me up at any moment. As I looked at my hands before me, pressed against the wall, I realised I couldn't feel them. Both hands were completely numb.

Slowly, my head began to clear, and I straightened up again as my legs grew firmer. I held my hands up before me, and flexed them both several times. At first I could only see the fingers moving, but then the usual sensations crept back. No feeling of cold, or even pins and needles. I looked at my hands as though they'd betrayed me. It's always the extremities that go first. The first sign that for all my torc could do, the poison was still progressing, and my body was breaking down. I wondered when my hands would go numb again, and whether I'd get the feeling back next time. Or what would fail me next. As if I didn't have enough to worry about . . .

Molly was right beside me, watching silently and trying to keep the concern out of her face. I could tell she wanted to say something, but because I didn't, she couldn't. I smiled at her, to show I was back, and then gestured with an almost entirely steady hand at the opposite wall.

"Well, here we are. The Wulfshead Club. How do you want to play this?"

"We can't go in as Eddie Drood and Molly Metcalf," she said, her tone indicating she would accept the change of subject, for now. "Too many complications, and too much back history with the club and its patrons. Some might have heard that you're ... not yourself, and try to take advantage. And for those who haven't heard anything yet, best not to drop any clues."

"Right," I said. "I do have the feeling that we're still banned. As Eddie and Molly. We made a hell of a mess of the place, last time we were here. It's going to be hard enough to ask casual questions about Dr DOA, without having to fight off heavily armed bouncers at the same time."

"I'm sure they'll have forgotten all about our little upset," said Molly. "Well, no, they won't have forgotten, but if they banned anyone who got a little rowdy now and then, they wouldn't have any customers left."

"Of course," I said, "we're not just anyone."

"Damned right," said Molly.

"In order to make it easier for us to pursue our enquiries, I'll go in as Shaman Bond," I said. "People are always glad to see Shaman, that charming rogue about town."

"You like being him," said Molly, "I often think, more than you like being Eddie. Which is ... just a bit weird."

"Shaman doesn't carry the weight of my family's history around with him, and he hasn't done the kind of things I've had to do. But he'll still die when I do. That doesn't seem fair."

"Okay," said Molly. "Moving on ... I'll go in as Roxie Hazzard, well-known mercenary soldier and adventurer for hire. She's a cover persona I often use when I have to work in the Nightside and don't want to carry

Molly Metcalf's personal and professional baggage in with me."

I looked at her. "And why have I never heard anything about this Roxie person before?"

"Because you didn't need to know," Molly said loftily. "A girl's entitled to a few secrets."

"And you have more than most," I said generously. "Has Roxie been involved in anything, or done anything, that Shaman might know about?"

"I wouldn't have thought so," said Molly. "Shaman's never been to the Nightside. Has he?"

I smiled. "Not officially. I have my secrets too, you know."

Molly laughed, and closed in on me. "Tell me all, right now, or it's tickle time."

"Later," I said.

Molly dropped me a wink, snapped her fingers, and just like that, she was somebody else. Molly Metcalf blinked out of existence, to be replaced by a tall, muscular figure with frizzy brick-red hair and a harsh, handsome face. She wore a heavy black leather jacket over a simple blue jumpsuit, with thigh-high calf-leather boots, and a length of steel chain wrapped around her waist. She looked like she could punch out a rabid Rottweiler and look good doing it.

"Okay, that is incredible," I said. "I'm looking at you through my Sight, backed by all the power of my torc, and I still can't see a trace of Molly Metcalf anywhere."

Roxie Hazzard grinned back at me, and when she spoke, even her voice had changed to a low, sultry growl with a hint of an accent I couldn't place.

"That's the idea, lover. The change has to be complete, to go undetected in places like the Wulfshead and the Nightside."

"Is it just an illusion?" I said. "Or have you undergone an actual physical transformation?"

"Allow a girl a few trade secrets," said Roxie. She struck a pose, showing herself off. "So, do you fancy me like this?"

"I'm going to be in trouble whatever I say, aren't I?"

She laughed happily; a low, throaty sound. And then we both looked round sharply. There had been movement, and the sound of movement, farther down the alley. Deliberately made, wanting to be noticed. I looked hard into the shadowy depths of the alleyway, but couldn't see anything. I glanced at Roxie, and she shook her head quickly. We started down the alley together, and I quickly discovered that while she might look like Roxie, she still moved like my Molly. Like a predator, always ready for trouble.

Half-way down the alley, a figure stepped out of the shadows to confront us. Even though there was nowhere he could have come from, no way he could have got that close without us noticing. As though he'd just appeared out of nowhere. Which is never a good sign. I stopped, and Roxie stopped with me. The new arrival stood very still, waiting for us to make the first move.

A tall, almost spindly figure in a grey hoodie over grey slacks and grubby trainers. So he could disappear into the shadows whenever he felt the need. He had the air of someone used to hiding from unfriendly eyes. He pushed his hood back, to reveal a pale, youthful face with short black hair and heavy stubble. His eyes burned fiercely, and his thin lips were pressed tight together; holding harsh emotions within. There was something of the wild about him, ready to fight or flee, as necessary.

I relaxed a little as I recognised his face, but only a little. His presence here made no sense.

"It's all right, Roxie; I know who this is. Allow me to present to you the current Jack a Napes. One of the good guys. I've worked with him. Jack a Napes is a title, but you can't inherit it or assume it. You can only get it by the acclaim of your peers, in the relevant under-ground communities."

"Never heard of it, or him," said Roxie.

"You wouldn't have," I said. "He doesn't move in your circles. Or mine, normally. Shaman Bond, not the other guy, knows him."

"Your life can be very schizophrenic at times," said Roxie.

"We knew you were going to say that," I said.

"So who or what is a Jack a Napes?" said Roxie. "And why is he just standing there, looking at us like that? In fact, I really don't like the way he's looking at us."

I didn't either. Jack a Napes was, if not actually an old friend, certainly an old colleague. He should have been pleased to see Shaman Bond. Instead, he was standing stiffly, half-hidden in the shadows, and I could all but smell the tension coming off him. He had the air of a man who'd come looking for a fight. Which really wasn't like him.

"Jack!" I said loudly. "It's me, Shaman!"

"I know you," he said.

I waited, but he had nothing more to say. His voice sounded harsh and threatening, even defiant. Really not what I remembered.

"Jack a Napes is the latest in a long line of English trickster adventurers," I said quietly to Roxie. "The name goes back centuries, championing any number of causes. Each new Jack a Napes gets to decide what he's going to dedicate his life to. He's part of the Robin Hood tradition, battling authority figures on behalf of those who can't defend themselves. There are any number of old songs and stories about various Jack a Napes, but he's never been romantic enough, or safe enough, for the mass media."

"So what's the current Jack a Napes all about?" said Roxie.

"He's part of the Animal Liberation Force," I said.

"Frees animals from science labs or breeding farms, bad zoos, and circuses. Anywhere he believes the animals are being mistreated. He's very fond of animals; not so much of people."

"How does he know Shaman Bond?"

I kept a careful eye on Jack a Napes, but he still didn't move a muscle. I raised my voice to make sure he could hear me. Hoping my words would remind him of the Shaman Bond he used to know.

"I was sent to break into a secret Government research facility, not far from Porton Down. The scientists there were running drug trials on monkeys, trying to blow their little minds with massive doses of psychedelics. To see what would happen to primate minds without the human ego and complexity to get in the way. All they had to show for it was a whole bunch of confused and really pissed-off monkeys, more likely than most to shit in their hands and throw it at their tormentors. According to a whistle-blower, who'd left in a hurry ten minutes before being fired, the scientists were about to kill and dissect all the monkeys, and harvest their brains. They had plans for those chemically altered brains. Jack a Napes broke into the facility to liberate the animals, and found me already there."

"Hold everything," said Roxie. "Since when did your family have a soft spot for animals?"

"I was there to stop what was supposed to happen next. According to the whistle-blower, the scientists were planning to use all those brains to create an organic computer. Not a new idea; it's been tried many times before, with all kinds of animals. It never ends well. I hadn't expected to run into Jack a Napes. I introduced myself as Shaman Bond, so as not to freak him out, and he persuaded me to help him smuggle the monkeys out of the facility, to where he had friends waiting with transport. They left, and I went back inside and burned the place down. Jack a Napes didn't care about the scientists, and after what I'd seen in the files, about what they'd done and planned to do, neither did I.

"Some time later, I tracked down the politicians and businesspeople behind the scheme. Because monkeys were just the first step; stage two called for harvesting the homeless. Jack a Napes never knew what I did to the people in charge. At least, I hope not. He was always a gentle soul."

"I like the sound of this Jack a Napes," said Roxie, "or rather I would if he weren't still looking at us like that. What's wrong with him?"

"I don't know," I said. "He shouldn't even be here; he's not a part of the Wulfshead scene. He shouldn't even know the club exists."

"Really don't like the way he's looking at us," said Roxie. "Like he's betting on which way we'll fall, after he's ripped our throats out with his bare teeth. And what he'll do to the bodies afterwards. Is he usually this creepy?"

"No," I said, "he isn't."

"We can't hang around here all night, waiting for him to get off the pot!" said Roxie. "We have things to do!"

"I know!" I said. I took a step forward and addressed Jack a Napes directly. "Jack! You know me!"

"I know you, Eddie Drood," said Jack a Napes. "I know you too, Molly Metcalf."

"Hey!" said Roxie. "He shouldn't be able to see me when I'm being Roxie!"

"It's time for you to pay for your sins, Drood," said Jack a Napes. He sounded like he meant it.

I looked at Roxie. "Okay, something is very wrong here. There's no way Jack a Napes could know I'm a Drood. He shouldn't even have heard of the Droods. He isn't part of our world."

"And he just used the exact same words as the Manichean Monk, on Cassandra Inc's airship," said Roxie.

"You're right," I said. "But Jack a Napes wouldn't

know someone like the Monk either. No way their paths would cross."

"It can't be a coincidence," said Roxie. "Not the same threat, in the same words, from two people who should have no quarrel with you."

"Somebody else must be behind this," I said.

"Want me to ask him who?" said Roxie.

"I think I'd better do it," I said. "You'd scare him."

"Damned right," said Roxie.

I took another step forward, and Jack a Napes smiled unpleasantly at me. His hands came up, clenched into white-knuckle fists. I kept my voice carefully calm and reasonable.

"What are you doing here, Jack?"

"Looking for you, Drood."

"But we only decided to come here a few hours ago!" Roxie said behind me.

"I know what I need to know," said Jack a Napes. "I see you, wherever you are, whoever you are."

"Okay . . . ," said Roxie. "That wasn't at all spooky."

"What's going on here, Jack?" I said.

"Word is out, Eddie," said Jack a Napes, his voice openly mocking now, "that you're weakened, vulnerable. What better time to make you pay for what you and your family have done?"

"That's what the Manichean Monk said!" said Roxie.

"Who put out the word, Jack?" I said. "No one's supposed to know but me and my family."

"And the man responsible," said Roxie.

I glanced back at her. "Why would he want everyone to know?"

"Why did he want to kill you?" said Roxie.

Jack a Napes made an impatient sound to draw our attention back to him. He wanted to be the centre of attention.

"Did you know the Monk, Jack?" I said.

"You could say that," said Jack a Napes. "I know you killed him, Eddie. Threw him off an airship."

"That's not what happened!" I said.

"Don't let him get to you, Eddie," Roxie said quietly. "That's what he wants."

"I never did anything to hurt you, Jack," I said. "Neither has anyone else in my family."

"Your family murdered the only person I ever loved," said Jack a Napes.

"What?" I looked at him, honestly baffled. "That can't be right; I'd have heard . . ."

"It's time," said Jack a Napes. "Time for you to suffer, the way I have." He smiled slowly, a cold, anticipatory smile, out of place on his youthful features. "Maybe I should kill your woman first, right in front of you."

"Okay," said Roxie. "That's it. He just crossed the line and he's going down. I don't care if he is an old friend of yours."

"Molly, please," I said. "There's something going on here, something I don't understand . . ."

"Time's up, Drood!" said Jack a Napes. "Time to pay for all your sins!"

"That's the Monk again!" said Roxie. "That's what he said!"

Jack a Napes strode forward, and Roxie got ready to meet him, but I stopped her with a quick gesture.

"No, Molly."

"Why not?"

"Because I don't want Jack hurt," I said. "He's one of the good guys. I don't believe he's in his right mind. Someone's got to him."

Roxie shrugged. "Okay, but he doesn't look to me like he wants to be talked out of it."

"I have to try," I said.

"Of course you do," said Roxie. "You're one of the good guys."

I put myself between Jack a Napes and Roxie, holding my hands out placatingly.

"Don't do this, Jack. You can't hurt me. I have armour."

"I know," said Jack a Napes. "So do I now."

He ripped open his shirt collar to reveal a dully glowing brass torc at his throat. It was old, really old, and a thing of power. I could feel its presence, as though some ancient predator long thought extinct had just stepped into a jungle clearing and showed its teeth.

"That's not a Drood torc," said Roxie. "What is that, Eddie?"

"I'm not sure," I said.

"You should know Druid magic when you see it," said Jack a Napes. "This is Lud's Ward. Lost for centuries, but I tracked it down. Just so I could use it against you, Drood. As long as I wear Lud's Ward, any attack on me is automatically turned back against the attacker. The best kind of defence; you don't dare hurt me."

"You always were the most passive-aggressive terrorist I ever knew," I said. "But how is that thing going to help if I just stand here and refuse to attack you? You can't make me fight you."

"I don't care what you do," said Jack a Napes. "I'm going to kill you with my bare hands, for what you did. I've waited so long for this . . . to make you pay for what you put me through."

"I haven't done anything to you! This is all some stupid mistake!"

"No mistake," said Jack a Napes. "Your family destroyed my love, and my life. I can't get to them, but I can get to you."

"Jack," I said, "this isn't like you."

"It is now," he said.

He launched himself at me, still smiling that fixed, hateful smile. I just had time to think there was something wrong in the way he moved, and then Jack a Napes' clawed hands were reaching for my throat. Roxie stabbed one hand at him, and the air between them crackled with unnatural energies. I tensed for a moment, before recognising it as a simple immobilization spell. But the magic didn't even reach Jack a Napes; it rebounded and blasted Roxie right off her feet. She hit the ground hard. Jack a Napes laughed softly; it was a satisfied, happy sound. And I finally accepted this wasn't the Jack a Napes I'd known. That gentle soul was gone, replaced by a killer. And I'd had enough of him.

I armoured up, and almost gasped as new strength and a marvellous sense of well-being slammed through me. I hadn't realised how run-down I'd been feeling, until I didn't feel it any more. I pushed that thought aside for later and went to meet Jack a Napes. I still didn't want to hurt him, but he wasn't giving me any choice. I couldn't let him hurt Molly.

I punched him in the face with a golden fist. A blow hard enough to ensure any normal man would sleep through the rest of the day. It felt like I'd punched a mountain; something implacably hard and unyielding. My fist was stopped dead, just short of Jack's face. He grinned at me, savouring the moment, as I took a punch in the face so hard, I cried out in spite of myself.

I staggered backwards, my head ringing inside my armour. I hadn't realised how literal Lud's Ward was. My face pulsed with pain. I looked up to find Jack a Napes lunging at me, hands outstretched and his face full of a terrible anticipation.

Both hands fastened around my throat. Steel-hard fingers, inside my armour, choking the breath out of me. That shouldn't have been possible, but Lud's magic was old magic, predating the Droods. I threw myself back and forth across the alley, trying to break his grip, but I couldn't. He thrust his face into my featureless golden mask, still smiling, and he didn't look like Jack at all. I grabbed hold of his wrists with my golden hands and tried to crush them, and then cried out and had to stop as my own wrists were crushed. I tripped him, and we both crashed to the ground. I'd hoped the impact would shake him free, but it didn't. I wound up flat on my back, with him kneeling on my chest and strangling the life out of me.

His face was very close now, twisted with hate. I hit him again and again in the ribs, but only I felt the blows. My lungs strained. I couldn't breathe. I couldn't believe this was how I was going to die. In a filthy back alley, at the hands of an old friend, for reasons that made no sense at all. The thought infuriated me, so much it cleared my head and I knew what to do.

I reached through my armoured side with my armoured hand. The two surfaces melded seamlessly together, allowing my bare hand to reach deep into my pocket, and the pocket dimension I keep there. It was hard to concentrate, with Jack a Napes' hands closing my throat and his laughter in my face, but I pulled out the handful of small plastic boxes the Armourer had given me. I dropped two, but kept hold of the green one. Then all I had to do was hit the button on the top and activate the neural inhibitor.

Jack a Napes howled miserably, his whole body convulsing as the field generated by the box scrambled his thoughts. His hands jumped away from my throat, and he fell backwards off my chest, scrabbling helplessly on the ground beside me. I sat up, breathing hard and fighting to get air into my lungs again. The box worked because Lud's Ward didn't recognise the electro-magnetic field as a physical attack. It was too old to know about science. I grabbed up all the plastic boxes and thrust them back into my pocket. And then I went after Jack a Napes. Because the neural inhibitor's effects wouldn't last much longer.

I grabbed hold of the brass torc round his neck, and crushed it in my golden hand. The torc shattered and fell apart. Because up close and personal, old Drood magic was never going to be a match for Ethel's new strange matter. Jack a Napes sat up suddenly, and pushed me away. His face was clear, his thoughts working again. For a moment he didn't realise what had happened, and then he put a hand to his torc, found the crushed remnants of Lud's Ward, and let out a wordless cry of rage.

He scrambled back up onto his feet, and I got up to face him. He reached behind his back, and brought out a glowing dagger. I really hadn't expected that. Jack a Napes never used weapons. Never. Where the hell could he even have got such a thing? Presumably, the same place he got Lud's Ward. Someone else must have provided him with both. Whoever was behind his attack, and that of the Manichean Monk.

Dr DOA?

Normally, I would expect any enchanted weapon to shatter against my armour, or skid harmlessly away. But after Lud's Ward . . . it was always possible Jack a Napes had found the one enchanted weapon that could hurt me. He lunged forward, the glowing dagger leaping for my heart, and I had no choice but to defend myself. With my armour on, he might as well have been moving in slow motion. I had all the time I needed to move inside his reach and punch him hard in the chest. Crushing his heart.

I felt it convulse under my fist. Jack a Napes' hand opened, and the glowing dagger fell to the ground. He looked surprised, and then all the expression just dropped out of his face. He fell to his knees, fell back, and lay still. I armoured down and knelt beside him. He looked up at me, barely breathing. He was already dead; he just didn't know it yet. All the hate and rage had left his face; he looked like the Jack a Napes I remembered. The man I thought I knew. His dying eyes struggled to focus on me. I leaned over him as he said his last words.

"Shaman? Why . . . ?"

And then he died.

I sat down hard on the alley floor. I'd just killed a man I respected, and he died not even understanding why I'd done it. I felt tired, worn-out, and this wasn't just because I was no longer wearing my armour. I felt like I'd lost my way. Every breath hurt my bruised throat, and my sides ached from the punishment I'd taken from my own attacks. I tried to work out what had just happened, and couldn't. Was that what happened when you knew you were dying? Everything just stopped making sense?

Roxie knelt beside me. "Taken out by my own spell. I'll never live it down. Are you all right, Eddie?"

"Not really, no," I said.

She looked me over quickly. "Are you injured anywhere?"

"Probably."

She tried to work a simple healing spell on me, and swore harshly when nothing happened.

"It's the torc," I said. "It's working so hard now to protect me from the poison, it won't allow anything to affect me. I'll be okay in a minute. I've had worse. Just let me . . . get my breath."

She sat down on the ground beside me and leaned against my shoulder. She looked like Roxie, but she felt like Molly. We sat together for a while, saying nothing. My breathing slowly eased, and my various aches and pains retreated a little. I looked at the dead Jack a Napes.

"What am I going to do now, Jack?"

Roxie misunderstood me. "Leave him here. Our business in the Wulfshead won't wait. The club Management will see the body is taken care of."

"I've killed again," I said.

"You had no choice!" Roxie said fiercely. "It wasn't your fault!"

"He was almost a friend," I said. "One of the good guys."

"He didn't act like one," said Roxie. "Someone must have messed with his mind."

"Maybe," I said.

I started to get to my feet, and then stopped as I saw the dagger lying on the ground beside me. I armoured up my right hand, picked the knife up by the hilt, and looked the weapon over. The blade wasn't glowing any more. It seemed like just an ordinary knife, one he could have got anywhere. I snapped the blade in two, just in case, and threw the pieces away. I made my armoured glove disappear. The temptation to wrap myself in my full armour, and feel strong and well again, was almost overwhelming, but I couldn't afford to give in to temptation. Because if I hid away in my armour, I might never come out again. And I still had work to do that couldn't be done by a Drood.

I got to my feet, slowly and carefully, making the odd pained noise as my injuries protested. Nothing was broken. It was just pain. Roxie got up too, standing close, ready to help if needed. She thought I didn't see the concern in her eyes. I looked down at the dead man, one last time.

"He deserved a better death than this."

"We all do," said Roxie.

I looked at her. "Once we're inside the Wulfshead, we need answers, but we can't tell anyone why. No one can know Eddie Drood is . . . compromised."

"If Jack a Napes is anything to go by, I think that ship has sailed," said Roxie. "The word is out. People know."

"We can't afford to assume that," I said doggedly. "The longer it takes for word to get around, the more time we'll have to operate freely. Before the predators start circling . . ."

"Is that really it?" said Roxie. "Or is it that you just don't want your friends to know that you're dying?"

"I haven't got time to deal with sympathy," I said.

"But they could help! Go places we can't, talk to people who wouldn't talk to us!"

"Molly . . ."

"You have to be the hard man, don't you, Eddie?"

"Yes!" I said. "I have to be! Because it's the only way I can do this."

"No one will think you're weak," said Roxie, "if you ask your friends for help. Are you really ready to risk your life, rather than have them think less of you?"

"That isn't it," I said. "You don't understand."

"What? What don't I understand? Explain it to me!"

"Dr DOA got to me in my family home," I said. "Where I should have been safest. The only way he could have done that was with the help of someone who knew how to get to me. Someone I thought I could trust."

"Someone inside your family?" said Roxie.

"And if Dr DOA can get to my family, he can get to my friends. There's only one person in my life I know I can trust, and that's you."

"All right," said Roxie. "What do we say when people want to know why we're asking questions about Dr DOA?"

"Shaman Bond always wants to know things," I said. "I spent years establishing his insatiable curiosity. Everyone will just assume he's working on some new con, or asking on someone else's behalf. Because that's what he does. I'll concentrate on Dr DOA; you see what you can find out about the Survivors. Who they are, what they do, and how best to get in to see them, uninvited."

"No problem," said Roxie. "People will talk to Roxie Hazzard, because she has a well-established tendency to kick the crap out of people who give her a hard time."

I smiled briefly. "Remind me; what is the difference exactly between Roxie Hazzard and Molly Metcalf?"

"Roxie wouldn't put up with half the crap from you that Molly does."

"Fair enough," I said. "Let's go crash the Wulfshead."

I walked over to the opposite wall and growled certain Words at it. A silver door appeared, set flush with the brickwork and deeply etched with threats and warnings in angelic and demonic script. I could read most of them; there was nothing new, and nothing that bothered me. I was pretty sure some of the earliest examples had been written by members of my family.

"This is Shaman Bond," I said to the door.

"And Roxie Hazzard!" Roxie said proudly.

I pressed the palm of my left hand against the silver slab. The metal felt hot and sweaty, like a living thing. I didn't flinch. I'd encountered worse in my time. There was a worryingly long pause, and then the door swung open, acknowledging our right to enter, which was just as well. The door has been known to bite the hands off people whose names weren't on the guest list. Probably just as well for the door. With the mood I was in, I was more than ready to armour up and kick the door right off its hinges if it gave me any attitude. Perhaps the door sensed that.

I strode in, with Roxie strutting proudly at my side. Not so much like conquering heroes, though; more like supplicants in the underworld.

Inside the Wulfshead Club, it was all mayhem and music. Neon strip lighting, furniture so modernistic, you couldn't tell what it was supposed to be half the time, and a long high-tech bar that looked more like a modern art installation, designed by someone with a real fondness for absinthe. Giant plasma screens covered the walls, endlessly broadcasting intimate and indiscreet details from the lives of the rich and famous. Without their knowledge or approval. Glimpses into secret headquarters and hidden bunkers, film stars at play and politicians making deals, little gods and lesser demons lying down together. The very latest music slammed and pounded on the air, while girls with hardly any clothing on danced their hearts out on spot-lit miniature stages. Just because they could.

The Wulfshead is where the weird people go; the heroes and the villains, the living and the dead, and all the others stuck somewhere in between. To drink and gossip, draw up plans for the saving or damning of civilization, to look for a new con or pick one another up. Just like any bar in London, really, except that the clientele are a little more exotic. Laughter and tears, romance and death threats; all human and inhuman life is here, ready to embrace you. If you can stand the pace.

The usual familiar faces were making the scene. Waterloo Lillian, the transvestite showgirl, looking impossibly glamorous in her dark fishnet stockings, crimson basque, and tall ostrich feathers on her head, was arm-wrestling with Janissary Jane, the mercenary demon fighter. Up close, Jane's combat leathers smelled of smoke and fire and dried blood, just like always. A man who claimed to be immortal was earnestly discussing quantum theory with a serial reincarnator, over a bottle of wine that was old before Atlantis sank. A nurse with a starched white uniform half-soaked in fresh blood chewed hungrily on a human heart, while a halo of flies buzzed round her head. And Monkton Farley, the famed consulting detective, stood with his back to the bar, holding forth to a crowd of adoring disciples while they hung on his every arrogant word.

The roar of conversation rose and fell as everyone swapped the latest news, hammered out dodgy deals, and plotted to throw some poor unfortunate to the wolves. Games were played, reputations were made and ruined, and a good time was had by all. I nodded to Roxie, and we split up, heading off through the packed crowd in different directions. I took my time, smiling and nodding to everyone and working the crowd with practised charm. I had questions, and I was determined to get answers, but I couldn't afford for anyone to see how desperate I was. As long as I was the casual, easy-going Shaman Bond, people would tell me anything, just for the joy of spreading the news and a chance to do someone else down. But if they got the idea the information had a value, then the price would go up. And up. I didn't have the time or the inclination to bargain, and I didn't feel up to just beating the information out of people. Besides, that was what Eddie Drood did. Not Shaman Bond. Just another reason why I prefer being Shaman.

I looked round the club, taking a breather for a moment. I'd known good times and bad at the Wulfshead. With friends and enemies, and a whole lot of people who drifted back and forth between both. It seemed to me I should be feeling better because I was moving among my own kind, in so much good company. But if anything, the sheer seething vitality of the crowd just made me feel worse. Like I didn't belong here any more. This was a place for people with plans, and hopes, and a future. Part of me just wanted to turn and leave, run away from something I couldn't be a part of any more. But I didn't. I had a job to do. So, as on so many occasions before, I put on a smile I didn't feel and went to work.

I don't think Roxie even noticed my moment of melancholy. She was too busy grinning at everyone and waving happily to old friends. Playing up to the crowd, laughing and sparkling effortlessly. Everyone seemed pleased to see her, and only too ready to buy her many drinks. She clapped people on the shoulder and on the back, kissed cheeks and mouths, and knocked back any drink anyone cared to put in her hand. She was loud and lewd, big and boisterous, and laughter followed wherever she went. It was a hell of a performance. A small part of me was angry that she could be having such a good time while I was dying.

I felt angry at the crowd around me. How could all these people be enjoying themselves so much? Didn't they know I was dying? Well, no, of course they didn't. That was the point. But I still felt jealous of their happiness, of their casual assumption that they still had years ahead of them. Time to do whatever they wanted. I'd never been scared of death in the field; in the heat of the moment, going head to head with some powerful opponent over something that mattered. But this slow departure from life, having it all taken away from me bit by bit, seemed so horribly unfair.

I surprised myself then, with a sudden harsh smile. It wasn't like me to brood. I'd fight my death like I'd fought every other adversary, with everything I had. Because that was what I did. I plunged into the crowd again, greeting familiar faces, exchanging gossip, and quietly slipping in the odd question about Dr DOA. I kept crossing paths with Roxie as we moved back and forth, following the same leads to the same people. No one seemed too surprised that Shaman Bond and Roxie Hazzard should know each other. Shaman was famous for knowing everyone. But I was surprised to discover just how many of our mutual friends and colleagues knew the Roxie of old. And didn't seem to connect her with Molly Metcalf at all. Or did they know, and were just pretending to be polite? Not for the first time, I wondered how many of the club's regulars had always known Shaman Bond was also Eddie Drood. And kept quiet, to keep the peace. Everyone wears a false face of some kind at the Wulfshead Club.

I made my way to the long bar, and ordered my usual ice-cold bottle of Beck's from one of the many bartenders with exactly the same face. Because they were all clones. The Management ensure loyalty in their staff by growing their own. You really don't want to know about their retirement plan. You can order any kind of drink at the Wulfshead bar. Succubae's Tears, Muse's Breath, and Quetzalcoatl's Revenge. None of which are trade names. Ponce de Leon's sparkling water and Shoggoth's Old Peculiar. Rumour has it the club's Management keep their bar stock in another dimension. Because they're afraid of it. My Beck's went down nice and easy, soothing my throat and easing my aches and pains, and I was surprised to find I'd emptied the bottle. I went to ask for another, and then stopped myself. No telling what booze might do to me in my current condition. I put the empty bottle down on the bar and turned my back on it. I had to be on top of things while I still had things that needed doing.

I hated having to make such decisions, hated not being able to be effortlessly strong and confident, like I used to be. Just another thing Dr DOA had stolen from me. Just another reason to track him down and take it out on him.

It occurred to me then that I could just stop here at the Wulfshead. Abandon the chase, give up on my revenge, and spend what time I had left enjoying myself with friends. I could go out easily, among good company. But a cold hard part of me would never accept that. I had been wronged, and I would have my vengeance no matter what it cost me. I put on my smile again and went back into the crowd.

I moved easily through the closely packed people, letting the crowd's currents take me where they would, smiling and nodding to people who nodded and smiled at me. Shaman was glad to see everyone, and they were always glad to see him. Because Shaman always knows the best stories and the latest gossip, and is always ready to lend an ear to a new plan, or a heart's pain. And he's always good for a laugh. But no matter which conversation I joined, I always found a way to steer it round to Dr DOA. Who was he? Where was he? How could he be contacted?

But it turned out that as far as most of the club's patrons were concerned, Dr DOA was just another urban legend of the hidden world. Some people believed in him; some didn't. Some thought he was the semi-public face of a secret society, so the world wouldn't be able to work out why they were killing off certain significant people. Others believed he was just a front for a Drood assassination squad. Though others quickly pointed out that the Droods have never been bashful about anything they do. Someone else suggested Dr DOA was a franchise; that someone was secretly funding any number of Dr DOAs, making it possible for anyone to become the anonymous killer, for the right money. And thus have their true motives obscured, hidden behind the mystery that was Dr DOA. I quite liked that idea, but couldn't believe my family wouldn't already have known all about it. And done something about it, long ago. We don't like competition.

There were all kinds of stories about Dr DOA, and once I'd started the ball rolling, people stumbled over one another to chime in with the ones they'd heard. It was never anything that could be confirmed. He was a man or a woman, a group or an organisation. Or just a mirror for our paranoid times, because someone had to take the blame for all the murders that were never solved. No one in the Wulfshead had ever met him, or known anyone who had, and no one wanted to. And absolutely no one would admit to doing business with him, for fear of reprisals. From his victims' friends and relatives, or from the man himself. The only thing everyone would agree on was that it was very dangerous to go looking for Dr DOA. People who did tended not to be seen again.

Finally, reluctantly, I approached Monkton Farley. The two of us go way back, even though we'd never admit it in public. He was currently dressed to the height of Nineteen Twenties fashion, from the elegant pinstripe suit to the immaculate white spats on his gleaming shoes. A handsome-enough fellow, if you could overlook his open disdain for anyone who wasn't as smart as he thought he was. I stood at the edge of the crowd that had gathered around him. Everyone was listening breathlessly to the details of his latest triumph, the Case of the Disembodied Body. He'd been relating the story when Roxie and I arrived, and he was still telling it now. He seemed no nearer to arriving at a conclusion, so I decided I'd just have to break into his monologue and hope his devoted disciples didn't strike me down for blasphemy. But when I tried to push my way through, they immediately closed ranks to keep me out. Partly to keep me from interrupting their hero, partly to keep an outsider out. They were the true fans, and only they were entitled to get close to the great man.

I could have forced my way through them easily enough, but I was being Shaman Bond, so I just looked over the heads of the crowd and caught Farley's eye. He broke off from his story, sighed quietly, and signalled to his followers to let me through. They moved aside, reluctantly and resentfully, and I nodded easily to Monkton Farley as I strolled through the ranks to stand before him.

"Shaman," he said. With the voice of the unjustly put-upon.

"Hello, Monkton," I said. "You're looking very yourself. Wondered if you could help me with something."

"What seems to be the problem? Someone stolen your charisma?"

The crowd laughed loudly. Until I looked thoughtfully around me, and all went quiet again.

"It's about Dr DOA," I said.

An excited murmur ran through the ranks of admirers. Everyone looked expectantly at Farley to see what he would say.

"I know the name," he said. "And the reputation. A very discreet and very dangerous man."

"You're the first to admit he's more than an urban legend," I said. "Have you encountered him, yourself?"

"Not personally, no," said Farley. "The proof being that I'm still here. You're about to ask me why I haven't used my amazing deductive abilities to track him down and bring him to justice, aren't you? Unfortunately, I can only follow the evidence. And Dr DOA doesn't leave any. But rest assured; I have no intention of giving up on the man."

"Well," I said, "that's good to know. Any ideas on useful directions I might look in?"

"Why would you want to?"

I fixed him with a look. "Family business."

He nodded reluctantly. "I have heard . . . that the poison he uses is always the same. Completely unstoppable because it is not of this world. Which of course suggests that Dr DOA himself might also be not of this earth. I would therefore suggest that Black Heir might be able to tell you something. Chasing up the loose ends of close encounters is supposed to be its remit, after all."

"Thank you, Monkton," I said. It was a useful suggestion.

"Anything, for your family," said Monkton Farley.

Which was as close as he was ever going to come in public to admitting he was half Drood. I nodded to him and moved away, leaving him to his admirers. All of whom scowled at me as I passed; they were jealous of my personal moment with the great man.

Roxie was immediately there at my side. "I might have found someone who can help."

"Anyone I know?" I said.

"Yes. But not in a good way."

"That covers so many people in my life . . . Which possibly says as much about me as it does about them. Who is it?"

"Persecution Psmith."

"Oh hell."

"Precisely."

The old Puritan adventurer was sitting alone at the farthest end of the long bar, from where, perched carefully on a bar-stool, he was looking out over the club. One of the few people I know who can do that and still retain their dignity. People around him were careful to maintain a very respectful distance. Partly because he was famously not the sociable sort, and partly because even in a club like the Wulfshead, infamous for attracting any number of genuinely dangerous individuals, everyone still had enough sense to be scared of Persecution Psmith. I wondered why he even came to the club, where he always made a point of drinking alone. Perhaps because even an old gore crow like him still felt the need for company. Sometimes. He turned unhurriedly to watch us approach, even though I was sure no one would have informed him we were coming.

No one knows how old he is. Stories about his exploits go back centuries. Most of them highly moral tales, in a disturbing sort of way. He still dressed in the Puritan garb of the Seventeenth Century; drab dull black without a trace of colour anywhere, under a swirling night-dark cloak. His long face was drawn and gaunt, etched deep with lines of harsh experience. His dark eyes blazed with a fierce dedication to his cold cause, and his hooked nose and flat mouth gave him the look of some brooding bird of prey. He killed bad people. Or people he decided were bad and needed killing. One of the scarier agents for the Good. Pity and mercy were not in him.

Roxie stopped in front of him and nodded easily, entirely unimpressed. Psmith managed a small smile for her. I nodded politely and he nodded back, but he kept his attention fixed on Roxie.

"Still getting into trouble, child?" he said, his voice like a low rumble of thunder.

"Whenever possible," said Roxie.

"You two know each other?" I said. "How . . . No. I don't want to know."

"Very wise," said Roxie. "Persecution Psmith, allow me to present Shaman Bond."

"Your reputation precedes you, Mister Bond," Psmith said gravely. He didn't make it sound like a good thing.

Just meeting Psmith's cold gaze made me feel guilty. Psmith was famously morally upright, without any weaknesses or trace of sin in his past. And he was always unflinchingly hard on those who had such failings. An uncompromising judge, jury, and executioner. I felt like I wanted to confess to him, for the good of my soul. From Roxie's easy-going smile, it seemed unlikely she felt the same.

"What's that you're drinking?" I said, nodding to his glass on the bar.

"Water," said Psmith.

"Not even sparkling," said Roxie. "Puritans . . . Why do you even bother coming in here?"

"If you're hunting sinners," said Psmith, "you have to go where the sinners are."

"Not for the company?" I said.

He surprised me then, by taking the question seriously. He thought for a while, his eyes far away. "I sometimes think I've lived too long . . . and outlived all the softer emotions. I am a thing of cold purpose now, and nothing more. Perhaps I come here to remind myself of what it feels like, to be just a man. Because the day I forget that is the day I become as bad as the things I have given my life to hunting."

I felt a need to press him on that. "No friends? No family?"

"No," said Persecution Psmith. "I gave them all up, to become what I am. I gave up my life in return for more years to fight evil."

"Like the Walking Man?" said Roxie.

"Not really. No."

"Was it worth it?" I said. I was genuinely interested as to what his answer would be.

"Some days I think one thing; sometimes another. Revenge is a harsh mistress. But then, I think both of you already know that, Eddie Drood and Molly Metcalf."

"Of course you know," said Roxie. "You know everything."

He smiled briefly again. "Not everything, child. What is it you want from me?"

"Wait a minute," said Roxie, glancing at me. "You made a deal . . . for more years. What kind of deal?"

"Not one I'd recommend," said Psmith.

"Drowning men will clutch at the grubbiest of straws," I said.

"Only if they give way to despair, and give up on hope," said Psmith. "Years aren't everything."

"Why would someone like you want to help us?" I said. "Everyone knows you don't approve of morally borderline types. Like Droods or witches."

"Because I cannot turn away from a call for help," said Psmith.

"Even from people like us?" said Roxie.

"Especially from people like you. And because you're going after Dr DOA. Yes, I've heard. And I approve. I can't find the man; perhaps you, with your connections, can. It would do my old heart good to know someone had taken him down. I suggest you start with the OverNet."

Now, that did catch me by surprise. The OverNet is the Internet's shadowy twin. Where all the darkest and most dangerous sites and contacts can be found. Information too disturbing to be shared with the everyday world. Online translations of the *Necronomicon*, the *Book of Eibon*, and the *Mysteries of the Wurm*. Chat rooms for vampires and ghouls, and aliens looking for hints on how to pass as human. Answers to questions that sane people would know better than to ask. And, supposedly, home to the most powerful search engines available with access to even the most restricted areas. If you can hack your way through the jungle of rumours, half-truths, and deliberate misinformation, there are dreadful truths and wondrous secrets to be found.

"What do you know about computers?" said Roxie.

"In my early days, I used a bloodhound's good nose to hunt down sinners," said Psmith. "Now I must use the Devil's tools to locate the Devil's followers. What has the world come to, when Satanic Churches have their own websites and advertise openly for new members? I am busier than ever, these days—so many souls to save or condemn, and so little time. Sometimes I think I can't wait for Judgement Day to arrive just so I can get some rest."

I decided to take the hint. "Thank you for your help. We'll be going now."

Roxie glowered at Psmith. "Burned any witches lately?"

"I never burned any witches," Psmith said calmly. "Though I have hanged quite a few."

I took Roxie by the arm and hauled her away, before things could become suddenly and violently unpleasant. You don't live as long as Persecution Psmith without becoming very hard to kill. Roxie waited till she was sure we were out of his earshot before nodding reluctantly to me.

"Actually, that wasn't such a bad idea. Whoever wants to hire Dr DOA must have some means of contacting him. And the OverNet is less ethical and more secure than most when it comes to putting people together."

"Agreed," I said. "But you can bet my family's computer people are already all over that side of things. If there's information to be found, they'll find it. I can't believe it will be that simple. Dr DOA hasn't lasted this long by leaving any kind of trail. Monkton Farley suggested we try Black Heir."

Roxie sniffed. "If Black Heir knew anything that important, it would have been put up for sale by now. Even Dr DOA couldn't poison a whole Government department to keep it quiet."

And then we both stopped as the Midnight Masque stepped out of the crowd to block our way. Tall and slender, fashionable as a glossy magazine spread and twice as glamorous, with a burst of peroxide white hair to set off the jet-black featureless mask that covered her whole face. A lady of the evening, or any time of day if you had the money, the Midnight Masque can be anyone your heart desires. Her blank face reminded me uncomfortably of my own golden mask. But hers can change shape to become anyone you want. Even the face you lust after in your most secret dreams.

"Stop asking questions about Dr DOA," she said bluntly, in a voice very unlike her usual sultry murmur.

"Why?" said Roxie, just as bluntly.

"You stay out of this," said the Midnight Masque. "This is between me and Shaman."

"In your dreams," said Roxie.

"Anything you have to say to me, you can say in front of Roxie," I said to the Midnight Masque.

"Oh, it's like that, is it? I hadn't heard. Anyway, stop asking after Dr DOA! I don't want you drawing his attention to the Wulfshead and those of us who drink here. You're putting us all at risk!"

"Really?" I said. "Even inside the Wulfshead, with all its security and protections?"

"We can't live here," said the Midnight Masque. "We all have to go home, eventually. Who's to say Dr DOA isn't in here right now? Moving unseen and unknown, listening to everything we say, making notes and taking names? Deciding who to punish, to make a point?"

"Oh, grow a pair, Enid," said Roxie.

"That's not my name!" said the Midnight Masque. "That hasn't been my name for years!"

"Yeah, right," said Roxie.

"Sorry, Enid," I said, "but I need answers."

"Why?" said the Midnight Masque. "What could be so important to you that you have to put all of us at risk by trying to find him?"

"Oh hell," I said. "Why do you think?"

Her voice softened immediately. "Oh . . . Oh, Shaman, I'm so sorry. I didn't know. Of course, I get it now. You do what you have to."

She put a comforting hand on my arm and her face changed, taking on the familiar features of Molly Metcalf. Roxie smiled. I was careful to say nothing. The Midnight Masque took her hand off my arm, and Molly's face faded back into the featureless black mask. The Midnight Masque turned away and disappeared back into the crush.

"Okay," Roxie said to me. "That was actually rather sweet."

"Not particularly helpful, though," I said.

Janissary Jane approached Roxie, ignoring me. Up close, she smelled of blood and death and quite a lot of gin.

"Roxie, word is, the Twilight King is putting together an army of mercenaries to fight demons in the underverse. Good money, bad odds. You interested?"

"Maybe later," said Roxie.

Jane passed her a card. "Contact information. It'll be good for another thirty-six hours, and then we're off."

"You're going?" said Roxie.

Janissary Jane shrugged. "It's a war, isn't it?"

She moved away. I looked at Roxie. "She is dead, isn't she?"

"Died some time back, for us," said Roxie. "I didn't have the heart to tell her. Must be some Time-Travel thing."

"That's the Wulfshead for you," I said.

Roxie tapped my arm and indicated with her head to where Monkton Farley had dispensed with his admirers and was now slow dancing with Waterloo Lillian. They seemed quite taken with each other.

"Do you think he knows?" said Roxie.

"Oh, he must," I said. "Great detective like him."

"Well, if he doesn't, he's going to get a really big clue later on."

"You are an awful person, Roxie Hazzard," I said solemnly.

And then I looked past her, to where Harry Fabulous was standing at the edge of the crowd, trying surreptitiously to get my attention. Harry used to be the best Go To Guy for absolutely everything you could ever want that was bad for you, physically and spiritually. You want someone to paint your portrait, or take your photo, like Dorian Gray? Want to smoke some Martian red weed, or be bitten by a vampire dominatrix in some underground BDSM club? Want to dance with the Devil in the pale moonlight? Then Harry Fabulous was your man.

A furtive, seedy presence, in clothes so casual they were actually characterless, Harry looked like he dressed in a hurry while someone he didn't want to meet was coming up the stairs. He looked like he could use a shave, and probably a bath. Apparently, he had a close encounter with something really nasty in the back room of some Members Only club in the Nightside, and now he was desperately doing good deeds, hoping against hope it wasn't too late to redeem his soul. Harry never talked about what happened. And given some of the things he was prepared to talk about, whatever it was must have been really bad. I only knew as much as I did because the Droods know something about everyone. I said as much to Roxie.

"Even what goes on in the Nightside?" she said.

"Especially what goes on in the Nightside," I said. "Know your enemy."

I made my way through the packed crowd to where Harry was waiting, with Roxie just calmly following on behind. I looked casually around. No one seemed to be paying us any attention, but this was the Wulfshead, after all. Harry nodded briefly, flashing his meaningless smile.

"Hello, Eddie," he said. "Molly."

"Hello, Harry," I said. "Still running scared of the afterlife?"

"I could ask you the same question," said Harry. "My soul may be stained, but at least I still have one. Can a Drood say the same?"

"My family is really going to have to do more work on the PR side," I said.

"Never mind that!" said Roxie, scowling heavily. "How do you know who we really are, Harry Fabulous?"

He shrugged. "The club Management told me."

"Do they know what happened to you in the Nightside?" I said.

"Why do you think I run their errands?" He glanced around quickly, and then leaned in close. "The Management have learned you're looking for Dr DOA. Because you're his latest victim."

"How do they know that?" said Roxie.

"How do they know anything?" said Harry. "Because they're the Management."

"Can they help me?" I said.

"Come into the office," said Harry, "and we'll discuss it."

He led the way into the Management's private office at the rear of the club. I'd been there once before, and it hadn't changed. Just a bare room, with a desk and some chairs. No windows, and no other way in or out. Harry sat down behind the desk, and Roxie and I sat facing him.

"I was sorry to hear about your condition, Eddie," said Harry.

"Who else knows?" I said.

"Word is getting out," said Harry. "I know some places where they're holding celebrations and street parties."

"Eddie's saved the whole world, more than once!" said Roxie.

"Did you expect them to be grateful?" said Harry. "You can't be a Drood, and do what Droods do, and not make a whole lot of enemies."

"Why are we here, Harry?" I said. "Do the Management have a cure for what's killing me?"

"No," he said. "But they can help you find Dr DOA."

I nodded. "I can settle for that."

Harry looked up at the ceiling. "Do it."

The whole room shuddered for a moment, and then was still.

"What was that?" said Roxie, ready to jump out of her seat.

"Just activating the room's security," Harry said quickly. "Nothing to worry about. The door is locked, and the club's protectors are watching over us."

"You mean the Roaring Boys?" I said.

He nodded quickly. No one likes talking about the club's mysterious and notorious enforcers. "They're currently protecting this room from all forms of surveillance. Even Heaven and Hell would have a hard time listening in, with the Roaring Boys on the job."

"Have you any idea who or what the Boys really are?" I said.

"No," Harry said very firmly. "And I don't want to know. You live longer that way."

"All right," I said. "What's this all about, Harry?"

"The Wulfshead Management still owe you a favour, for cleaning up the mess made by MI Thirteen when they tried to bug the club."

Roxie looked sharply at me, silently demanding to know why I'd never mentioned this to her before. I gave her a look that said *Later* and she reluctantly subsided again. I looked back at Harry.

"How can the Management help me?"

"With your permission, I'd like to bring someone in on this," Harry said carefully. "You aren't going to like or approve of him, but I guarantee you really need to talk to the guy."

"I'm in no position to be choosy," I said. "Right now, I'd accept help from my worst enemy."

"Funny you should say that," said Harry. "But before I invite him in, you have to give me your word that you won't kill him."

"This is going to be really bad, isn't it?" I said. "Okay, you have my word."

Harry looked at the door. "Open!"

The door unlocked itself, and a young man walked in. My first thought was that a homeless guy had somehow wandered in off the street. He looked even more of a mess than Harry. The door shut and locked itself behind the newcomer, and he glared at me sullenly. He looked like he slept rough, ate out of Dumpsters, and stole anything he could get away with. His grubby clothes came from charity shops, and his attitude was that of a dog kicked too many times. He glowered sourly at me, and then at Roxie.

"Eddie Drood and Molly Metcalf. I can't believe it's come to this . . ."

I looked at Roxie. "Some days, I don't know why we bother . . ."

"This is Django Westphalion," said Harry.

Roxie looked at the young homeless guy. "Really?"

"No," said Django. He looked at Harry. "Has he sworn not to kill me? Am I safe?"

"With a name like that, probably not," said Roxie. "Hey, why didn't you ask me to swear as well?"

"The Drood gave his word, Django," said Harry. "And I'm sure he'll stand between you and Molly, if need be."

He seemed to be enjoying the situation a little too much for my liking. Django sniffed loudly.

"Bet you never thought you'd meet someone who's sunk lower than you," he said coldly.

"It does warm the inner man," said Harry. "Now, you wanted this meeting. Talk to the Drood."

Django fixed me with a challenging stare. "I can get you into Under the Mountain so you can meet with the Survivors. If anyone can save you, they can."

I sat up straight in my chair. "How?"

His whole form changed, right in front of us. Becoming an exact duplicate of Harry, then Molly, then me, and finally back to Django Westphalion.

"Because I'm one of the few surviving Immortals," he said defiantly. "That ancient and glorious family the Droods massacred, at Castle Frankenstein. Because of you, there's only a handful of us left now, scattered across the world, hiding in the shadows. On the run from everyone."

"Well, that's what you get," I said, entirely unconcerned. "For being a family of complete bastards and utter shits. You treated all of human history as your own private playpen and hunting ground. You can't really be surprised that everyone wants you dead."

He sneered at me. "You can talk, Drood."

"Why are you willing to help him?" said Roxie.

"I hate all the Droods, and him especially," Django said sullenly. "But I owe the Wulfshead Management more than I can ever hope to repay. It has been made clear to me that if I cooperate, they are willing to wipe my debts clean, and not throw me to the Roaring Boys."

"Because the Management owe you, Eddie," said Harry. "And they really don't like being beholden to anyone."

"You want to talk to the Survivors," said Django. "Well, I can arrange that, because I have a standing invitation to drop in anytime I feel like it. I've been allowing the Survivors to experiment on me. Because all the members of my family were shape-dancers, the Survivors hope to find something in my genetic makeup that can be transferred to them."

"Why would you agree to be their lab rat?" said Roxie.

"Because they pay," said Django. "It's a hard life, when you have to go in fear of everyone." He snarled at me. "I used to have the whole world at my feet, and now it's at my throat. If it were up to me, I'd let you die, Drood. And then join the queue to piss on your grave."

"I'll leave you to work this out," said Harry, getting to his feet. "You don't need me any more. And you're probably about to discuss things I'm better off not knowing."

The door opened and closed behind him. The rest of us were too busy glaring at one another to care.

"So, how are you going to get us inside Under the Mountain?" said Roxie. She sounded suspicious. I didn't blame her.

"Only way in is by teleport," said Django. "The Survivors' base is set up inside a massive cavern, deep inside a mountain. No actual entrances or exits. They do like their privacy. And given some of the things I've seen them do to their lab rats . . . it's just as well."

"Do you have a dimensional Door?" I said.

"I have a personal teleport bracelet," said Django. "Alien tech. Those in my family were always great beachcombers. How do you think I was able to escape your family's massacre of my people at the Castle? And stay one jump ahead of all my many enemies?"

He pulled back his filthy sleeve to show off a chunky brass bracelet on his wrist, studded with what looked like semi-precious stones for controls. Steampunk tech. Probably lifted off the body of some poor alien, trying to hide from his own kind among Humanity.

"So what do we do?" I said. "Hold hands?"

He sneered at me. "I'd rather die, Drood. No, just stand close, within the field of the bracelet."

We all stood together in the middle of the room. Roxie wrinkled her nose at Django's rather pungent smell as his fingers danced over the controls, and then, just like that, we were somewhere else. Standing in a huge, brightly lit stone cavern, surrounded by dozens of heavily armed guards, all of them pointing weapons at us.

CHAPTER SIX

Good Living, and Bad

There are times when having an awful lot of guns pointed at you can be a good thing. When you've been having a really bad day, for example, and you are definitely feeling the need to take it out on somebody. I took one look at the dozens of heavily armed and armoured guards training their guns on me and on Roxie, smiled nastily, and armoured up. Shocked gasps sounded from all sides, along with a pleasing number of involuntary noises suggesting awe, dismay, and stark terror. Reliable indications that a Drood was in the room. Roxie surrounded herself with a screen of fiercely spitting magics, and some of the guards actually started to back away. Others were already quickly lowering their weapons, while trying very hard to look like the whole thing had been some terrible misunderstanding. I turned to Django Westphalion, grabbed him by the throat with one golden hand, and lifted him off his feet.

"Why did you warn them we were coming?"

"I had to!" He clawed at my golden wrist with both hands, but couldn't break my hold. "I had to give them advance warning so they could lower the security shields to let us in!"

I hate it when they start being reasonable. I reluctantly let go of him, and he fell on his arse on the stone floor, breathing hard. One of the few good things about Immortals is that you never need to feel bad about assaulting them. Because you can always be sure they've done something to deserve it. Django scrambled backwards across the floor, glaring at me venomously.

"You forget, I'm a shape-changer! I can turn into a monster and tear you apart!"

"Really?" I said politely. "A monster? Like what, precisely? What have you ever been, or even seen, that you think could take a Drood in his armour? You don't even have a weapon on you, do you?"

He scowled sullenly. "The Survivors won't let you in if you're carrying any kind of weapon. They agreed to make an exception for your armour only because they're so keen to get their hands on a Drood."

"Well," I said. "That doesn't sound at all ominous."

"Stand still!" shouted one of the guards. "I am in command here, and I order you to put your hands in the air and lower your armour!"

I turned to look back at the guards. I'd actually forgotten about them, for a moment.

"Does that even sound like something I'd do?" I said. "Get rid of the one thing that's protecting me from your guns? Which, I can't help noticing, some of you are still pointing at me. Never a good idea with a Drood. We take such things personally. Now, be a sensible chap and order all of your men to lower their weapons. And then nobody needs to get hurt, damaged, or horribly maimed."

"Right," said Roxie, grinning broadly. "What he said."

Most of the guards were clustering together in little groups now, in the mistaken belief there was safety in numbers. I stared unhurriedly around me, letting them all get a good look at my featureless golden face mask. There's something about its complete lack of eyeholes that really upsets people. Some of the guards had automatic weapons, some had energy guns obviously derived from alien-developed tech, and a few were putting their faith in magical artefacts. I glanced at Roxie.

"You take the hundred to the left. I'll take the hundred to the right."

"Love to," said Roxie. "I hate being made to feel unwelcome."

"Surrender!" the guard leader said just a bit hysterically. "I demand that you surrender!"

"You just can't talk to some people," I said.

I took a step forward and all the guards opened fire at once, hitting me with everything they had. I stood my ground, quite casually, and let them get it out of their systems. My armour soaked up bullets and the energy beams with equal indifference, and it took no damage at all. A few magical energies crackled on the air around me, trying to force their way in and failing. I put up with this just long enough to really discourage the guards, and then I launched myself at them.

I was in and among them before they could even adjust their aim. I knocked them off their feet with great sweeps of my golden arms, tore weapons out of their hands, and threw them this way and that, and punched out anyone whose face I didn't like. I picked guards up and threw them away, and they went skidding helplessly across the stone floor. Some kept firing, hoping point-blank range would make a difference. It didn't. I picked these guards up and used them to hit others. From all around me came cries of rage and frustration, pain and horror, and it was music to my ears.

It felt good to have something to strike out at. Somebody to punish for the rotten day I'd had. But I was still careful not to hurt any of them too badly. I came here to ask the Survivors for help, after all. Littering the arrival chamber with dead bodies would not make a good first impression. Besides, I didn't do that anymore. No matter how brassed off I was feeling.

But no one attacks a Drood and gets away with it. Some things just can't be permitted.

Roxie was keeping herself occupied, and enjoying herself immensely. She might look every inch the mercenary adventurer, but she still had command of all her witchy unpleasantness. Nothing the guards fired at her was even getting close, and she was having a great time turning weapons into snakes, scorpions, and lobsters that went straight for the genitals. Apparently, her sense of humour remained the same no matter who she was being. She gestured languidly, and a whole bunch of guards' armour disappeared, replaced by flowery frocks, basques and stockings, and some quite distressing bondage outfits. At which point, most of the guards threw their weapons on the floor, stuck their hands in the air, and did their best to look like they were really very sorry. Some were clearly only moments away from bursting into tears. I thought Roxie was being quite restrained, for her. She hadn't turned anyone into a toad, or a squelchy thing with its testicles floating on the surface. So far.

"Stop this right now! All guards will stand down immediately!"

The loud authoritative voice caught everyone's attention. Those guards still standing immediately lowered their weapons and stepped back, doing their best to look like it was all nothing to do with them. I dropped the two guards I'd been about to slam together, and Roxie dropped the one she'd been punching in the face. Django Westphalion stayed where he was, curled up in a ball in a far corner. The newcomer with the imperious voice turned out to be a distinguished-looking young man in a white doctor's coat. Handsome enough, in a bland sort of way, with a ready smile and a discerning gaze. His only striking attribute was a shock of pure white hair, quite at odds with his apparent age. He strode across the great stone chamber, heading straight for me and ignoring the various injured and unconscious guards along the way. The guard leader, who'd been keeping well back all through the fighting, fired off a snappy salute at the newcomer, and was roundly ignored. Roxie strolled over to join me, smiling unpleasantly. The newcomer planted himself in front of us and flashed his most accommodating smile.

"Please, do accept my apologies, on behalf of the Institute. This has all been a terrible misunderstanding. You are our honoured guests."

Behind him, the guard leader looked like he couldn't believe his ears. Clearly, he'd been told something very different. Those of his men still on their feet just looked relieved they didn't have to fight any more. The newcomer gestured quickly, and the guard leader rounded up his men and led them away. Detailing some to help the injured and carry off the unconscious. It wasn't quite a retreat, but enough of one to satisfy my pride. Roxie made a rude noise at their departing backs. The newcomer cleared his throat, just a little theatrically, to draw our attention back to him. He was all smiles, apparently entirely unperturbed by my armour or the stray magics still swirling around Roxie. If anything, he seemed fascinated by both. He extended a welcoming hand to me, and I armoured down so I could shake it. He watched my armour disappear with interest, and then pumped my hand enthusiastically. Roxie dismissed her magics, and he made a point of shaking her hand too. I looked at Roxie.

"Who do you want to be here?"

"Think I'll go back to being Molly. She can be more frightening."

"I've always thought so," I said generously.

Molly Metcalf replaced Roxie Hazzard, and the young man laughed out loud, applauding delightedly.

"Marvellous! Simply marvellous! Eddie Drood and Molly Metcalf! All in one day . . . I'm so happy to meet you both."

"Something of a first," murmured Molly.

Django Westphalion slouched over to join us, and glowered at me. "You're on your own now, Drood. I was told you're dying. Good. Hope they invite me to the autopsy, so I can spit on your insides."

He left the chamber as fast as he could without actually looking like he was running away. He chose a different exit to the one the guards used, confirming that he knew his way around Under the Mountain. The newcomer looked after him, sighed in a disappointed sort of way, and then turned back so he could smile at me and Roxie some more.

"Allow me to introduce myself. I am Dr Melmoth, research scientist, and Head of the Science Division here at the Survivors' Institute, Under the Mountain."

"Aren't you a bit young to be in charge of things?" said Molly. "What are you, twenty-two, twenty-three? Or have you been trying out a youth serum?"

"Oh no," Melmoth said cheerfully. "I just acquired a morbid fear of death at a much younger age than most. Hence the hair. As a result, I determined to do something about it and became a highly motivated boy genius. The Survivors snapped me up at the first opportunity."

Melmoth had a flighty, almost giddy air to him, for someone who claimed to be so traumatized by death. Presumably a coping mechanism. He took in the expression on my face, and chuckled understandingly.

"Fear can be a marvellous motivator. Particularly

when there really is something to be scared of. As you'd know now better than most, Eddie. No need to tell me about your little problem. I've been briefed."

I had to raise an eyebrow at that. "Really? Who by?"

"The Wulfshead Management," said Melmoth. "They vouched for you, or you wouldn't be here. We don't allow just anyone into Under the Mountain. Not without knowing as much as possible about them in advance."

"You know the Wulfshead Management?" said Molly.

"Well, not personally . . . but the Institute has had dealings with them. Hasn't everybody? Now then, I want to reassure you, Eddie, that you've come to the right place! Oh yes! We've heard about Dr DOA, and his singular poison, but we've never had a chance to examine one of his victims while they were still alive. Oh, we're all really looking forward to seeing what we can learn from you, Eddie! Though I have to say . . . everyone here is frankly amazed and just a little flattered that the Droods should hold our research in such high regard. That you would come to us in your hour of need."

I heard a question in his voice that I had no intention of answering. It wouldn't help anything for him to know that to us, the Survivors were just a name in an old book. Better to be diplomatic; especially where my family's reputation is involved. Let the world think we know everything. Because mostly we do.

"Can you help me?" I said bluntly.

"Of course, of course! Place your trust in us, Eddie, and I promise that you won't be disappointed!" Melmoth grinned broadly, rubbing his hands together in anticipation. "We do love a challenge!"

"Yes," said Molly. "But can you help him?"

"We specialize in hopeless cases, Ms Metcalf," Melmoth said almost reproachfully.

"What is it you actually do here?" I said. "You understand there isn't a lot of information about you, out in the world."

"Of course, of course, just as it should be." Melmoth shot me a knowing wink, bouncing lightly on the balls of his feet in his eagerness to impress me. "Our work requires security. And privacy. We deal in the one thing everyone wants, after all—more life. Basically, Under the Mountain is one big research installation. Into all the problems that flesh is heir to. Research into every form of illness or physical breakdown. How our bodies sustain us, and why they fail us. We are interested in everything there is to know about life. We're looking for the cure, you see."

"The cure?" said Molly. "To what?"

"To everything!" said Melmoth. "To death itself!"

"Okay . . . ," said Molly. "How's that going?"

"We're making progress," said Melmoth. "Oh, and thanks awfully for bringing Django back. We have a whole new bunch of really interesting tests to run on him. And he's always so hard to get hold of."

"Will he enjoy these tests?" I said.

"I shouldn't think so, no," said Melmoth. "He didn't enjoy any of the others."

"Good," I said. "You do realise he's not actually immortal? That's just the family name. He's only very long-lived."

"Well, that's a good start, isn't it?" said Melmoth. "It's his ability to change his shape that we find so fascinating. Complete control over his physical structure, right down to the cellular level. Flesh that can adapt itself to any number of changing conditions! If we could only learn to duplicate that . . ."

"How's that going?" said Molly.

"We're working on it," said Melmoth.

"How long have the Survivors been working on this cure for death?" I said.

"Afraid you're asking the wrong man," said Melmoth. "I'm a relative newcomer to the Institute. They offered me the best-equipped laboratories in the world, and no problems with funding, and I couldn't say yes fast enough! I believe the Survivors, as an organisation, have been around for decades. There are scientists who've spent their whole working lives Under the Mountain. There's nothing like knowing you're engaged in the Greatest Work of Our Time to attract the best minds. Of course, it helps that we deal in pure science here; no moral or ethical restrictions to get in the way of whatever we decide is necessary. We pride ourselves on being very open-minded. It is, after all, the final result that matters. Putting an end to dying will justify everything we've done."

"But you must have human subjects to experiment on," said Molly. "How do they feel about these . . . moral ambiguities?"

She didn't sound too pleased with what she'd heard so far. Molly didn't have much use for morals or ethics herself, but she believed everyone else should. There's no one more judgemental than an ex–supernatural terrorist. If Dr Melmoth recognised the open disapproval in Molly's voice, he didn't seem to care.

"They're all volunteers," he said. "Sometimes for the money, more often because there's something wrong with them, that the world can't put right. Or it's a friend, or family, and then they volunteer their lives in return for the Institute's helping those they care about. It's all so very public-spirited and uplifting! We treat all our subjects with the utmost care, Ms Metcalf. They are part of the Great Work."

"What successes have you had?" I said bluntly, trying to bring him back to Earth.

"What have you got that you can show us?" said Molly.

"Why don't I give you the unofficial tour of the Institute?" said Melmoth. "How would that be?"

"Unofficial?" I said.

"Well, we don't get enough visitors for there to be an official tour, you see," said Melmoth. "I think it best if I just . . . walk you round. Show you what there is to see. After all, we have nothing to hide! Nothing! This way, please."

"Given how many secrets you must have, and how strict your security is, and that you greet your visitors with a whole bunch of armed guards . . . I have to assume there are some things you don't want the outside world to know about," I said. "Why are you being so open with us?"

"Because we want you to trust us enough to place yourself unreservedly in our hands," Melmoth said earnestly. "We help you so you can help us. Lots of people here would just love to get their hands on a Drood. The things we could learn from you . . . while we're helping you."

"There is a limit to how much of myself I'm free to discuss," I said. "My family's security must always come first."

"Always?" said Molly. "Even when you're dying?"

"I'm still a Drood, Molly," I said flatly. "I have duties and responsibilities. Some secrets aren't mine to share. I won't risk the safety and security of my family, just for a chance to save my own skin. *Anything, for the family.* It's not just a T-shirt."

Molly shook her head. When she finally had enough control of herself to speak, her voice was low and bitter. "Even now. After everything they've done to you . . ."

"Well," I said, "that's families for you."

"Everyone here will be very grateful for whatever information you feel you can provide," said Melmoth. "Now, if you'd care to come this way . . ."

He led us out of the stone cavern, hurrying on ahead with great enthusiasm, almost skipping along. He plunged into one of the un-signposted openings in the cavern wall, and just like that, we were walking along a gleaming steel corridor. The change in atmosphere was dramatic, like jumping straight from the Past and into the Future. The curving steel walls were entirely featureless, with no visible seams, as though the whole corridor had been extruded in one piece. It stretched away before us, lit by glowing half spheres set into the curved ceiling at regular intervals. Molly strode along at my side, glaring suspiciously about her. Making no secret of the fact that she didn't trust Melmoth or our new setting. But then, to be fair, she felt that way about most people and most places. Melmoth just scurried along ahead of us, not even glancing back to see if we were keeping up. He hummed tunelessly to himself, hands thrust deep into his coat pockets, as though he didn't have a care in the world. And this from a man supposedly so traumatized by the very thought of death that his hair had gone white.

We finally emerged into a massive cavern, big enough to hold a dozen cathedrals. High above, an artificial sun illuminated a great concrete plaza, surrounded by huge concrete arches leading off in a dozen different directions. All of them entirely functional, and not in any way decorative. Just there to serve a purpose. The sheer size and scale were intimidating.

There was no one else about. Molly stuck close at my side as we stood just outside the tunnel mouth. I felt like a target. This would make a really good place for an ambush . . . by people who really wanted to get their hands on a Drood and know his secrets. Melmoth stopped some distance ahead and looked back as he realised we weren't keeping up with him. He smiled brightly, and gestured for us to come forward and join him.

"Please; there's nothing for you to worry about! Come and take a look; this is what you came here to see . . ."

He beckoned winningly for us to join him. When I went forward, I saw why he'd stopped. The concrete floor just ended, with no warning and no railing. Molly clung tightly to my arm as we both looked down. Past the drop-off, the cavern fell away farther than my eyes cared to follow. The cavern's walls were lined with houses and habitations, buildings and science labs. Futuristic structures, huge inscrutable machines, and tall towers linked by a delicate spiderweb of walkways. Fiercely shining lights and flaring colours, and everywhere people, small as ants in an ant farm, just going about their business.

A whole city, built inside a mountain.

I could see clear traces of alien and future tech. Apparently, the Survivors had been gathering things they could use for some time and weren't too fussy about the source. Because you couldn't get anything like this anywhere reputable. That meant the scientific black market—Black Heir, and all the more-furtive areas of the hidden world. To acquire all of this, the founding Survivors must have gone shopping with pockets full of money, greedy as magpies for every bright and shiny thing they thought they needed. I made a mental note to inform my family. Some markets are forbidden because you can't deal with those people, and some things not even a little bit people, without blood on your hands as well as theirs.

I couldn't help a small smile. Even as I was dying, I was still doing my job as a field agent. Molly, delighted with the view, was going *Oooh!* and *Aah!* a lot. I wasn't so sure. Something about these brightly lit, crowded-together rooms and windows made me think of cells. The solitary spaces of religious thinkers, of scientists and their apprentices; perhaps even the cells of some giant organism. A single engine driving some Great Work incomprehensible to the individuals who laboured on it.

I looked at Melmoth, and he looked eagerly back at me, waiting for a response.

"Impressive," I said. "Where do we go from here?"

Melmoth's face fell. He'd clearly been hoping for more. "This way, to the elevators."

He turned away from the long drop, and strode off towards one particular archway. I had to pull Molly away from the view so we could go after him.

"It must have taken some time, and a lot of resources, to build all this," I said to Melmoth's back. "So, who paid for it all?"

"Is there anyone more afraid of dying than a rich old man who's finally understood you can't take it with you?" said Melmoth, not looking back. "We're never short of donations, from all sorts of people in all sorts of places. Every one of them desperate for a chance to cheat the Reaper. We make the results of our research known to all our patrons, in regular reports, but you'd be surprised how few of them want to try the things we have to offer. They all want to live on, but only on their own terms."

"And you?" I said. "Given your particular problem with dying?"

"I have the option to try anything I like," Melmoth said easily. "We all have. Perk of the job. But, as with so many of our more than generous benefactors, I'm waiting for just the right option. As to how this installation was constructed, everything you see was brought in through the teleport mechanism and assembled in place. Of course, it's not finished. We're constantly improving and upgrading the Institute."

"Where did the Survivors get hold of such a powerful teleport mechanism?" said Molly. "They're rare. I know where to look for a phoenix's egg and a Maltese falcon, but I'd still have trouble getting my hands on a teleport mechanism that could do all this."

"It was a gift," Melmoth said blithely. "From someone who wanted our services, but didn't have the money to pay for them."

"Was this someone human or alien?" I said.

He shrugged. "Who can say? We try not to ask personal questions. The point is, it often works out that way. We let word get out as to what we need, and people rush to press it into our hands, in return for what we know. People can be very generous when their backs are pressed against a wall with really big spikes on it."

"This particular benefactor, with the teleport," I said, "Any connection to Black Heir?"

Melmoth smiled. "I couldn't possibly comment."

"I could," said Molly.

"How many people work here?" I said quickly. "Under the Mountain?"

"Something like twelve thousand, I believe," said Melmoth. "In their own various disciplines. We are a broad and eclectic church. And that's not counting all the patients and volunteers, the security, and support staff. Let's go meet some of them!"

"Let's," I said.

We finally came to a pair of perfectly ordinary-looking elevator doors. Melmoth hit the call button, and the doors opened immediately, as though they'd been waiting for him. We all filed in, and Melmoth turned to a really long row of buttons, chose one near the bottom, and stabbed it dramatically with a long finger. The doors closed and down we went, into the depths of the city.

"How many floors are there?" I said, looking dubiously at the many buttons.

"Depends on your security clearance," said Melmoth. "Only a few have access to all departments, on all levels. Most people only work within their own speciality, never seeing anything beyond their own few floors. But you, as our honoured guests, get to see anything you want."

"How nice," said Molly.

Melmoth beamed at her. "It is, isn't it?"

His relentless good humour was beginning to get on my nerves. No one smiles that much without their brain being chemically challenged. It isn't natural.

The elevator seemed to descend forever. At least there was no music. Molly and I looked at each other, behind Melmoth's back. Molly's expression asked me how I wanted to play this, and I shrugged in my best *Take it as it happens* manner. Melmoth was humming again.

The doors finally opened onto what could have been an office floor in any building. Thick carpet, pleasant setting, cheerful atmosphere. Melmoth strode off down the corridor, leaving us to hurry after him, and led us to a surprisingly spacious room, packed with monitor screens showing views from all over the city. Dozens of people sat bolt upright in front of them, studying the views with great concentration. None of them looked round as we entered. Because we wouldn't be there if we didn't already have permission. I was starting to think nothing unexpected ever happened Under the Mountain. Because it wouldn't be allowed. Melmoth strolled around quite happily, peering over shoulders at various views.

"Behold!" he said grandly. "It's all here—scientific laboratories, medical wings, demon surgeons, and magical grottos. Hope, in every shape and form. Everything from genetic manipulation to radical surgical procedures, the grafting of exotic genetic materials, and forbidden alchemical practices. Nothing is considered out of bounds, Under the Mountain. Except failure, of course."

"Of course," I said.

I leaned forward. I couldn't help noticing the wide proliferation of armed guards, standing to attention outside closed doors, or patrolling brightly lit corridors in large groups. I pointed out a particularly heavily armed gathering, escorting a coffin on a hospital gurney. The coffin was wrapped in very heavy chains.

"Why do you need so many armed men, Dr Melmoth?"

"We give as much attention to internal security as external," said Melmoth. "Safety is paramount. And we do have the occasional problem with disturbed patients trying to escape from the secure areas. We can't allow that. Some are infectious, some present a danger to themselves and others, and some are simply deluded. The guards are there to protect the medical staff."

"Armed guards," I said.

"Well, of course."

"You shoot your patients?" said Molly.

"Only the ones who complain," said Melmoth. He chuckled happily. "Little bit of hospital humour there."

"Show me some of your success stories," I said. "Cases where you've actually achieved something."

"Of course!" said Melmoth. "We have nothing to hide. And much to be proud of."

And I thought, but didn't say, *Then why did I have to ask? Why didn't you volunteer to show them off?*

We left the monitor room, and not one single person turned to watch us go. In my experience, you don't get that kind of discipline without staff indoctrination bordering on brainwashing, backed up by severe punishments for even the smallest infringements. Under the Mountain was starting to feel less like a medical establishment, and a lot more like Fanatics "R" Us. Melmoth took us back to the elevator, and this time the doors actually opened as we approached. Bit of a giveaway, that. Someone was watching.

This time we stepped out into a warren of cheerfully anonymous corridors, and Melmoth hurried along quite happily, never once seeming unsure of his way. Voices spoke calmly from hidden speakers. Announcements, instructions, requests for particular individuals to hurry to a certain location. There was a general sense of urgency in these voices; of important things happening.

"This sounds more like a regular hospital," said Molly.

"It is!" said Melmoth. "In every way that matters. We work hard here, to save lives."

"At any cost?" I said.

"Where the alternative is death, yes," said Melmoth.

"You don't think the price of survival can sometimes be too high?" I said.

"What an odd question," said Melmoth. "Particularly from someone in your position . . . The whole philosophy of the Survivors is that we intend to go on living for as long as possible, no matter what the world puts in our way to try to stop us. And that, of course, means not being bound by unnecessary moral and ethical restrictions. We will use any weapon in our fight, because so will the enemy. Death pulls no punches, and neither do we. Anything less would be insane. We are at war with death."

"Couldn't everyone say that?" said Molly.

"Yes," said Melmoth. "But we mean to win."

To get to the hospital wards we had to pass through a series of heavy metal doors that opened only to number pads, voice recognition, and retina scans, and finally a DNA test. All of it enforced by armed guards with strict orders and no sense of humour. Dr Melmoth had to provide all the samples, because Molly and I firmly declined. I couldn't help wondering whether the doors were there to keep unwanted visitors out, or to keep the patients in. *We have a problem with disturbed patients trying to escape,* Melmoth had said. Were they that disturbed before the doctors got to work on them? At least the guards had enough sense to point their guns well away from me and Molly. Word had clearly got around, which was just as well. I wasn't in the mood to put up with any nonsense.

Once we were past security, the hospital ward looked much like any ward. Though one where the patients were clearly only hoping against hope that someday they might walk out of there. A quietly desperate place, full of people chasing their last chance. I'd already decided I would not be ending up in a place like this. Patients lay quietly and uncomplainingly in their beds, hooked up to intimidatingly large machines. Lots of attached tubes and wires, and incomprehensible readouts. None of the patients so much as turned their heads to look at us. Because if we weren't a doctor or a nurse, we didn't matter. We couldn't help them. These patients had only one thing on their minds.

Melmoth led us down the central aisle, smiling brightly at everyone, and delivering a running commentary on what was being done for each patient; drugs, spells, tailored nanotech. Mostly just to see what would happen. He didn't even lower his voice as he said that, but no one reacted. Nurses in traditional uniforms bustled back and forth, being quietly and firmly professional. Like bees moving among flowers, I thought, and carrying out a necessary function for their own purposes.

"No private rooms?" said Molly. "I thought you had unlimited funds."

"We prefer open wards," said Melmoth. "One case might provide useful information or insight into another. And this way, the patients can provide emotional support for one another. Since we can't allow visits from friends or family or loved ones."

"Not at all?" said Molly.

"Security must be maintained," said Melmoth. "The patients go along; they understand what's at stake here."

"What happens to patients who get cured and want to go home?" said Molly.

"A little light editing of the memories and they're free to go, of course," said Melmoth. "We're not monsters, Ms Metcalf."

"But if your cures don't work, then your patients die here alone," I said.

"My dear Eddie, we all die alone in the end," said Melmoth. "Now, let me show you some of our successes!"

Beyond the wards lay an open courtyard, full of men with metal parts. No artificial limbs, no Six Million Dollar Men with super abilities and telescopic eyes. Just rough-and-ready cyborgs; men with bulky pieces of tech jutting out through splitting skin, with bulging cameras where an eye should be, and artificial backup organs on the outsides of their bodies. Some had heavy packs on their backs to power internal motors; others were attached to standing machines, big enough to generate the forces necessary to keep them going. Some cyborgs looked more human than others. They clumped heavily back and forth, like tin soldiers with unreliable mechanisms, every gesture slow and awkward because it had to be thought out in advance. Joints and connections sparked, and bulging implants made loud complaining noises. The new bodies worked and they functioned; but that was the best you could say about them.

"Not exactly aesthetic, I know," said Melmoth. We were standing right there with the cyborgs, but he didn't lower his voice. "Still, these are all prototypes. First we make it work; then we make it pretty. We're learning something useful from all of them to be applied to the next generation."

"Can any of these people ever leave here, and go home?" said Molly. "Looking like that?"

"No," said Melmoth. "The implanted tech belongs to us. We developed it, and we're not ready to share it with the rest of the world, just yet. But everyone here signed a contract, of their own free will. They were dying. They're all grateful for the extra time these procedures have bought them."

"Yeah," I said. "They look grateful."

"Ask them!" said Melmoth. "Talk to them. They have much to be grateful for. They don't feel pain, heat or cold, hunger or thirst. They never get tired, and they'll last for years."

He broke off as one of the cyborgs started screaming, in a flat, mechanical voice. The sound was horrible, like a machine having a mental breakdown. He lurched back and forth, holding his sutured head in both hands, while the other cyborgs backed jerkily away.

"I can't feel anything! Anything! How can I be alive if I can't feel? It's like being locked in a box with all my skin cut off. I can't even remember what it was like to feel anything. I hate this. I hate this."

He beat at his head with his fists, and tore off one of his ears. He looked at it for a moment, as though trying to remember what it was, and then threw it away. He ripped the camera out of his eye socket and crushed it in his hand. There was no blood. He tore tech implants out of his arms and chest, leaving trailing wires that sparked and smoked, along with the odd spurt of machine fluids. Muscular orderlies in hospital whites came running forward to restrain him. The cyborg struck out at them with his unfeeling fists. Still screaming. Molly grabbed my arm.

"Do something, Eddie! Help him!"

I armoured up and walked towards the cyborg. He turned awkwardly to face me. The taut skin on his ruined face couldn't show emotion, but his words did.

"Please," he said. "Kill me."

I took him in my golden arms, and held him close. A doctor edged in behind the cyborg, and jabbed him in the back of the neck with a long needle. The cyborg sighed once, and collapsed. I lowered him gently to the ground, and the orderlies picked him up and carried him away. It took all of them to do it. I went back to Molly.

"That was it?" she said. "That was all you could do?"

"I don't want to kill any more," I said. "And he chose this." It sounded unconvincing, even to me. But I couldn't say, *I don't want to upset Melmoth. I might need him.*

"I'm sure he'll feel better tomorrow," said Melmoth. "Once we've adjusted his brain chemistry."

The other cyborgs were moving restlessly around again, trudging back and forth in their enclosure like animals in a zoo with nothing better to do. If they were at all upset by what they'd just seen, they had no way of showing it. They were too busy concentrating on the new limits of their miserable mortality.

"Is this what you want done to you?" said Molly.

"No," I said. "Not under any circumstances."

Melmoth shrugged easily. "Then let's go look at something else."

In a small closed-off area, we looked out on another world, viewed through a one-way mirror. A wide-open moor stretched away before us; a place of dark shadows and drifting mists, muddy ground and stinking bogs, and scrubby, malformed vegetation. All of it under a night sky lit by the blue-white glare of a huge new moon. It was a cold and desolate place, nowhere anyone sane would choose to live.

"Of course, most of that isn't real," said Melmoth. "It's part recreation, part holographs. To make the patients feel at home."

"What patients?" said Molly. "I don't see anyone . . ."

"There," I said, pointing.

Silent figures went slinking through the darker places. There was nothing human in the way they moved. They leapt and pirouetted, crouched and scrabbled, appearing and disappearing like animated scraps of nightmare whimsy. Drifting across the moor like tumbleweed moved by moonbeams, with flashes of flailing overlong arms and legs. The occasional roughly human shape stood out briefly, in silhouette against the full moon.

Melmoth worked a set of controls below the one-way mirror, and although the moonlight grew no brighter, somehow we were able to see everything much more clearly. The patients were long-bodied and inhumanly slender, with stick-thin arms and legs. They skittered and scurried, like daddy longlegs dancing across the moorland. They looked like people who'd been stretched on a rack and then left that way. Even their skulls were horribly elongated, with glowing eyes and pointed ears.

Several came together to form a group, or pack, and went haring off in pursuit of one desperately fleeing individual. They hunted him down, leaping through the moonlit night and cutting off every escape like a cat playing a mouse, and then they brought him down, killed him, and ate him. Stuffing the steaming flesh into their sharp-toothed mouths with calm complacency.

"Why did they do that?" said Molly.

"Something to do with herd instinct, we think," said Melmoth. "They can always tell when someone doesn't belong. We think the rejects must have too much of their original humanity in them."

"Why didn't you do something to help him?" said Molly. "He was one of your patients too!"

"They all signed releases," said Mclmoth. "They agreed to the new kind of life they would be joining. This is a part of their natural order now, their continuing life cycle. Purging the herd to keep it pure. It would be self-defeating to interfere. And we are learning so much from them."

"Like what?" I said.

"I'm afraid that's classified," said Melmoth. "Proprietary information, and all that."

"And they chose to become like this?" said Molly.

"They all accepted the grafts of elven genetic material," said Melmoth. "As an alternative to dying. Some were quite keen to become elves. Of course, this isn't exactly the result any of us were expecting when we started out . . ."

"I'd rather die than be something like that," I said.

"When the time comes, you may feel different," Melmoth said complacently. "They did. There's something about being shown a coffin with your name on it that does tend to concentrate the mind wonderfully."

"Hold it," said Molly. "Where did you get your hands on elf genetic material? Interbreeding with humans has always been one of the elves' greatest taboos. I can't believe they'd go along with this . . ."

"You'd be amazed what certain individuals will agree to," said Melmoth. "Under the right conditions."

"Something's happening," I said. "Look . . ."

The elven hybrids were darting agitatedly back and forth. They plunged across the moors, in and out of the mists and shadows, in increasingly large groups, as though searching for something. Finally, they all came together and circled round and round the same spot, before crashing to a halt and freezing in place. Some kind of communication was going on among them, though there wasn't a sound to be heard. And then they all turned their heads at once, to look in our direction. As though something had caught their attention.

"Can they see us?" said Molly.

"Of course not," said Melmoth. "They shouldn't even be able to detect the viewscreen, let alone know what it is. It's just not present, in their world."

"Are you sure about that?" I said. "Because they're certainly looking at something."

The whole group surged forward, dozens of elven hybrids leaping and scurrying over the uneven ground, heading straight for us. They crossed the moor at incredible speed, arms and legs pale flickers in the moonlight. Their stretched faces were fiercely intent, and their wide smiles showed vicious teeth.

"They can't see us!" Melmoth insisted.

"They know we're here!" I said. "Look at them."

They slammed to a halt just short of their side of the viewscreen, and then milled back and forth, crawling around and over one another. And then one stopped, raised a clawed hand, and tapped one heavy claw against the other side of the screen. Scraping the claw slowly across it, testing to see what it was. And one by one, others came forward to do the same. They were trying to get out. To get to us.

"They can't get through," said Melmoth.

He sounded like he was saying it more to reassure himself than us. One hybrid closed his hand into a bony fist and punched the other side of the viewscreen. Immediately, all the others joined in, hammering with all their strength. They made no sound at all. Molly glared at Melmoth.

"Shouldn't you be sounding an alarm?"

"It's a silent alarm," Melmoth said numbly. "So as not to upset the patients. It sounded the moment their behaviour changed. Help is on its way."

The door behind us slammed open, and a single woman came hurrying in. Not a guard, and not obviously a doctor; just a short and stocky middle-aged woman in ethnic Gypsy wear, complete with any number of bangles and necklaces. Dark curly hair, lots of makeup, and the swagger of someone who knows for a fact that they're always going to be the most important person in any room. She smiled at me, letting me know she knew I was attracted to her. I was pretty damned certain I wasn't. She nodded familiarly to Molly, and scowled at Melmoth.

"All right, what have you done to get them this stirred up?"

"Nothing!" said Melmoth. "I've never seen them like this . . . Oh, Eddie, Molly, allow me to introduce my colleague, the Soul Witch. Head of the Magical Division, with full responsibility for situations like this. Whatever this is. The most powerful witch in the world."

Molly bridled immediately. "Oh yes? Then why have I never heard of her?"

"Because unlike some of us," said the Soul Witch, "I don't feel the need to advertise." She moved in close to the viewscreen, ignoring the rest of us to look closely at the elven hybrids as they hammered silently and determinedly on the other side. "I did tell you this might happen, Melmoth. We don't understand enough about what the genetic grafts do to these people to be able to predict their behaviour. They're magical creatures, with more than human senses."

"But why can they see us now, when they couldn't before?" said Melmoth.

"They've always been able to see us," said the Soul Witch. "They just didn't care before. Something must have changed, to set them off . . ." She turned suddenly to look at me. "Of course, it's the Drood! They can sense his torc, its power, and they want it. Get him out of here, and they should settle down again."

The viewscreen didn't break or shatter; it just suddenly wasn't there any longer. Instead, a great gap appeared in the wall, opening onto the dark and shadowy moor. A cold wind came blasting in, bringing with it the scent of muck and mud, rot and decay. The elven hybrids launched themselves through the opening, fighting one another in their eagerness to get to me. I armoured up and they swarmed all over me, clawing at my armour and snapping at my face mask to try to get through, to get at me. I grabbed hold of them and threw them away, but they just came straight back again. More and more of the hybrids hurled themselves at me, trying to drag me down through sheer weight of numbers. I stood my ground and clubbed them off me, one at a time.

I had to hit them hard to make them let go. Bones broke and skulls shattered under the impact of my golden fists, but it was the only way. Nothing I did slowed their attack. Their blood-red eyes were full of a terrible hatred, and their heavy teeth snapped and ground together viciously. I kept clubbing them off me. Bodies littered the floor and did not rise again. I tried to tell myself, *They're not people any more.* It didn't help.

Molly circled around me, blasting individual hybrids with quick bursts of magic. Some withered, some caught fire, and some blew apart like sacks of blood. Most just fell away dead. Because of their strong magical nature, Molly could only take them out one at a time, and there were always more, scrambling through the opening from the moor.

"Stop killing them!" yelled Melmoth, dancing agitatedly around in the background. "Please stop killing them! They're patients! Valuable research subjects!"

And then he broke off as one of the hybrids turned abruptly to look at him. Melmoth froze where he was. The hybrid took a step forward, grinning nastily. Melmoth produced a piece of high tech from his pocket and pointed it at the hybrid.

"Please stand back. I don't want to have to hurt you."

The hybrid laughed silently, and took another step.

"Reject," Melmoth said sadly.

He did something with the tech in his hand, and the hybrid dropped dead to the floor.

More and more came streaming through the opening where the viewscreen used to be, throwing themselves at me in a blind fury. They didn't seem to care how many had already died at my hands. I was almost buried under a great clawing blanket of the things, reduced to striking out blindly with my golden fists. And then the Soul Witch said a single Word, and they all dropped off me in a moment. They cried out silently, pressing their hands to their elongated heads, and then turned as one and fled back through the opening. Back onto the moor, and the world that had been made for them. I shook the last few off me, and they fell lifelessly to the floor. The Soul Witch gestured briefly, and the one-way viewscreen returned. On the other side, the elven hybrids were scattering across the misty moor, disappearing into the shadows and going to ground. I armoured down and nodded my thanks to Molly. She looked even more tired than I felt, but she still found the energy to glare at the Soul Witch.

"What took you so long?"

"It's all in the timing," said the Soul Witch.

Melmoth looked at the dead bodies littering the floor and shook his head. "Such a waste . . ."

"What did you do to them?" I said to the Soul Witch.

"I accentuated the elven material in their bodies," she said calmly. "So they couldn't bear to be in a human place." She smiled at Molly. "I'm surprised you didn't think of it."

"I was busy!" snapped Molly.

I looked thoughtfully at Melmoth, who'd only just realised he still had the piece of tech in his hand and was putting it away.

"What did you do?" I said.

"What I can make, I can unmake," said Melmoth. "Such a waste of good material . . ."

"Never mind," said the Soul Witch. "We're bound to learn something useful from the autopsy. You know you always enjoy that."

"Yes," said Melmoth, cheering up. "There is always that to look forward to."

The Soul Witch gave me a hard look. "This was all your fault, Drood. Disturbing our patients with your presence. This isn't a zoo."

"The Drood wanted to see what we'd achieved," Melmoth said quickly, "before he would agree to become a patient. And you know how much . . ."

"Yes, yes, I know. This fascination of yours with Droods will be your undoing." The Soul Witch took one last look at the moor, now entirely quiet and empty, and turned away. "From now on, I suggest you view our test subjects only from a safe distance. For their safety as well as yours."

I took the opportunity to study the Soul Witch with my Sight. Ever since she'd arrived, I'd had the feeling there was more to her than met the naked eye. And sure enough, through the Sight, I could tell she didn't just have a soul . . . She had several. Stacked inside one another, like Russian nesting dolls. The Soul Witch . . . Was she an eater of souls, a container of ghosts, or a preserver of personalities? I quietly drew Molly's attention to the Soul Witch, and Molly nodded quickly to confirm she'd Seen it too. And then shrugged, to indicate she didn't understand it either. While I had the Sight, I took a quick look at Dr Melmoth, who turned out to be just as interesting. The man was positively stuffed full of life energies. Far more than one man should ever have. No wonder he was so up all the time.

I really don't like it when people keep secrets from me. It's supposed to be the other way round.

The Soul Witch turned her back on the moor, and left the room without another word. Melmoth looked expressionlessly after her. I allowed my Sight to drop. I didn't think he'd be able to tell what I'd Seen, but there was no point in taking chances. A secret known is an ace up your sleeve.

"Marvellous woman, the Soul Witch," Melmoth said finally. "Full of character! And a complete pain in the arse to work with." He smiled apologetically at me. "I'm afraid you're not seeing us at our best. Perhaps we should call off the tour."

"I've seen nothing yet to convince me you have anything to offer that I'd want done to me," I said grimly.

"Then on we go," said Melmoth. "You're really a very hard man to please, Eddie."

There was the group mind that remembered being human, but wasn't any longer, and the single mind downloaded from clone to clone as the same disease kept killing its body. The tenth generation had so little personality left, they might just as well have lobotomized it. Various attempts to transplant useful vampire and ghoul traits, all of which resulted in people who would have been better off all the way dead. Combinations of living and nonliving materials, man and machine forced together in unhealthy proximity, and all kinds of extreme cutting-edge scientific and magical measures. All of these people were alive when they should have been dead, but none of them looked particularly happy about it.

We moved on, through more of the featureless steel corridors. I hadn't seen a single thing I approved of so far, and certainly nothing I was prepared to let them try out on me.

"None of the subjects you've seen will live forever," said Melmoth, "but they're all promising starts."

"I was expecting to see some Frankenstein-style patchwork efforts," said Molly.

"I'm told there were several such attempts, back in the early days," said Melmoth. "But the practice was soon dropped. Too many problems with tissue rejection. How the Baron overcame that remains a mystery. We have reached out to many of his surviving creations, through the Spawn of Frankenstein network, but they refuse to talk to us. Or allow us access to any of their medical records. They're being very selfish, holding back such important information. I can only assume they have issues with medical science."

"I wonder why," I said.

"Precisely!" said Melmoth.

"What about the genetic material you extracted from the Immortal, Django Westphalion?" I said. "Any progress with that?"

"So far, it's proved utterly incompatible with the human genome," said Melmoth. "In fact, it's killed everyone we've tried it on. In appallingly unpleasant ways. We think it's something to do with not being able to control the shape-dancing ability. Whatever originally changed the Immortals from their baseline humanity altered them to such an extent that strictly speaking, they shouldn't be considered human any longer. And so far, Django has proved most secretive, not to mention intransigent, when it comes to discussing his family background."

I thought about that as we walked down the steel corridor. Given that the Immortals were originally created by the other-dimensional fugitive known as the Heart, who also adapted my family's DNA so we could bond with our torcs . . . I had to wonder about the state of my own humanity.

Melmoth might not have noticed how disappointed I was, but Molly had. She put her arm through mine and squeezed it reassuringly.

"We're bound to find something, Eddie. We haven't seen everything yet."

"I'm not sure I want to," I said. "Is it just me, or have all these cures for death been just a bit weird?"

"I'm assuming that's because they've tried all the usual things, and none of them worked," said Molly.

"Or maybe they've spent too long living Under the Mountain," I said. "And the isolation has driven them all batshit mental."

Melmoth must have caught some of that, because he stopped and considered me thoughtfully.

"I'll admit we have no cure for death itself, just yet. So for now we have to be content with little victories."

"I haven't seen anything I'd consider even a little victory," I said. "Don't you have anything that would just . . . give me back the years I was going to have?"

"Please," said Melmoth. "Come with me to our main medical facilities. Our very best people are waiting to give you a thorough examination and discover exactly what's happening in your body right now. There are all kinds of less-dramatic procedures we could try, once we have a better understanding of your current condition."

"I don't know . . . ," I said.

"We've come all this way, Eddie," said Molly. "We have to let them try. Please, Eddie . . ."

I sighed, and allowed myself to be persuaded.

The main facilities turned out to be a huge open laboratory, containing the kind of medical equipment I'd previously seen only in my worst nightmares. Alien computers and futuristic tech, prods and probes, scalpels and saws, and a whole bunch of intricate steel instruments just casually lying around on trays. Most of which looked horribly invasive.

The doctors and nurses were all very busy removing the other patients so they could give me their full attention. Some of the departing patients were protesting furiously, arguing that they'd paid good money . . . until it was explained to them that I was a Drood, at which point they decided to leave quietly. Some actually got up off their beds and walked. All but one, a large and portly gentleman who tried hard to appear dignified while holding his hospital gown together at the back.

"I am not going! I will not be pushed to the back of the queue! Don't you know who I am?"

"Do you know who that is?" said Melmoth. "That is Molly Metcalf."

The large gentleman left, very quietly and very quickly.

I smiled at Molly. "Your reputation precedes you."

"That's what a reputation is for," said Molly.

Once all the patients were gone, the doctors and nurses gathered together to look me over. I could see awe and excitement in their faces, and something that might have been a kind of hunger. *They've waited a long time to get their hands on a Drood* ... I felt like an antelope that had wandered into the lions' feeding ground. I stared them all down, as coldly as I could. Dr Melmoth quickly came forward, smoothing the way with soothing words, and everyone relaxed a little. Except me. One of the doctors wheeled a tall standing screen forward, and they all took it in turns to study me through it.

"It's so they can see your torc," Melmoth explained. "Most have never seen one before."

"I should hope not," I growled. "I'm still not sure about this. I've already told you; my family's secrets are not on the table."

"You can't put unreasonable obstacles in our way and still expect us to work miracles," said Melmoth. "Who knows what piece of hidden information might turn out to be just what we need to save your life?"

"No," I said. "I'm sorry, but no. And if you keep pushing it, I am leaving ..."

"That's enough!" said Molly. Her face was flushed with something more than anger. She glared at me, and her voice was harsh. "Stop making problems, Eddie, and let them do their job! I didn't come all this way just to watch you turn your back on the only people who might be able to save you!"

"You've seen what they do here," I said carefully. "Think what they might do, with access to Drood secrets."

"I don't care about your damned family! I only care about you. Now let them do what they need to, so ..."

"All right," I said. "For you, Molly." I turned to Melmoth, keeping my face and voice stern. "Nothing invasive. And no wandering off the beaten path. You stick to identifying the poison in me, and what can be done about it. Nothing else. I will defend my family's secrets, even at the cost of my own life. Or yours."

"Of course, of course," said Melmoth. He shot a hard look at the other doctors. "I'm sure we're all comfortable with those very reasonable restrictions."

The doctors didn't look like they were, but they all managed some kind of nod.

"Okay," I said. "Do you want me to strip naked?"

"Not unless you feel you really want to," said Melmoth. "We have first-rate scanners here."

I was persuaded to lie down on a quite extraordinarily uncomfortable bed while the medical staff took it in turns to wheel various pieces of unfamiliar equipment into place around me. And then point them at me. The machines made all kinds of interesting noises, as though determined to establish their importance, but whatever they were doing, I couldn't feel it. My torc didn't even tingle. The staff members scanned me thoroughly from head to toe, looked inside me from a whole bunch of different angles, and then displayed what they'd found on oversized monitor screens. I didn't understand half of what I was looking at, but the doctors seemed very impressed. There was a lot of pointing, followed by heated discussions that started out as whispers but quickly escalated to loud disagreements and shoving matches. Melmoth had to intervene several times to keep people from coming to blows. I might have been wrong, but the watching nurses seemed to find this all very entertaining.

The doctors then took a large number of blood samples from various places, with really long needles. I didn't enjoy that at all. One of the younger doctors got a bit testy with me over that. He put on an officious face and a condescending voice.

"Oh come on!" he said. "It's just a few needles . . .

Who would have thought a big bad Drood would turn out to be such a crybaby?"

Molly grabbed his shoulder, spun him round, and punched him out. He hit the floor hard and had to be dragged away. Everyone was a lot more polite after that. A lot of the nurses grinned at Molly, in a way that said, *I've always wanted to do that.*

Molly held my hand through all of the tests. One of the doctors asked, very politely, if they could sample my spinal fluid. And my bone marrow. Another wanted deep-tissue extractions from various major organs. They assured me these were all very simple procedures, which could be carried out under a local anaesthetic. I declined. The doctors tried to argue with me, insisting that they knew best. I stopped them with a look.

"You don't insist to a Drood," I said. "Let's see what you can do with what you've got, first."

The doctors turned to Melmoth, and he nodded reluctantly. "Eddie Drood is our guest. We are here to help, not pry." He stopped as a thought struck him. "I know you won't agree to a DNA test, but how about a semen sample?"

Molly grinned suddenly. "I could give you a hand . . ."

"No," I said very firmly.

The medical staff then took it in turns to hit me with a series of prepared questions, first about my medical history, and then about my torc. What it was, how it worked, how it was protecting me from the poison. I didn't have answers to most of the questions, and I refused to talk at all about the torc. The doctors switched to psychological questions about my childhood, my upbringing, my feelings about my parents, my sex life . . . I refused to answer any of those either, though Molly seemed quite ready to discuss that last one.

"Come on!" she said. "This is for Science!"

"No it isn't," I said.

I could tell some of the medical technicians were

surreptitiously trying to scan my torc while I was being distracted with questions. I could feel it tingling at my throat. I wasn't worried. My torc was quite capable of looking after itself. One of the machines suddenly exploded, another went up in flames, and one just disappeared. Everyone became even more polite after that.

Melmoth darted all over the place, peering over shoulders and sticking his nose into everyone's work. Always ready to offer an opinion or debate each new piece of evidence. The medical staff seemed used to it, in a long-suffering sort of way. As Head of the Science Division, the white-haired young man was presumably beyond criticism by the rank and file. When the staff members finally ran out of unpleasant things to do to me, they split up into small groups to discuss their findings, and what it all meant. There was a lot of furtive glancing back at me, but no one said anything to me.

Molly was gripping my hand so hard by now, it hurt.

"Well?" I said finally. "Talk to me! Have you found anything useful?"

Melmoth had been darting agitatedly back and forth among all the groups, so the doctors looked to him to be their spokesman. I sat up on the bed to face him.

"We've learned a great many things," he said carefully. "But not much we didn't already know, or at least suspect. We've located the poison in your system, but we have no idea what it is. None of us has ever seen anything like this. Its chemical composition makes no sense. And we have seen a great many unusual things in our time Under the Mountain."

"Could this unknown poison be of alien origin?" I said, just as carefully. "As in, from another world?"

That stopped them all short. They looked at one another and consulted their notes again. More whispered discussions, some of them quite energetic. Melmoth moved from group to group, getting a consensus, before coming back to me.

"We've checked the poison against all the examples of alien material we have on file, but we haven't been able to establish a match. That doesn't mean the poison isn't alien; just that it's not from anywhere we've encountered before."

"You've had aliens here?" said Molly.

"No one wants to die," said Melmoth. "Anything else would have to come under patient confidentiality. Suffice it to say, every alien species we've encountered has turned out to be totally incompatible with the human genome. An alien poison should have no effect at all on a human body."

"So Monkton Farley was wrong," I said. "I must make some time to rub his nose in that."

The doctors and nurses looked at me silently. They'd done all they could, with what they'd got. They looked to Melmoth.

"I'm afraid the situation is brutally simple, Eddie," he said, curbing his normal enthusiasm. His new composure gave his voice a certain grim gravity. "Your body is breaking down as the poison advances, and will continue to do so. Until it can't function any longer. Your torc is fighting a valiant rearguard action, slowing the poison's progress and keeping you alive, but it's burning up your body's resources to do it. Anyone else would have been dead long ago . . . but it seems there is a limit to the miracles even a Drood torc can perform. The best we can suggest . . . is that you allow us to remove your mind from its dying body and download it into something else."

"My mind?" I said. "What about my soul?"

"We deal in science here," said Dr Melmoth. "For that side of things, you would have to consult the Soul Witch. Or Bishop Beastly. He's our Head of Death-related Studies." He smiled briefly. "We do our best to cover all possible areas . . ."

"Bishop Beastly?" said Molly. "That's a name and a half. Why . . . ?"

"Because he loves animals."

"Oh . . . ," said Molly.

"No," said Melmoth. "I mean like Saint Francis of Assisi."

They were trying to cheer me up. I could tell. It wasn't working.

Molly was more disappointed than I was that the doctors couldn't help me. She let go of my hand and sat down on the bed with her back to me. So I couldn't see her face. I wasn't disappointed, because I never really thought they could do anything. Droods have the best medical people and equipment in the world. I only agreed to come to Under the Mountain because . . . well, because there was always a chance. Molly had allowed herself to hope. I knew better. Hope just gets in the way of doing the job. Melmoth cleared his throat to draw my attention.

"The medical staff have asked me to say . . . they are willing to keep working on your blood and tissue samples. Who knows what we might discover, in time . . ."

"No," I said. "I want all my blood and tissue samples assembled here and destroyed, right now, right in front of me. Don't even think about keeping anything back. I'd know."

"Of course you would," murmured Melmoth.

I watched closely as they destroyed the various samples, one after another. Until one of the doctors refused to hand over his.

"This is a Drood!" he said. "We may never get a chance like this again! Science must take precedence over one patient's foolish and selfish wishes!"

I got up from the bed, and he fell quiet. I armoured up, and the medical staff all but fell over one another, backing away from me. Shock and even horror filled their faces. It was one thing to have heard about golden strange matter, and quite another to face a Drood in his armour. I raised one golden fist, and slowly grew spikes out of the knuckles.

Melmoth took the samples from the no-longer-protesting doctor, and I watched silently as they were destroyed. The medical staff didn't say a word. The doctor who'd spoken out couldn't even look at me any more, because when he did, he started shaking. I suppose I should have felt like a bully, but I didn't. When it was all over and done with, Melmoth gestured quietly to the doctors and nurses, and they all quickly filed out. I waited until only Dr Melmoth was left, before armouring down again.

"Drama queen," said Molly.

I sat back down on the bed, trying to hide how bone-deep tired I felt. All my muscles were aching, like I'd just run a marathon. The urge to hide inside my armour and never come out again was growing stronger. Molly realised something was wrong. She sat beside me, and glared at Melmoth.

"There must be something you can give him! Some drug that would just . . . keep him going!"

"It's the torc," Melmoth said kindly. "It won't let us interfere. It's practically running Eddie's body now. That's why I suggested downloading Eddie's mind. His body is on its last legs, and it's only going to get worse."

He produced a silver hip flask from inside his coat, and handed it to me. I tried it. Pretty good brandy. I took a long drink, savouring the warmth as it went down. It didn't make me feel any better, but that would have been asking too much, anyway. I passed the flask to Molly, and she took a good belt before handing it back to Melmoth. He took only the merest sip, before putting the flask away.

"You're still welcome to try any of the solutions you've seen," he said.

"No," I said. "Thank you."

As far as I was concerned, that was it. I was ready to go. Melmoth must have sensed that, because he leaned in close and lowered his voice, even though we were the only ones there.

"Before you leave . . . I really would be very grateful if you'd step into my private office. Just for a moment."

I wasn't keen, but given how much of his time and attention he'd already granted me, with not so much as a word about payment, I felt I owed him that much. I looked at Molly, and she shrugged, so I nodded to Melmoth.

His private office turned out to be pretty basic, just a desk and some chairs. No comforts, no personal touches, all the papers on his desk neatly arranged. No windows, of course. It reminded me of the Management's office, at the Wulfshead. Melmoth sat down behind his desk, and Molly and I sat down facing him. Melmoth started to say something, and then stopped. He didn't seem too sure about where to begin.

"Would you like a cup of tea or something?" he said.

"No," I said. "Nothing. Just get to the point."

Melmoth laced his hands together on top of the desk and leaned forward, lowering his voice conspiratorially.

"If it were up to me, I wouldn't be bothering you with what is, after all, internal Survivors business, but there are people above me I have no choice but to answer to. And they insisted I ask you, so . . . You must have wondered why we've all gone out of our way to be of assistance to you, and never once raised the question of payment. Or even asked a favour of your illustrious family."

"The thought had crossed my mind," I said.

"Right," said Molly.

"We wouldn't normally even allow a Drood access to Under the Mountain," said Melmoth. "We were pretty sure your family wouldn't approve of many of the things we do here. And your relatives do have a tendency to shut down anything they disagree with. Often quite suddenly and violently."

"But you couldn't resist the chance to examine a real live Drood," I said.

"That was undoubtedly part of it," said Melmoth. "But we need your help. Your investigative skills. Someone here . . . is killing people. How he gets away with it is a mystery. We have surveillance coverage in every room, every corridor, every lab. Everyone is under constant observation, for their own protection. The staff and the patients. But someone is killing people when no one is watching. It has to be someone fairly high up who knows our system and its inevitable blind spots."

Molly and I looked at each other, and then sat up straight, giving Melmoth our full attention.

"You have a murderer running loose inside the Institute?" I said. "And your security people haven't been able to find him?"

"Exactly!" said Melmoth. "Which should be impossible, given their resources and manpower."

"Who's been killed?" said Molly.

"Seventeen victims, so far," said Melmoth. "Twelve men, five women. All medical staff. Never a patient or a volunteer."

"So he's targeting well people," I said.

"That seems likely, yes," said Melmoth.

"How did they die?" I said.

"Another part of the mystery. No wounds, no injuries. Just . . . found dead. We thought the first few were natural causes. But seventeen, in less than a week?" Melmoth shook his head. "Could there be any worse crime than to kill someone who's dedicated their life to preventing others from having to die?"

"Have you questioned the Immortal?" said Molly.

"Of course!" said Melmoth. "First suspect we looked at. But it couldn't have been Django Westphalion. He wasn't present in Under the Mountain when the murders occurred. And even with his teleport bracelet, he couldn't get in without contacting us first, to get the security shields lowered. A lot of people wanted it to be him, just on general principles. We have some idea of the many sins his family is responsible for, down the centuries. But . . . no. It can't be him. Hard as it us for us to accept, the murderer has to be one of us. The people who really run things here are the Overseers. They founded the Survivors, and still set general policy. They insisted I bring you in on this."

"Hold it," said Molly. "Some of the original founders are still alive?"

"Apparently," said Melmoth. "I've never met them. Don't know anyone who has. Anyway, they felt we needed an experienced outsider. Someone with an independent background. We were still arguing over who might be suitable, when Django said Eddie Drood wanted to come here. We took that as a sign. Your reputation as a solver of mysteries precedes you. And you too, of course, Ms Metcalf."

"Of course," said Molly.

I looked at her, and we both got up and moved to the far end of the office so we could talk quietly together.

"We don't have time for this," said Molly. "We can't take on a lengthy murder investigation. We just can't. Not now. I mean, even talking to all the right people will take ages."

"We have to try," I said.

"Why?" said Molly. "We've spent too long here already! Wasting our time . . . your time. You're the one who's always in a hurry."

"They helped us, so we have to help them," I said. "Sometimes it really is that simple."

"Even when you're dying?" said Molly.

"Especially then," I said. "We have to do right, when it matters. Because if not us, then who?"

"You've been getting broody again," said Molly. "You know I hate questions like that."

"Yes," I said. "I know. Don't worry; this won't take long."

She looked at me sharply. "You've already figured something out, haven't you? You know something!"

"Let's say I've seen something," I said.

I turned to Melmoth. "We need to talk to the Overseers."

He shook his head. "No one talks to them. Even the three Department Heads have no direct connection. All instructions arrive anonymously, from outside Under the Mountain. Just as well; it means we get left alone to get on with our work."

"Why do they need to be anonymous?" said Molly.

"Since we don't know who they are, we can't speculate as to their motives," said Melmoth. "Well, actually we can and we do, but . . . we don't dare ask them. Not if we want to go on working here."

Molly looked at me. "Does this remind you of the Wulfshead Management?"

"The thought had crossed my mind," I said.

"With your permission," said Melmoth, "I'll call in the other two Department Heads."

"Yes," I said. "I think that would be wise."

Melmoth raised his voice. "Come in!"

The door opened and the Soul Witch swaggered in, with a general air of *I'm here, so the party can start now.* She was followed by a large, more-than-portly gentleman in a full scarlet cardinal's gown, complete with a tall golden mitre. I wondered how he kept it balanced on such a round head. His face was all curves and dimples, with deep-set eyes and a knowing look. For a man of his size, he moved with surprising grace, and I sensed a real strength buried under all that bulk. He bestowed a warm and avuncular smile on me and Molly, but I wasn't convinced.

"This is Bishop Beastly," said Melmoth. "Head of Death-related Studies."

"Bishop?" I said. "Of what Church, exactly?"

He smiled a fat smile. "All of them, dear boy. This is no place to be making enemies."

He chuckled loudly, and ripples spread across his vast form like a slow earthquake. He insisted on shaking my hand, and then Molly's, with his huge podgy fingers. For a man who looked like he never said no to a second helping, or turned down a dessert, there was nothing weak about his grip.

"What do you do here?" I said. "Exactly?"

"I cover the spiritual side of things," said the Bishop. "Because someone has to. These two deal in body and mind; I deal in those matters that concern the spirit. What good does it do to survive, if in the process you compromise your soul?"

"Have you seen some of the things they're doing here?" I said.

"Alas," said the Bishop, "my position is largely advisory."

Dr Melmoth and the Soul Witch exchanged a knowing glance behind the Bishop's back.

"I saw that," said Bishop Beastly.

"No you didn't," said the Soul Witch.

"I didn't need to," said the Bishop. "You're so predictable." He smiled knowingly at me and Molly. "Think of me as the designated conscience of this facility. Someone has to be in a position to say, *No, no farther; that is a step too far.*"

"Either you're not saying it enough, or they're not listening," I said.

"It is that kind of facility," Bishop Beastly admitted. I didn't care for his smug and superior attitude, like the cat that always expects to get the catnip. I also got a definite feeling of undercurrents of violence running deep inside him, just waiting for an outlet. For an excuse to punish someone. The Soul Witch and Molly were looking at each other thoughtfully, like two predators agreeing to share the same watering hole for as long as it suited both of them.

"When you stare into the Abyss," said Molly, "remember that the Abyss stares also into you."

"The trick is not to blink first," said the Soul Witch.

"How long do you expect this investigation of yours to last?" said the Bishop.

"Exactly," said the Soul Witch. "Some of us have important work to be getting on with."

"Not long," I said. "In fact, I'm almost done."

"What?" said the Bishop.

"I know who the murderer is," I said.

"You do?" said the Soul Witch.

"Do tell," said Melmoth.

"It had to be someone really high up," I said. "With access to all areas, including the security centre. Someone who knew the surveillance system inside out, so they could avoid the cameras and be in a position to give orders so the security people would stay away from the right places at the right time. Which meant it had to be one of you three. And you forgot, Dr Melmoth; I may be dying, but I'm still a Drood. We don't trust anyone, even when they seem to be doing their best to help us. Thanks to my torc, I have the Sight, and while you've been studying me, I've been studying you."

Molly and the Soul Witch looked intently at Melmoth, and their eyes widened.

"Yes!" said Molly. "I can See it!"

"Dear God," said the Soul Witch. "Melmoth, how could you?"

"I'm feeling very left out," said Bishop Beastly. "What are all of you Seeing that I'm not?"

"Dr Melmoth is saturated with life energies," I said. "I saw them earlier. Far too many for one man to have come by honestly. I might not have understood the significance of that if I hadn't just had an interesting experience with something similar. When you said the bodies were found dead with no obvious wounds or injuries, Dr Melmoth, it all made sense. You've been killing people by sucking out their life energies and storing them inside you."

"Why?" said the Soul Witch. "Why would you do this, Melmoth?"

He smiled suddenly; it was a happy and entirely unrepentant smile. He stood up behind his desk and looked uncaringly around him, like a great man being bothered by questions unworthy of him.

"I came here to find a cure for death, to save my own life. Because one human lifetime seemed such a pitifully small thing, when there was so much waiting to be learned and mastered. I came to Under the Mountain with the highest of hopes, only to find that for all the techniques being practised here, for all the endless studies and research . . . none of you had come up with anything I could use to save myself. So I found a shortcut. A way to take life from others, and make it my own. It wasn't as if they were doing anything useful with it . . . The stolen energies extended my life. The years my victims would have had became my years. And I went on killing because . . . Well, you can never have enough life, can you? No matter how many years I took, it wasn't immortality. I knew I would use up all the energies eventually, and still die. Which was, of course, completely unacceptable."

"Dear Lord," said Bishop Beastly. "How could we have had such a monster in our midst, and not have known it?"

"Oh please," said Melmoth. "Like there's any shortage of monsters here."

"What do we do now?" said the Soul Witch. She seemed genuinely stunned.

Melmoth turned his smile on her. "You can share in my discovery. You and the Bishop. Through me, you can live lifetimes, enjoy far more years than you ever anticipated. All you have to do is hold Eddie and Molly in this room while I make my escape. I'll come back, after they've left, and show you how to live. Really live."

"Yeah, right," said Molly. "Like they're going to fall for that one . . ."

"How do we know you'll be back?" said the Soul Witch. Her voice was flat and harsh.

"Well," said Melmoth, smiling more engagingly than ever. "I guess you'll just have to trust me, won't you?"

He came out from behind his desk. Molly and I started forward, and then had to stop as the Soul Witch and Bishop Beastly moved to block our way. Melmoth waggled the fingers of one hand in a quick good-bye, and then was out the door and gone. The Bishop moved quickly to fill the doorway, while the Soul Witch stared challengingly at Molly.

"You can't trust him!" I said. "Hasn't what you've just heard proved that? He's got to be heading for the teleport station, and once he's gone, you'll never see him again!"

The Bishop and the Soul Witch glanced at each other, and shrugged pretty much simultaneously.

"It's nothing personal, I assure you," said the Bishop. "But faced with such an opportunity . . ."

"We'd be mad not to take it," said the Soul Witch.

"Quite," said the Bishop.

"We can't risk losing out on the prize we've been chasing all our lives," said the Soul Witch. "There's nothing like being around the dying all day to make you even more concerned with living."

I took a step towards the Bishop, and he seemed to expand to fill the doorway even more completely. His smile had become unbearably smug. "Once I have set myself in place, my dear Drood, I am very hard to move. I'm actually very holy, you know, and protected by the powers above."

"You're protecting a murderer," I said.

"No one's perfect," said the Bishop.

I considered armouring up and forcing my way past him, but something in his pose gave me pause. He might be bluffing, or he might not. In a place like this, who knew? But then, a man of the cloth wouldn't last long in a place like this unless he knew how to defend himself . . .

While I was still thinking that, Molly took a step forward, and she and the Soul Witch stood face-to-face; like two gunslingers meeting in the middle of Main Street. There was a sudden tension in the air, as powerful forces gathered. The two witches moved their hands slightly and adjusted their postures; professional fighters taking the measure of each other. And then the Soul Witch seemed to suddenly *unfold*, as all the souls stacked within her came forth, superimposing their presence upon and around her. Smoky ghosts, uncertain presences, made up of mists and tatters. The Soul Witch gestured, and the ghosts sprang forward like attack dogs, half of them heading for Molly and the others for me.

They swirled around Molly, circling her rapidly, unable to reach her. I armoured up, and they climbed all over me, trying and failing to force their way through my armour. They wrapped their smoky arms around me, holding me in place. They had the weight and gravity of unquiet souls with unfinished business. But when I tried to hit them, my golden fists passed right through them. They were only solid when they chose to be.

I still had my Sight. I could See the shining threads that connected each individual soul to the Soul Witch. And it was the easiest thing in the world for me to grab hold of the nearest shimmering threads with my golden hands and snap them. The souls convulsed as the strings that connected the puppets to their puppet master disappeared, and then I heard silent voices crying out, *Free! Free at last!* as the ghosts disappeared. The Soul Witch swore angrily, and pulled the remaining souls back from Molly and into her.

While the Soul Witch was distracted, Molly slammed her hands together. The whole office was suddenly full of a blindingly bright light. Even I was dazzled, inside my golden face mask. I could hear the Soul Witch and the Bishop crying out in shock and horror. The light hammered against my armour like a hailstorm of burning coals. When the light finally faded away and I could see again, it was all over.

The Soul Witch was curled up in a ball on the floor, murmuring, *Don't, please don't . . .* over and over again. The table and chairs had been burned to ashes, and all four walls showed heavy scorch marks. Molly was untouched. I nodded to her respectfully.

"Damn," I said. "You've still got it, Molly. You are still professionally scary."

"When I have to be," said Molly. "Believe it."

"How much magic have you got left?" I said.

"Maybe one or two spells. I'm back to running on fumes."

"Hang in there," I said. "We've still got work to do."

We both turned to look at Bishop Beastly, standing in the doorway. Completely untouched by what had just happened. He smiled briefly.

"I really am very holy. Witchery can't touch me."

I raised one golden fist. I didn't even have to do the spiky-knuckles bit before he raised both fat hands placatingly.

"But I know a lost cause when I see one." He moved away from the door. "Feel free to go after Dr Melmoth, with my blessing."

"If he's escaped, because you've slowed us down . . . ," I said.

"He won't," said the Bishop. "Trust me."

"Yeah, right," said Molly.

Out in the corridor there was no sign of Melmoth any-where. Just a single technician, hurrying along. He took one look at us, and turned quickly to hurry off in some other direction. I caught up with him, took a hold of his coat, and picked him up off the floor.

"Which way to the teleport station?" I said.

"I can't tell you that!" said the technician, trying hard to look everywhere but into my featureless golden mask. "Security must be preserved!"

Molly leaned in beside me and smiled unpleasantly at him.

"Hi! I'm Molly Metcalf!"

"It's not far!" said the technician. "Down the right-hand corridor, take the elevators at the end, all the way to the top floor. Please don't turn me into something."

I dropped him, and we hurried down the right-hand corridor.

"Still scary," I said.

"Damned right," said Molly.

We found the elevators, and I armoured down while Molly hit the call button. And then we had to just stand there and wait. Elevators have no sense of urgency. The doors finally opened, and we stepped inside. I hit the top button, the doors took their own sweet time closing, and we started up. Molly and I stood together, watching the floor lights change.

"He could already have reached the teleport sta-tion," I said. "He could already be gone. And we haven't got time to go chasing after him. I don't suppose you could . . ."

"No, I can't just transport us there!" said Molly. "I told you; I'm wiped out. I couldn't even produce a top hat from a rabbit. Isn't there any way to make this ele-vator go faster?"

I studied the controls again, just on the off chance. "Apparently not."

We waited, and waited, until the doors finally opened onto a wide-open space, with no one about and any number of corridors leading off. There was a sudden commotion down one of the corridors, so we ran towards it. We burst into what had to be the teleport station, a number of carefully delineated departure pads surrounded by unfamiliar equipment. And standing very still, his hands in the air and well short of the pads, was Dr Melmoth, guarded by a dozen heavily armed security men. Two seriously spooked technicians were staying well back, pressed up against the control panels. One of the security guards nodded to me.

"We've been waiting for you, Drood. Bishop Beastly phoned ahead and got us here in time to prevent Dr Melmoth from leaving. He's not going anywhere. Unless he does something really stupid, and then my men will see just how many holes they can shoot in him before he hits the floor."

"Of course," said Molly. "Phones trump slow-moving elevators any day. Why didn't we think of that?"

"Well?" I said. "Do you have Security's phone number?"

"No one loves a smart-arse," said Molly.

Melmoth glanced around him, careful not to lower his hands even a little bit. He looked the guards over, dismissed them with a sniff, and smiled at me.

"Tell you what, Eddie. I'll share my discovery with you, if you'll get me out of this. You want to live, don't you, Eddie? What I've got can't cure you, but it could give you many more years!"

"You're the second person to make me that offer today," I said. "The price is still too high."

"Wait," said Molly. "What is it you've got, Melmoth?"

"Molly . . ."

"Hush, Eddie! Don't you want to know?"

I nodded to the security guard. "Let him show us what he's got. Unless it looks like a weapon, and then . . ."

"He's dead meat," said the guard.

Melmoth made a face at him. "You just can't get good help these days."

He lowered one hand, reached slowly and carefully into his coat pocket, and produced a small blood-red crystal. He held it out before him so we could all see. It didn't look like much; just a gleaming crimson stone, in which dark shadows curled slowly.

"This is what I found, hiding unsuspected among a consignment of alien artefacts we received from Black Heir. I've no idea what it is, or what strange world it might have come from; but all you have to do is point it at someone, and their life jumps right out of them and into you. Just make a wish . . . and all their years are yours. Your problems could be over in a moment, Eddie . . ."

"And how many more people would have to die, to keep me going?" I said.

He gave me his best engaging smile. "Only little people."

"Forget it," said Molly. "I know what that is, and it's not what Melmoth thinks. It's not even alien; it's a vampire jewel. What you get if you take a vampire and reduce it down to its basic essence. Nasty thing." She looked coldly at Melmoth. "The jewel steals life energies, but that's all. It can make you stronger, but it can't grant you one extra day of life. You've been killing people for nothing . . ."

"No . . . ," said Melmoth. For the first time, he looked genuinely upset. "No!"

He jabbed the blood-red stone at Molly, but before I or any of the guards could react, Molly gestured sharply, and the crimson jewel leapt out of Melmoth's hand and into hers. He dropped to his knees and rocked back and forth, shaking his head.

"All those people I killed . . . and I'm still going to die! It's not fair!"

The Soul Witch came in with Bishop Beastly. She looked pale, but back to herself again. She nodded to me, ignoring Molly.

"Leave Melmoth to us. He will be punished."

"Are you going to kill him?" said Molly.

"No," said Bishop Beastly. "I don't think any of us are in the mood to be that merciful. Too many good people have died."

"Thought you were very holy?" I said.

"Not all the time," said the Bishop. He smiled at Melmoth. "Vengeance is mine."

"Ours," said the Soul Witch.

"Quite so, my dear," said Bishop Beastly. "Dr Melmoth can serve as our latest guinea pig, for all the most dangerous and extreme experiments. For as long as he lasts. Who knows; maybe through him we'll find something that does work."

"Okay," said Molly. "I can live with that."

She tossed me the vampire jewel. "Be a love, Eddie, and destroy that thing. No one in this madhouse can be trusted with it."

I armoured up one hand and crushed the blood stone. When I opened my golden hand, just a little powder fell away. Bishop Beastly nodded to the security guards, and they grabbed hold of Melmoth and hauled him out of the chamber. He fought them all the way, kicking and screaming. Because he had better reason than most to know what lay in store for him.

"Now, if you'll excuse us," said the Soul Witch, "we need to make a report to the Overseers. And arrange for a new Head of the Science Division. The work must go on. Because there really aren't any shortcuts."

"The technicians will see you on your way," said the Bishop. "Safe journey. Don't feel you have to hurry back any time soon."

They left, not looking back. The two technicians looked at Molly and me with shocked, vaguely traumatized eyes. And that was when Django Westphalion came storming in through a side corridor, bearing an energy weapon so big he needed both hands just to aim it. The technicians dived for cover again, while I armoured up and put myself between Molly and the Immortal. He opened fire, and a beam of energy shot out, so fierce it seemed to slice a path through reality itself to get to me. The beam slammed into my armoured chest, and the golden strange matter soaked it up like a sunbeam. Django cursed bitterly and threw the weapon to the floor.

"It's not fair! It's just not fair!"

Molly came out from behind me, and advanced on the Immortal with a determined look in her eye. "I have put up with enough shit for one day."

Django saw her coming, and bent down to pick up the energy weapon again. Molly got there first, and kicked him in the face while he was still bent over. He fell backwards, and she was on him in a moment, beating the crap out of him. Just on general principles. I armoured down and watched her do it. After all, it wasn't like she could do him any real damage. His shape-changing abilities would repair any injury. From the amount of noise he was making, it still hurt like hell. Served him right, the treacherous little toad. Molly finally stepped back, breathing hard, and I approached her cautiously.

"Feeling better now?"

"Much," said Molly.

I nodded to the Immortal as he pulled himself back together again. "Sorry about that, Django. But she needed someone to take out the day's frustrations on, and you were dumb enough to give her an excuse." I picked up the energy weapon and crumpled it into scrap with my golden hands, before throwing it aside. "Why did you want to shoot me, anyway? You know I'm dying."

"Not fast enough," Django said spitefully, rising painfully to his feet.

"Tell me something," I said. "That teleport bracelet of yours, the one you used to bring us here. Where did you get it?"

"Why should I tell you anything, Drood?"

I looked to Molly. "Ready for Round Two?"

"Oh yeah . . . ," said Molly.

"Black Heir!" Django said quickly. "I got it from Black Heir."

"That's the second time that name has come up," said Molly. "I think we need to pay Black Heir a visit."

"Right," I said. "I still haven't given up on the idea that Dr DOA's poison isn't from around here. It would explain a lot. And Black Heir knows about things like that."

"Will its people talk to you?" said Molly.

I grinned. "I wasn't planning on giving them a choice."

I grabbed hold of Django's arm and took the bracelet away from him. He started to object, and then fell sullenly silent when I looked at him.

"Can you work that thing?" said Molly.

"Looks straightforward enough. Particularly after some of the things the Armourer's given me."

"How am I supposed to get home?" said Django.

"Walk," said Molly.

I turned to the teleport technicians, who had reluctantly emerged from cover again. "Send the Immortal away. Preferably somewhere very removed from anywhere civilised."

"No problem," said the head technician. "We never liked him. No one here does."

"Of course not," said Molly. "He's an Immortal."

I threw Django Westphalion onto the nearest teleport pad, and the technicians quickly threw a whole bunch of switches. Django glared at me.

"I'll get you for this! I'll make you pay for this, Drood!"

"Join the queue," I said.

He disappeared. The head technician smiled ingratiatingly at me. "You know, you don't need the bracelet. Our equipment can send you anywhere in the world."

"No offence," I said, "but I never trust other people's equipment. It's always possible your bosses don't want us to be able to report on what we've seen here. They might have given you secret orders, to send us somewhere very remote. Or even have us arrive in pieces. So if you'll just drop your security screens, we'll be on our way."

"And no messing with the screens," said Molly. "I'd know. And I'd be very upset."

"It's true," I said. "She would."

The two technicians exchanged a look, admitting nothing, and got to work. And then both of them froze, staring at the controls in front of them.

"That's not right," said the head technician.

"What isn't?" I said.

"Something's coming," he said. "Coming in, from outside. As though they were just waiting for us to lower the shields."

"But that's not possible!" said the other technician. "Not without knowing our exact coordinates! We're not expecting anyone, are we?"

"No. We're not."

"Well . . . raise the shields again!"

"Too late!"

A figure appeared suddenly on one of the teleport pads. A large black warrior woman, in heavy jade armour deeply etched with mystical symbols. She was tall and majestic, lithely muscular, with a broad, high-boned face. Her hair was styled in bright green cornrows. She carried a glowing sword on one hip, and a double-headed axe on the other. Two bandoliers crossed her impressive bosom, bearing luck charms, killing objects, shaped curses, and pre-prepared spells. Weaponized magic. She stared at me with cold, cold eyes.

"I am the Demon Demoiselle," she announced in rich, carrying tones.

"Never heard of you," I said. I looked to Molly. "Have you heard of her?"

"No," said Molly. "And I've heard of everyone who matters."

"Your sins have found you out, Eddie Drood," said the Demon Demoiselle. "Time for you to die, for what your family has done."

"It's those same words again!" I said. "This is some new gang, or maybe a conspiracy."

"Why is everyone suddenly so keen to kill you?" said Molly. "They never wanted to kill you before you were dying."

"Yes they did," I said.

"Of course," said Molly. "You're a Drood. I was forgetting."

I turned to the Demon Demoiselle. "Do we really have to do this? It's been a long day, I'm tired, and I'm not in the mood."

"I will kill you, Drood, for what you've done!"

"No you won't," said Molly.

She snapped her fingers, and the teleport pad activated itself. The Demon Demoiselle blinked out of existence. The two technicians hurried to reset the security measures so she couldn't get back in.

"Thank you, Molly," I said. "I didn't want to have to kill someone else."

"I thought as much."

"I thought you were out of magics."

She grinned. "I may have quietly sucked a few energies out of the vampire jewel before I gave it to you."

"Of course you did," I said. A thought struck me. "Do you have any idea where you just sent her?"

"Of course! Remember the reservoir, where we crashed Cassandra's airship?"

"Ah," I said. "I hope she can swim."

"From the look of her, she could probably walk on water," said Molly.

"True. Okay, off to Black Heir's Headquarters. We'll take a look at what its people have, which they're almost certainly not supposed to have, and find out what they know about Dr DOA."

"Maybe they can help you," said Molly. "All the weird shit they've picked up down the years, they must have something. But, Eddie . . . where will we go if they can't?"

"We just keep following the leads," I said steadily. "Dr DOA has to stay lucky to stay hidden; we only have to get lucky once."

"Maybe," said Molly. "But he hasn't survived this long just by being lucky."

"I know," I said.

CHAPTER SEVEN

Buried Treasure

The problem with using unfamiliar teleport mechanisms is that you're never quite sure what to expect. Sometimes it feels like being torn apart and then slammed back together again; sometimes like a side trip through a Hell dimension with hellhounds on your trail; and other times like being turned briefly inside out after a very heavy lunch. Django Westphalion's teleport bracelet was surprisingly easy on the nerves. One moment Molly and I were in Under the Mountain, and the next we were standing near the top of a steep hill overlooking the sea. Somewhat to my relief, we seemed to be where we were supposed to be. At Black Heir's Headquarters, right on the edge of the Cornish coast. (First rule of staying alive: Never trust an Immortal.) I grinned at Molly.

"A very smooth arrival, with everything inside me still where it ought to be. We should send Django a nice thank-you note."

"No we shouldn't," said Molly. "The only thing I'd send him would be a death threat, with postage owing."

At which point we disappeared and reappeared again, this time some ten yards farther away. Molly grabbed hold of my arm, and then we disappeared again, reappearing right on the cliff edge. So close, a part of the rocky edge actually crumbled and fell away under my feet. Molly tried to pull me back, and a whole section of the cliff edge dropped out from under her feet. I hauled her away just in time, and we both stumbled backwards, putting some distance between us and the long drop.

"It's the teleport bracelet!" said Molly.

"I know!" I said.

"Well, shut it down!"

"I'm trying!"

I fumbled at the controls, but they were all flashing wildly. Rather than risk the damned thing teleporting us blindly again, and maybe right over the edge this time, I ripped the bracelet off my wrist and threw it on the ground. I stared at it fiercely, my gut muscles tensing, while Molly held on to my arm with both hands so we couldn't be separated. I slowly relaxed as the bracelet just lay there on the dirt path, trying to look innocent. The control crystals were still flickering unsteadily.

"Could be a malfunction," I said. "Or maybe I did something wrong . . ."

"Hell with that," Molly said immediately. "We know who's to blame. The Immortal planned this."

"Well," I said, "it wouldn't surprise me if he sabotaged the bracelet. The Immortals always did delight in thinking ahead, when it came to plotting their revenges."

I stooped down over the bracelet to examine it more closely, but it disappeared. I shot a quick glance at my wrist, in case the bracelet had tried to reattach itself, but it hadn't.

"Did you hear something?" said Molly.

There had been the sound of a splash, far below. I moved cautiously back to the cliff edge and peered over the side. Molly clung grimly to my arm, ready to haul me back, but she couldn't resist leaning over for a quick look herself. A long way below, the sea crashed heavily against jagged black rocks. If the bracelet had fallen into those turbulent waters, the odds were it wouldn't be coming back.

"It's gone," I said as we stepped back from the edge.

"Good," said Molly. "But how are we going to get moving again, after we're done here? Ask Black Heir to call us a taxi?"

"I can always call home," I said. "And I still have the Merlin Glass. If I can persuade it to behave."

Molly pulled a face. I didn't blame her. I took a moment to look out over the view and appreciate it. Because I wasn't sure how many views I had left. Dark waters, under a lowering late-evening sky. Heavy foam splashing over ragged rocks as the tide came crashing in to pound on them. No seagulls on the wing, no ships out at sea. Just the ocean, nature in the raw, savage and brutal and completely indifferent to the transient human eyes that found a cold beauty there.

"How are you feeling, Eddie?" Molly said quietly. "I mean, really?"

"Really?" I said. "Hanging on by my fingernails, but still on top of things. I've got enough left to get me where I'm going."

I turned my back on the view, and looked up the long dirt path to the old house at the top of the hill. I could tell Molly wanted to talk some more, but I had nothing else to say. She sighed, just a little, and joined me in studying the house. It had clearly started out as a grand Victorian mansion, more than big enough to hold an organisation the size of Black Heir, with enough room left over to store any number of secrets. Black Heir did love to keep things to itself; until it could sell them.

The house was a wreck, with a battered exterior, broken slates on the roof, and a couple of squat brick chimneys that would have to be seriously upgraded before they could even pass muster as a fire hazard. No lights on anywhere, and heavy wooden shutters covered all the upper-floor windows. The house wasn't short on character, though. It seemed to crouch sullenly, like an old predator past its prime, trying to summon up enough courage or spite to be dangerous one more time. I'd seen photos of the place, in files at Drood Hall, but nothing in them had suggested the dark malevolent power of the old house. This was a place where bad things were plotted, and done, because Black Heir had always gone its own way. And if it could trample over everyone else in the process, so much the better.

"Very Gothic," said Molly. "Reminds me of all the covers on those cheap paperback Gothic romances I used to devour as a teenager."

"Much about you suddenly becomes clear," I said. "Still, what better aspect to hide its true nature as a gatherer of high-tech trinkets that fell off the back of a starship?"

"Why have its Headquarters here, so far from anywhere?" said Molly.

"Its old Headquarters used to be up in Yorkshire," I said. "That was back in the Forties, when, according to Uncle Jack, flying saucers were dropping out of the skies and crashing into fields all over the north country. Don't ask me why. Maybe something about the scenery reminded them of home."

"So why move all the way down here?" said Molly.

"Partly because the organisation outgrew the old place, but mostly because it got sloppy with procedures and was in danger of being noticed. Black Heir had to pull a disappearing act, to avoid answering some very awkward questions from some very awkward customers. As to why here, exactly, no doubt it had its reasons.

Probably entirely selfish ones. Black Heir has always been run by scavengers, pirates, and borderline criminal scumbags. They're in it for the money, not the service."

"Then why does your family support them?"

"Because they're our scumbags, and besides, they're very good at what they do. These days."

Molly scowled at the crumbling old house, as though it had personally offended her. "You know, it never occurred to me to ask before, but . . . why is it called Black Heir? I mean, black for black market; I get that. But . . . heir? Heir to what?"

"Well . . . ," I said patiently.

"Oh God, you're about to lecture me, aren't you?"

"You asked. Black Heir started out as an underground criminal organisation, looting alien tech left behind from close encounters that went seriously wrong. Its members took the name when they came to work for us, because they're heir to an earlier organisation that my family had to shut down with extreme prejudice. They had ended up crossing too many lines, and almost started a war between this planet and several different alien species. Scavenging is one thing; disrespect to the alien dead is quite another."

"What did they do?" said Molly, her eyes glowing. She never could get enough gossip.

"Apparently," I said, "they were running a thriving trade in dead aliens. Organs and tissues and so on as ingredients for really alternative medical treatments. Like tiger parts and monkey glands in certain traditional remedies. There was also a market for complete corpses, for very rich people with their own private museums and rabid collectors' mania. Always desperate for something unique, to one-up their friends and colleagues. I'm told there was even a very specialized market for live aliens."

"For private zoos?" said Molly.

"Occasionally. But some people will have sex with anything. If only for the bragging rights."

"Oh *ick*," said Molly. "And can I also add *ew*."

"Quite," I said. "My family shut it all down. Stamped out the trade at both ends, and disappeared a hell of a lot of people. War was averted, and Black Heir stepped up to become the new authorized vultures on the scene."

"So your family is responsible for Black Heir," said Molly. "I should have known."

I shrugged. "There has to be someone to clean up after alien and other-dimensional incursions . . . And you can't expect people to do the work of vultures and still act like gentlemen. Besides, no sane person would take the risks. Clambering around inside crashed alien ships is a lot like defusing an unexploded bomb, with the added risk of being poisoned, irradiated, or horribly transformed, as well as just killed. I once had to help clean out a crashed starship that was infected with alien parasites. Poison wouldn't kill them; we ended up having to chase after the little bastards with lump hammers."

"Does your family have any history that isn't completely appalling?" said Molly.

"Give me time," I said. "I'll think of something."

I returned my attention to the old dark house. Vaguely worried it might have crept up on us while I wasn't looking. But the house was entirely still and silent, and the only sounds in the evening were the low murmur of the wind and the distant crush of surf on the rocks below. Black Heir's Headquarters looked grim and desolate and lonely. The house at the end of the world.

"Why are you looking like that?" Molly said. "Is there something wrong with the house?"

"It's a house at the end of its life," I said slowly. "Everything it was, everything it was for, is over now. It reminds me . . . of me."

"Stop that," Molly said firmly. "Don't beat yourself up; you have any number of enemies ready to do that for you. Now, changing the subject. Have you ever been here before?"

"No," I said. "My family doesn't interfere in the everyday business of other agencies. Well, not directly, anyway. We just keep a watchful eye, and hand out spankings as necessary."

I knew I was spending too much time talking when I should have been moving, but I felt oddly reluctant to get any closer to the old house. Something was wrong here. I could feel it.

Molly looked around her. "Shouldn't there be some kind of security?"

"Yes," I said. "There should. Everything from guards and guard dogs, to land mines and force shields. And all kinds of nasty surprises. Black Heir has a lot of enemies and a lot to protect. At the very least, someone should have noticed our arrival by unscheduled teleport, and sent some security personnel out to check who we are and what we're doing here."

"No lights anywhere."

"I had noticed. An ominous detail, in an ominous setting."

"Highly Gothic," Molly said dryly. She grinned suddenly. "Ten to one, there's something awful in the attic."

"No bet," I said.

"What have the Droods got in their attic?"

"The remains of people who asked too many questions."

Molly looked at me. "I can never tell when you're joking, with your family."

"Neither can I," I said.

I strode forward, up the dirt path to Black Heir's Headquarters, and whatever lay in wait for us. It concerned me that I didn't even know why I was feeling so worried. I'd been in a lot scarier situations than this and never let it get to me. Could Dr DOA's poison be affecting my mind as well as my body? That would be something to worry about . . . I increased my pace, refusing to be intimidated, even by myself. Perhaps especially by myself. Molly had to hurry to keep up. Our footsteps sounded very loud in the quiet, warning the house that company was coming. I kept looking around for some kind of security, or defences. I even used my Sight briefly, but there was nothing.

The great old house loomed over us as we drew closer. Still not a single light showing in any of its windows, nor any sign of a face looking out.

"Is anyone here going to be glad to see us?" said Molly.

"Almost certainly not," I said. "Black Heir is currently even more than usually annoyed with my family since the organisation lost out on taking control of the Department of Uncanny, when Charles and Emily decided to take it on. Black Heir sees that as a Drood takeover . . ."

"Charles and Emily . . . ," said Molly. "Good people. Are your parents back with your family?"

"Yes, and no," I said. "Which I think says more about my family than it does about my parents. But you can bet Mum and Dad will make sure that Uncanny soon establishes its own identity and agenda, entirely separate from the Droods. Someone has to be the conscience for my family."

"I thought that was you," said Molly.

"I won't always be here," I said.

Molly stopped so abruptly, I had to stop with her. She glared at me, eyes bright with angry tears she refused to shed.

"I can't do this, Eddie! I can't keep on doing this . . . Pretending you're all right, and that everything's going to be all right. I just can't!"

She put up a hand when I tried to answer her, and

turned away. I had to wait, until she had control of herself again.

"I'm sorry," she said finally. "I thought I was stronger than that."

"Me too," I said. "We have to keep going, Molly. It's all we've got."

Molly scowled fiercely at the old house. "There had better be someone in there who can help you, even if it's only with information on Dr DOA, or I will burn the place down around their heads!"

"Be my guest," I said generously.

She let out a brief caw of laughter, and just like that, she was herself again.

"What do you think?" she said. "Would we be better off going in as Shaman Bond and Roxie Hazzard?"

I thought about it, and then shook my head. "No. They'd be too small fry to be allowed in. Black Heir might be happy to make deals with Shaman or Roxie, in the street or in the clubs, but they'd never be invited into Headquarters. Black Heir would never trust a pair of rogues like Shaman and Roxie with access to its secrets. Its people will let me in as Eddie, because they'll be afraid of upsetting my family. And they'll let you in as Molly Metcalf, because they'd be afraid of upsetting you." I smiled. "That's always been the best way to deal with Black Heir, from a position of power, and fear. Keeps the organisation respectful . . . and less likely to plunge an alien knife into our backs."

We finally came to a halt before the front door; a huge slab of dark-stained wood, with no name or number, no bell or knocker, not even a letter box. Some doors are there just to keep people out.

"Not exactly welcoming," said Molly.

"I think that's the point," I said. "You don't put your Headquarters on top of a hill in the middle of nowhere, unless you really don't want to be bothered."

I banged on the door with my fist. The sound was

flat and muffled, as though the heavy wood was soaking up the vibrations. I felt like kicking the door, but restrained myself. Dignity at all times. After a lengthy pause, the door swung slowly back, without even the faintest of creakings from the hinges. Standing in the doorway was an old man in a shabby black suit who looked like he had answered an ad for *wrinkled retainer*. He stared flatly at Molly and me, volunteering nothing. He might have been tall once, but age had stooped him right over. He was almost unhealthily thin, so that his suit hung loosely around him, with nearly enough room in there for someone else. His bald head was graced with just a few flyaway grey hairs, and his heavily lined face was punctuated by a beak of a nose and tightly pursed lips. As though the whole world had left a bad taste in his mouth. But there was still a spark in his deep-set eyes. He looked like a sudden breath of wind might blow him away, yet there was something in the way he blocked the doorway that suggested he might still prove hard to move, if he put his mind to it.

"Yes?" he said, in a way that made it clear he didn't expect anything good to come from the answer.

"I'm Eddie Drood," I said. "This is Molly Metcalf."

"They're gone," he said immediately. "Black Heir. Packed up everything and moved to the new Headquarters, in London. No one here now. I'm all that's left. The Caretaker." And then he stopped, and smiled suddenly. It changed his whole face and demeanour. There was mischief in that smile, and a hint of old secrets faithfully kept. He tapped the side of his nose meaningfully with one finger, as though inviting us to consider the implications of what he'd just said. "It might not have got the Department of Uncanny, like the organisation had been expecting, but it did get new Government funding, and an extended remit to operate, until Uncanny is up and running again. Black Heir is going to be very busy. For as long as it can get away with."

I looked to Molly. "While the cat's preoccupied, the packrats will steal everything that isn't nailed down. And when it is, they'll steal the nails too. You can also bet Black Heir will grab as much new territory as it can, which it won't want to give up."

"It's going to be a problem, isn't it?" said Molly.

"Of course," I said. "That's why the Government did this. Stirring things . . ." I smiled coldly. "But once my parents have got Uncanny going, they won't take any nonsense from the likes of Black Heir."

And then I stopped. I'd run out of things to say. I hadn't realised how many hopes I'd pinned on Black Heir's being here, so I could question its people about Dr DOA. I'd been sure they'd know something, and now there wasn't even anyone to talk to. I'd come all this way for nothing. An empty trail, and a dead end. I was lost for anything to say or do. I realised the Caretaker was still looking at me.

"Might as well take a look around, while we're here," I said with a confidence I didn't feel. "See if they left anything useful behind. Bound to be something . . ."

Molly nodded and smiled determinedly. She could sense my mood, and was trying hard to be cheerful and supportive. It was a brave effort.

"Bound to be!" she said.

"You're welcome to come in, I suppose," said the Caretaker. "But there's nothing here. They took everything that mattered with them."

"But not you," I said.

"Someone has to do the dusting," said the Caretaker. "And answer the door to unexpected visitors. Come in . . . Watch your feet! I've just cleaned in here."

Once inside, he gestured for us to move on down the dark, shadowy hall while he closed the front door. Given his age, and the obvious weight of the door, I was surprised he could move it. I was ready to give him a hand, but he managed easily enough. Hidden counter-weights, probably. I half expected him to creak more than the door did. Only a handful of light bulbs still glowed in the chandelier hanging overhead, and the flat yellow light barely reached from one end of the hall to the other. The long wood-panelled walls looked like they'd been stripped clean, with patches to show where pictures had hung until very recently. No furniture, no fixtures or fittings, but there were a great many scratch and scuff marks on the bare wooden floorboards, to show where heavy things had been moved across them on their way to the front door.

"Damn . . . ," said Molly. "They even took the carpets."

"Oh, there used to be a lot of stuff here," said the Caretaker. "You could hardly move for interesting items. Used to be a whole row of standing suits of armour, right there. Nothing a human being could get into, but very decorative. And glass display cases, crammed full of alien flotsam and jetsam. Their equivalent of scrimshaw. All gone now. Black Heir never likes to give up on anything it owns. Or thinks it might be able to sell one day. It took everything but my memories."

"You know Black Heir is going to shut this place down, sooner or later," I said. "Do you have somewhere to go?"

"Bless you, sir," said the Caretaker. "Black Heir will never sell this place! Blow it up, maybe . . . Far too many secrets, and far too many weird things that the world never got to hear about. As long as I'm here, its people won't do anything." He tapped the side of his nose again, just a bit roguishly. "They know better than to bother me. This is my home."

"Do you have a name, Caretaker?" said Molly.

"Oh yes, miss." And then he turned away, hobbling proudly down the hall like it was his own private kingdom. "You're welcome to the run of the place," he said, not even glancing back over his shoulder. "There're still a few things of interest left, as long as you're not too choosy. All the internal security measures have been shut down. I think."

He turned slowly to look back, and gave Molly and me a perfectly unpleasant smile before wandering off down the hall. His shoulders were shaking slightly, as though he were giggling to himself. Molly looked at me.

"After you," I said.

We took our time, walking around the ground floor. Nothing but empty rooms now, just dimly lit spaces, and even more shadows. A few old-fashioned fireplaces without even any ash in them, and bare floorboards that creaked complainingly under our feet. The air was flat and stale, as though the windows hadn't been opened in a long time.

"Notice something?" said Molly. "No dust, no cobwebs, not even a trace of dirt or grime. Even the windows look to have been cleaned recently. I'll say this for the Caretaker; he keeps the place spotless."

"Don't suppose he's got anything else to do," I said. "I hope his own quarters are a bit more comfortable."

"Is it worth asking him about Dr DOA, do you think?"

"He's just the Caretaker," I said. "I doubt Black Heir's people told him anything they didn't have to."

We tramped up the bare wooden steps of the staircase to the next floor, but it was just more empty rooms, only darker because of the closed wooden shutters. Our footsteps echoed loudly. It felt like walking round an old deserted cemetery.

"Do you want to go up, and take a look at the attic?" I asked Molly. "I'll hold your hand."

"If there'd been anything there worth looking at, they would have taken it," said Molly. "Or buried it out back. I'm surprised they didn't rip up the floorboards and take them as well."

"The people here didn't want to leave any trace of themselves behind," I said. "Nothing to show what they did here; nothing that could be used against them."

Molly nodded absently as she looked up and down the empty landing. "You know, this old house reminds me of Monkton Manse on Trammell Island. Where I lived with my parents, before they were murdered. I never liked it. Another house with too much history and that no one ever loved."

"Don't," I said. "You'll get me started on Drood Hall."

"Do we even know anyone who had a happy childhood?" said Molly.

"Give me time," I said. "I'll think about it."

We went back down to the ground floor, making as much noise as we could, to drive away any ghosts that might still be lingering. I took another close look at the heavy scrape marks on the hall floor. A lot of really heavy things had been moved through the entrance hall, in something of a hurry, going by the amount of damage to the floorboards.

"I can understand Black Heir wanting to move to London," said Molly. "To take advantage of the situation there before Uncanny can get its feet under the table. . . . but why leave in such a rush? The signs here almost suggest a panic."

"We could be reading too much into this," I said. "I might not study my family's weekly briefing sheets as thoroughly as I should, but if there had been any real trouble here, I'm sure there would have been something about it."

"Whatever happened here, we missed it," said Molly.

"I thought that!" I said. I looked up and down the shadowy hall. "Is it worth wasting any more of our time? I mean, we've seen all there is to see."

"Are you sure we've come to the right place?" said

Molly. "Just because this was Black Heir's official Head-quarters, it doesn't necessarily follow that this is where it kept the good stuff."

"I used to be in charge of the family, remember?" I said. "It was my job to know about places like this. I used to get regular briefings on what went in and out of here. This is definitely the right place!"

"All right!" said Molly. "You know, you've got very testy since you started dying."

"I wonder why," I said.

We shared a small smile.

"If the good stuff isn't here . . . ," I said, "then it must be somewhere else."

"You've been hanging around Monkton Farley too long," said Molly. "You'll be deducing things next." And then she stopped as a thought struck her. "How does Black Heir collect the things it salvages? Does it have field agents? Does it have contacts in the alien communities here on Earth to tell it where to look? Can it track starship landings?"

"I don't know," I said.

"You were in charge of the family!" said Molly. "It was your job to know things!"

"I knew what I needed to know," I said with great dignity. "I had departments for everything else. They knew things, so I didn't need to. Until I did."

"And here I thought you knew everything . . ."

"I do! Mostly. And when I don't, I fake it."

"Now he tells me." Molly looked to the rear of the hall. "When in doubt . . . try the cellar. That's where all the really interesting and disturbing things always are, in deserted, spooky old houses."

"There'll be rats," I said. "I hate rats. And spiders."

"I'll hold your hand," said Molly.

We searched the whole of the ground floor, but couldn't find any way down. I was ready to call the Caretaker back, when Molly gave a sudden sharp cry of triumph and pointed at one section of a wall. Like a hunting dog that's just spotted prey lurking in the undergrowth. I leaned in close and discovered quite a large door cunningly concealed in the woodwork.

"I'm impressed," I said. "You have keen eyes, to go with your innately suspicious nature."

"I spent a lot of time looking for hidden doors and secret panels in the walls of Monkton Manse, back when I was a kid," said Molly. "It was something to do while the grown-ups were busy plotting terrorist outrages and violent insurrection. I learned to recognise the signs. Things that don't quite fit, two different kinds of wood that don't belong together, and the fact that if you actually use your eyes, you can see the outline of a bloody big door!"

She pushed hard against the concealed door, but it didn't want to move. I briefly armoured up one arm, and gave the door a hard shove. It jerked back a good couple of feet, revealing nothing but darkness. A strange, unpleasant smell wafted out. I coughed a few times, and Molly wrinkled her nose.

"What is that?" she said.

"Beats the hell out of me," I said. "I've never smelled anything like that before, and I have smelled some pretty weird things in my time."

"I won't ask," said Molly.

"Best not to," I agreed. "Not a good sign, though . . ."

"We're looking for things not of this earth," said Molly. "A smell even you don't recognise is probably a really good sign."

I reached through the opening and ran my fingers across a bare stone wall until I found the light switch. I tried it, without much hope, but a fierce light immediately snapped on, illuminating a set of rough stone steps descending farther down than I could follow. I squeezed through the gap, onto the top step. That strange, unpleasant smell was even stronger. Molly quickly squeezed in beside me and peered down the long stairway.

"That's a hell of a lot of light bulbs that they didn't take with them."

"They must be planning to come back, for whatever's down there," I said. "Which means it has to be worth taking a look at."

"Told you," said Molly. She shot me a mischievous glance. "If you don't mind the rats, and the spiders."

"You kick the rats; I'll stamp on the spiders."

"I'm calling the RSPCA on you."

I started down the stone stairs. There wasn't any railing, and the rough steps weren't wide enough for the two of us to walk down side by side, so Molly settled for crowding my back and peering over my shoulder. I expected the air to grow colder as we descended into the depths, but instead it felt increasingly unpleasantly warm. A damp, sweaty heat that reminded me uncomfortably of a greenhouse, where living things are forced into growth against their will. It didn't take long before we'd gone down farther than the house went up, with no end in sight. I had to wonder whether this could be the real Black Heir repository. The part of the iceberg that mattered.

Some time later we reached the bottom and found our way completely blocked by a solid steel door. The gleaming metal slab had no details, no markings, and no handle. Just a single and very singular lock, set flush with the metal. I didn't even want to think how they'd got a slab of steel this big down the narrow steps. I leaned in for a closer look at the lock. I'd never seen anything like it, and I know locks. Molly, both hands on my shoulders, was peering past me. The mechanism boasted a number of flickering lights, and there was something off, something wrong and maybe even disturbing, about those lights.

"That is not normal," said Molly. "I know locks. I mean, really know them, and I've never seen anything like that."

"Probably alien," I said. "Typical of Black Heir. Hide away all the good stuff where no one else can get at it. Maybe some of it was so big, it couldn't be moved without drawing attention to itself, so it's still there. And that's why the Caretaker was so sure Black Heir would never sell the house."

"We have to get in there and take a look," said Molly. "I mean, it's practically our duty."

"When you're right, you're right," I said.

"Damned right," said Molly.

I armoured up my right hand, and sent a series of golden filaments sneaking into the lock, to work out its secrets and open it up. But the lock's workings were so complicated, and so alien, my armour couldn't seem to make any sense of them. I tried to see the insides of the lock through my armour, but it was like looking into a series of distorted fairground mirrors. In the end, I just gave up and pulled the filaments back into my glove.

"That," I said, "has never happened to me before."

"I'll bet you say that to all the girls," said Molly.

I gave her a look. "You think you can do better?"

Molly sniffed at the lock. "If I had my magics, I'd be making that thing sit up and beg by now."

"How long before you recharge?" I said.

"I am not a battery! It'll take as long as it takes."

"Now who's getting testy?" I said.

"Don't push your luck, Drood."

I armoured down my hand, and retrieved the Merlin Glass from its pocket dimension. The silver-backed mirror settled comfortably into my hand, showing me my own scowling reflection. Molly put a gentle hand on my arm.

"You sure this is a good idea, Eddie?"

"No," I said. "But I didn't come this far to be beaten by a locked door."

I tried to get the Merlin Glass to show me a view of what lay on the other side of the door, but the Glass refused to cooperate. It stubbornly remained just a mirror, showing me nothing but myself. I tried to shake it out to Door size, so it could transport us past the locked door, but it stayed the same size no matter how hard I shook it. In the end, I lost my temper and went to smash the Glass against the door. Molly cried out and grabbed my arm with both hands, stopping the mirror just a few inches short of the door. I tried to pull free, but she wouldn't let me. I started to shout at her, and she stopped me with a serious look.

"This is Merlin's work, remember? Who knows what breaking the Glass might let loose?"

I went cold all over as I realised what I'd almost done. I stopped fighting Molly, and she slowly let go of my arm. Watching me closely, in case I lost control again. I breathed steadily, trying to slow my racing heart. What the hell had I been thinking? I never lose my temper that easily; I just don't. All Droods are trained from an early age, in all the rigours of self-control. Because our armour can kill with the slightest thoughtless act. I felt like I'd just had a really narrow escape, as though Molly had pulled me back from the edge of an extremely long drop. I nodded shakily to her.

"Thanks."

"Eddie? What just happened? That wasn't like you."

"I don't know," I said. "Maybe I got too close to the alien tech. Maybe the Glass messed with my head. And maybe . . . Dr DOA's poison isn't just a threat to my body." I smiled humourlessly. "Like we don't have enough problems. If I start losing control, Molly, losing my mind . . . you have to get me home. Whatever it takes. My family has protocols in place to deal with

Droods who can't control themselves, and their armour."

"I often wondered what happens to a Drood with Alzheimer's," said Molly, trying for a light touch and failing.

"We put them to sleep," I said flatly. "It's the kindest way. For them and for us."

"What?" Molly stepped back from me. She looked genuinely shocked. "You kill them? Why not just take their torcs away?"

"Because they wouldn't cooperate. And taking the torc by force would kill them anyway," I said. "God knows how many I killed when I took my family's torcs away the first time. I never asked, and the Matriarch was kind enough never to tell me."

"Eddie . . . I never knew. You never told me . . ."

"It's not something we talk about. But we all know the risks. We know our duty, to the family and the world. A Drood in his armour is scary enough when he knows what he's doing. A mad or wandering mind, in Drood armour . . . doesn't bear thinking about."

"I can't take you back to your family so your relatives can just put you to sleep!"

I looked at her steadily. "If I get to that stage, it would be the last kindness you could do for me."

"I won't do that, Eddie. I can't."

"Yes you can," I said. "And you will. Because you know all the alternatives would be worse."

I slipped the Merlin Glass carefully back into my pocket dimension, armoured up, and hit the steel door as hard as I could. I had a lot of frustration in me, and I put everything I had into that punch. My golden fist slammed to a halt, jarring my shoulder, and the steel door sounded loudly, like a struck bell. But when I brought back my hand, I'd barely dented the metal. I hit it again and again, hammering away at the steel slab until it jumped and shuddered in its frame. The metal dented and even buckled in places, but the steel wouldn't break and the door wouldn't budge. In the end, I was forced to stop, and just stood there, breathing hard.

"That is not steel," I said after a while. "I've ripped steel like paper with my armoured hands. This is just something that's been made to look like steel. As alien as the lock."

"Maybe the Caretaker's got a key," said Molly.

"If he had, would he tell us?"

I hit the door with my golden shoulder, throwing myself at it again and again. In the end, the door didn't give, but the hinges did. They sheared clean through, and the door tore itself away, blasted inwards to measure its length on the floor beyond. It made a hell of a racket as it landed, and the echoes took a long time to die away. I looked back up the stairs to see if the noise had attracted the Caretaker's attention, but apparently not. I armoured down, and stepped cautiously forward to peer through the new opening.

"Don't you think you should keep your armour on?" Molly said tentatively.

"No telling what its presence might trigger once we get in there," I said. "God alone knows what kind of booby traps Black Heir will have left in place. I can always call it back in an emergency."

"Famous last words," said Molly.

I stepped cautiously through the doorway, and Molly was right behind me.

Lights slammed on the moment we entered. I froze where I was, but nothing else happened. Just automatic systems, triggered by our entrance. Molly eased in beside me.

"Where are the lights coming from?"

"All around," I said. "Everywhere . . ."

"There's something wrong with this light, Eddie. It's like looking at everything through dirty water."

"Maybe whatever they've got here needs alien light."

I moved slowly forward. As my eyes adapted to the fierce lights, I realised the open space before us was much bigger than it had any right to be. It was huge, massive. At first I thought we'd entered some giant cavern, hollowed out of the heart of the hill . . . but the curving walls and high ceiling were both made from the same strange metal. Nothing I'd ever seen before. It had a dull purple-green sheen, actually uncomfortable to human eyes. I moved forward very cautiously, refusing to let Molly hurry me.

We'd emerged along a narrow extended walkway, attached to the far wall on one side, and just a frighteningly long drop on the other. Weird machinery bulged out of the metal wall. It was made up of sweeping organic curves, melding and even melting into one another. As though someone had turned up the heat at the last moment. Weird lights flared and subsided inside them. There was a constant sense of being watched, by unseen, unfriendly eyes.

Some of the machines were barely waist high; others towered high above us. I had no idea what any of them were, or what they were for. Nothing I was looking at made any sense. There were things like stalagmites and stalactites; silicon coral rising up and hanging down, streaked with uneasy colours and deeply etched with what might have been circuits, or instructions, or something else entirely. Strange structures made out of metal rods twisted and turned around one another, in patterns it hurt my mind to look at. Shapes that seemed to slide away from my gaze, resisting interpretation. And more, still more . . .

It was like the places we walk through in dreams, packed with things beyond understanding, full of awful significance. The whole setting seemed more and more dreamlike the farther I ventured into it. But was this my dream, or an alien's? I felt lost, disorientated, divorced from the world I knew and understood.

"You know what this is, don't you?" Molly said quietly. "What this has to be?"

"We're moving through the remains of a crashed alien starship," I said quietly. "The house must have been built over the crash site to conceal it."

"How long ago?"

"God knows."

"Is it safe to go on?" said Molly.

"There can't be anything too dangerous down here," I said, trying hard to convince myself. "Black Heir's people would have shut down anything that posed a threat, so they could work here safely."

"This is all just so . . . fascinating," Molly said breathlessly. "Wonderful . . . I've never been inside a real alien spaceship before."

"Not many have," I said. "Despite what you hear on chat shows."

Molly reached out a hand to touch something that sparkled invitingly. I moved quickly to intercept her hand.

"Don't touch anything!"

"Why not?" Molly said immediately. "You said it was safe!"

"If you know what you're doing," I said.

"And you do?"

"You'll notice I'm not touching anything," I said.

"Where's the fun in that?" said Molly. She sniffed disdainfully, but kept her hands to herself as she looked around. "Do you recognise anything? Like what species would have a ship like this?"

"Beats the hell out of me," I said. "I really should have paid more attention in class when they were teaching us about aliens."

"How could you be bored by aliens?"

"You didn't know our teacher." I craned my head right back, looking up and out to try to get some sense of the scale of the ship. "I'll have to contact the family to have a proper investigative team sent in. If we haven't encountered this species before . . ."

"Aren't you sure?"

"I'm not as sure about a lot of things as I was before I came in here," I said. "Something about this structure, this technology, interferes with human thinking. Undermines it. We don't belong here."

"It feels like we're not on Earth any longer," said Molly. "Like none of the usual rules apply here."

"Wouldn't surprise me," I said. "That's aliens for you."

"Look at the size of this ship . . . It's huge! You could throw cathedrals around in here. How could anything this big crash on Earth, and no one notice?"

"Really good shields?" I shrugged. "It depends on how long ago it was. It's always possible something really important was happening, and my family got distracted. It does happen. We can't watch everything."

"I always thought being inside an alien ship would be . . . inspiring," Molly said slowly. "Or frightening. But I can't seem to get a feel for any of this. It's all just too . . . different, for anything I feel to have any meaning. I don't know what to make of any of this."

"A common reaction," I said. "I'd like to say you get over it, but . . . aliens are never what you expect. That's sort of the point."

I stood on the edge of the walkway and looked down. The immense open space just dropped away, beyond any point I could see. Not because it was dark, but because it was just so far. The buried starship consisted of level upon level, plunging away into the earth, far beyond any human scale. But here and there, very human-looking ladders had been set in place to connect the various levels. All the way down, into the depths. Black Heir's work, so its people could get around. Like insects crawling through some great and intricate clockwork mechanism.

Too small even to make out the shape of the pieces, let alone understand the overall purpose.

I went over to the nearest ladder, grabbed hold of the top, and gave it a good tug. It seemed solid and sturdy enough.

"What's holding that ladder in place?" Molly said dubiously.

"Looks to me like it's been glued," I said. "Maybe nothing else would take . . ."

"Glued? Are you kidding me?" Molly said loudly. "I'm not trusting myself to superglue!"

"It's probably not any earthly glue," I said.

"Is that supposed to reassure me?"

"Apparently not. Look, I'll go first."

"Damned right you will," said Molly. "You've got armour. You'll probably bounce."

I climbed down the first few rungs, stopped, and bounced up and down a few times. "See? Perfectly safe."

"This had better be worth it," Molly growled. And scrambled down after me, light as a feather.

I went down two more levels, just to see if there was any difference, but it all appeared the same. Weird technology, disturbing sights, and enigmatic vistas. I looked over the edge again and couldn't see any point in going farther. Just more and more levels, with no end in sight. And I didn't want to get too far from the entry point, and our only way out. Molly peered into the depths.

"Do you suppose the engines are still down there? Somewhere?"

"I doubt even Black Heir has the expertise to safely remove an alien stardrive," I said. "More likely it would sell the entire ship, after stripping it of everything it thought there was a market for, and then the engine would be part of the deal for the ship."

"You sound like you've had some experience of this," said Molly.

"My family has acquired its fair share of alien tech," I said. "Our Armourers can't invent everything we need. And we have to keep up with everyone else."

I pulled armour out of my torc to make a face mask so I could use its augmented Sight to study the deepest parts of the ship. But something in the depths turned my gaze away, even when I tried infrared and ultraviolet. I sent the armour back into the torc. Molly punched my arm.

"Next time, give me some warning! That expressionless face freaks me out."

"That's sort of the point," I said, rubbing my arm. "Any of your magics come back yet? Anything that might help?"

"No. Just a few tingles. I've been working it hard today. And stop asking me! You can't hurry it. I'll tell you when I've got something!"

"Don't shout at me when I'm dying," I said. "I feel very strongly that I should be excused shouting."

"Okay," said Molly. "You're taking advantage now."

We shared a smile.

I moved along the new level, looking closely at everything and keeping my hands to myself. Molly moved along with me, unusually quiet.

"There are gaps here," she said finally. "In between the tech. What could make gaps like that?"

"Black Heir," I said. "See the tool marks? Human tools. Things have been removed . . ."

"Salvage," said Molly. "Buried treasure."

"Black Heir's people kept the existence of this ship to themselves," I said, "because they didn't want to share."

"No wonder they didn't want to sell the house."

"But the Caretaker did talk about Black Heir being ready to blow it up . . . You think he knows about this?"

"He's the Caretaker," said Molly. "Who knows what he knows."

We finally came to a row of tall transparent tubes,

each one big enough to hold two or three people. It was full of a strange glow that seemed to swirl slowly, like a fog made of light. Looking directly at it was actually painful, but when I concentrated, I could just make out a dark form in each tube, half-concealed in the light. What I could see made me glad I couldn't see more. They were all twice the size of anything human, ugly and distorted, without even a nod to human ideas of symmetry or aesthetics. Alien. Not of this earth. The fierce light seemed to curl protectively around the dark shapes.

"Damn," said Molly. "Look at the teeth on that. Have you ever seen a species like this before? Aliens aren't my field. I've always been more into demons."

"I had noticed," I said. "No, I've never seen anything like this. They look . . . seriously dangerous. But you never can tell, with aliens. Beauty is in the sense organs of the beholder."

"Don't get too close!" said Molly as I leaned in for a better look.

"It's all right," I said. "These are stasis tubes. To protect and preserve the bodies."

"Bodies?" said Molly. "They're dead? Are you sure?"

"I seem to feel it," I said slowly. "Can't you feel it?"

Molly shook her head uneasily. "Maybe."

"Dead so long, they're almost mummified, despite everything the tubes could do to preserve them," I said. "The original crew. Killed in the crash, I would think."

"Not by Black Heir?"

"No. The bodies have been here too long for that. The ship was here before the house."

"So how did Black Heir's people find out about the ship?" said Molly.

"Good question," I said. "Someone must have told them. I'm going to have to talk to my family about this. It would appear someone has been keeping secrets from us, and we can't have that. Secrets are our business, and we don't like competitors."

I knelt down to study the bottom of the tube. A ring of what might have been controls surrounded the base, but they were nothing I could understand.

"Careful, Eddie," said Molly.

"Don't worry," I said. "It's not like I could wake them up. They've been dead for a very long time."

"I can't believe I'm having to be the sensible one," said Molly.

"You'll get over it," I said. I stood up again. "I think the crew members were in these tubes when the ship came down, to protect them, but there must have been a massive systems failure on impact. I don't think they ever got to wake up. Those who weren't killed outright by the crash just slept on until they died. And then the tubes preserved their bodies. They came all this way . . . just to die in their sleep without ever seeing where they'd arrived."

"Is it possible your family does know about this ship?" Molly said carefully. "It oversees Black Heir; you said so yourself."

"Maybe," I said. "We have extensive files on all the alien species currently visiting this planet. More than you'd think. Aliens hang around the earth like winos outside a bar. And for much the same reasons . . . Just because I don't recognise this particular species doesn't mean no one in my family would. Specialist departments, remember? My family is responsible for overseeing most of the Pacts and Agreements that keep the various alien species from misbehaving while they're here."

"Hold it again," said Molly. "Who set up these Pacts and Agreements in the first place?"

"The Organisation," I said.

"Never heard of them," said Molly.

"Not many have," I said. "And that's the way they like it. The Droods aren't the only really secret agents. The point is, we're supposed to be kept informed about all crash sites so we can keep an eye on them. Remember the group that Black Heir replaced, and what they got up to? If Black Heir's people have been keeping all this to themselves, so they could be sure of exclusive salvage rights, they must have been pretty confident that no one else knew about it."

A transparent tube slammed down from up above, so fast it seemed to just appear around Molly. Neither of us had time to react. Molly bounced off the inner wall, and then hammered on it with her fists, but she couldn't break it. She spun round and round inside the tube, searching for weak spots, and then she dropped her hands and looked at me desperately. She raised her voice, and it came to me quite clearly.

"What is this, Eddie?"

"Black Heir must have left some security protocols in place here," I said, trying hard to sound calm. "Something to protect its buried treasure from outsiders. We must have triggered it when we got too close to the tubes."

"Well, why did it grab me and not you?"

"Because I'm a Drood."

I got down on one knee and studied the controls round the base. They were the same as before, and they still didn't make any sense.

"I don't like to touch any of this, in case I make things worse," I said finally.

"How could it be worse?" Molly said loudly. "I'm trapped in here! Just hit something!"

I tried everything, but nothing worked. The system was locked.

Molly swore flatly, and I looked up immediately. The swirling light I'd seen in the other tubes was rising slowly up inside Molly's tube. It had already enveloped her ankles. She kicked out at the eerie glow, and her foot moved jerkily through it, as though encountering resistance. She cried out briefly, and I was quickly up on my feet again.

"Molly? Are you all right?"

"Eddie, my feet have gone numb. I can't feel them. And the numbness is crawling up my legs, along with the light. Damn . . . I'm starting to feel tired. Drowsy."

The tube was trying to preserve her. As it had failed to do with the alien crew. And there was no telling what effect the light would have on her human physiology. I armoured up, yelled for Molly to back away, and then hit the transparent wall with all my strength. My golden fist just skidded away, leaving the tube unmarked. I hit it again and again, putting all my strength into each blow, but I couldn't even crack the material. I stood back again, breathing hard, and Molly looked at me with bleary eyes.

"Have you got anything on you that might help, Molly?" I said loudly.

It was clear she was being affected by the rising light. It was past her knees now, and still climbing. She patted vaguely at her sides with her hands, but couldn't seem to make them work. As though she'd forgotten what they were, or what they were for. Her eyes kept closing, and she had to fight to force them open again.

I forced myself to be calm, so I could think. If my armour couldn't do the job, what else did I have that might? The Armourer's parting gifts. I reached through my armoured side and brought out the plastic boxes I'd been given. They looked very small in my golden palm. The neural inhibitor wasn't any use, and neither was the truth inducer or the chemical nose. I put them back and searched through all my other pockets. And found a left-over portable door, from an old case. A simple black blob that could spread out to make an opening in anything. I slapped the black blob against the tube's outer wall. If I could open up a hole big enough for Molly to step through . . . I let go of the blob and it just fell away, unable to get a hold on the alien material of the tube wall. I watched numbly as it fell to the floor.

Molly sank slowly to her knees, half disappearing

into the swirling, rising light. She slumped forward against the tube, her face pressed against the inner wall. Her features were slack, her eyes closing. I knelt down facing her, and slammed my hands against the outside of the tube, desperate to get her attention.

"Molly!" I shouted. "The wristwatch! Remember the wristwatch the Armourer gave you! It's a time compressor, speeding up the age of everything it touches . . . Molly! Put your watch against the tube and hit the damned button!"

She forced her eyes open, and looked at her left hand. She pressed the watch against the inner wall, and then her eyes closed again. I beat on the wall with both hands, shouting her name again and again. Her other hand rose slowly up out of the churning light, found the watch, and fumbled at it for an agonizingly long moment before she found the button, and held it down. Cracks immediately appeared in the tube wall, shooting off from her arm in all directions, splitting and branching. And still, the tube held. I stood up and hit the tube with all my armoured strength. The tube shattered into a hundred jagged pieces, and I reached in, grabbed Molly, and hauled her out of the wreckage. The glowing light surged up, as though angry at being cheated of its prey. I backed quickly away, hugging Molly to me, and the light faded away and was gone, unable to maintain itself outside the tube.

I had to hold Molly up as her legs dangled uselessly. Her face rested against my golden chest, her eyes closed. I shook her hard, and said her name insistently until she frowned petulantly and tried to push me away with her weak arms.

"Leave me alone. I'm tired. Let me sleep."

"We have to get out of here, Molly. Molly!" I armoured down so she could see my face. "Molly, please . . ."

Her eyes opened, and she looked at me for a long moment. "Eddie . . . ?"

She got her feet under her and stood up straight, shaking her head to clear it. I let go of her, ready to grab hold again if her strength appeared to be giving out. She looked back at the shattered tube, shuddered briefly, and then peered solemnly at her wristwatch.

"It seems . . . the new Armourer does good work."

"Sometimes," I said.

"Oh look; it's stopped."

"You can wind it later," I said patiently. "We have to get out of here, Molly. God knows what other booby traps Black Heir might have put in place."

"Bastards," Molly said succinctly.

A painfully loud siren blasted into life, a sharp mechanical sound that went right through my head. Molly clapped both hands to her ears. The siren cut off, and then repeated itself briefly at regular intervals. Molly lowered her hands and glared about her.

"What the hell is that?"

"Sounds like a timer," I said. "Oh hell, it's a countdown. Remember what the Caretaker said, about Black Heir being ready to blow everything up? He meant the ship! Black Heir would rather see all of this destroyed than risk it falling into someone else's hands. Black Heir's people always were dogs in the manger."

"Have we got time to get out of here?" said Molly.

"What do you think?"

"Bastards! We have to find the bomb and shut it down!"

I looked around. The ship stretched away in every direction, back and forth and up and down. Miles and miles of alien tech, and the bomb could be anywhere.

"It can't be part of the ship," I said, "or it would have gone off when the ship crashed."

"Not if it was an auto-destruct," said Molly, "that the crew never got a chance to use."

"So Black Heir found it and set its own timer in place

so it could control it!" I said. "That means Earth technology, and I can track that!"

I armoured up again and concentrated. My senses are always sharper, clearer, when I'm in my armour. First, I tuned out the siren, and then I boosted my hearing, listening for the timer. And there it was, just three decks down. We were in with a chance. I yelled to Molly to follow me and ran for the nearest ladder. I scrambled down three levels and looked quickly about me. The Earth tech had been attached directly to the gleaming ship wall, sticking out like a sore thumb. I ran over to it and examined the simple mechanism at close range. Molly soon caught up, breathing hard.

"Rip the bloody thing off the wall!"

"No," I said, not looking away. "That could trigger the explosion. Maybe if I press my chest against the bomb, my armour will absorb the explosion . . ."

"You can't risk that!" said Molly. "Even if your armour did soak up the blast, the impact would still probably kill you."

"Molly, I'm dead anyway. No point in both of us dying . . ."

"No! Think of something else!"

Not alien tech. Earth tech . . . I pressed one golden hand carefully against the timer, and sent golden tendrils easing into the mechanism. They found their way in without any problem, and then it was the easiest thing in the world to sever the connections between the timer and the bomb. The siren snapped off, and a blessed silence returned. I pulled the tendrils back out, armoured down, and let out a long sigh of relief. Molly hugged me tightly, pushed me away, and glared about her.

"I am sick to death of this ship, Eddie. Let's get out of here."

"Sounds good to me," I said.

I led the way back to the ladder, and then we both

stopped as we spotted a single transparent tube, standing alone and half-hidden in the shadows. It was broken, and empty. The shattered pieces pointed outwards. This tube had been smashed open from the inside.

"One of them survived," I said. "One of them got out . . ."

"Yes," said the Caretaker, standing behind us.

We both spun round to face him. He wasn't stooped over any more. Standing up straight, studying us thoughtfully with clear, intelligent eyes, he didn't look nearly as old and decrepit as he had before. He smiled gently.

"This is why I stayed. Everyone else was happy to go to London, but I couldn't leave my family. I had the ship's mechanisms make me over into a human form, right after the crash. Standard procedure. And I lived among humans for so long . . . I almost came to think of myself as one. But in the end, I just couldn't go."

"Does Black Heir know who, and what, you are?" I said.

"No," said the Caretaker. "I could never trust Black Heir's people with that kind of knowledge. They just thought of me as the long-standing Caretaker, who came with the house. Perfect camouflage."

"Why did you let them gut your ship?" said Molly.

"It was never going to fly again," said the Caretaker, "and nothing here was any use to me."

"You must know the rest of your crew is dead," I said carefully. "Why have you stayed, all this time?"

"Because the ship's beacon is still working," said the Caretaker. "Signalling to the stars that one of us is still alive. Someday, my people will come looking. To take me home again. Are you going to make me leave here?"

"No," I said. "This place, this ship, still needs a Caretaker."

We left him there, looking around and remembering old times.

"Are you going to tell your family about him?" said Molly.

"I don't think so," I said. "My relatives don't need to know about another beachcombing alien. And it won't be the first secret I've kept from them, after all."

"You old softie," said Molly.

We left the house and trudged back down the dirt path. Night had fallen, and the stars were out. The moon was hidden behind clouds. The cold night air was bracing, even refreshing, after the hothouse environment of the crashed ship. I breathed deeply to clear my head of many things. I went to the cliff edge to look out over the sea again. The sea was still crashing against the black rocks far below, wearing them away moment by moment. The ocean was patient. It had all the time in the world. Molly stood beside me, giving me some space, and some time. The cold wind surged around me, pulling at my clothes like someone impatient for me to be moving on. Like the death that haunted my every moment. I felt cold, and worn down. I looked to Molly. Her concern was clear in her face, but she didn't say anything. I reached out an arm to her, and she moved in close, so she could lean against me while I put my arm around her shoulders. She felt warm and comforting. Someone I could lean on, when my strength gave out.

"Bit of a wasted journey," I said. "No one here to ask about Dr DOA. No new leads to follow. We've wasted our time, and come to the end of the trail. Nothing left but to go back to Drood Hall. And hope they've come up with something."

"There is one place I've been thinking about," Molly said carefully. "Somewhere . . . from my past."

I looked at her. There were undertones in her voice I didn't like. "Where did you have in mind? And why haven't you mentioned it till now?"

"This is from way back in the day, when everyone called me a supernatural terrorist . . ."

"Because you were," I said, briefly amused. "I was there, remember? Trying to stop you."

"The point is," said Molly, "back then, I mixed with some pretty extreme people. Because I needed all the allies and support I could get, in my vendetta against your family. I couldn't afford to be choosy. And I never actually cut my ties with a lot of them. Some were friends, as well as useful allies. I've been out of touch with most of them for ages . . . Partly because I was trying to be a different person; partly because I knew they wouldn't approve of you. But I always kept the lines of communication open . . . just in case. I needed to feel there was somewhere I could go if I ever really upset your family."

"I often feel the same way," I said. "Why do you suppose I maintain so many safe houses?"

"There's a place where we all used to meet," said Molly. "Very secret, and very secure. I'm pretty sure no one but us ever knew about it. If I put the word out, that I need help, I think a lot of the old gang would still turn up. They could help, Eddie! They're all . . . creative people. They might know Dr DOA, or know about him, or know of something that could save you."

"They'd help a Drood?" I said.

"They'll help save the man I love," said Molly. "Or there will be trouble."

I thought about it, and then nodded. Any port in a storm, when the ship is sinking. "How are you going to contact them, with your magics gone?"

She gave me a look, and brought out her cell phone. It was bright pink, with a Hello Kitty design.

"You sure you can get reception here?" I said. "We're a long way from anywhere."

"It's not that kind of phone," said Molly. "This is part of the magical network. And it's always fully charged. Good thing one of us thinks ahead."

She turned the phone on, selected some names from the menu, and spoke into the phone.

"This is Molly. Everyone who hears this, I need help. Big-time. Get back to the old clubhouse, and I'll see you there. Don't keep me waiting."

She shut the phone down and put it away.

"That's it?" I said.

She gave me a superior smile. "Magic gets the job done while Science is still looking for its trousers. And it's not wise to stay on the phone too long. It can attract the wrong kind of attention."

"As opposed to the sort of people you're trying to contact?" I said.

"Don't be a smart-arse," said Molly.

"All right," I said. "Where do we have to go, to meet these old chums of yours? The Wulfshead?"

"Not really their scene," said Molly. "They don't like public places."

"If they're the kind of people I'm starting to remember, that's understandable," I said. "Where would they feel safe?"

"Ah . . . ," said Molly. "You're really not going to like this."

"There hasn't been much about today I have liked," I said. "Go on; surprise me."

"Where can you go," said Molly, "when the whole world will kill you if it can get its hands on you? You go underground. All the way underground. Down a disused coal mine in Wales, the Deep Down Pit. Closed in the Eighties and abandoned, so we moved in and made use of it for ourselves. It's been left untouched and forgotten ever since. I haven't been back in ages. I don't know who will turn up . . . But if anyone knows how to save a life, it's the kind of people who put so much thought into how to take them."

"Thank you," I said.

She glanced back at the old house, which stood silhouetted against the night sky and the stars. "You were wrong, Eddie. It's not the end of the road. It's still a home, to the Caretaker. What more proof do you need that there's still hope?"

I smiled, and nodded. Because she still needed to believe that.

CHAPTER EIGHT

Haunted by the Past

S ome of us are haunted by the past, and some of us are hunted by it. Because it's not just the things we do that define our lives, but also the people whose lives we destroy along the way. Often without even meaning to. But then, no one ever said being the good guy was going to be easy. Or everyone would be doing it.

"So," I said to Molly, trying for a confidence and cheerful attitude I really wasn't feeling, "how do we get to this Deep Down Pit?"

"There is only one way," said Molly. "When it feels like the whole world wants you dead, it helps to have only the one entrance point to worry about. So we blew up all the entrances to the mine, collapsed the main tunnels, and spread nasty rumours about poison gases, rock falls, and hauntings, to keep people away. We did everything short of putting up a large sign, *Entering this mine can cause erectile dysfunction and exploding haemorrhoids.* The only way into the Deep Down Pit is by teleport."

"Like Under the Mountain," I said.

"Exactly. Some techniques are just classic. Unless you know the correct passWords, you can't even find the arrival point."

"You and your friends clearly put a lot of thought into this," I said. "Along with blind terror and blatant paranoia."

"We needed to feel safe," said Molly. "The point is, we're going to have to try the Merlin Glass again."

"Just when you think the day can't get any worse . . . ," I said.

I took the Glass out and held it up before me. Molly leaned in close, and we both studied the hand mirror carefully. When it wanted, the Glass could look remarkably innocent.

"Do you have any idea why sometimes it works and sometimes it just thumbs its nose at you?" said Molly.

"Pure cussedness," I said. "I'm sure if only I could listen in on the right frequency, I could hear it sniggering. But I . . . have had enough." I brought the mirror in close, so my face filled the reflection. I looked more than usually tired and angry, and not at all like someone it would be wise to mess with. "Listen to me, Glass. Either you behave properly this time, or you are going over that cliff edge and into the ocean. Because if I can't trust you to do what I need, when I need you to do it, then I can't see a single reason why I should hang on to you."

"I love it when you get all masterful," said Molly.

"No you don't," I said.

"I was being supportive!"

"Well, assuming that I have just successfully intimidated a Glass made by the most dangerous sorcerer who ever lived, I'm going to need the exact spatial coordinates for the Deep Down Pit's arrival point."

"Don't look at me," said Molly. "I haven't got a clue. All I ever needed were the right passWords, and then my teleport spell would lock on and take me there."

"Okay . . . ," I said. "That should still work. Concentrate on the passWords, and the Glass will pick them out of your head and do the rest for us."

"You're kidding me!" said Molly. "That thing can read minds?" She scowled at the hand mirror suspiciously, and I moved it just a little out of her reach. Molly has always had impulse-control problems.

"Trust me," I said. "That's not even in the top ten of the most disturbing things the Merlin Glass can do."

"Now you tell me . . . ," said Molly.

She frowned, concentrating on security protocols from years past. When both the good guys and the bad guys wanted her dead, often with good reason. My face in the hand mirror disappeared, replaced by an impenetrable darkness. I frowned and moved the Glass back and forth, but the scene it was showing didn't change.

"Really don't like the look of that," I said.

"What else were you expecting to see?" said Molly. "The depths of an old abandoned mine?"

"This just gets better and better," I said. "Any shields and protections in place that we need to worry about?"

"No," said Molly. "We figured they'd just attract attention."

"But what if one of you has talked since then?" I said. "Or was made to talk?"

"Unlikely. But even so . . . we filled most of the tunnels with booby traps, deadfalls, and really unpleasant surprises. We weren't there to enjoy scenic walks, after all; just hole up until the heat died down, or people forgot why they were mad at us. Or decided they needed us to do something for them that no one else could."

"And these booby traps . . ."

"Are probably still in place."

"Better and better . . ."

"Stop complaining and get on with it," Molly said ruthlessly.

I shook the hand mirror out to Door size, and the Glass obeyed without any problems or hesitations. As though keen to demonstrate how cooperative it was being. The Door hung on the air before us, still showing nothing but a darkness deeper than the night. It was like looking into the depths between the stars.

"I'm still not sure about this . . . ," I said.

Molly put a hand on the small of my back and gave me a good hard shove. Sending me stumbling forward, into the dark on the other side of the Door.

I reached out instinctively with both hands as I left the light behind me, but there was nothing there. Just a hard floor under my feet, and a sharp drop in temperature. I shuddered briefly. The air was stale and dusty. Molly barged into me from behind, and I almost cried out.

"Stay put," she said while I was still persuading my heart to start beating again. "I want to make sure we're in the right place."

"I'm not going anywhere," I said with great certainty.

A sullen glow appeared on the air next to me, surrounding Molly's upraised hand. A dim, anaemic glow, not much more than the last gasp of a dying firefly. But enough to show the strain on Molly's face as she dredged up the last scraps of magic left in her.

"Impressive," I said solemnly. Because the last thing she needed was me being considerate.

"Oh shut up," she said. "Make the most of it; it won't last."

She held her hand up as high as it would go, to spread the dim glow around, but it didn't have the strength to travel far. I was just able to make out a medium-sized room, with a bare floor, rough stone walls, and a disturbingly low ceiling. Some uncomfortable-looking furniture, two tall standing cupboards, and some abandoned workstations with dusty papers still scattered across them. A stained and curling poster, still clinging stubbornly to one wall, proclaimed, *Smash the system. Any system.* Heavy shadows surrounded Molly's flickering light as though the room didn't want to be seen too clearly. I turned to the Merlin Glass behind me, and it immediately shrank back down and shot forward to nestle into my hand. I put it away.

"As safe houses go, this had better be very safe," I said.

"Don't start," said Molly.

"Come on; it's not exactly luxurious, is it?"

"It's a hideout, not a holiday home. And it's been abandoned for years. What were you expecting—a rocket base inside a hollowed-out volcano?"

"Just once, it would be nice," I said wistfully. "What was this, originally?"

"Some kind of storeroom, back when this was a working mine," said Molly. "All we cared about was that it was a long way from the surface."

I avoided looking at the low ceiling, because I really didn't want to think about the tons of rock pressing down above us. I moved carefully forward, doing my best not to trip over anything. Not sure what I was looking for, or even if there was anything worth looking for, but trying to show a polite interest. Molly opened one of the cupboards and rooted energetically through the packed shelves, picking things up and throwing them aside, while the light around her upraised hand rose and fell as her concentration wavered.

"What are you looking for?" I said.

"Something I left here," said Molly, not even glancing back at me. "A little insurance, in case I ever had to come back. I've left useful bits and pieces scattered across abandoned hiding places all over the world . . . Ah! Yes!"

She turned around, grinning broadly, and held up a very familiar-looking blood-red stone.

"A vampire jewel!" Molly said triumphantly. "Told you I'd seen one before."

"So you did," I said. "But what use is that going to be? If you're planning to drain some life energy out of me, I feel I should remind you there's a hole in my bucket."

"It's all right, sweetie; I haven't forgotten why we're here. I left some magics stored in this jewel, in case I ever needed a recharge in a hurry."

She closed her hand tightly around the crimson stone, and her other hand blazed with a sudden fierce light. Enough to fill the whole room. Molly whooped loudly, while I had to turn my head away.

"All right, I'm impressed! Now dial it down; you're blinding me!"

She reduced the light to a bearable level, still smirking, and pocketed the vampire jewel while I took another look at our surroundings. They hadn't improved. Still resolutely cheap and shabby, like the kind of boarding house where you just know the water is always going to be cold. And that there will always be something lurking at the bottom of the communal toilet bowl. But I did spot a light switch on the wall beside me. I reached out and threw the switch, and a single hanging light bulb came on, dispensing a surprisingly warm and comfortable glow. Molly and I looked at it, and then at each other. She dismissed her magical light and lowered her hand.

"Have you got your own generator down here?" I said.

"Well, yes, we used to," she said. "But I can't believe it's still working after all these years."

"Unless someone's been maintaining it," I said.

We both nodded slowly as the same thought came to us. I lowered my voice before I spoke again, and Molly moved in close.

"Could there still be somebody here?" I said.

"There shouldn't be," said Molly. "We all abandoned this dump the moment we had our own places. It was only ever intended as a stopgap, because we'd pissed off too many people. There's nothing like being trapped in a confined space alongside people you've got hardly anything in common with, to make you truly desperate to get the hell away from them, first chance you get."

"And there you have summed up my entire relationship with my family," I said.

"But we always swore we'd never tell anyone else about this place," said Molly. "In case we ever needed it again."

"You told me," I said.

"Because I had to!"

"Exactly," I said. "Very old saying: *Three people can keep a secret, if two of them are dead.*"

"And not always then, in our line of work," said Molly.

"Precisely," I said. "Could one of your old associates have come back here? Or sent someone? Does everything in this room look as it should?"

Molly peered around her, taking her time. "It seems . . . just as grim and nasty and soul-destroyingly depressing as it always did. But then, needs must, when the Devil dogs your heels . . ."

There was no sign anyone had been here before us. A thick layer of dust lay over everything, apart from the floor. Which was surprisingly clean. And when I opened up the second cupboard, the shelves were packed with food and drink. In modern packaging, with current sell-by dates. Nothing particularly tempting; mostly generic health foods. High in nutrition, low on taste sensations. Bottled water, not even sparkling. All of it easy to prepare, and long-lasting. Enough to keep one person going for quite a while . . .

"I hadn't heard anyone was here," said Molly, frowning. "But then, I haven't heard anything from most of these people in a long time. Even when we were hiding out together, we kept to ourselves, mostly. Minded our own business. All we ever had in common was our Cause."

I nodded to the poster on the wall. "Smash the System?"

"It's a dirty job," said Molly, "but someone's got to do it."

"Okay," I said. "I think you need to come clean with me, Molly. Who exactly are these old friends of yours that you've been so very careful not to name?"

"Because I knew you wouldn't approve of them! And most of them were never friends; just colleagues. People with a common cause against common enemies. Like your family."

"I need names, Molly. I need to know who or what we might be dealing with here."

"All right! The Ghostly Gunman, the Fury, the Damned . . . people like that."

"Wonderful," I said. "Terrific! A hitman, a supernatural terrorist, and a complete bloody psychopath! These are the people you've called back to help me?"

"When your friends can't help you, who is there left to turn to, except your enemies?" said Molly.

I had to smile, just a little. "All right, that does sound familiar. From the time we first got together, when I was on the run from my family."

"You don't have to trust these people," said Molly. "I don't trust most of them. But some were friends, and some were allies. We learned to stand up for one another, because the whole world was at our back and at our throats. You don't forget connections like that." She stopped, and scowled at the food and drink in the open cupboard. "This can't be one of us. I would have heard!"

"You know what?" I said. "Whoever it is, it's none of our business. If someone wants to hide out here, I say fine. We're not here for them."

"Right!" Molly said brightly. "We can just stop here and wait for the others to join us. I'm sure someone will be able to help you, Eddie. These were all very gifted, very knowledgeable people."

"Who almost certainly won't want to kill me in interesting and appalling ways, because I'm a Drood."

"Don't worry, sweetie. I'll protect you."

We arranged ourselves as best we could on the extremely uncomfortable chairs, and waited. After a while, for want of anything better to do, we fell to discussing old times. It always amazes me how far Molly and I have come, from the people we used to be. The loyal blunt instrument of an ancient family, and a second-generation freedom fighter with a mad-on for the whole world.

"Do you miss the old days, Eddie?"

"When we were fighting on different sides?" I said. "And doing our best to kill each other on a regular basis?"

"Not so much that side of things," said Molly. "I was thinking more about . . . when we were both so sure of what our side was. When you still had faith that everything you did for your family was always going to be right, and I still had faith in the rightness and necessity of my cause. When we both thought we were changing the world for the better, with everything we did."

"When you were out to kill every authority figure in the world? Good or bad."

"I had issues. And anyway, a girl should have ambition." Molly sighed heavily. "Life was so much easier then, for both of us. When we never had to question anything."

"Easier isn't always better," I said.

"Ignorance can be bliss."

"It's still ignorance."

"We did have some good times, though," Molly insisted. "Come on; admit it."

"It was more like a game then," I said. "But still the kind of game where people could get hurt. And not always the people who should get hurt."

"You remember it your way; I'll remember it mine," said Molly. "As far as I'm concerned, they were all great adventures!"

"Yes," I said kindly. "I suppose they were."

Each of us, in our own way, was trying to comfort the other. We sat some more, and waited some more. Talking listlessly about this and that. I shifted uncomfortably on my chair and glanced at my watch.

"Shouldn't some of your friends have turned up by now?"

"Yes," said Molly, frowning. "Somebody should have."

"You want to try contacting them individually, on your special little fairy phone?"

"No," she said. "They'll either turn up, or they won't. You can't talk these people into anything. They're not exactly amenable to reason. Bribery, maybe."

"I could always threaten them with my family," I said. "That usually works."

"Not this bunch," said Molly. "They'll come in spite of your being a Drood, but only because it's me that's asking."

"Could they have arrived somewhere else?" I said. "Just how big is the Deep Down Pit?"

"Big," said Molly. "The tunnels go on for miles. That was the point, so that even if our enemies did break in, they'd never be able to find us. The whole Pit is basically one big maze. But this room was always the designated arrival point. You have to enforce a certain discipline, when people are teleporting in and out."

"But it would be possible for someone to arrive at some other point?" I said.

Molly frowned. "I suppose so. Why?"

"Because I think I just heard someone moving about," I said quietly. "Right outside that door."

We both rose silently from our chairs and moved over to stand by the room's only door. It was so quiet, I could hear Molly breathing. She raised an eyebrow to me, asking if I could still hear anything. I shook my head. I took a careful hold of the door handle, and it turned easily in my grasp; but when I tried to open the door, it was locked. I armoured up and all but tore the door out of its frame as I hauled it open.

Outside, Molly and I moved quickly to stand back to back as we looked up and down the mine tunnel. It was all rough-hewn stone walls and timbered supports, in a tunnel barely wide enough for three men to walk abreast. And a ceiling so low, it made me want to duck my head. Everything looked solid and safe enough, but the only light was what came spilling from the room behind us, and it didn't have the strength to travel far. Both ends of the tunnel were lost in darkness. Anyone could have been watching us from out of that dark. I listened hard, but all I could hear was my own harsh breathing, and Molly's. I armoured down. Molly raised one hand and summoned her magical light again. It pushed the darkness back in both directions, but there was still no sign of anyone. Molly lowered her hand, the light snapped off, and the darkness surged forward again.

There were footprints in the thick layer of dust on the floor. I knelt down to inspect them more closely, and Molly crouched down beside me.

"Clues!" she said happily. "I love it when there're clues!"

"I'm seeing more than one shoe size here," I said. "So, more than one person. Some prints appear to be a lot older than others . . ." I stood up slowly, grimacing at sudden pains in my back and thighs. I must have made a sound, because Molly put out a hand to help me. I let her.

"Lots of footprints here, Molly. For a supposedly abandoned meeting place. You'd better brace yourself."

She batted her eyelids at me flirtatiously. "Why? What did you have in mind?"

"I'm about to put my mask on," I said patiently. "And I don't want you beating me up again."

"I should hit you more often," said Molly. "You're not usually this considerate."

"Don't get used to it."

I masked my face, carefully checked with Molly to make sure she wasn't freaking out, ignored the face she pulled at me, and boosted my senses. I peered into the darkness at both ends of the tunnel, using infrared and ultraviolet, but the empty mine shaft just stretched away into the distance. I focused on my hearing, and all kinds of sounds came clearly to me, from all directions. From above and beyond, as well as in adjoining tunnels. None of what I was hearing sounded in any way human, but things were definitely moving around, in the deep-down tunnels. The slow, steady tread of something impossibly heavy, every footfall crashing down like a jackhammer. Low insect chitterings like a swarming tide of cockroaches. And something that might have been a huge worm, squeezing through a mine shaft that was only just big enough. It's amazing the images your mind can produce to explain the sounds you hear, in a dark tunnel miles underground, far away from sunlight and sanity.

I tried to tune out everything but human sounds, and found I couldn't. It required a skill at fine-tuning that was simply beyond me. I made a mental note to put in some practice later. You never know what you're going to need out in the field. I shut down my enhanced senses, sent the golden face mask back into my torc, and turned to Molly.

"There're a lot of things down here with us that aren't in any way people. And not good things, from the sound of it. Was it always like this?"

"I have no idea what it's like now," said Molly. "I haven't been down here in ages."

Which wasn't, I couldn't help but notice, exactly an answer to my question.

And then we both fell back, as a wild other-earthly light blasted suddenly out of a side tunnel I would have sworn wasn't there just a moment before. A dark human figure came drifting down the tunnel towards us, half-hidden in the dazzle. It was a woman, advancing steadily along the new passageway, her every movement invested with intimidating purpose. A woman with murder on her mind. You learn to recognise things like that, working in the field. If you want to keep on working in the field.

Molly and I stood together, and stood our ground. Facing the light and ready for anything, we thought.

The woman with a killer's eyes finally stepped out of the light and into our tunnel, as though emerging out of a dream and into reality. The entrance disappeared behind her, cutting off the other-worldly light. Molly made a soft, almost shocked sound of recognition. The new arrival was tall and gaunt and no longer young. She would have been good-looking if her face hadn't been deeply carved with harsh lines of pain and loss, rage and resolve. She wore long robes of stark black and white, perhaps chosen to match her pale face and night-dark hair. Her thin-lipped mouth was stretched in a mirthless grin, and she had a cold, dangerous presence, backed up by those dark fanatic's eyes. She looked only at me, ignoring Molly.

"Eddie Drood," the woman said in a voice like a knife cutting into flesh. "You're mine at last. I will kill you for what your family did."

"Angelica?" said Molly.

"Not now, Molly. I'm working."

"Hold everything," said Molly. "You know her, Eddie? You know Angelica Wilde, the Fury?"

"We've met," I said. "Though not what you'd call personally. There was a time the Fury worked alongside my family. In common cause, against common enemies. I was there when she took down the Cannibal Colonels. I was in the background, but I was there."

"So you know what she is," said Molly.

"Only what I read in the files," I said. I looked to Angelica, to see if she wanted to interrupt, but she seemed content to just glare her hatred at me for the moment, so I went on. "A long time ago, Angelica Wilde went to Greece and slept overnight in an old tomb. She had a vision, and came out of that tomb blessed with ancient power. People called her the Fury after that, because of who she was and what she did. Like the old-time relentless pursuers of sinners, she tracked down bad guys the law couldn't touch, and handed out her ideas of justice. Give me that old-time religion . . . She did good work. Until it all went wrong."

"But Angelica used to be one of my closest friends!" said Molly. She couldn't seem to decide which of us she wanted to glare at more. "She brought me here, to the Deep Down Pit, when we'd both made the world too hot for us." She stepped forward, putting herself between me and the Fury, and forcing Angelica to look at her. "I never knew you knew Eddie!"

"Only professionally," I said, wondering just how I'd been put on the defensive.

Angelica Wilde ignored me now, her cold gaze fixed on Molly. "Don't wait for any more of the old gang, Molly. No one else is coming. Nobody trusts you any more. You betrayed the Cause. The Droods murdered your parents, and you ended up sleeping with one!"

"Life is complicated," said Molly. "Love, even more so. If you hate Eddie so much, and I'm still waiting to hear why, exactly, why did you answer my call? You and I, we haven't been that close in years."

"I'm not here for you!" said Angelica. Her mad gaze snapped back to me. "I'm here for the Drood. Who do you think has been organizing all the attacks on him? I sent them! I possessed the Manichean Monk, and Jack a Napes, and the Demon Demoiselle. I filled them with the Fury, took control of them, and sent them to kill you, Eddie Drood!" She laughed at the look on my face. An ugly sound, full of bitter satisfaction. "I watched you fight them, through their eyes; heard them scream as they died . . . and I laughed and laughed. I didn't just make you kill again, Drood; I made you kill innocents."

For a moment I couldn't speak, honestly shocked. "Why? Why would you do that? I barely know you!"

"A chance to kill a weakened, vulnerable Drood? To make your relatives suffer, as they made me suffer? I jumped at the chance!"

"Why?"

"Your family murdered my husband!"

Molly looked at me. "Okay, lost again. I never even knew she was married."

"Armin del Santos," I said.

"Yes," said Angelica, "you remember that name, Drood. The only truly good man I ever knew. Honest, honourable, and completely dedicated to the Cause, so your relatives killed him. Just because they could. It's time for you to die, Eddie; to pay for your family's sins."

She struck a mystical pose, and magical energies snapped into place around her. Molly quickly struck her own pose, surrounding herself with crackling magics. I didn't armour up; I didn't want to escalate things. Or attract attention to myself. The two women glared into each other's faces, making subtle adjustments in their stances and gestures. Barely restrained forces seethed in the narrow tunnel. Two equally matched, equally dangerous women met each other's gaze unflinchingly. Neither of them prepared to back down; both ready to fight to the death over me.

I didn't feel the least bit flattered.

The Fury turned her glare on me and gestured sharply. Dozens of snakes rose up out of the unbroken stone floor, writhing and coiling. Some big enough to crush a man, others small enough to have really nasty neurotoxins in their poison. I grabbed Molly by the arm and hauled her back, out of range. She didn't even look at me. I armoured up, and Angelica's face became even colder.

She stabbed a long finger at me, and the snakes surged forward. Shooting across the stone floor with incredible speed, launching themselves at me before I could even react. The largest specimens wrapped themselves around my legs, while others shot up my armoured frame and snapped into place around my waist and back, my neck and head. They seethed all over me, clamping down like the grip of death itself. And all the time dozens of smaller snakes butted their blunt heads against my armour, striking again and again with fanged mouths.

If I'd been scared of snakes, it would probably have been fairly upsetting, but I've never been bothered by them. Spiders, now, that might have been different. And it wasn't like the snakes could get through my armour. They could crush and constrict all they liked; I barely felt their presence. The ones trying to bite me were lucky they hadn't broken their fangs. I'd already studied the snakes carefully through my mask to make sure they weren't illusions or magical constructs, but they gave every appearance of being just snakes, compelled by the Fury's will. So I just pulled them off me, a few at a time, and threw them as far as I could down the tunnel.

"Eddie, what are you doing?" Molly said from a cautious distance behind me. "Kill the damned things!"

"No," I said. "It's not their fault."

"You always choose the oddest times to get sentimental, Eddie," said Molly.

"You're not bothered by snakes, are you?"

"Maybe just a bit."

"Don't worry," I said. "I'll protect you."

She sniffed loudly, and stabbed one finger at the snakes still crawling all over me. Half of them disappeared, and the others jumped off, hit the ground, and streaked away as fast as they could go. Molly smiled smugly. I turned my featureless golden face to the Fury, who glared defiantly back at me. She held out an open hand, revealing a palm full of small ivory pieces.

"I will show you fear in a handful of teeth," she said. "Behold the Hydra's children . . ."

She scattered them across the floor between us with one sweep of her hand. And everywhere a tooth hit the stony ground, a human skeleton sprang up. More and more of the bony things just appeared out of nowhere, standing straight and tall; a complete collection of bones with nothing connecting them but the will of the Fury. The bones were old and brown, cracked and pitted, as though they'd been in the ground a long time. The grinning skulls turned slowly to orientate on me, fixing me with their dark, empty eye sockets.

"Molly?" I said, not taking my eyes off the skeletons for a moment. "What am I looking at? Exactly?"

"I think . . . those are the remains of all the miners who ever died in this mine," said Molly. "They have that feel about them."

"I'll take your word for it," I said.

More and more appeared, until there were dozens of them; a skeletal army for the Fury, packing the tunnel from wall to wall. Bony feet clattered noisily on the stony ground as they stirred restlessly in place. And then the Fury spoke a single Word, and they all came charging forward at once, smiling their death's-head grins and reaching out for me with clawed, bony fingers. And I had a sudden flashback to being terrified by a similar scene in a movie I saw as a kid, *Jason and the Argonauts*. I grinned behind my golden mask. Time for some payback, and just maybe a little serious therapy.

I launched myself right into the midst of the skeleton army, and hit them so hard with my golden fists that skulls shattered, bones flew on the air, and splintered pieces fell to clatter on the floor. I scattered the skele-

tons with great sweeps of my golden arms, breaking
them up and throwing them this way and that. But the
bones just leapt up off the floor and re-formed themselves, while the ones I threw away came swarming
back, driven on by the Fury. They hit me from every
direction at once, swarming all over me, bony hands
pounding and clawed fingertips scratching harmlessly
across my armour. Just the sound sent hackles rising on
the back of my neck. The skeletons beat at me with their
bony fists, tried to crush me in their skeleton arms, even
tried to bite me with their bared teeth. Doing their best
to drag me down through sheer strength of numbers.

The overwhelming proximity of so much death had
a cold, numbing effect, even past my armour's protection. Everywhere I looked, fleshless faces grinned back
at me. A sudden panic rushed through me as I thought,
Is this what death is? Is this what's waiting for me? And
then, just as quickly, anger rose up to push back the
panic. *Hell with that. I'm not ready to die. Not yet.*

Molly jumped back and forth behind me, blasting
skeletons to pieces with quick mystical gestures. And
the ones she blasted didn't get back together again. But
she could only take out one at a time while her magical
resources were limited, and there were so many of them.
I could hear her language getting worse. And Angelica
Wilde just stood and watched, smiling. Savouring the
thought of my death.

I raised my Sight, and immediately made out a network of shimmering threads hanging on the air and connecting the skeletons to the Fury. I reached out, ignoring
the bony things as they swarmed all over me, and it was
the easiest thing in the world for me to break all the
threads with one swift gesture. But nothing happened.
I was so outraged, I just stood there for a moment. It
should have worked. It worked the last time. It felt like
the universe had cheated. The Fury laughed at me.

"I filled my children with the power of the Fury, with my rage for revenge. Nothing can stop them now but your death, Drood. They'll never stop coming for you, wherever you are. An army that will never grow tired, never give up; an army that can't be killed because it's already dead!"

"Hell with that!" Molly said loudly. "Eddie, the power's not in her; it's in the teeth! The Hydra's teeth!"

She gestured sharply at the ivory pieces lying scattered across the stone floor, and every one of them glowed brightly in the tunnel's gloom. With one great shrug, I threw off the skeletons still hanging on to me, and hurried forward before they could come at me again. I stamped on each glowing tooth as I came to it, crushing them to dust in a moment. The skeletons began snapping out of existence. I danced up and down the tunnel, my golden boots slamming against the stone, and when the last tooth was gone, so was the skeleton army. Angelica Wilde was so mad, she actually stamped her foot on the floor.

"I have other weapons!" she screamed. "Other traps! You'll never see them coming! And you'll never get out of here alive!"

She turned suddenly and ran off down the tunnel, disappearing into the darkness. By the time Molly could generate a handful of light, the Fury was gone. I started after her anyway, ready to pursue her into the dark, but Molly stopped me with a hand on my golden arm.

"No, Eddie. We booby-trapped the hell out of these tunnels back in the day. Remember?"

"I'm in my armour," I said.

"Some of these traps were designed with Droods in mind," she said. "They're seriously powerful and seriously nasty. We all had a lot of enemies in those days, and a lot of time to sit around, thinking up new ways to maim and murder anyone dumb enough to come bother us where we lived. Angelica wants you to go chasing after her, straight into whatever she's got waiting."

"She can't have done much," I said. "She hasn't been here long."

"Time doesn't mean anything where the Fury's concerned," said Molly. "She can bend the whole world to her will. If she stops being mad long enough to concentrate."

"If she was that powerful," I said, "you and I would be dead by now."

"If you weren't a Drood," Molly said steadily, "and I weren't the wild witch of the woods. Our basic natures protect us from the Fury's gods-given abilities. You might say, when they look at us, they recognise one of their own. That's why Angelica has been using snakes and skeletons, and possessing other people."

"She made weapons out of people," I said. "Including one man I genuinely respected. She made me kill innocent bystanders . . ."

"Try not to hold that against her," said Molly. "You've seen her eyes, heard her speak. Losing her husband drove her crazy."

"I know," I said. I armoured down so she could see my face. "She's your friend. We could just leave. She's not why we're here, and if no one else is coming, we have no reason to stay. I feel . . . a certain responsibility for the way she is. You get used to feeling like that, with my family."

"No. We can't do that," said Molly. "She'll never stop trying to kill you. She'd just find more innocents to possess and send after you. What happened with her husband? Why did your family kill him?"

"We didn't," I said. "It's a long story . . ."

"We have time," said Molly. "I need to know, Eddie."

"Armin del Santos called himself the Rage," I said. "Because he hated all forms of authority. Good or bad. As a young man, he went walkabout in Australia and ended up at Ayers Rock. He fell asleep on top, and entered the Dreamtime. The underverse. When he came out again, he was changed, charged with old-time power. Determined to tear the world down, so he could replace it with something better.

"As long as he stuck to the usual targets, my family had no problem with that. He brought down a few Big Bads even my family had been having trouble with. But then he moved on, to radical politics. Fighting the system was one thing; deciding to kill everyone involved in it, no matter what side they were on, was never going to be acceptable."

"So Armin was a supernatural terrorist?" said Molly.

"Nothing more terrifying than a good man who chose to embrace extreme solutions," I said. "And then he met up with Angelica Wilde, and radicalized her."

"The Rage and the Fury," said Molly. "They were made for each other."

"Unfortunately, yes," I said. "And they became far more dangerous together than they'd ever been on their own. Anyway; while she was away, massacring a group of slavers who specialized in abducting children left orphaned by natural disasters . . . the Rage decided to do something really big. His wedding present to her; something big enough to impress the whole world. He was going to destroy the city of London. The politicians, the businesspeople, all the Government apparatus . . . and everyone else along with them. His plan was to open up a new entry point into the Dreamtime, and drop the whole city into it. But it never occurred to him that a door opens both ways. And that the Dreamtime contains a lot of things that have no place in the waking world. My family received a warning from someone or something inside the Dreamtime. Six field agents were sent to shut Armin down, and of course he fought them, every inch of the way."

"Did they really have to kill him, to stop him?" said Molly.

"They didn't kill him!" I said. "I'm not entirely sure they could have. Whoever or whatever came back from the Dreamtime, looking like Armin del Santos, wasn't exactly human any more."

"Human enough to love Angelica," said Molly.

"Yes . . . In the end, the field agents opened up their own entry point, with the help of our unknown friend on the other side, and pushed Armin back into the Dreamtime. To learn a better way."

"So he's not dead?"

"Not necessarily," I said. "Though he's never come back out . . ."

"If you told Angelica this . . ."

"We have, many times! She refuses to believe anything that comes from a Drood."

"She might believe me," said Molly.

"If you can get her to listen," I said. "You're the one who betrayed the Cause, by loving a Drood."

"We have to try, Eddie. She was my friend."

"All right," I said. "Let's go find her. See if we can stop this madness from going any further."

"You'd do that?" said Molly. "After everything she's done?"

"She's not entirely responsible," I said. "I get that. And besides, she's your friend."

Molly placed a gentle hand on my chest, and I put my hand on hers.

"You're a good man, Eddie," Molly said quietly.

"I can be," I said. "For you."

We made our way quietly and cautiously through the interconnecting tunnels of the Deep Down Pit, which were lit only by Molly's magical light. She sent a ball of the stuff bobbing along on the air ahead of us, leaving her free to sweep one hand back and forth before her like a glowing metal detector. Searching out hidden traps and nasty surprises. But much to her surprise, she couldn't find anything. Not because it was so well hidden, but because there wasn't anything there to be found.

"There really were some nasty things hidden away here," she said, scowling so hard, it must have hurt her face. "I put some in place myself. And I discussed the merits of a lot of the others with my friends and colleagues. It was something to do, to pass the time. To see who could be the most extreme, and ingenious, and thoroughly unpleasant. You know what I can be like when I get competitive."

"Yes," I said. "It's not a pretty sight. Don't hit! What sort of things did you come up with?"

"Oh . . . floating transformation curses, invisible trapdoors over infinite drops, concealed teleport pads to send the unwary somewhere unwelcoming. The usual . . ."

"And you didn't tell me about any of this before you brought me down here, because . . . ?"

"Because I knew you'd whine like a little girl! And I never thought I'd be taking you on a guided tour." She stopped suddenly and shook her head. "They're all gone. No trace of a trap or an ambush anywhere. It's like someone just . . . tidied up and removed them all."

"Who would do that?" I said.

"I don't know. They'd have to know where everything was, and the only proper ways to defuse them . . . and we were the only people who knew that."

"It's clear someone else has been living here," I said. "Given the working generator, and the food in the cupboard, maybe they did it so they could move around safely."

"But they'd still have to know how! And none of us ever intended to remove the traps, in case we might need them again!"

"Things change," I said.

We headed deeper into the mine, through endlessly branching tunnels and passageways, walking in the pool of light provided by Molly's floating sphere. With darkness ahead, and darkness behind. The air was starting to get really stale now, and worryingly cold. Now and again I patted my pocket to reassure myself that the Merlin Glass was still there, if we did ever need an emergency route to the surface.

"Are you sure we're going the right way?" I said finally.

"It's been a long time since I was last here," said Molly. "But don't worry; there are signs on the walls only those of us who put them there can see. No one's messed with them. As far as I can tell."

And then she stopped, and looked around, frowning. I looked quickly up and down the tunnel, but couldn't see anything.

"I've been assuming Angelica would follow the old signs, like me," said Molly. "But that side tunnel she appeared from; that was new. She made it. Maybe she doesn't need the signs to navigate . . . Put on your mask, Eddie. Look for signs of Angelica's work."

I set my golden mask in place, and boosted my Sight and hearing as much as I could stand. But the dark was just as dark, and there wasn't a sound anywhere. As though the whole mine were holding its breath. I armoured down, and gave Molly the bad news.

"If someone with Angelica's power wants to stay hidden," I said, "it'll take more than Sight to find her. She could be hiding inside one of the walls, in her own personal tunnel. But to attack us, she'll have to reveal herself."

"So what do you want to do?" said Molly. "Keep going?"

I looked up and down the empty tunnel again. "Maybe we'd do better to set up a secure position, inside heavy-duty protections, and let her come to us. Meet her from a position of strength."

"She's the Fury," said Molly. "Powerful, and crazy.

A bad combination. Do we really want to give her the advantage of surprise as well?"

"Let's keep going," I said.

The tunnels seemed to stretch away ahead forever. My feet ached from slamming endlessly against the stone floor, and my back ached from always having to bend forward so I could avoid banging my head on the low roof. Worrying creaking and groaning came from every side, as though the tunnel supports were seriously considering throwing up their hands and saying, *To hell with it.* Stumbling around in the dark, in pursuit of a crazy woman endowed with godlike abilities, was starting to seem like an increasingly bad idea. There were definite limits on how far I was prepared to go for someone else's friend.

And then we both stopped, and crouched down to examine fresh footprints in the dust on the floor. Too big to be Angelica's, they just started, walked away, and then stopped. As though whoever made them could appear and disappear at will. We straightened up again, and looked carefully around us. Molly brightened her floating light to an almost painful intensity, but it still couldn't illuminate the whole length of the tunnel. There was always a darkness where the light couldn't go.

And I was hearing things again, without needing the extra boost from my mask. Things were moving all around us. Growing louder, and more distinct, the deeper we went. As though they didn't feel the need to stay hidden any longer. Sounds from ahead and behind, from tunnels on the far side of the stone walls, from above and below. Definitely not human sounds. I glanced at Molly, to make sure she was hearing them too, but all of her attention was fixed on the way ahead.

"There's something in this tunnel with us," she said quietly. "I can't see it, but I can feel it."

I actually felt a little relieved to have it confirmed I wasn't just hearing things. I made sure my voice was calm and steady when I answered her.

"Any idea what it might be?"

"There were always things down here with us," Molly said reluctantly. "We never tried to find out what, working on the principle that if we didn't bother them, they wouldn't bother us."

"You must have some idea," I said.

"You dig deep enough," said Molly, "you can find some really old things, sleeping in the earth."

"If it turns out to be a Balrog," I said, "I shall be departing at speed. Try to keep up."

"That's what I'm Tolkien about," said Molly.

We laughed briefly together, and then stopped. There was always the chance something might hear us, and come to see what was making all the noise. Some things you really don't want to disturb, even if you are a Drood and Molly Metcalf.

"It could be something Angelica's called up," said Molly.

"Or something that's been here all along," I said. "What if we've just wandered into something's living room?"

"Do you want to turn back?" said Molly.

"Do you?"

"Definitely considering it," said Molly. "But . . . Angelica was my friend. At a time when I really didn't have many."

"Then we keep going," I said.

"After you," said Molly.

"Ladies first," I said generously.

We didn't get far before the tunnel floor slanted sharply down, plunging even deeper into the earth. The air was getting hard to breathe, and so cold, that both of us were shaking and shuddering. Molly called up an envelope of warm fresh air for us to move in, but almost immediately something really big started moving in a nearby tunnel. Its tread was heavy enough to shake the floor under our feet. Nearby tunnel supports made loud complaining noises, and long streams of dust fell from the ceiling.

"Lose the heat," I said quietly. "It's attracting attention."

The whole tunnel trembled as painfully loud, utterly inhuman sounds burst out of the tunnel ahead. The sound of something hunting that had just caught a scent. The horrible noise went on and on, long after living lungs should have been incapable of sustaining it. And then it just stopped, leaving behind a silence that was somehow worse. Something was listening, to see what we would do.

Molly dismissed the heat and air envelope, and the cold slammed down hard again, hitting me like a blow. Dust in the air scrabbled around inside my throat, but I wouldn't let myself cough. The ominous quiet continued. Molly and I stood close together, not moving. She pulled her magical light back into her hand, so it only just covered the two of us. The dark in the tunnel surged forward, in front and behind, like a predator sensing a weakness. Molly glanced at me and then shut down the light completely. Rather than risk having it draw something to us. The darkness was close, almost suffocating. I reached out in the dark, and Molly's hand clasped down tightly on mine. The silence went on and on, and after a while, Molly cautiously raised her light again.

"Extend the light ahead of us, Molly," I said quietly. "Slowly and carefully."

She nodded quickly, and the light inched forward, a cool, characterless glow that illuminated every inch of the old tunnel, not allowing even the smallest shadow for something to hide in. The light moved on and on, revealing nothing . . . and then stopped abruptly.

"Sorry," said Molly. "That's as far as I go. I'm burning through my magical energies a lot quicker than I expected. And we really don't want to still be here when the light goes out."

"Dim the light back to just us," I said.

She nodded, and the light returned in a series of quick jumps. The darkness ate up the tunnel again, almost hungrily.

"Are there any more energies stored in the vampire jewel?" I said.

"A few," said Molly. "For real emergencies. I don't think this qualifies, just yet. So, do we go on?"

"We go on," I said.

And then Molly gestured urgently, to indicate she'd heard something up ahead. We both stood very still, listening hard, and I heard footsteps. Slow, cautious, entirely human. I murmured in Molly's ear.

"Angelica?"

"Could be," Molly said just as quietly. "It's about bloody time. How do you want to handle this?"

"Talk to her. Reason with her. Hope we don't have to kill her."

"Works for me," said Molly. And then she frowned. "We're going to have to split up, Eddie."

"What?"

"Will you hush!"

"You want to go off on your own, without me?" I said.

"This might not be Angelica," Molly said patiently. "We don't know who else might be down here. We need to come at whoever this is from two different directions, cut them off and trap them between us, with no way out."

"Can you maintain a light around me while you're not here?" I said.

"No."

"I'm really not happy about this."

"Oh come on!" said Molly. "You're not afraid of the dark, are you?"

"Down here?" I said. "Yes! With good reason! There really are bad things in the dark, just waiting for a chance to creep up on me!"

"I won't be far," Molly said soothingly.

"I am really not a happy bunny," I growled. "But, for the purposes of this very cunning trap of yours, I am prepared to be a big brave Drood, and stand alone in the dark as bait in your trap. So you can get behind our prey and chase it to me. But you'd better not be long."

"Got it," said Molly.

She kissed me briefly on the forehead, and set off into the dark. Taking the light with her. The gloom closed in around me, like a great blanket intent on suffocating the life out of me. I armoured up and felt a bit better. I'd fought gods and monsters in my armour, and made them cry like babies. And I was just in the mood to do it again. Bring on your monstrosities from the lower depths, and I would make them rue the day they were spawned.

After a while, I heard footsteps coming my way. Hushed, cautious, very human footsteps. And with them, a flicker of light. I turned on my infrared and braced myself, ready to face the Fury again. But when a glowing crimson figure appeared, it was quite definitely male. Another shape, which I recognised as Molly, moved behind it. She had trapped someone between us, in a tunnel with no side exits. The infrared image drew closer, like a crimson ghost stumbling through the dark. I waited till he was almost upon me, and then made my armour glow fiercely. Hitting him right in the face, like a spotlight. Revealing just an old man, in ragged clothes. He cried out and threw up an arm to shield his face. He turned to run and then stopped as he found Molly right behind him, blocking his way.

He stood frozen in place for a long moment, and then turned reluctantly back to face me. He had unhealthily pale features, under dirty grey hair. His mouth trembled, and his eyes darted back and forth, looking for a way out that wasn't there. Molly raised her glowing hand and filled the tunnel with light. I armoured down, but the old man still looked just as scared. Molly took one look at the old man's face and recoiled with something like shock.

"Ben?" she said. "Is that you? What the hell are you doing down here, after all these years?"

He looked at her, his face blank. His clothes were filthy dirty, and he wasn't in much better shape. His hands were shaking, and not from the cold. His face was heavily lined, and his eyes were worryingly vague, but they slowly came alive as he looked at Molly. He seemed, finally, to know her.

"Molly Metcalf . . ."

"Yes, Ben. It's me. You remember me . . ."

"Care to introduce us?" I said. "Who, exactly, have we caught? And could we perhaps throw him back, because up close, the smell of him is bringing tears to my eyes."

"This is Ben Luger," said Molly. "He used to be part of my old gang." She patted the old man on the arm, as though comforting a nervous dog. "Back in the day, they called him the Ghostly Gunman."

I studied the old man with new interest. I'd heard that name before; knew some of his legend. But I still nodded for Molly to tell the tale, because her voice seemed to calm the old man.

"One of the best-paid political assassins in the business," said Molly. "Ben could teleport into anywhere, drop his target, and never be caught by even the best security. Until finally, inevitably, he was. You never should have gone after Hadleigh Oblivion, Ben. You should have known the Detective Inspectre was way out of your league."

Ben nodded slowly. He'd seemed to come back to himself as he heard Molly recount his life. When he spoke, his voice was harsh and strained, as though he hadn't used it for some time.

"I knew that, Molly. Of course I knew that. But the money was just so good, so tempting. I could have retired on it. I never stood a chance. Hadleigh Oblivion scared the crap out of me . . . and I ran. Ran for my life, and my sanity. And he saw to it that everybody knew. So much for my fearsome reputation . . .

"I ran away from everyone I knew, and from all the people who were suddenly feeling brave enough to come after me, now they didn't have to be scared of my reputation. I ran back to the only place I'd ever felt safe. The Deep Down Pit. I've been here ever since. Hiding. For years . . . I'm not even sure how many. Time seems to pass differently, down here in the dark. When you're on your own . . ."

His face had gone vague again, as though he were musing, remembering. I moved in beside Molly, still careful to give the old derelict plenty of room.

"This old man was part of your group?"

"He's not old, Eddie," Molly said tiredly. "He's the same age as me. Look at what being down here has done to him!"

"Going up against Hadleigh Oblivion probably took its toll as well," I said.

"Ben?" Molly said carefully. "What have you been doing all these years?"

His face snapped back into focus. "Thinking. Repenting. Oblivion opened my eyes, you know. Showed me how wrong I'd been. All the people I killed, all the suffering I caused . . . He made me feel every bit of it. He made me see the truth of my life, and it was a hard lesson. I ran away from the world, and myself, because I didn't want to be able to hurt people any more. I've kept myself busy, exploring the Deep Down Pit and mapping it. There's far more here than we ever suspected, Molly! I shut down all the booby traps so I could move around. And so no one could be hurt by them."

"What is it that lives down here?" I said. "We've been hearing all kinds of things . . ."

"We give each other plenty of room," said Ben, nodding happily. "And they discourage anyone from coming after me."

"We found food stores in the arrival room," said Molly.

"Oh yes," said Ben. "I still have a few friends. They don't visit; I wouldn't want them to. But they teleport in fresh supplies, now and again. When they remember. The rest of the time, I make do."

I didn't like to think about exactly what Ben Luger might find to eat and drink, in the dark, when he had to.

A new fear appeared in Ben's face. He looked ready to bolt or ready to fight us if we tried to stop him.

"Have you come to take me back, to stand trial for all the terrible things I did?"

"We're not here for you, Ben," Molly said gently.

"It's been so many years," I said, "I doubt anyone's still looking for you. Your legend survives, but not much else. You've imprisoned yourself down here for so long, I think you've done your time. We could take you with us when we go, if you want. My family could set up a new identity for you so you could start a new life . . ."

But he was already backing away from me, shaking his head, horrified at the thought of having to leave the safety of the Deep Down Pit. And perhaps even more afraid of a world he would no longer recognise or understand. He pushed past Molly and ran for his life, disappearing back into the comforting dark. Molly didn't try to stop him, so I didn't either.

"It's a hard life, being a supernatural terrorist," Molly said finally. "It breaks as many as it makes."

"And no man runs faster than those pursued by their own demons," I said.

"I'd hate to end up like that," said Molly.

"You won't," I said. "Not while you've still got me."

Her head whipped round sharply. "Did you hear that?"

"Hear what?"

"Something just changed," said Molly. "I felt it. Angelica changed something."

"Would I be correct in assuming that is not good?"

"What do you think?"

"Okay . . . ," I said. "Any idea what, or where?"

"This way," said Molly.

She led me back the way we'd already come. Moving quickly, as though worried it might already be too late to do whatever needed doing.

"We're going back to the arrival room?" I said. "How the hell did she slip in behind us?"

"She always did know these tunnels better than me," said Molly, not looking round.

"Now you tell me," I said.

We hurried down tunnel after tunnel, plunging out of one and into another, until finally Molly crashed to a halt, breathing harshly. I looked quickly round, but couldn't see anything. I was getting really tired of that. Molly pointed to a section of the tunnel wall up ahead. I moved carefully forward, and there in the rough stone was a dimensional Door. I didn't need to put on my mask to sense the fierce dimensional energies surging around the ordinary-looking wooden door, with no frame or hinges. I could feel the limitless possibilities, of all the places it could take me, tingling against my skin like background radiation. A small brass combination lock had been set into the wood of the Door, just where you'd expect a handle, to select the Time/Space coordinates for wherever you wanted to go.

"What the hell is something that powerful doing down here?" said Molly. "And before you ask, yes, I'm sure it wasn't here before. This is new. Angelica's doing."

"The only way to discover the Door's current setting would be to open it," I said. "And I am ready to class that as a really bad idea."

Angelica Wilde appeared, just suddenly standing in the tunnel, from where she faced Molly and me. As though she'd been there all along and we hadn't noticed her because she wouldn't let us. She was smiling that awful cold smile again, reminding me uncomfortably of the death's-head grins on the skeletons she'd sent against us. If anything, she looked even crazier.

"The Door is my bait, my trap," she said. "I knew it would bring you here. To me."

"All you had to do was stand still," said Molly. "We've been looking for you."

"Of course you have!" said Angelica. "You want to kill me. You have to kill me, because you know that's the only way you can stop me from killing Eddie. But I won't go down alone. This Door opens onto the bottom of the North Sea. Just think of all the pressure, all the tons of water, pressed up against the other side of that Door. Ready to flood into this tunnel the moment I open it! Even you and your armour couldn't survive that, Eddie Drood. And don't think you can use your Glass to escape; I'm suppressing it."

"But you'd drown with us!" said Molly.

"It'll be worth it," said the Fury. "To have my revenge at last. You think I want to go on living without my husband?"

"What if I could give him back to you?" I said.

She looked at me. Thrown completely, by the one thing I could say that she wasn't expecting. I moved over to the Door, armoured up my hand, and sent golden tendrils surging into the lock. I entered the access codes for the Dreamtime, which were still fresh in my armour's memory from a recent case I worked with the Soulhunters. The combination lock spun frantically, and then slammed to a halt. I whipped out the golden tendrils, and the Door opened, onto the Dreamtime.

It swung back into the wall, and light blasted out into the mine tunnel. A glorious illumination, like no other light in the world. Older, purer; primordial. Sounds rang out from behind the Door, wild and free, like mountains singing to one another at the dawn of the world. I raised my voice and addressed the Dreamtime.

"Armin del Santos, come out! Your wife is waiting for you."

And out he came, stepping through the Door and into the tunnel, as though it were the most natural thing in the world. A tall, handsome young man, in a checked shirt, blue jeans, and cowboy boots. His face was full of a wonderful calm. He smiled at Angelica, and she tried to smile back as tears ran down her face. She didn't look crazy any more.

"They told me you weren't dead," she said numbly, "but I wouldn't believe them. Oh, my love, my love, you haven't aged a day in all these years . . . And I have. Don't look at me. I'm not the woman you knew."

"That's why I'm here," said Armin. "Come with me, Angel."

Angelica looked into the marvellous light spilling out from beyond the Door, and slowly shook her head. "I can't. I don't belong in a place like that. Not after everything I've done."

"Yes you do," said Armin. "Because of everything you've done. That's the point. The beginning of the world is a new beginning for everyone."

He took her by the hand and led her through the Door, into the Dreamtime. To learn a better way, like him. The Door closed itself behind them. I grabbed the combination lock with my golden hand and ripped it right off the Door so it could never be opened again. From this side.

Molly threw her arms around me and hugged me tightly. "I do love a happy ending!" And then she let go and stepped back, smiling just a little shakily. "Now all we have to do is find one for you."

"That would be nice," I said solemnly.

And that was when a voice spoke to us, from beyond the Door. It didn't sound like anything that belonged in the Dreamtime. A professionally warm and confident voice, like a cold-calling salesman.

"Hello there! Do I have the honour of addressing Roxie Hazzard?"

Molly looked at me.

"Whatever you do, do not say, *Come in,*" I said. "Don't even think it loudly."

Molly put on her Roxie voice, and addressed the Door. "Who the hell are you, and what do you want?"

"Yes, that sounds like Roxie Hazzard," said the Voice. "Word has reached me that you have been trying to locate Dr DOA. I've been trying to contact you for some time to discuss this, but you're very hard to pin down."

"Yeah, well, I get around," said Roxie. "I've been busy. How did you find me here?"

"I didn't," said the Voice. "Someone else did. Now, why are you so keen to talk to Dr DOA?"

"Because I want to hire him," said Roxie.

"And who do you want killed?"

"Molly Metcalf," said Roxie.

"Ambitious," said the Voice. "And expensive. Luckily for you, the Doctor is in. Go to the Hiring Ground in London and ask for the Psychic Surgeon. He'll be there for the next two hours. He can put you in touch with Dr DOA."

The Voice fell silent. Roxie called after him, yelled at him, even kicked the Door, but the Voice was gone.

"Interesting," Molly said finally, in her own voice. "He knew enough to find me here, but he didn't know Roxie is Molly. And the Hiring Ground? That's pretty down-market for someone as supposedly exclusive as Dr DOA."

"Maybe that's the point," I said. "Who'd expect to find someone like him in a place like that? Still; the Psychic Surgeon? That scumbag . . . Do you know him?"

"Not personally," said Molly, "but like a great many people in our line of work, I know of him. Scumbag pretty much sums him up."

"Basically a con man," I said. "Though a lot of his powers are supposed to be the real deal. The man who can cut bad things out of your soul. Molly, this has to be some kind of trap."

"We have to risk it!" said Molly. "Because it's the only lead we've got, and because we've nowhere else to go . . ."

I nodded. "Then it looks like this is a case for Shaman Bond and Roxie Hazzard!"

"Damned right!" said Roxie.

CHAPTER NINE

Hard Times Make for Hard Choices

D r DOA. The man who murdered me. In my sights at last.

After getting sidetracked by so many distractions, it felt good to have a solid lead at last. Assuming nothing else went wrong, of course. I retrieved the Merlin Glass from its pocket dimension and held it out before me. The hand mirror stared innocently back, as though the thought of misbehaving had never even occurred to it. But there was still something about the way my reflection was looking back at me that I really didn't like. It seemed to be smirking rather than smiling, and there was something about the eyes . . . I looked like I knew something I didn't. On an impulse, I pulled several extreme faces, and my reflection duplicated them all perfectly.

"Eddie, what are you doing?" said Molly. "Trying to break it?"

"Just testing," I said.

I looked around, and found Molly had transformed

herself into Roxie Hazzard. The tall muscular redhead in a black leather jacket, with a length of steel chain wrapped around her waist. Every inch a warrior woman. She grinned at me cheerfully, and I nodded back respectfully.

"Yes," I said. "Where we're going, that's the kind of look that will get us answers."

"You negotiate," said Roxie, "and I'll intimidate."

"I can be intimidating," I said.

"Of course you can, dear," said Roxie.

"I'm a Drood!"

"Trust me, I haven't forgotten. It's just that you've been trained, while I have natural talent." She stopped, and looked at me seriously. "We're getting close to Dr DOA, Eddie. I can feel it."

"We've been invited to meet a go-between," I said. "A meeting that will almost certainly turn out to be a trap."

"Then we'll just have to make sure that it's our trap," said Roxie. "Because I have the bit between my teeth, and I am not letting this lead get away from me."

I hefted the Merlin Glass in my hand. "I hate depending on this, when it's so important . . . but I take it you don't have enough magic in you to transport us to the Hiring Ground?"

"I've barely got enough left to teleport us to the surface," said Roxie. "Never mind all the way to London. Physical transport is hard; it takes a lot of power. You're basically slapping the universe in the face to get its attention, telling it you're not where it thinks you are but somewhere else, and then slapping it again if it looks like arguing. You can do that only so many times before the universe starts slapping back."

"I don't know why I ask you questions," I said. "I'm never any happier for knowing the answers."

"What's the best way into the Hiring Ground these days?" Roxie said briskly. "It's been a long time since

I showed my face there, as Molly or Roxie. Is it still a major shithole?"

"I doubt very much that it's changed for the better," I said. "But I haven't been there in ages either. Assuming the old entrance points are still valid . . . I think our best bet would be around the corner from Kings Cross railway station."

Roxie pulled a face. "Not the most salubrious of areas."

"Then Shaman Bond and Roxie Hazzard should fit in nicely," I said. "I'm told parts of the area are very nice these days, thanks to recent regeneration. Mind you, they keep saying that about most of London, and I'm rarely impressed."

"Just being near the Hiring Ground probably lowers the area's tone," said Roxie.

I held the hand mirror out before me. "Give me a view of the Kings Cross area, near the Hiring Ground."

My reflection disappeared immediately, replaced by a bustling scene of London at night. Bright lights and loud traffic, and all kinds of people surging back and forth, hurrying on their way to somewhere important. Every single one of them staring straight ahead, to make it clear they were minding their own business. Taxi drivers leaned constantly on their horns, while big red London buses pulled out in front of everyone and bounced slower-witted cyclists off their heavy sides, just because they could. Trucks weighed down far beyond the legal limits carried the kind of goods you were never going to get a receipt for. And everyone else just tried to stay out of everyone else's way.

"Some years back, I remember watching a BBC documentary about Kings Cross," I said. "They claimed the station area was rife with prostitution and drug trafficking. I used to go through there on a regular basis when I was a London field agent, and I never saw anything. Mind you, I was probably too busy looking for monsters and aliens and the like."

"I suppose that world is a lot like ours," said Roxie. "Unless you know what to look for, you're never going to see it. Two worlds existing side by side, barely touching. Parallel, but separate."

"A lot like our world, and the everyday world," I said.

"Except the hidden world is much more glamorous," said Roxie.

"Well, of course," I said. "We're in it."

I shook the hand mirror out to Door size, and the view became an open window. A breeze blew through from Kings Cross, bringing with it enticing scents from a dozen ethnic restaurants and the smell of massed vehicle emissions. The roar of the traffic almost drowned out the roar of the crowds. I strode through the Door, with Roxie right on my heels. Out of the dark of the Deep Down Pit, and into the darkness of Kings Cross at night. No one noticed our arrival. I shook the Glass down and put it away.

"At least the Glass is behaving itself," said Roxie.

"For now," I said.

Roxie linked her arm through mine, and we set off down the street. People moved quickly to get out of our way, without quite seeming to realise they were doing it. Perhaps because sheep can always sense wolves in their midst. No one looked twice at Roxie's colourful outfit; in this part of London, she was almost dowdy, compared to some of the fashions on display. Sharp suits and pretty frocks; punks and hippies; every subculture you could think of and every fetish under the moon.

"I never knew the leather-and-straps look was so in," I said.

"You need to get out more," said Roxie.

I laughed briefly. "I was always a lot more innocent

than was good for me. For years, I thought BDSM stood for 'Belle Dame sans Merci.'"

"Not a million miles off," said Roxie. "Where are we going, Eddie?"

"Down here," I said.

I took a sudden side turning, and just like that, the whole nature of the area changed. The crowds disappeared, while the general ambience made a rude gesture and lurked in corners. Boarded-up and whitewashed windows to every side, shops that were never open, and shadowy people just standing around for no obvious reason. I walked straight past them as though I belonged there, and they just assumed I did. It's all in the walk. A few people glanced at Roxie, and she glared right back at them. No one looked twice. Wolves can always recognise an alpha predator.

I stopped before an old-fashioned red public telephone box, pressed up against a stained brick wall. The box had seen better days, some forty years ago. The glass panes were cracked or broken, the paintwork was chipped and grubby, and the phone had been ripped out. Some of the locals had been using the box as a toilet. Quite recently. Roxie turned up her nose.

"I thought all these old telephone boxes had been taken away, long ago."

"Most have," I said. "But not this one. Partly because it still serves a purpose, but mostly because it never was on any official list. I doubt there was ever a working phone in the box; it's just protective camouflage."

I pulled open the door, stepped inside, and gestured for Roxie to join me. Together, we filled all of the available space. Roxie wriggled deliberately and gave me a bright smile.

"Okay, now what?"

I gave the back of the box a good hard shove, and it swung open into the brick wall, accessing a great open hall. I stepped into the building beyond, and Roxie hurried after me. I let go of the door, and it swung quietly shut again.

"Welcome to the Hiring Ground," I said.

"That's it?" said Roxie. "No security guards or protections?"

"Getting in is easy," I said. "Getting out again, alive and intact, is something else."

Roxie looked around. "I was right. Still a shithole."

The Hiring Ground was one big open area, with a tall arched ceiling. Packed from wall to wall with booths and stalls and trestle tables, and the occasional expensive commercial stand. People everywhere shouted their wares, while vendors at the booths competed to see who had the loudest sound systems. Crowds of extremely assorted people bustled up and down the narrow aisles, all of them talking at once. The volume was painfully loud, but no one seemed to give a damn. There was a certain grubby vitality to the place, but I didn't care for all the greed and avarice on open display.

"Reminds me of the Nightside," I said.

"No," Roxie said immediately. "The Nightside is all about sin. The Hiring Ground specializes in commerce. Not that sin is excluded, you understand, as long as someone thinks they can make a profit from it. The Hiring Ground is all about money."

"Just remember," I said. "We're not here looking for bargains."

"There's always time for shopping!" Roxie said cheerfully.

"You buy it; you carry it."

The Hiring Ground goes back to Victorian times, though there are stories of earlier venues that go all the way back to the Roman city of Londinium. Unlike the much better-known and far superior Hiring Hall, which I'd visited not long ago on a case involving a plot to steal the Crown Jewels, the Hiring Ground is an altogether more desperate and sinister affair.

The Hiring Hall can boast stands and booths for any number of Governments, Spy Organisations, and important Special Interest Groups. A place to make the kind of deals that matter, with people who matter. The Hiring Hall attracts the upper crust and the upper levels—gods and monsters, rogues and villains, and creatures of the night. All very up-market, and no one ever makes any trouble because of the dozen or so big brass golems standing around the perimeter. Just waiting for a chance to make a nasty example of someone. The Hiring Hall is an ancient market for civilised people.

The Hiring Ground is where you go when you're looking for dirty deeds done cheap and nasty. Neutral ground for mercenaries and adventurers, con men and killers, ghouls and ghosts . . . all of them desperate for a paying gig, and no longer in any position to be choosy about what it might involve.

Grubbily dressed vampires and shabby werewolves thrust flyers for specialized sex clubs into people's hands as they passed. No one ever said no, but no one ever kept them. Blinking on and off like faulty light bulbs, ghosts flickered from stall to stall, looking to hire themselves out with offers of everything from subsidized hauntings to pestering debtors. It's a hard life when you're dead, and your options are limited. Ghouls slouched around, showing their toothy grins, always ready to dispose of an unwanted corpse. Because they'll eat anything, up to and including toxic waste spills. A bunch of alien Greys, in ill-fitting black suits and designer sunglasses, politely indicated their ability to make anyone disappear. Short term or long term.

There were stalls selling very special weapons to kill the kinds of things that shouldn't exist in a sane and rational world. Or specialized burglary tools, for getting in and out of haunted houses. Coats made from the pelts of creatures that don't officially exist. Wines so potent you could get drunk just reading the labels on the bottles. Sex toys for mutant women, surgical tools for operating on alien hybrids, and bodily by-products of the rich and famous (carefully bottled and authenticated, and useful in all manner of unpleasant ways).

Every single bit of it desperately down-market, sleazy, and disreputable; nothing you'd want to brag about buying afterwards. The Hiring Ground is where you go when no one reputable will let you past their doors. Do I really need to tell you that most of what's on display is not what it claims to be? That most of it is going to be faked, adulterated, or a complete con? The Hiring Ground is home to the fraudulent, the forger, and the confidence trickster. Buyer beware, and be sure to count your fingers after you've shaken hands on the deal.

Roxie wrinkled her nose. "I wouldn't have thought it possible, but this place has gone even more down-market. I used to hang out here a lot in my younger days, as Molly and Roxie. When I was still finding my feet in the hidden world. Looking for causes worth fighting, causes that would pay enough for me to live on. Vendetta may satisfy the soul, but it doesn't put a roof over your head or food on the table."

"What kind of jobs did you end up doing?" I said, genuinely curious.

She shrugged. "Mostly strong-arm stuff. Bodyguarding and general security. For the kind of people and places no one else would touch. Overseeing the transport of very special items from one location to another. Helping collectors get their hands on the kinds of things that are never going to appear on the open market, and then keeping them alive afterwards. A lot of it was about keeping people alive, when someone else wanted them dead. Usually with good reason." She stopped, and looked at me directly. "I never killed anyone for pay, if that's what you're asking."

"I wasn't asking," I said.

"The Hiring Ground's got a lot worse, since my day,"

said Roxie. "These crowds have the look of people prepared to do absolutely anything for money."

I had to agree. There was a general air of desperation. Of people who'd fallen so far, or been pushed so far, they were ready to accept any job, any danger, any humiliation, for fear they might never find another opening. Those at several of the larger booths were recruiting mercenary fighters for armies at war in other dimensions. The sides weren't clear, but then, it wasn't the cause that mattered. Just the money. I was astonished to see none of the booths carried the official Seal of the Guild of Mercenaries, guaranteeing proper levels of training and equipment, and a return home afterwards for the survivors. I could remember a time when no one would sign up unless the Seal was there. But now the attitude of the recruiting officers was apparently *If you don't want to do this, someone else will. And you'll miss out. Don't come back whining tomorrow, because we won't be here and neither will the job.*

There were long lines at each of the booths, and no shortage of men and women willing to take some king's shilling. More meat for the grinder.

Those at other booths were looking for paid volunteers to act as test subjects for new drugs, spells, and nonlethal weaponry. Good money but not great, and absolutely no safety guarantees. Take it or leave it. An awful lot of people looked happy enough to take it. No questions asked, apart from *Where do I sign?* and *How soon do I get paid?*

"You know," I said to Roxie, "a good ambulance chaser could clean up around here."

"You really think the Hiring Ground would let a lawyer or a union rep through its doors?" said Roxie.

"When times are hard, the choices get harder," I said. And surprised myself with the bitterness in my voice.

"I'm surprised your family allows a place like this to exist," said Roxie.

"If we did shut it down, another would only spring up somewhere else," I said. "Just as bad, if not worse. At least we know about this one and can keep an eye on it. Just the knowledge that we're watching keeps people from doing anything too extreme."

"Define extreme," said Roxie.

And I didn't have an answer. We moved on past stalls and tables, taking our time so as not to appear in a hurry. Someone would only take advantage. I saw several faces I knew, all of them doing things or agreeing to things that disappointed me. After years of enforced absence, the Pariah Priest was back on the job, looking to sign people up to be possessed for a short period. So that certain angelic and demonic assignments could be carried out on the mortal plain. The removal of the possessing agent was guaranteed, but not the state of the body after the agent was finished with it. Roxie stepped in front of the booth, and glared at the Pariah Priest until he was forced to acknowledge her presence. He scowled right back at her.

"What do you want, you infamous child?"

"Who's doing the possessing?" said Roxie. "Agents for the Light, or the Darkness?"

"What does it matter?" said the Pariah Priest, smiling smugly. "You aren't responsible for anything the agent does with your body; you're just renting it out."

"What about after-effects?" said Roxie. "Having Heaven or Hell camp out in your head is like having the afterlife take a toxic dump in your soul."

"Why do you think the pay's so good?" said the Pariah Priest.

Roxie would have pressed that more, but the long line in front of the booth was growing restless, and she reluctantly stepped aside to leave them to it. You can't help people who don't want to be helped. I spotted a familiar face in the queue.

"Jack Shelter," I said. "You used to have a solid rep as a poltergeist handler. What are you doing here?"

"Might ask you the same thing, Shaman," said Jack. "There's been a real downturn in the building trade. I had to lay all of my people off, until there was no one left to lay off but me."

"But why this?" I said.

"When times are hard, you have to go where the work is," said Jack. "At least the Hiring Ground is hiring. A lot of places aren't."

I moved on, with Roxie a silent unhappy presence at my side. We stopped before another booth, where a platinum blonde beauty wearing hardly anything at all was fronting a concession called Lust from the Dust. Roxie squeezed my arm tightly.

"I know her!" she said. "That's the Chakra Cutie! Used to train girls to weaponize their sexuality. She's one of the old gang I was expecting to meet at the Deep Down Pit."

"Does she know you as Roxie or Molly?" I said.

"Oh yes . . . We go way back."

Roxie planted herself in front of the Chakra Cutie while I listened to the spiel. The Cutie was shilling for a company looking to hire bright young things to channel dead movie stars. So their fans could have sex with them. A new twist to the oldest profession. I leaned in to murmur in Roxie's ear.

"Pardon my ignorance, but . . . this is a con, isn't it?"

"Of course it's a con! They're just looking for young people without much personality of their own, who can be trained to fake it."

"Don't they always?" I said.

The Chakra Cutie finally accepted that Roxie wasn't going anywhere, and cut off her spiel to glare coldly at her.

"What do you want, Roxie? I'm working here! And anyway, I'm not talking to you! Drood lover!"

"Really?" said Roxie. "You're going to claim the moral high ground, when you're fronting a knocking shop? There was a time you would have fire-bombed places like this."

"Times have changed," said the Cutie.

"Even so, Hooking from beyond the Veil?" said Roxie. "That was an old con, even when we were starting out."

"The money's good."

"It would have to be," said Roxie.

"You want me to call booth security?" said the Chakra Cutie. "Have them throw you out?"

Roxie smiled slowly. "I would love to see them try."

I took her by the arm and moved her firmly away. "We're not here to start fights and get ourselves noticed. We can't afford to be distracted."

"I know," said Roxie. "We're here for you. But . . . I can't believe it's all got so damned sleazy! The Hiring Ground was always the bottom rung of the ladder, but this is just blatant exploitation."

"Hard times make for hard people," I said. "At both ends of the queue."

Everywhere we went there were people we knew, who knew us, and none of them seemed at all surprised to see Shaman Bond and Roxie Hazzard at the Hiring Ground. No one offered anything but a sad smile, a resigned shrug, and a general attitude of *It comes to us all, in the end*.

"I feel like burning down the whole place," said Roxie. "Just on general principles."

"Then where would these people get work?" I said.

"Don't be reasonable," said Roxie. "I'm not in the mood to feel reasonable."

"Can't recall a time when you were," I said.

She managed a small smile. "Let's just do what we came here for and get the hell out."

It took us a while to track down the Psychic Surgeon. He might have been a Major Player once, but these days, his stall was a lot farther from the main drag than it used to be. *It comes to us all . . .*

The Psychic Surgeon was a fleshy, middle-aged man, in clothes so colourful, he would have looked over-dressed on a golf course. He had fierce eyes and a strident voice, and a distinct if somewhat disturbing presence, like a wolf with a big smile and some foam on its chops. He targeted anyone who came near his slightly shabby stall, boasting of his past triumphs and the extraordinary extent of his abilities. A lot of people stopped to listen, but not many stayed.

"I am the one and only Psychic Surgeon! I can operate on you with my mind; add or remove moods, modify memories, and cut away inhibitions! I can boost your talents and accentuate your attitudes! I can do surgery on your soul and make you a better person! Or, at least, a different one!"

He was quite happy to demonstrate his abilities on the people gathered before his stall, without warning or apology. He was certainly impressive enough, but the casual cruelty implicit in his demonstrations put a lot of people off. He made a man forget his own name, and a woman weep inconsolably over the death of someone she'd never heard of. He made two strangers fall passionately in love, and he set an old married couple at each other's throats. All for the entertainment of the crowd, and himself. But most people just drifted away, before he could do something to them. The Psychic Surgeon grumpily released his hold on the people he'd affected, and they hurried off, shaking with reaction. The Surgeon shouted after them.

"You'll be back! I can make you happy! Make your enemies miserable! Cut away all the parts of you that are holding you back! You need me!"

Roxie tried to get his attention, but he just waved her away.

"Not now, girlie. I'm working."

"Girlie?" Roxie said dangerously.

He looked back at her, and then smiled suddenly. The stage persona was gone in a moment, and he was just a calm, somewhat fatigued businessman.

"Roxie Hazzard; mercenary for hire, no job too dubious. And Shaman Bond, plausible rogue about town, always looking for a little trouble to get into, but never around when the authorities turn up."

I looked at Roxie. "He's heard of us."

"Who hasn't?" said Roxie.

"You made good time getting here," said the Psychic Surgeon.

"You even look at my aura wrong," said Roxie, "and I will rip your head right off."

She was being more than usually brusque, because she couldn't afford him looking past Roxie to see Molly. Or my torc. The Psychic Surgeon just shrugged.

"I get that a lot," he said.

"Isn't there any hall security?" I said. "To protect people from people like you?"

"Not any more," said the Surgeon. "They got in the way of business. The official attitude these days is *Enter at your own risk*. And don't be too upset by my little exhibition. Half of that crowd works for me. The point is to get people talking, and then they'll come and see for themselves. At which point I shall be their kindly old physician, there to help them with all of life's little problems."

"Can you?" said Roxie. "Really?"

He shrugged. "Depends on the problem. I can cut things out, or move them around; but I can only work with what's there." He looked me briefly up and down. "Want an upgrade on your charisma? A voice that compels, or a look that seduces? I'm doing a special on confidence boosters. Two for the price of three."

"That's not right," I said.

"You see! They're working!"

"Never mind that crap," said Roxie. "We're not here for what you have to offer."

"You sure?" said the Surgeon. "I could always cut away Shaman's bothersome independence; make him live only to serve you."

Roxie smiled at me. "The thought does have its attractions . . . but no."

"You just can't help some people," said the Psychic Surgeon.

I fixed him with a cold stare. "I've been having a really bad day. I could use someone to take it out on."

"Never make an enemy; that's what I say," said the Surgeon. "What can I do for you?"

I looked at Roxie. "See? I can do intimidating."

"I knew you had it in you," said Roxie. She fixed the Psychic Surgeon with her own cold glare. "Can you really put us in touch with Dr DOA?"

"Hush!" the Surgeon said sharply. "That's not a name to use in public."

He looked around quickly, and just a bit dramatically, to make sure no one had overheard. Though we would have had to be shouting at the tops of our voices to cut through the general bedlam. The Psychic Surgeon closed up shop, by setting in place a large sign: *The Psychic Surgeon is out. Do not mess with his things, or he will cut off your libido.* He then led us to a private shielded-off area at the rear of his stall, surrounded by standing wooden panels engraved with ancient Chinese characters. I nodded. I'd seen that kind of security before: Stay inside the circle and no one could overhear you.

"Are you sure that's enough?" said Roxie. "In a place like this?"

"Even God would have to turn up his hearing aid to listen in on us," said the Surgeon. "Now, what do you nice young people want with Dr DOA? I mean, yes, I get it; you want the wild witch of the woods dead. And like anyone sane, you'd much rather someone else did the dirty work and took all the risks. But why choose Dr DOA? There's no shortage of people with grudges against Molly Metcalf, who'd be happy to do the job for a lot less than the Doctor will charge you."

"I want Dr DOA," said Roxie, "because he never fails. He's there for when they really, absolutely, have to die. That's what I'm paying for."

The Surgeon nodded. "No offence, dear, but are you sure you can afford a service like this?"

"Money is no object," said Roxie, "where Molly Metcalf is concerned."

"That's what the Doctor likes to hear!" the Surgeon said cheerfully.

"Do you know him?" I said. "I mean, personally? I don't think I've ever heard of anyone who could claim to have met the Doctor in person."

"I can put you in touch with the man," the Psychic Surgeon said carefully. "For a percentage of the fee. But I've never even been in the same room as the Doctor. Ours has always been a strictly business relationship. I prefer to maintain a safe distance from that man, and what he does."

"I'm still not entirely convinced he exists," said Roxie.

The Surgeon sneered at her. "I could drop some names of the Doctor's more-recent accomplishments. People who died from apparently natural causes, or were quite blatantly poisoned. Enough to convince. But you already know all that, or you wouldn't be here. You can strike a deal with me, or you can walk away. The Doctor won't care. And I only care in as much as it affects my percentage. There's never any shortage of people wanting to hire Dr DOA. For reasons of his own, he has chosen to move you to the front of the queue. He hasn't told me why, and he doesn't need to. He doesn't need to tell me anything, and mostly he doesn't."

"I heard he killed a Drood recently," I said. "Is that right?"

"You do get around, don't you, Shaman?" said the Surgeon. "Yes. I heard that."

"So who hired the Doctor to murder a Drood?" I said. "Who could be crazy enough to seriously piss off the world's most dangerous family?"

"The Doctor never talks about his clients," said the Surgeon. "That's part of what you're paying for."

"Where is he?" said Roxie. "Where can we find Dr DOA?"

He started to say something, and then stopped. He looked at us both thoughtfully. "I see minds differently from other people. Comes with the job. I can see strengths and weaknesses, and all the colours and flavours of thought. And there's something not quite right about you two. Roxie, why are you so keen to have Molly Metcalf killed?"

"You've heard of her, haven't you?" said Roxie.

"Well, yes . . . ," said the Surgeon. "Good point."

"And we aren't dumb enough to try to do it ourselves," I said.

"Understood," said the Surgeon.

"We need to be sure Dr DOA really can dispose of the wild witch," I said. "After all, a lot of powerful people have already tried to take her down. She's still here, and they're not."

"The Doctor can get to anyone," said the Psychic Surgeon. "I can tell you're serious about wanting to meet him, but . . . I'm also getting the impression that you want information . . . Yes! You want to know who hired the Doctor to kill Eddie Drood! Why would you want to know that?"

"I told you to stay out of my head!" said Roxie.

The Psychic Surgeon fell back a step, quickly raising both hands. "Please! It's your business. I really don't care. But the Doctor might . . ."

He looked around, peering past the standing wooden panels at the people passing by, and when he was sure no one was paying any attention, he produced a piece of folded paper and offered it to Roxie. She looked at it suspiciously and gestured for me to take it. I did so, while Roxie glared at the Surgeon.

"I didn't come all this way for a note! I was promised a meeting with Dr DOA!"

"No you weren't," the Psychic Surgeon said calmly. "I chose my words very carefully. You were promised a connection, and that's what you get. The Doctor knew you'd come; don't ask me how. He had that message already prepared for you, and delivered to me by private messenger. And his instructions were that you are not to read it until after I am gone." He smiled briefly. "Whatever it is, I don't want to know. I'm better off not knowing. I make murders possible, but I'm never a part of them."

"You haven't even peeked?" I said.

"Of course not! He'd know!" The Surgeon actually shuddered briefly. "I value my business relationship with the Doctor. And I value being alive."

I hefted the folded piece of paper. "This will take us straight to Dr DOA?"

"If he wants you to find him," said the Psychic Surgeon. "And please, never contact me again. Even for the kind of people the Hiring Ground attracts these days, you two are just too disturbing."

"That's it?" said Roxie. "You've nothing more to say?"

"Not a damned thing," said the Psychic Surgeon. "You can go now."

"That's what you think," said Roxie.

She grabbed hold of his jacket lapels with both hands, lifted him up onto his toes, and then dropped her Roxie look to show him her real face. The Surgeon made a shocked sound. He brought up his hand, and suddenly it was holding a scalpel made out of shimmering light. He moved to slash her across the throat, but the scalpel fell apart before it could even touch her, breaking up in the face of Molly's protections. I knew she had them, but my heart still missed a beat. The Psychic Surgeon whimpered as he looked at his empty hand, and then turned reluctantly back to look at Molly.

"You're not just a mercenary. Who are you? What are you?"

She pulled his face forward so she could smile right into it. "I'm Molly Metcalf. And you are in real trouble."

That gave him the strength he needed to pull free from Molly's grasp. He ran blindly, not even noticing I was in his way. He lashed out at me with his restored glowing scalpel. I armoured up, and the scalpel exploded into sparks as it hit my golden chest. The Surgeon cried out and fell back, looking at his empty hand as though it had betrayed him. I armoured down, so as not to attract attention. I looked quickly around as Molly grabbed hold of the Psychic Surgeon again, but everyone passing by seemed to be determinedly looking somewhere else. Partly because the Hiring Ground exists only by everyone minding their own business, but most likely because the Psychic Surgeon had no friends here. He looked from Molly to me and back again, and seemed to shrink in on himself.

"The wild witch and a Drood," he said faintly. "He knew . . . Dr DOA knew! And he didn't tell me. The bastard . . . He sent you here so you'd kill me!"

"Not necessarily," I said. "Tell us what we want to know, and you could still walk away."

He looked older, all his arrogance and authority falling away. If he hadn't seemed so pathetic, I would have enjoyed seeing him take such a fall. It felt like bullying a child. And then I remembered all the murders he'd made possible, fronting for Dr DOA, and I hardened my heart.

"Why contact Roxie Hazzard, in the Deep Down Pit?" I said. "Why tell us to come here?"

"Because I was told to!" said the Surgeon. "Dr DOA set it up."

"Why?" said Molly.

"I don't know!" the Psychic Surgeon said miserably. "He doesn't tell me anything; I just work for him. I'm not a violent person; I'm just a frontman! He contacted me originally, completely out of the blue. And then he told me how the deal was going to work. I wasn't going to argue; not with a man like him. I just went along."

"Why?" I said. "Why get involved in so many deaths?"

"Because the money was good! Times are hard . . ."

"You must know more about the Doctor's methods than anyone else," said Molly. "Tell me how to save Eddie!"

The Surgeon looked at me. "You're him? You're the Drood he poisoned? How are you even still alive?"

"There must be some way to save him!" said Molly, shaking him hard.

"You can't!" said the Surgeon. "No one ever survives Dr DOA! That's the point. I'm amazed he's lasted this long. There's nothing you can do! Nothing anyone can do. I'm sorry . . ."

"There's nothing you can think of that might help?" said Molly.

"No!" said the Psychic Surgeon. "Nothing!"

"Then I don't have any reason to keep you alive, do I?" said Molly.

She let go of his lapels, grabbed his head with both hands, twisted savagely, and broke his neck. She let go of him, and he fell to the floor. I looked down at the body and couldn't honestly say I felt anything. He'd made so many murders possible, including mine. I took a deep breath and looked at Molly.

"You can't kill everyone who annoys you."

"Watch me," said Molly. "If you're going to die, then everyone responsible is going to die with you."

"That won't save me," I said.

"I have to do something!" said Molly.

"There's still hope," I said. "Dr DOA wanted to meet me. That must mean something. Let's see what he has to say."

I turned the folded paper over. On the outside it read, *For the attention of Shaman Bond and Roxie Hazzard.* I opened the paper, and inside it said, *Hello, Eddie and Molly. I'll meet you back at Drood Hall. In the Armoury. Come now, and come alone.*

The message was handwritten. Something about the hand looked familiar, but I couldn't place it. There was no signature. Molly read the message and looked at me.

"Okay, I'm lost. He knows who we are. How is that possible?"

"Because I was right all along," I said. "Someone inside my family made this possible. Gave Dr DOA all the details. We have to go back, Molly, and finish this."

"Face-to-face with Dr DOA at last," said Molly. "Do you care if I kill him?"

"If he can't help me," I said, "then we don't have a reason to keep him alive, do we?"

CHAPTER TEN

Home Again, Home Again

I brought out the Merlin Glass, and immediately all hell broke loose. Alarms and sirens, bells and whistles, followed by the sound of raised voices, accusations and counter-accusations, insults and tears, and a great many people running for the exit. I looked past the standing wooden posts and saw some people grabbing up armfuls of goods, while the more experienced just abandoned everything and ran. Either because they were anticipating a raid, or for fear they were about to be found out. An awful lot of people had an awful lot to feel guilty about in the Hiring Ground.

I looked innocently at Molly. "Did I do that?"

"Looks like the Hiring Ground does have some security measures after all," said Molly. "And given that we are currently standing over the body of a man I just killed, I don't think we should still be here when the security patrols come looking."

I nodded. "Time to go home, Molly."

"Can the Glass take us straight to the Armoury?" said Molly. "I thought there were all kinds of protections in place, to keep people from just dropping in uninvited."

"Oh there are," I said. "Protections and defences like you wouldn't believe. We'll have to go the long way round."

I ordered the hand mirror to show me a view of the Drood grounds, as close to the Hall as possible. Instead, the Glass showed me an inside view of the Armoury. I stood there and looked at it.

"What?" said Molly, looking at my face. "What's wrong? The Glass isn't playing up again, is it?"

"That . . . shouldn't be possible," I said, indicating the view. "Even the Merlin Glass shouldn't be able to pierce the Armoury's defences, and it definitely shouldn't show me something I didn't even ask for!"

"You're the one who said it reads minds," said Molly.

"Not like that," I said. "And not without permission."

"Are we stranded here?" said Molly. "Because if the Glass can't get us out, I think we need to blend with the crowd and run. A group of heavily armed men are heading our way, and they do not look in the mood to ask polite questions. All right, we can probably take them, but . . ."

"Yes," I said, "it has been a long day, hasn't it?" I glared at the Merlin Glass. "Work, you bastard. Take us home."

I shook the Glass out to Door size, and it opened onto the Armoury. I had a moment to think there was something wrong with what I was seeing, and then Molly was right behind me, shouting, *Go! Go now!* So I just plunged through, with Molly crowding my heels. The Glass immediately shrank back to hand-mirror size, without waiting to be asked, and nestled comfortably into my hand. Like a good dog expecting praise.

The shouting and general clamour from the Hiring Ground were gone, replaced by utter silence from the Drood Armoury.

And that was when I realised what was wrong. The Armoury was completely deserted. Not a soul to be seen anywhere. No lab assistants, going about their usual destructive and homicidal business. No ongoing experiments, no explosions from workstations or muffled screams from the firing range. It was eerie; like turning on your favourite soap opera and seeing nothing but an empty set. I'd never seen the Armoury like this before. Except in the fake Armoury, in the Shifting Lands, where duplicates of my parents had tried to murder me. That had been a trap, and this felt like one too.

I stood very still, looking carefully around me. Something was seriously wrong. There's always something happening in the Armoury; the assistants work in shifts, twenty-four hours a day. Because the family never knows when it might need some new weapon or device. And because you have to keep the lab assistants busy, to stop them from getting into mischief. But all the workstations had been abandoned, some with projects left half-finished. There were even cups of tea and coffee with the steam still coming off them. Whatever had happened here, it had happened suddenly and very recently.

"Okay . . . ," said Molly. "I am going to go out on a limb here and say this is not good. In fact, it's downright creepy. Where is everybody?"

I called out to the Armourer. My voice echoed in the quiet, but there was no response. So I called out to Ethel, and she answered me immediately. There was no trace of her usual rose-red manifestation. Just a quiet voice, hanging on the air.

"You're in danger, Eddie."

"Not even a welcome home?" I said. "Typical. What's happened?"

"We're not sure," said Ethel. "Someone sounded the Emergency Evacuation Alert from inside the Armoury. The one that means *Everyone get the hell out and run for your lives; an experiment has just gone horribly wrong.* And given the kinds of things that go wrong in the Armoury on a regular basis, to sound that Alert would have to mean that the Hall itself was in danger. The Armourer organized a complete evacuation of the Armoury, actually manhandling a few who didn't want to leave, made sure everyone was accounted for, and then sealed the blast doors. To ensure the emergency was contained inside the Armoury. But once Maxwell and Victoria started asking questions, it quickly became clear no one would admit to sounding the Alert. No one knew anything about an experiment gone out of control. And when the Armourer tried to get back in, to investigate the situation, they found the entrance codes had been changed. By someone still inside. The family is working on a way to get back in. How did you manage it?"

"The Merlin Glass," I said. "And the only way that would work . . . is if someone had shut down the Armoury's shields and protections. Which has to mean someone is in here with us. I was right all along, Ethel; there's a traitor in the family."

"Not another one," said Ethel. "It's getting so you can't trust anyone . . . You're going to have to be very careful, Eddie. I can't see what's happened, or who's responsible, or where they are. And I should be able to. It might be best for you and Molly to just leave the way you came. We don't know who or what we're dealing with."

"All the more reason to stay," I said. "We can't leave the Drood Armoury in the hands of a traitor. God alone knows what an enemy could do with unrestricted access to the kinds of weapons and equipment they work on here. It's unthinkable."

"No it isn't," said Molly. "I've thought about it a lot, every time your family has really pissed me off. Whoever it is, we have to stop them. Before they do any of the things I've thought about."

"Eddie . . . ," said Ethel, "the Matriarch is getting ready to authorize the Alpha Red Alpha Protocol."

"Oh shit," I said.

"What?" said Molly. "What Protocol? Eddie, why are you looking like that?"

"In the worst emergency situation," I said, "the family can activate the Alpha Red Alpha mechanism by remote control and use it to drop the whole Armoury into another dimension. So that whatever appalling thing is happening, it won't reach the Hall. We can always build another Armoury."

"Listen to me, Eddie," said Ethel. "I've been thinking about this, and you really need to—"

Her voice cut off.

"Ethel?" I said. "Ethel! Talk to me! What is it I need to do?"

But there was nothing; only the uninterrupted hush of the deserted Armoury. I looked to Molly.

"Okay, I am seriously worried now."

"What could be powerful enough to silence Ethel?" said Molly.

"Nothing I know of," I said. "But then . . . whatever it is, it's been hiding from her all this time."

"And it's in here with us right now," said Molly. "Maybe we should leave. We're not exactly operating at our best. And . . . I don't like this situation, Eddie. Far too many unknowns. It's not running away when you're retreating in the face of far superior numbers."

"Are we?" I said.

"Sure as hell feels like it," she said. "Someone's running a game here, and we don't even know the rules. So let's be sensible, just for once, and refuse to play the game."

"Sounds like a plan to me," I said.

I held up the Merlin Glass, but before I could order it to take us anywhere, the hand mirror tore itself out of my grip and leapt up to hang on the air before me. It grew quickly to Door size, of its own volition, while still remaining a mirror. I'd never seen it do that before. The full-sized mirror stood before me, showing me my reflection. But there was something wrong with it. It was my face staring back at me, but I didn't like the look on my face. And then I realised that while Molly was standing right beside me, she wasn't in the mirror. My reflection stirred and smiled unpleasantly at me. And then it stepped forward, out of the mirror, to stand before me.

"Well," I said, because I had to say something. "I really wasn't expecting that."

"He looks like you, Eddie," said Molly, "But he looks wrong. He doesn't feel like you."

"I should hope not," said my double, still smiling his smile, and for a moment all I could think was, *Do I really sound like that?* "I'm not Eddie; I'm my own man. I am Edmund Drood. Your equivalent, Eddie, from the Other Hall. You remember the Other Hall from the Other Dimension, the one that briefly replaced yours. The Hall from another world, where all the Droods had been wiped out. I did that. I had my family members killed; watched them be overrun and put down like the rabid dogs they were. I had them all slaughtered, and I gloried in it. Come on, Eddie . . . Don't tell me you never thought about it. After everything they did to us . . ."

"You killed your own family?" said Molly.

"Well, not me personally," said Edmund. "Not on my own. I put together an army, and then turned it loose on the Hall. After I'd sneaked in first and shut down all the defences and protections. The way I did here." He smiled reflectively. "My poor family . . . They never knew what hit them. It was easier than you'd think, to build my army. I had no idea there were so many other people who hated my family almost as much as I did." He laughed quite happily. "I wanted to be free of my family. Free of all its unreasonable demands and expectations, and the stifling weight of its history. Imagine my surprise when at the height of my triumph—when the massacre was over and I was busy dancing in the ruins— my Hall was suddenly transported here, and me with it!

"I didn't know what was going on, so I hid inside the Merlin Glass. I knew its protections would be strong enough to conceal me from everyone. From inside the Glass, I could see everything and learn all about this amazing new world I'd arrived in. It took me a while to understand what had happened, and a while longer to learn how to use the Glass to send me anywhere in the world I wanted. Imagine how I felt to discover a whole new Drood family, still alive . . . And someone who looked just like me, but wasn't anything like me. So, I stayed hidden. I knew what your family would do if it found out who I was and what I'd done. And besides, I had plans to make. To deal with this new family."

"You've been hiding inside the Merlin Glass all this time?" I said.

"At first, I was in the Glass from the Other Hall," said Edmund. "But then your Armourer merged my Glass with yours, when yours was damaged. And I went with it. Which allowed me to follow your activities very closely. I've been popping in and out of the Glass ever since, going back and forth in the world and walking up and down in it. Making all kinds of useful contacts."

"You're why the Glass has been defying me!" I said.

He smiled modestly. "A man's entitled to a little fun."

"But why did you have Dr DOA poison Eddie?" said Molly.

"Haven't you got it yet?" said Edmund. "I am Dr DOA! I had to do something in this world, to raise enough money and power to help me take down this new family of Droods. The Glass meant I could go anywhere, get to anyone . . . But after a while, I just couldn't stand it any more. I wanted Eddie dead. Because I knew he'd be the only one who could stand against me and prevent the destruction of his family. The only real threat to my continued existence. You could call it self-defence. And anyway; you had to die, Eddie. For not being like me."

"But what's your grudge against this family of Droods?" said Molly. "Whatever the members of your family did to you . . . they're all dead! These are new people."

"They're still Droods!" said Edmund. "I'll never feel safe while a single Drood is left alive."

"Why reveal yourself to me now?" I said.

"You started looking for me," said Edmund. "I suppose that was inevitable, once I poisoned you. But you were never supposed to last this long . . . At first I was content to just let you stumble around, because you weren't getting anywhere. But it occurred to me there was always the chance you might talk to the wrong person, pick up some clue, find some way to stop me . . . So I contacted the Psychic Surgeon and gave him a message to pass on to Roxie Hazzard in the Deep Down Pit. I always knew where you were, as long as you had the Merlin Glass. I brought you to the Hiring Ground, just so you would dispose of the Psychic Surgeon. I knew you'd want to, and he had outlived his usefulness. And then my little note brought you home, after I'd prepared the ground. I didn't want us to be interrupted. So here we are, Eddie and Edmund. Face-to-face at last. Because I want this over and done with."

"How have you stayed hidden from everyone?" I said. "From Ethel?"

"I made an accommodation with the Merlin Glass,"

said Edmund. "Or rather, with Something I found inside it."

"Something?" I said. "Or Someone?"

"That's my business," said Edmund. "The point is, I've been able to keep my presence hidden from all manner of prying eyes. Including that dimensional parasite you all bow down to."

Molly stepped forward suddenly, fixing Edmund with a fierce, dangerous look. "You must have a cure for the poison you use. That's all I care about. Save my Eddie, and I give you my word I won't kill you."

"A cure?" said Edmund. "Are you mad? There is no cure! I brought the poison with me from my world. Just a little something I used to have fun with. I never even looked for a cure. Why would I?"

Molly made a low, defeated sound. I understood how she felt, but I still had work to do.

"Well," I said. "I guess everyone has to face their evil twin at some point. You brought me here. Now what?"

"You were supposed to be dead long before this," said Edmund. "I'm still not entirely sure why you're not. Must be something to do with your armour having a different source than mine."

"Where does your armour come from?" I said. "When I searched the Other Hall, when it was here . . . the Heart had already abandoned it. And you never had an Ethel."

"Like I'd tell you," said Edmund. "All that matters is, I can't bear to have you around any longer. Your mockery of me, your very existence, offends me."

"Funny," I said, "I feel the same way about you."

"Thought you might," said Edmund. "Come on, you know some things are just inevitable."

We both armoured up in a moment and went for each other. Molly backed quickly away, but I barely noticed. All I could think of was getting my hands on Edmund. My shadow self; my murderer. We slammed against each other with the force of living mountains. Golden fists pounded featureless masks, with a sound like golden bells dying. I couldn't hurt him, and he couldn't hurt me . . . but we tried. With all our strength and passion, we tried.

We each struck terrible blows that would have shattered walls and brought down buildings. We beat and clubbed at each other, and our armour took it all. We fought and wrestled, equally strong, equally matched. I grabbed up a workstation and broke it over his head. He threw me through a metal tower. We raged back and forth through the Armoury, breaking everything we touched and smashing through everything that got in our way. Now and again we'd snatch up some abandoned weapon and try it on each other. But though the air shimmered with strange energies, and fires started up all around, we never came to any harm. We were Droods in our armour, and nothing could touch us. We rampaged up and down the length of the Armoury, sometimes wrapped in explosions from the things we destroyed, like the only real things in a paper world.

Driven by a rage not born of reason.

Until Molly suddenly yelled for both of us to stop. And there was something in her voice that commanded our attention. We broke apart, both of us breathing hard from our exertions, and turned to look. Molly was standing by a hidden control panel she'd uncovered in one wall. Her hand hovered over a big red button.

"This is the Armoury's self-destruct control," she said loudly. "For when the Alpha Red Alpha Protocol can't be used, but the Armoury still has to be destroyed to protect the Hall. Your uncle Jack showed it to me, Eddie, because he thought someone outside the family should know. Just in case. He trusted me to do the right thing, when it mattered. The forces this button will unleash are enough to finish off even a Drood in his armour. They had to be, to ensure the Armoury was completely destroyed. So stand down, Edmund. Or I swear I'll kill us all."

"Now, why would you do that?" said Edmund. He sounded honestly curious.

"Eddie's dying," said Molly. "If you can't or won't save him, then I have no reason to let you live. And I don't want to live, without my Eddie. At least this way I get to take you with us."

Edmund armoured down. He smiled at me, and winked at Molly. "Nicely played. But the game's not over yet. And you won't kill me until you're sure I've told you the truth about a cure."

The Merlin Glass shrank down to mirror size. Edmund grabbed it out of the air, turned, and ran for the rear of the Armoury. I armoured down as Molly came running over to hold me. I clung to her like a drowning man. We were both shaking.

"Was that button really . . . ?" I said.

"Yes."

"Were you bluffing?"

"I'll never tell," said Molly.

"We have to go after him," I said, "before he can escape through the Merlin Glass."

"How do you know he hasn't already?" said Molly.

"Because he's still got something planned," I said. "He must have some kind of trap set up, just in case he couldn't finish me off."

"Then let's go trigger his trap and break it over his head," said Molly. "And then feed him the pieces."

"Sounds like a plan to me," I said.

We went after Edmund, taking our time because we knew he wasn't going anywhere. But when we finally caught up with him, at the far end of the Armoury . . . I was still shocked to see what he was doing. Someone had brought the Alpha Red Alpha mechanism up from under the Armoury. And Edmund was at the controls.

It looked just as big and complicated and unnerving as I remembered. A huge plunging waterfall of solid crystal, with glowing wires running through it like multicoloured veins. Etched from top to bottom with row upon row of ancient abhuman symbols. So old I didn't even recognise the language. And inside all of that, a massive hour-glass some twenty feet tall. Wrought in solid silver, with glass so perfect it was barely visible. The top half was full of shimmering golden particles, which Edmund had just set in motion. They tumbled into the lower half with slow, terrible purpose.

I moved cautiously forward with Molly close at my side, trying not to be noticed. Edmund, intent on the controls, didn't even look up.

"What's he doing?" Molly murmured.

"Nothing good," I said quietly. "No one's really understood how that mechanism works since Uncle Jack died."

"Who knows what Edmund knew, in his own world?" said Molly.

A Doorway suddenly appeared, not the usual kind; it was more a tear in reality itself. Edmund left the Alpha Red Alpha mechanism and plunged through the new opening. I ran after him, with Molly racing along at my side, and all I could think was, *I can't let him get away. Not after all this* . . . I ran through the Doorway, and then stopped so abruptly, Molly had to hang on to my arm to stop herself.

We were in the ruins of a wrecked and abandoned Armoury. I'd seen it before, in the Other Hall, from Edmund's world. I heard a sound behind me, and spun round just in time to see Edmund slip back through the Doorway. Turning, he laughed once in my face, and then the tear in reality disappeared. Shut down from the other side.

"Open it!" said Molly. "We have to go after him!"

"We can't," I said numbly. "Look around. There's no Alpha Red Alpha mechanism in this Armoury. We're trapped here. He's won."

We stood together, in the Armoury of the Other Hall, in a different world. With no way home.

Read on for an excerpt from Simon R. Green's next Secret Histories Novel,

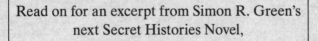

Moonbreaker

Available from Ace in June 2017

t wasn't my family's Armoury, but it looked enough like the one I knew to send a chill down my spine. The same long series of stone cellars, with colour-coded wiring tacked haphazardly to the walls. But here the workstations were abandoned, the firing ranges were empty, and wreckage and rubble lay everywhere. The Armourer and his white-coated lab assistants, who should have been running wild with out-of-control experiments and weapons that endangered the lives of everyone around them, were gone—long gone. Slaughtered by the Droods' many enemies, after my other self shut down the Hall's protections and sabotaged its defences. The Armoury was still and silent now, its many wonders trashed or looted. Like some ancient burial chamber despoiled by grave-robbers who could never hope to appreciate the treasures they carried away or left trampled under foot.

The only sounds disturbing the graveyard quiet came from Molly. Her language started out bad and quickly escalated, as she swept her hands back and forth through the empty space where the dimensional gateway had been just a few moments before. She was trying to find some trace of it with her magics, so she could call it back and force it open, but she wasn't getting anywhere.

"Molly," I said thoughtfully.

"What? I'm busy!"

"Look what's back."

She turned around, and there was Alpha Red Alpha, towering over us. The great dimensional engine itself. Molly glared at it.

"That wasn't there a moment ago."

"I know."

"So what was it doing? Hiding from us?"

I shrugged. "That's Alpha Red Alpha for you."

I looked carefully at the massive and never fully understood mechanism, designed to be the Droods' last line of defence. So that if the Hall ever found itself faced with a threat that couldn't be stopped, the engine would translate the whole building into another dimension, another earth, where it could safely remain until the threat was over and the Hall could be brought back again.

Either the family here never got a chance to use it, or Edmund did something to it.

Alpha Red Alpha: a gigantic hour-glass shape immersed inside a frozen waterfall of gleaming crystal, shot through with sprawling circuits, like ragged veins. It was hard to make sense of, hard even to look at, as though it existed in more than three dimensions . . . And if there were any controls, I couldn't make them out. Only my uncle Jack, when he was Armourer, really understood Alpha Red Alpha.

"Can your magics get us home, Molly?" I said. I was pretty sure I already knew the answer, but I needed to hear her say it.

"Not a hope in hell!" Molly scowled at Alpha Red Alpha as though she was seriously considering giving it a good kicking, just on general principle. "I don't even know where home is from here! You can't navigate all the different Earths and all their different histories without being really sure of the exact Time/Space coordinates involved."

"And there's no trace left of the dimensional Door we came through?"

"No." Molly's shoulders slumped, and she suddenly looked tired and worn-down. We'd put a lot of effort into chasing Edmund, and it was catching up with both of us. "Edmund must have locked the door from his side, using the other Alpha Red Alpha." She looked at me sharply. "If he's smart enough to operate it, why can't you?"

"Because he's spent ages learning how to work it," I said.

"If he could figure it out . . ."

"I don't have enough time," I said.

Molly nodded reluctantly. "Does this machine look the same to you as the one in our world?"

"Hard to tell," I said. "Just looking at the damn thing hurts my eyes. It's . . . different, but I couldn't tell you how. I am sure it wasn't standing here the last time we visited this Armoury."

"Edmund must have moved it," said Molly. "So he could set his trap."

"How?" I said. "Look at the size of it! You couldn't shift something this big with a power loader and a stick of dynamite!"

"I don't know," said Molly. "And don't you snap at me, Eddie Drood! Edmund's just another version of you, which means really this is all your fault!"

"Somehow I knew it would be," I said.

We shared a quick smile, and went back to studying the dimensional engine. It stared silently back at us, giving away nothing.

"Edmund must have been coming and going between the two Earths for some time," I said. "But how could he have used my Hall's Alpha Red Alpha without the Armourer or his staff noticing?"

"That still leaves the Merlin Glass," said Molly.

"Without my noticing?" I said. Molly started to bristle again, and I realised we were dangerously close to another argument we couldn't afford, so I changed the subject. "We have to get back to our world, Molly. My whole family is in danger from Edmund as long as he's running around our Hall, unsuspected."

Molly leaned in suddenly and kissed me.

"What was that for?" I said.

"Because that is just so typical of you, Eddie—thinking of others, instead of yourself. We have to get back because you're running out of time."

"Trust me," I said. "I hadn't forgotten."

"Any chance there might be a manual for Alpha Red Alpha in the Library?" said Molly.

"Unlikely," I said. "My uncle Jack was the only one who ever had any control over the machine. Max and Victoria like to say they do, now they're Armourer, but that always sounded like whistling in the dark to me. They're probably still trying to make sense of whatever notes Jack left behind. And he only ever partly understood how the damn thing operates, anyway."

Molly looked at me sharply. "How can your people not understand how it works, when you invented it?"

"Alpha Red Alpha was reverse-engineered from alien tech," I said patiently. "Like most Drood weapons and devices. That's why we're always a step ahead of everyone else."

"I thought it was because you had the best scientific brains!"

"We do," I said. "That's how we're able to reverse-engineer alien tech so successfully. We have come up with some amazing things on our own; science and the supernatural are our playthings. But we are all of us standing on the shoulders of giants. Sometimes alien giants."

"Hold it," said Molly. "I thought Black Heir was in charge of clearing up after alien incursions and salvaging all the tech that gets left behind?"

"They are," I said. "But Black Heir answers to my

family. They make sure we always get the good stuff. And, in return, we keep everyone else off their backs."

"How does any of this help us now?" said Molly.

"It doesn't," I said. "But it has given me an idea . . ." I armoured up my right hand and extended it toward the dimensional engine. "You know how I use my armour to hack computers and make them do what I want? I'm hoping it might be able to do the same with Alpha Red Alpha. Enough to get us back home, at least."

"Go for it," said Molly. "I stand ready to applaud, jump up and down, and whoop with joy."

Golden tendrils eased out from my fingertips, only to stop well short of the machine's crystalline surface. They wavered uncertainly on the air and then snapped back into my glove. I looked at my hand, and even shook it a few times, as though that might persuade the armour to cooperate, but nothing happened. I let the golden strange matter disappear back into the torc around my throat.

"Okay," said Molly. "What just happened there?"

"Apparently, Alpha Red Alpha is so . . . different, my armour couldn't make any sense of it," I said slowly. "In fact, if I didn't know better—and I'm not sure that I do—I'd say my armour was afraid of it."

"Your torc has picked one hell of a time to have performance issues," said Molly. "So, there's nothing we can do? We're trapped here?"

"Lost and alone, in a world without Droods," I said.

She sniffed. "You say that like it's a bad thing."

We both managed a small smile.

"I refuse to give up," said Molly. "It's not in my nature. What else can we do?"

"First," I said, "we go exploring. Take a walk through the Hall and get a good look at where we are and what we've got to work with. There might be something we can use to get us home."

"Hark!" said Molly, cupping one hand to her ear. "Is that the sound of whistling in the dark I just heard?

Eddie, we need to get the hell out of here, and make our way to the Nightside! You can get anywhere from the Nightside."

"That's assuming this world has one," I said.

"Every world has a Nightside," said Molly.

"Now, there's a horrifying thought," I said. "But even so; it could be very different from the one we know."

"The whole point of the long night is that you can find anything there," Molly said briskly. "Particularly if it's something the rest of the world doesn't approve of." She paused and looked at me seriously. "How are you feeling, Eddie?"

I knew what she was really asking: How much time did I think I had left? And how much longer would I still be able to fight my corner?

"I'm angry enough to keep going," I said steadily. "Edmund screwed up. He should have killed me while he had the chance. In fact, I have to wonder why he didn't."

"Because he couldn't," said Molly. "You're a better fighter than him, and he's always known it. That's why he poisoned you and ran away."

"I will get us home," I said. "And I will find him and make him pay. Whatever it takes."

"That's more like it," said Molly. "That's my Eddie."

She hugged me hard, and I let her do it. Because it was important one of us had faith in me.

After a while, we moved off through the unfamiliar Armoury. It didn't take long to confirm what I'd already suspected—the whole place had been picked clean. Not a weapon or useful device to be found anywhere. Everything was covered in thick layers of dust, from the smashed and abandoned computer stations to the deserted weapons galleries. Tangled wiring hung down from the walls in thick clumps, as though someone had tried to tear them down. Walking through the silent

Armoury was like moving through a tomb: a place of the dead, abandoned to Time. Where only the past had any meaning.

"There's really nothing left," I said finally. "My family is just history here."

"Hold it together, Eddie," said Molly. "There's still work to be done."

Everything looked much as I remembered it from my last visit. There were gaps everywhere from where things had been taken, but no signs of actual fighting. The war had been lost up above, in the Hall, where the Droods made their final stand and were slaughtered, to the last man, woman, and child . . . Afterwards, the triumphant killers went storming through the Hall, looking for loot, and finally ended up down here. I hoped the Armourer was dead before that happened. He would have hated to see what the barbarians had done.

"Could there be . . . hidden caches somewhere?" Molly said hopefully. "Weapons or other things that only the Armourer would know about?"

"Just the Armageddon Codex," I said. "And according to the recorded message I triggered the last time I was here, the Armourer found time to seal the Forbidden Weapons inside the Lion's Jaws, so the enemy couldn't get to them."

And then I stopped, and thought for a moment. This family's Armourer had been my uncle James, not Uncle Jack. Here, Jack had been the famous field agent, while James had stayed home to be Armourer.

"You're scowling," Molly said accusingly. "Which is rarely a good sign. What are you worrying about now? Is this some new problem, and if so is it something I can hit?"

"This family's Armourer left a message for me in the Lion's Jaws," I said. "Remember?"

"I was here with you," said Molly, "There is nothing wrong with my memory."

"I was just wondering if there might be another message," I said.

"Worth a try, I suppose," said Molly. "Where are the Jaws?"

"I'm surprised you don't remember," I said.

"Don't push your luck, Drood."

The Lion's Jaws were in the exact same place as in my Hall: right at the back of the Armoury. A massive carving of a lion's snarling head, complete with mane, perfect in every detail. It had been fashioned out of rough, dark stone, and wasn't stylised in any way. It looked like the real thing, only twenty feet tall and almost as wide. I stood before it, looking steadily into the Lion's angry gaze. Molly stuck close beside me, scowling unhappily and just a bit warily into its eyes. Which was a perfectly normal reaction for any sane person. The Lion's Jaws don't just look dangerous.

"I have to wonder," I said, "whether this might have been carved from life. Very big life."

"Maybe we should look around for a really big wardrobe," said Molly.

"Don't even go there," I said.

The eyes gleamed, and the snarling jaws seemed only a moment away from lunging forward to snap my face off. The Lion's Jaws were created to give access to the pocket dimension where my family stored their most powerful and dangerous weapons, the kind you use when you need to destroy a whole army or monstrous invaders from another dimension. The Forbidden Weapons, for when reality itself is under threat. To open the gateway, you had to place your hand between the stone teeth. And if you weren't a Drood in good standing, and your heart wasn't pure, the Jaws would bite your hand right off. (The pure-at-heart bit was supposed to be just a legend, to scare away people with no good reason to be troubling the Jaws, but with my family you never knew.) The last time I'd been here, just my touch had been enough to trigger a recorded message from the Armourer James. A warning—and a last plea for revenge on those who'd destroyed the Droods.

I took a deep breath, and laid my hand flat on the great stone mane. Nothing happened. The old message was gone. Which meant the only thing left to try was putting my hand inside the Jaws. Even in my Hall, in my Armoury, I would have hesitated, but here . . . I wasn't even sure these Jaws would recognise me as a Drood. Armouring up wouldn't help, because these Jaws wouldn't be expecting Ethel's strange-matter armour. So I flexed my fingers a few times, breathed steadily until I was as calm as I was going to be, and then thrust my bare hand into the snarling mouth. My heart hammered as I fought to hold my hand steady, but the Jaws didn't move . . . and there was no second message. I snatched my hand out and stepped back.

"Nothing?" said Molly.

"I wouldn't say that," I said. "Something really unpleasant very nearly happened in my trousers. But no message."

"You're the one with the excellent memory," said Molly. "Was there anything in the first message that might prove useful to us now?"

"Not really," I said. "Though it did reveal some interesting differences between this family and mine. They still had a Heart, to provide their torcs and armour. Their Matriarch was Penelope, and the Armourer James said he destroyed the key to the Lion's Jaws, so at least we can be sure the Armageddon Codex is secure."

Molly looked dubiously at the Jaws. "What if someone tries to force them open?"

"It would be the last thing they ever tried," I said. "Let's get out of here. This whole place feels like someone is dancing on my grave."

*   *   *

Molly had to conjure a glowing sphere to lead us up the long flight of stairs to the ground floor. We needed the eerie green light to push back the darkness, because none of the lights were working. The thick layer of dust on the stone steps made it clear no one had been this way in a long time. Our footsteps sounded loud in the quiet, as though warning we were coming. The trapdoor at the top was still lying open, just as I'd left it the last time I was here. I frowned as I emerged cautiously and then hauled Molly up into the dimly lit room. The great open space looked just the same. Nothing had been touched, all the rubble and destruction left exactly as it was. Bright sunlight slanted through the shattered window, thick with curling dust. Molly dismissed her conjure light and looked quickly around her, but we were completely alone.

"Why has no one moved in?" I said, speaking loudly to show I wasn't intimidated by the setting or the hush. "I'd have thought someone would have taken possession of the Hall by now, if only for bragging rights."

"Maybe everyone thinks the place is haunted," said Molly. "Droods are dangerous enough when they're alive . . . And there's always the chance they didn't get everyone. The Hall could have been deliberately left empty, to draw back any Drood who wasn't here when the hammer came down. Bait in a trap. Just another really good reason why we should forget the sightseeing and get the hell out of here."

"I can't help thinking Edmund marooned us here for a reason," I said.

"He dumped us here because this is the only other Hall he had access to," said Molly. "And, anyway, what better place to leave you than a world where everyone wants to kill Droods? I mean, more than usual."

"I need to know more about this Hall," I said. "I need to know why this version of my family had to die."

"Of course you do," said Molly.

*   *   *

We went wandering through deserted rooms and empty corridors, stepping carefully around and over the wreckage and piled-up rubble. The walls were pocked with bullet-holes, and showed signs of bombs and incendiaries. No bloodstains. The Droods had died in their armour, fighting till the last. As we moved on, it became clear the whole building had been stripped clean. The accumulated loot and tribute of centuries was gone; every priceless statue and painting, every piece of antique furniture, and all our trophies. Every bit of Drood history and every precious thing I remembered . . . gone. Nothing remained to show my family had ever been here.

It felt like someone had stolen my life and pissed on my heritage.

"I never liked living here," I said finally. "Ran away to London first chance I got . . . and only came back when I was forced to. But I still hate to see the Hall looking like this. Like the king of the beasts dragged down by jackals."

"Can't say it bothers me," said Molly. "A Hall without Droods actually feels safer, like a predator whose teeth have been pulled."

"Thank you, Little Miss Tact."

"Don't get maudlin on me, Eddie. This isn't your Hall, and it wasn't your family. Hell, if Edmund's anything to go by, you should be grateful you never knew them."

"They were still Droods," I said.

I stopped in the middle of a large airy meeting place, where my family liked to sit and drink tea first thing in the morning. To read the world's newspapers and discuss the day's events, before setting about our various business. A civilised way to start the day. I looked around slowly, half expecting to see ghostly figures with familiar faces . . . And then I frowned.

"Oh, what now?" said Molly.

"All the way here, I've been spotting small differences," I said slowly. "Doors where there shouldn't be any, corridors opening onto halls that shouldn't exist, familiar routes that end abruptly at blank walls . . . I haven't seen any major changes—this is still the Hall I know—but it worries me that all these little differences might add up to a Hall and a family I might not recognise at all."

"I do have some experience travelling in other earths," said Molly. "Often it's the small differences that can be the most disturbing."

I looked at her. "And you never got around to telling me about these little side trips before because . . . ?"

"I don't have to tell you everything," Molly said haughtily. "I do have a life of my own, away from you. Oh, don't look at me like that, Eddie. It's just that sometimes . . . I feel the need to get away from everything. And where better to do that than on a completely different Earth?"

"I never feel the need to get away from you," I said.

"And you're the only thing in my world that doesn't occasionally drive me crazy," said Molly. "Settle for that."

"All right," I said. "What could be so disturbing about this strange new world?"

"Well, to start with, people we saw die could still be alive here. And vice versa, of course."

"But not my family," I said. "It was a nice thought, that some might have escaped the massacre. But Edmund seemed quite convinced all of this world's Droods were dead, apart from him."

"He should know," said Molly. "He betrayed them."

I shook my head slowly. "How could any version of me be so . . . vicious? What could have happened to me in this world to turn me into a cold-blooded killer who happily arranged for his whole family to be slaughtered?" I had to stop and breathe deeply for a moment, to bring my emotions under control. "The Armourer James said his family drove Edmund out. That he went to ground and disappeared."

"So he never hooked up with me?" said Molly.

I tried to smile, just for her. "No wonder he went to the bad."

"Eddie, you need to forget about these other Droods," said Molly. "It's just holding you back. We need to concentrate on finding something that can help you. Maybe even find a cure . . . Eddie? What's wrong?"

"I don't know," I said. "I'm just . . . tired."

Exhaustion hit me like a sucker punch. It was all suddenly too much, being so far from home, trapped in a distorted mirror of everything I knew. With death hovering over me like a vulture, just waiting for me to weaken. My vision darkened, my knees buckled, and I started to fall. Molly was quickly there to grab me and hold me up. Leaning in close so she could shout in my ear.

"Eddie, come on! You can't give up now. There's still things that need doing, people who need killing, and I can't do it all on my own! I need you! You're a Drood, dammit—act like one!"

That's my Molly. Always telling me what I need to hear, whether I want to hear it or not.

I forced the weakness back, refusing to be beaten by anything that got in the way of what needed doing, even myself. Perhaps especially myself. I stamped my feet hard until my legs straightened and my head came up. Molly saw my face clear and immediately stepped back to let me stand on my own. Watching me carefully, until she was sure I could manage without her. I gave her my best reassuring smile.

"It's all right, Molly. I'm back. You didn't really think I'd leave you here alone, did you? I can be strong for you."

"I know that," she said. "You just forgot for a moment. Look, have you seen enough of this Hall? Can we go now?"

"Not just yet," I said. "A thought has occurred to me."

"Oh, that's never good," said Molly. "What is it this time?"

"The last time we were here, we visited the Old Library and found a book set out on a reading stand. Left there for us, to tell us things we needed to know. And while we were there . . . something spoke to us."

Molly shuddered briefly. "Yes . . . A voice, from out of the dark between the stacks. It knew our names. But it really didn't sound like anything I wanted to stick around and meet."

"In our Old Library, there's always the Pook," I said carefully. "The Librarian's not-quite-imaginary-enough friend. Maybe whoever left that book out for us might be ready to help us again."

"Okay," said Molly. "I have to say, that doesn't strike me as one of your better ideas. Our Pook is disturbing enough. I'm not even convinced he's real, just something that followed the Librarian home from the Asylum for the Criminally Insane."

"True," I said. "But I always got the feeling the Pook was on our side."

"Yes . . . ," said Molly, drawing the word out till it sounded more like *no*. "I suppose it's worth a try. We could use someone here on our side."

I frowned as another thought hit me.

"Oh, what is it now!" said Molly.

"There are no bodies in the Hall," I said slowly. "There were bodies the last time we were here. Dead Droods in their armour, the golden material half-melted and fused together. I hadn't thought anything could do that to Drood armour. But I haven't seen a single body anywhere."

"Maybe they were harvested by this world's Black Heir," said Molly. "So they could reverse-engineer their own armour."

"They would have known better," I said. "This world's armour came from the Heart and drew its power from the life energies of sacrificed Droods. The kind my family used to depend on, until I put a stop to it. But that never happened here."

"Don't start blaming yourself for things you didn't do," Molly said sharply. "Whatever kind of Droods they were, they weren't your family."

"They were a version of my family," I said. "With familiar names and faces." I broke off as a really disturbing thought hit me. "Molly, could the Heart still be here? I know we checked the Sanctity last time and there was no sign of it, but could it be . . . hiding somewhere? Hoping for a Drood to return?"

"You are not thinking of making the Heart your ally!" said Molly.

"Hell no," I said. "I just want to know if I'm going to have to kill it again."

Molly's eyes became cold and distant as she sent her witchy Sight racing through the Hall. I looked quickly around, my hands clenched into fists, my skin crawling in anticipation of the attack I knew I'd never see coming. And then Molly relaxed, and shot me a reassuring smile.

"Take it easy; there's no trace of the Heart anywhere in the Hall. Or on the grounds, or even on this plane of existence. It probably ran off to some other dimension the moment it saw the Droods were losing."

"Well," I said, relaxing a little in spite of myself, "that's something, I suppose. One less thing to worry about."

"Now you see what I mean, about small differences adding up to big changes," said Molly. "Because of this, you never uncovered the truth about the Heart. These Droods were never freed from its control. With Ethel's more advanced armour, they might have stood off their attackers." She stopped, and looked at me sharply. "Hell, I'm amazed this world even exists, given you and I weren't here to save it from some of the threats we've faced."

"And yet the world still turns and life goes on," I said. "So someone must have stepped up to save the world in our absence. I find that comforting."

"You would," said Molly. "I wonder what price the world had to pay, to be saved by someone else."

"You would," I said.

ABOUT THE AUTHOR

Simon R. Green is the *New York Times* bestselling author of the Secret Histories Novels, the Novels of the Nightside, the Ghost Finders Novels, and the Death-stalker series. He lives in England.

CONNECT ONLINE

simonrgreen.co.uk
twitter.com/thesimonrgreen

The
Secret
Histories

by Simon R. Green

The gritty, humorous urban fantasy series
starring Drood. Eddie Drood. Of the powerful
clan tasked with protecting humanity from
the supernatural forces of darkness. He keeps you
safe by fighting off things that go bump in
the night. You're welcome.

Find more books by Simon R. Green
by visiting prh.com/nextread

"A literary love letter to the spy thrillers of the
'60s mashed up with every sort of paranormal
weirdness under the sun."
—SFRevu

"A hard-boiled, fast-talking, druidic James Bond
who wields ancient magic instead of a gun . . . a witty
fantasy adventure."**—*Library Journal***

simonrgreen.co.uk
SimonRGreenAuthor